THE LAST THING CLAIRE WANTED

THE
LAST
THING
CLAIRE
WANTED

A WINE COUNTRY COLD CASE

KARIN FITZ SANFORD

LEVEL
BEST BOOKS

Author Photo Credit: Sterling Mohar Photography

First edition

ISBN: 978-1-68512-162-4

Cover art by Level Best Designs

This book was professionally typeset on Reedsy.
Find out more at reedsy.com

In memory of my parents, Jack and Evelyn Fitzgerald,
and for my husband, Allen Sanford

Praise for The Last Thing Claire Wanted

"With vivid and gripping characters, an intricately woven plot, and a history that sticks its claws in you and doesn't let go, Karin Fitz Sanford leaves readers with something truly remarkable. A brilliant debut!"—Amanda Jayatissa, ITW Thriller Award-winning author of *My Sweet Girl* and *You're Invited*

"*The Last Thing Claire Wanted* will keep you on the edge of your seat. In a suspenseful tale of dark secrets threatening an entire family, former FBI Agent Anne McCormick finds out that not all secrets are meant to be discovered. Sanford's rich characters coupled with crisp pacing and twists you won't see coming make her an author to watch."—James L'Etoile, author of *Dead Drop*, and *Black Label*

"With beautiful prose and enough twists and turns to keep me reading long into the night, Karin Fitz Sanford's thrilling debut novel explores the lasting effects of trauma and the extraordinary lengths to which people will go to protect their family and legacy. Anne McCormack is a flawed but likeable protagonist, relentless in her pursuit of the truth, even as deceptions and danger mount all around her. I can't want to see what other long-buried secrets Anne uncovers in her future adventures."—Daniel K. Miller, author of *Fire on the Firth* and *Loch and Key*

Prologue

Santa Rosa, California

Just a few hundred yards from St. Paul's Parish School, the old adobe house stood in ruins in an overgrown and neglected orchard. It was fenced off and condemned by the city, but that only added to its allure for adolescent boys and the occasional vagrant. In a few hours, the crumbling adobe would be cordoned off with yellow police tape, and by Christmas, it would be bulldozed into a heap.

But on this fall afternoon, the four eighth-grade boys ignored the NO TRESPASSING sign on the chain link fence and got ready to climb over it like they did nearly every day after school. As far as they were concerned, the adobe house belonged to them; it was their secret place to sneak cigarettes, bitch about teachers, and look at old *Playboy* magazines that belonged to Scotty's older brothers.

"No outsiders allowed," said Tony, the one who liked to make the rules, "because then everyone would want to come, and then the priests and nuns would find out." They all agreed that nothing good ever came from that.

To keep from attracting attention, they had a ritual: the first boy would climb over the fence—or crawl through the opening cut in the chain link if he was feeling lazy—and when he got to the adobe, he would whistle for the next guy to start.

A few teachers and kids were still milling around the schoolyard, so they got off to a late start. Even the janitor was hanging around, picking up litter along the fence line and eyeing the boys with suspicion. They waited him out, shooting a few baskets until he finally turned around and disappeared into the janitor's shed.

Scotty was the first to climb over the fence. He landed on his feet, then took his sweet time getting to the adobe, dragging a stick along the worn path of tangled, tamped-down weeds. When he was within sight of their hideout, he heard a piercing scream. Then another scream, but it cut off abruptly, halfway through. His eyes darted in the adobe's direction in time to catch a glimpse of movement—it seemed barely more than a shadow of a figure fleeing from behind the old house. Scotty picked up speed. *Oh shit, who the hell...*

He raced to the adobe's rotting wood door and gave it a hard yank. When his eyes got used to the low light, he scanned the dusty interior and looked around for any disturbances. Was anything taken? Did someone find their stuff? He saw nothing but the same mildewed bean bag chair, same porn and cigarettes on the overturned crate, same dented cans and wrappers strewn about the ground. But someone had been there, something was off, and there was a slight metallic odor in the air.

In the far corner, he spotted a dark shape on the ground. He moved in slowly, cautiously, afraid of what he might find. An injured possum? Maybe a rabid dog?

Inching closer, he could see that the crumbled form was a small boy lying flat on his back, totally still. It looked like blood was trickling from the corner of his mouth. Scotty poked at the body with his branch. Nothing. He crouched down to get a closer look and froze. *Jesus.* He knew that face.

It was Tony's little brother. Danny Murray was dead.

I

PART ONE

Chapter One

Santa Rosa, September 26, 2019

Anne McCormack rolled off the futon, got to her feet, and checked her watch. *Seriously, not even ten o'clock?* She had over seven more hours to kill before she'd let herself leave the office.

She had already made the coffee and paid a few bills. Now what—check the obituaries again?

Wandering over to the tiny corner window, she gazed outside for what felt like the twentieth time that morning, seeing the same two russet-colored leaves dangling from a dry maple tree branch. She checked her phone for messages—again—though she hadn't left the room since the last time she'd checked. Nothing. Then glanced out the window. One of the two leaves had dropped to the ground while she wasn't looking. She felt encouraged. *Finally, some action around here.*

It was dawning on her that starting a new business—personal estate liquidation—after her FBI career had imploded two years before, probably hadn't been such a red-hot career move. The sign outside her office door read McCORMACK & CO. ESTATES SALES AND SERVICES. It might as well say "Slacker Sales and Services" for all the business she'd attracted in the last month.

She stared down at the futon. The futon was the problem, she decided. It symbolized inertia, laziness, and defeatism—a far cry from how she saw herself. It had to go. Thirty-two was way too young to be lying about all day. She rolled it up, lugged it to the far corner, and for good measure, gave it a hard kick. Satisfied, she decided to proof her website again (*the phone number must be wrong*), make new lists, do some cold calling. She was looking forward to lunch.

The phone rang.

It took her only five paces to get from one end of the office to the other where her desk was. Standing over the phone for a beat, she smoothed down the new black pants she'd slipped on that morning in the perpetual hope of stumbling upon a new client, and then picked up the call. It was Marty Holmes, her mentor in the estate sales business and former boss. When he'd hired her—right after she left the FBI—the first thing he told her was, "Estate sales are not garage sales, let's get that straight, right off the bat." The estate sales business, he explained, is about helping families dispose of the treasures left behind after a loved one's death, and then getting a big fat commission from the sales of said treasures.

After learning the ropes and making contacts, she'd handed in her notice. Which is how she'd ended up in this predicament: she owned a fledgling business with no business and few prospects.

"Hey, Marty."

"I've got a job with your name written all over it," he boomed.

"Oh yeah?" Two years as his assistant had taught her how jealously he guarded his profitable jobs. She was suspicious, but all ears.

"The deceased's name is Althea Jackson. No one's living at her house now, so the executor said to go on in. Come by the office and pick up the job folder and house key," Marty said, "and get back to me if you have any questions."

"Thanks for the lead," she said, surprising herself by how much she meant it: she needed this job. She had bills to pay and hours to fill. Besides, she needed something new to obsess over besides her miserable ex-husband.

"Well, don't thank me yet. No one here in my office will take it," he said with a little chuckle. "In fact, something might be a little weird, a little wacky, about this one. You still carry a gun?"

"Not often. Why?"

4

"Nothing, just curious," he said, "Anyway, look around the place and see if you're interested. Then give the executor a call if you want the job."

Anne was slipping on her jacket while he was still talking.

*　*　*

Some towns in Northern California have more Wine Country allure than others. Tourist buses zip past Santa Rosa to get to those towns: Healdsburg, Glen Ellen, St. Helena, Calistoga, Yountville, Napa, and Sonoma.

Santa Rosa residents are used to the snub and shake it off. Instead, locals take a what's-not-to-like attitude toward their hometown, citing all the things they *do* have: lakes to hike around, a mild Mediterranean climate, an airport, two malls, the Russian River Brewing Company, two Whole Foods markets, and enviable geographic proximity—the town is only a forty-minute drive to the Pacific Ocean; a sixty-minute drive to San Francisco; and about a half-hour trip to many of those tourist towns.

Anne was a local herself, except for her six FBI years spent in Virginia and Sacramento, and had heard all the stories about the town. About how, when Alfred Hitchcock needed an idyllic, all-American town for his 1943 film classic *Shadow of a Doubt*, he came to Santa Rosa. How 'Peanuts' creator Charles Schultz, who could have lived anywhere, made Santa Rosa his home. And every time she drove past the Luther Burbank Home and Gardens near the downtown, she recalled how the famed horticulturist had once called Santa Rosa "the chosen spot of all this Earth as far as nature is concerned."

On the flip side, Anne, along with every other kid in town, grew up with the ominous warning: "Don't go near the orchard!" because not everyone comes out alive.

Sitting in her thirteen-year-old blue Saab in Marty's parking lot, Anne scanned the loose pages in the manila job folder. The information was skimpy: Althea Jackson had lived her entire sixty-six years in Santa Rosa before dying of a heart attack two weeks before. Althea's daughter Vanessa Jackson, sole heir and executor, lived back East.

With the late morning sun glaring off her car window, Anne plugged

Althea's address into the GPS. It popped right up. Althea had lived in the middle of Santa Rosa's sketchiest neighborhood off Highway 101 near an industrial pocket on the south side of town—an area most law-abiding people shied away from. It was only ten minutes away.

Anne headed south on Highway 101 and was soon exiting the freeway, then turning into the entrance of an older mobile home park. She groaned aloud. *Good thing Luther Burbank never saw this place,* she thought. *This is nobody's idea of a chosen spot.* From the looks of it, the mobile park would be inhabited by drug dealers, lowlifes, small-time criminals, desperate single mothers, and shabby old bachelors—along with Althea Jackson and her so-called estate.

She passed the mobile home park's battered wood TRANQUIL ACRES sign, engraved with a warning: Adults Only. No Children.

Must be a retirement community, she thought vaguely as she drove toward Althea Jackson's address at the end of a cul-de-sac. She parked and sat for a moment, looking around, sensing a vaguely oppressive, almost eerie silence on the street.

Stepping out of the car, she shaded her eyes from the glaring sunlight. At first glance, Althea's vacant doublewide looked well maintained, a few grades above its neighbors. The striped turquoise/white awning was faded but fairly new, and the plants in the terracotta pots on the porch were still alive. Not too bad.

She heard the creak of a metal door and turned to see a disheveled older woman with short, spiky red hair step out of the trailer next door.

"Are you one of those estate liquidators?" the woman asked, approaching Anne. "Because Althea's daughter said someone would be coming by." She narrowed her eyes, scanning Anne from head to foot, then extended her hand. "I'm Judy Lyle, by the way. Me and my husband own this park."

"Anne McCormack." Anne shook her hand, then stepped onto Althea's porch. "Right, I'm here to see Althea Jackson's home."

"Well, you aren't the first. Four or five other cars have already shown up here, but they just did drive-bys. Guess they thought they were too good for mobile homes," Judy said with a mischievous gleam in her eye. "You're the first to actually *stop* your car."

Anne smiled wanly. What could she say— "Guess I'm the only one desperate enough for this job?" The sun was beating down on them, and Anne was eager to end the chit-chat and get inside.

"Well, if you take this job, you should know something," Judy said, picking up the water hose attached to Althea's house. "You saw the sign out front, right? That's not for decoration. This is 'sex offender housing,' as my card says." She reached into her pocket, pulled out a business card, and handed it to Anne.

"My husband Walter inherited this park twenty years ago. Back then, we used to have families here, drug dealers, prostitutes, all kinds. They were nothing but trouble. Lots of noise and fighting. Kept us up all hours of the night. So we got rid of all the families. Now we only rent to convicted sex offenders."

Anne nearly dropped her keys.

"Got about thirty of them here now," Judy said.

What? She'd heard about these kinds of trailer parks existing in Florida and Oklahoma, but Santa Rosa? Why didn't she know about this place? Maybe it was because her FBI years had been spent working violent crimes in Sacramento, not delving into the sex crimes of Sonoma County. Besides, no one she knew had ever lived here, not that she was aware of, anyway.

"Having sex offenders here drove out those damn drug dealers and hookers."

"How so?"

"Because we're always being watched by the sheriff's department, probation, corrections officers, newspaper reporters, you name it—all the people drug dealers don't want to be around, so they left. This is a clean park now, no trouble."

"Althea wasn't a sex offender herself, was she?" Anne asked. "Just asking because not many women would choose to live here."

"Ha! That's rich. No, she was my second cousin, and she'd visit me here sometimes, and then she decided to move in herself about five years ago. The rent's low, and she liked that," she said as she bent down to pick dry,

7

dead leaves off the rose plant.

"Me and her were the only women living here, but my husband watched out for us. Not that Althea needed it—believe me, she was tough. No one here bothered Althea. And of course, we got cameras everywhere," Judy said, pointing to security cameras lining the street.

"Besides, these guys don't mess with anyone here because they don't want to be kicked out. They got no place else to go."

Being a new business owner herself, Anne could appreciate that—as far as sustainable business models go—Judy's was golden. Repellent, maybe, but it had its own built-in checks and balances.

"I'll leave you now, young lady," Judy said. "But if you come back—if you take this job—always check in with me first so we can keep an eye on you. I'm armed, and I keep my eyes wide open."

"I'll be fine, but thanks for the word of caution," Anne said. Next time, if Judy wasn't around, she'd holster her gun inside her waistband instead of leaving it where it was totally useless: locked up inside the trunk of her car.

Anne went inside Althea's trailer, welcoming the cooler, slightly musty air, and locked the flimsy door behind her. She wasn't planning to stay long—just long enough to get a general idea of what would be sellable and what the heir would want to keep. She did a quick tour of the rooms. The furniture—the couch, chairs, and tables—were all worn and inexpensive; no one would pay much for them. Strictly Goodwill. But the home was surprisingly tidy, with everything in place.

She swept her hand idly along the top of the living room bookcase. It was only slightly dusty, as if Althea had dusted the day before she died. The bookcase held no books, just knick-knacks. But not ordinary Dollar Store knick-knacks, she noticed. These were all good pieces, expensive and out of place in this setting.

She gathered them onto the dining room table: a silver cigarette holder, a jade paperweight, an 18K gold men's Rolex watch, an heirloom jade ring, an ivory Buddha, and two diamond rings in velvet boxes. Each item was less than three inches in diameter. Pocket-sized.

Anne turned back to the file. Althea's occupation was listed as a residential housekeeper. *Hmmm.* She flipped the Rolex watch over and read the engraving on the back: Santa Rosa Mayor G. Murray, 1980-1991.

She took a few photos on her smartphone and checked the time. Nearly noon. Still time to go back to her office, write up a contract, and call Althea's daughter back on the East Coast.

An hour later, eating a turkey sandwich in front of her computer, Anne sent an email to Vanessa Jackson, then waited a half-hour before giving her a call. It was picked up immediately.

"Hello." The voice sounded wary.

"Hello, Vanessa Jackson? This is Anne McCormack, the estate liquidator who was just out at your mother's house. I'm wondering if you got the email I just sent you. I attached my terms and contract, along with references and some photos."

"Yes. Everything looks pretty standard," Vanessa said. "I guess you can get started. I'll sign everything and get them back to you."

"Actually, before you do, I'd like to discuss the photos," Anne closed her eyes, bracing for a fight. "I found those items at your mom's, and here's the thing: they seemed a little out of place...."

"Out of place? In what way?" Her voice took on an edge. "What exactly are you saying here?"

Whoa. Anne left the questions unanswered and waited for Vanessa to continue.

"Are you implying that she was too poor, too low class, to have nice things? That she stole them? Look, my mother worked for some of the finest families in town for over 30 years. Don't you think I'd have heard some complaints before this?" Her voice was sharply insistent, though, to Anne, it sounded like she was trying to convince herself.

"I don't know, Vanessa, and it's none of my business really," Anne said, now in full placation mode. "It's just that the watch has an inscription on the back of it. It was given to the mayor. I googled the records. The mayor was Gerald Murray. His family still lives in town."

Vanessa sighed and took a long pause. "I remember that family. I'd go there sometimes with Mom." Another pause.

"Listen, maybe Mom did have a little problem. Who knows? She never told me anything. Besides, it's water under the damn bridge."

More silence.

"Okay, go ahead and return the watch, but only if you promise to keep our names out of it. I don't want any trouble."

"Promise."

"And sell the rest of the stuff," Vanessa said.

"I'll write up a letter for you to sign that gives me your permission to—"

"Fine." The line went dead.

Chapter Two

Tuesday, October 1

C laire Murray never liked taking naps in the afternoon—never really approved of them. She especially didn't like taking naps outdoors, with its unpredictable breezes. But here she was, sitting in her wicker chair on the back deck with a book in her lap, waking up from a restless, dream-filled nap.

It seemed the older she got—she would be seventy-five next month, which was unbelievable to her—the lighter she slept. Almost as if her waking and dreaming states were melding together. The veil was thinning. And her loved ones, long dead, seemed closer at hand than ever, practically whispering in her ear.

Her small, black-haired spaniel jumped onto her lap. "So you want something, do you?" Claire's slender fingers mussed his shiny coat. After raising five children and a lifetime of work and social committees, Louie was her sole responsibility now. And that suited her just fine.

Much like this cottage. Of course, it was a far cry from the grandeur of the hillside home where she and Gerald had raised their family. They'd built that ultra-modern showplace during their glory years, as she thought of them now. It was all floor-to-ceiling windows, geometric angles, and high ceilings with a bedroom suite for each child. But she didn't miss that house, not one bit. Too large and too much work. Mostly, she didn't miss those dark final years, filled as they were with grief and trouble. Sadness seemed to have seeped into the walls.

Living here was her idea of freedom. She took exquisite pleasure in the simplest things, like getting up without an alarm. Going to bed when she wanted. Oatmeal for dinner? Who was to stop her? She even liked that her cottage was only a snug 700 square feet in all—squeezing in a bedroom, living area, bathroom, and a galley kitchen. Keeping it tidy was a breeze.

And oh God, the views. From the cottage's hillside vantage point, she could see the city lights below and lush greenery outside of every window. Looking west, out through the trees, she could glimpse the towering sign for The Parisian hotel, a landmark overlooking the town. That flamboyant, hot-pink neon sign gave off a garish glow that always made her smile.

She closed her eyes and adjusted her cashmere shawl, drifting into a familiar reverie of images and landing, as usual, on ones that defined her young married life—the formal Sans Souci dance at The Parisian; her strapless, pink satin dress; beautiful couples dancing; their explosive laughter at dinner parties. Her generation had smoked too much, drank too much dark liquor, and never exercised. *But God, we knew how to have fun.*

All right, enough. She could sit here all day and reminisce, or she could get dressed and be ready for the visitor who was coming in an hour: a young woman with an Irish last name—which she couldn't remember for the life of her—who had made an appointment to come by to return her late husband's watch. Maybe she would set out the fancy Danish butter cookies her daughter Joanne brought back from Solvang. And she could offer her guest a martini—because, of course, martinis and cookies.

Claire gently pushed Louie to the ground. "Sorry, Lou." She stood and was heading into the living room when a now-familiar wave of nausea come over her. She gripped the doorframe for support, but soon the nauseous feeling passed, almost as quickly as it had come.

The phone rang. She slowly crossed the living room and checked the caller ID before picking up: her youngest son Peter. "Hi dear, what's up?" Claire said, forcing cheer into her voice.

"Mom! Are you going to be around this afternoon?" Peter's voice rose a few octaves. "I need a little favor from you."

* * *

"Mrs. Murray? I'm Anne McCormack." Anne said, extending her hand to the older woman. From the open front door of the tidy cottage, Anne could see all the way through to the living room and the leafy views beyond.

"Of course, you're the young lady I spoke to about the watch." Claire shook Anne's hand and ushered her into the tiny foyer, locking the door behind them. "Nice of you to come. What will you have, some tea or wine? Or I can mix us some martinis if you're so inclined."

"Thanks, tea would be great," Anne said, though she didn't expect to be there long enough to drink it.

"I was surprised to get your call, but very pleasantly. I haven't thought of that watch in years." Claire motioned for Anne to sit in the living room and then stepped into the kitchen to make the tea. "Make yourself at home. I'll be just a minute," she called out.

Left alone in the living room, Anne surveyed her surroundings, casually at first, then with a growing interest she struggled to rein in. Where, she wondered, did her inexhaustible curiosity about other people's lives come from? It was as though she were still looking for a rule book on how to live, and she'd have all the answers if she just knew what kind of coffee they bought or what books they read. Her impulse to wander around people's private spaces, inspecting their belongings, was not always appreciated. But she couldn't help noticing Claire's antique furnishings, artwork—*Is that an original by Fernando Amorsolo?*—the crystal bowl filled with white roses, and rows of family photos in silver frames. Absentmindedly, she stood to get a closer look at the photos, then forced herself to sit back down again. *Not my client. Not my business.*

Claire entered the room carrying a silver tray loaded with a teapot, cups, and a plate of cookies. Anne jumped up to rescue the heavy tray and placed it on the coffee table. "Let me pour," Anne said.

"Thanks," Claire said, settling into the tufted loveseat. "And have a cookie. If you don't eat them, I'll just have to throw them away."

Anne laughed. That was exactly, word-for-word, how her grandmother used to guilt her into eating something. "Guess we can't let them go to waste," she said, reaching for a butter cookie.

Claire smiled and sipped her tea. "It was thoughtful of you to bring my husband's watch yourself instead of mailing or FedExing it."

"Well, it's an expensive piece," Anne said. "I wasn't comfortable having it delivered, especially since I live close by." She reached in her purse and pulled out an oblong black velvet box—along with her business card—and handed them to Claire.

"You talk like a jeweler, or at the very least, an appraiser—which I guess you are, in a way," Claire said, looking over the business card. She laid the velvet box beside her on the loveseat without another look.

"Among other things. But yes, I love research and art. Pricing things out. That's a big part of my job. I can't help but notice," she said, gesturing to take in the room, "that you have some lovely things." Anne's eyes roamed the room, landing on a recessed wall niche above the fireplace. It appeared to be a shrine of sorts, displaying three photos of the same small boy, a few toy cars, and a ceramic handprint. Claire's grandson? Maybe she would get a closer look on her way out.

* * *

While Anne was studying the room, Claire was studying Anne. In her early thirties, she surmised—younger than her own two daughters by a few years—with the budding self-assurance of a young woman coming into her own. On the tall and lean side, with shoulder-length tawny hair and intelligent brown eyes. Anne struck her as a trustworthy, competent person who got things done. Maybe a little skittish.

Claire shook her head and fleetingly wondered if she was reading too much into her first impressions. But she knew she was probably right. *What was that quote by Emerson? Something like "Who you are speaks so loudly I can't hear what you are saying."* Claire's intuition rarely failed her.

Claire brought her attention to the box, opened it, and lifted out the gold engraved watch her husband had received from the city over thirty years before. After they forced him to resign. At the time, she was deeply cynical about the gift, but hadn't shared those thoughts with Gerald, who seemed placated and even flattered by the watch. She wasn't in the least. To her, it was little more than a sorry-for-your-troubles goodbye gift—with a strong whiff of "but don't let the door hit you on the way out" about it. Though a widow for over twenty-five years now, since the evening he died in a car crash following hours of heavy drinking in a bar, she still felt fiercely protective of his memory. No matter how flawed he had been.

"I'm curious, how did you come by the watch?" Claire asked Anne. "It must be decades since it was lost—or more likely, taken."

"All I'm at liberty to say is that I found it in the course of working on a job," Anne replied stiffly, as if reciting a prepared speech. Her promise not to mention Althea and her daughter was firmly lodged in her mind. In the wake of the silence that followed, she added, "All I can say is that my client thought you should have it back. Sorry."

Claire took another tack. "Guess it really doesn't matter after all these years. It's just curiosity on my part. Do you have a list of your current clients for references? In case I need to use your services, of course."

Anne took a very long sip of tea. Then another.

Deciding that Anne clearly didn't like the question—and wasn't about to give up any names that might lead to the discovery of the thief—Claire dropped the matter.

"But seriously, I think I could use your help," she said. "I have a rented storage locker full of old furniture and boxes from all my house moves. I need to get everything inventoried and appraised, the sooner the better. I know it's not exactly up your alley, but if you have the time and inclination—"

"I'd be very interested."

"Great. That will help me get my things in order."

"And, of course, I do have references I can provide."

"I'll give you a call then," Claire said, standing up.

"I look forward to it."

As they headed toward the door, they passed by the wall niche. Anne paused in front of it. "Beautiful boy. Your grandchild?"

Claire stopped and gazed at the photos. "No, my son Danny. He was five years old when he died. He was murdered, actually," she said, her voice growing fainter. "He would be thirty-four years old now. No, wait, thirty-four and nine months. Ten months? I'm losing track...."

"I'm so sorry," Anne said, her face clouding with sympathy.

"They never did find the murderer, but it seemed like every detective in the county was on the case, at least for a while," Claire said. "I guess they weren't making enough headway, or maybe other cases took their attention from it. Anyway, they just stopped." She saw the concern on Anne's face and willed herself to regain composure.

"You know, Anne, your last name rings a bell. I seem to remember—"

The sound of the doorbell interrupted them. Louie barked out a greeting and waddled his way to the front door. They heard a key turn in the door, and in walked her son, tall and gangly with spiky brown hair and a wispy soul patch between his chin and lower lip.

"Hi, Mom, I'm home!" He hugged his mother.

Claire brushed off the comment and turned back to Anne.

"Anne, this is my son Peter, who does *not* live with me." She gave Anne a wry smile. "None of my kids do. Peter, this is Anne McCormack. Anne dropped by to return your father's watch," she said, showing him the watch she still carried in the palm of her hand.

"Don't remember seeing that before. Guess I was too young," he said. In one fluid motion, Peter reached for the watch and slipped it onto his wrist. He tilted his head back and squinted his eyes to admire it better. "Looks good on me, don't you think?"

Claire gave out with a long sigh and took Anne's arm. They brushed past him in the narrow foyer and went through the front door and out onto the walkway.

"I'll give you a call later this week so we can talk more about that job," Claire said.

"That'll be great."

"Oh!" Claire said, stopping short. "I remember what I was going to say before—about your last name. There was a young detective named

16

McCormack who worked on Danny's case. Would you happen to be related to him?"

"Yes, my Uncle Jack! He's retired from the police force now. He still lives in Santa Rosa, and I see him all the time. He's the reason I went into law enforcement—the FBI actually, which is neither here nor there since...." Anne's voice trailed off.

"Law enforcement?" Claire stared intently at Anne, then lightly gripped her elbow. "Come back inside, please."

Chapter Three

Tuesday, October 1

After Anne drove off, Claire collapsed onto the living room couch, her emotions bouncing from agitation because of her talk with Anne to worry about what Peter might be up to.

"Peter? Where are you?" she called out.

"In the back room."

Claire headed to the windowless utility room. Tucked behind the kitchen, it was really just an add-on shed—only big enough to fit the twin bed that was squeezed into the corner and little else. It had originally been a laundry room and still had chrome faucet fixtures jutting out from the walls for the long-departed washer and dryer, now relegated to the garage.

"What's going on?" she asked from the doorway. Peter was standing with his arms outstretched as if measuring the room's width. "You said you had a favor to ask. I'm very tired, so—"

"Okay, the thing is, there's a problem at the house," he said, lowering his arms, "and I need a place to crash right away." He gave her his sad, wide-eyed puppy-dog look, the one she'd hoped he would have retired by now due to its waning effectiveness.

He hurriedly went over his litany of reasons why he needed to move in: he was thirty-eight years old and too old to be living with three roommates who were total losers—they had drinking problems, minimum wage jobs, questionable hygiene, and worst of all, IQs that were half as high as his. And the galling part was they wanted *him* to move out.

"It'll only be for a few days. This will suit me fine. I've lived in worse places. Hell, I'm living in a worse place right now. One of my roommates—"

"I don't want to hear it," she said. His problems were endless.

"I was thinking Noreen would let me move in with her, but she never returned my calls. You'd think my own twin would—"

"Your sister has her hands full," Claire said.

"And Tony lives too far away," he said.

Tony, Claire's oldest son, lived fifty-five miles away in San Francisco with his third wife. Peter didn't even bother mentioning his oldest sister because everyone knew Joanne could barely stand to be in the same room with him.

"What makes you think there's enough room here? With all your stuff? Look at this!" Claire said, waving her hand vaguely at the five-by-eight-foot space, already crammed with the narrow bed, boxes, and Louie's dog bed.

But she had the sinking feeling that it was already a lost battle. He lifted his chin a few inches. The better to sniff his victory in the air, Claire thought.

"Okay, but only for a few days," Claire said to Peter's back as he headed out to his car to grab his pillow and backpack.

"I'm serious!" she said.

* * *

Claire awoke the next morning to the unfamiliar sound of someone moving around in her kitchen. It took her a minute to realize it was Peter. She heard Louie whimpering for his breakfast and then heard kibble being poured into the dog's bowl. She glanced at the clock on her bedside table: eight a.m. Peter was getting ready to go to his part-time job as a draftsman in an architectural firm.

Claire waited in her bedroom until she heard the front door slam.

She sat up slowly, feeling both tired and anxious about what the day would bring. Two months before, her bouts of nausea and exhaustion had been diagnosed by her physician as the flu, which he later upgraded to pneumonia—and which she didn't believe for one minute.

She had a slight cough, true, but nothing unusual. No, this was something different, she told him, unlike anything she'd ever felt before. But Dr. Rose insisted it was pneumonia, and since he'd been her personal physician for over twenty years, she let the matter drop. He didn't order any tests, but he did recommend drinking hot tea and getting plenty of rest. Then he left for a vacation in Hawaii.

While he was out of town, Claire's condition worsened and included stomach pains so she saw another doctor who ordered a series of tests. Those led to a scan and then to more tests.

At first, she only confided her fears to her oldest daughter Joanne and to her dearest friend Betty Fazio. And finally, to Tony, because he was her firstborn and the executor of her will, and he would need to know.

Today, she would meet with a new doctor and learn the final diagnosis, but she already sensed the news wouldn't be good. She went about her morning, making her bed, opening the back door for Louie, and heading into the kitchen for coffee.

She reached for the phone and dialed Joanne's number.

* * *

"Mom, I've been thinking about you all morning," Joanne said, looking out at the morning shadows from her third-story office window. She had a department meeting in ten minutes. "Are you sure you don't want me to come with you to the appointment? I could be there in forty-five minutes."

"Actually, that would be good, Jo, because I've changed my mind. I'd like you to be there with me."

Joanne sat up. Although this abrupt change in plans was unsettling, she was more unsettled by the vulnerability she heard in her mother's voice. She tried to recall the last time her mother had asked her for anything—had put her out in any way—and couldn't. Though their relationship was warm, it wasn't an easy and confiding one. Maybe they were too much alike, or perhaps the years after Danny's death created a barrier of reserve that was difficult to cross. But all in all, they were good. No real problems between them.

"Absolutely," Joanne said.

"And in other news," Claire said, "your brother moved in here yesterday. But only for a few days, or so the story goes."

"Oh, for Heaven's sake, Mom," Joanne said while emailing her colleagues to cancel the morning meeting. "You know he's never going to leave, don't you? He's there for good. You're going to have to sell the house to get him out!"

Claire laughed. They were on more familiar ground now.

"He has a decent job now—okay, a part-time job." Joanne leaned back in her chair, idly twisting the ends of her long, blonde highlighted hair. "Why not make him get a hotel room, or get an apartment, or even move in with that ex-wife of his? Come to think of it, I wouldn't wish that on anyone. She's back in town, by the way."

"Michele's back? Where did you hear that?"

"Through the grapevine—actually, it came from Noreen, who got it from Peter. He keeps in touch with Michele sometimes. You'd think he'd learn," Joanne said.

"Some people never do—"

"Peter obviously hasn't. I was hoping he'd be out from under Michele's blue-eyed spell by now," Joanne said.

The marriage between Peter and Michele had crashed and burned over fifteen years ago. Until her sister Noreen's text message last week, Joanne hadn't thought of Michele in years.

They were quiet for a moment, then Joanne broke the silence: "Well, I'm taking off—I'll see you in an hour."

* * *

"Could you be clearer? I'm just not understanding," Joanne said.

The young doctor apparently thought he'd been perfectly clear. But to Joanne, it seemed like he had been circling around the prognosis, being intentionally vague—using the words 'stomach cancer,' 'fast spreading,' and 'inoperable'—but making no mention of treatments. No conclusions. No timeframe.

"What about treatments?" Joanne persisted.

The doctor explained that in order to start treatments, they would need to know exactly where the cancer started—since the place of origin would determine the type of treatment. And to find out where it had started, they would have to do exploratory surgery. Which he didn't recommend.

"Why not?"

"The cancer has spread too far."

"So what you're saying is no treatments. No radiation or chemo? What stage is the cancer?" Joanne was frustrated, and it was showing. She felt her mother's hand touch her arm.

Nervously shifting his weight, he said, "There's no stopping the cancer. It's just a matter of time." The words chilled them into silence.

Claire finally spoke. "What would you do if I were *your* mother?"

He glanced out the window and then turned back to face Claire. His gaze locked on hers. "This happened in my family last year. We decided to put our mother into hospice care and let nature take its course."

"How much time do I have left?" Her voice was low, barely audible.

"It's difficult to know for sure, but I would say between six weeks and three months."

He slipped his pen into the pocket of his white lab coat, said he was very sorry, and then left them alone in the consultation room.

Neither of them spoke. Nothing was registering about this new reality. In the silence, Joanne could hear the faint sounds of the hospital intercom system outside the door. She struggled for control, knowing there could be none. *There are things I need to do—lists that need to be made.* She must make arrangements for hospice. Deliver the news to Tony, Noreen, and Peter. Call Betty. Have them pass the news along to the grandchildren, relatives, and Claire's friends. Enlist Tony's help: he could call the attorneys and check on insurance and finances. Hire caretakers. Order a hospital bed. Arrange for a wheelchair. Fill prescriptions. *There are countless, countless things that need to be done.*

For now, Joanne just put her hands on her mother's shoulders and kissed the top of her head.

Chapter Four

Wednesday, October 9

Anne rode shotgun alongside her Uncle Jack in his restored '65 Mustang convertible—its top down on this sunny fall afternoon—as they cruised to their favorite diner in downtown Santa Rosa. Anne fiddled with the CD player, trying to find a tune she recognized from her uncle's hoary collection.

"We need a little Tom Waits," he suggested. "The early years."

Anne dug out Wait's *Rain Dogs* CD and went straight to "Time," one of her favorites. "Something we can finally agree on," she said.

"Ah, my retirement theme song." Jack sang along, off-key in his raspy voice, messing up the lyrics as always.

"Or maybe your retirement song should be 'I'm a Lazy Sod' by the Sex Pistols," Anne said, pretending to search for the tune in his pile of CDs.

Jack nodded his head agreeably. "I swear, it's like you're channeling your Aunt Dot."

They circled the block and lucked into a parking spot right in front of Nell's Diner on Fourth Street. While Anne plugged a few quarters into the parking meter, Jack grabbed a manila folder from the back seat. Entering Nell's, the cashier greeted them and motioned toward their usual booth near the back of the diner. Jack always sat facing the entrance like many ex-cops did, so he could see the comings and goings. Anne sat opposite him, content to leave the diner surveillance to her uncle. They dutifully studied

24

the menu from front to back but decided on what they always decided on: country breakfast, hamburger and fries.

Their usual waitress, Kathy, came by to get their order. Jack told her that his old partner Dean would be joining them, so they would need a few more minutes.

"And I thought my day couldn't get any better," Kathy said, giving Anne a conspiratorial wink. Jack was in his mid-sixties, but traces of his boyish good looks lingered. He still had his mostly dark hair and was still trim, except for a little around the middle. As always, he was dressed for comfort: today, he was wearing a loose black T-shirt and faded jeans.

Jack dropped the manila folder onto the table. "My notes from the Danny Murray case. I can let you take them home, but I'll need them back."

"Walk me through it," she said in their blunt way of speaking to each other, the upshot of a lifetime of familiarity. Jack was her father's older brother—and as near to being a father figure as she had since her own had died of a heart attack when she was seventeen. Jack had walked her down the aisle when she married Gary, her now ex-husband. "I remember hearing some stories about the murder as a kid, but it's pretty vague to me," she said.

"It was a real sad case: a five-year-old kid on his way home from kindergarten, strangled to death in a dirty old shack. The town went crazy—nothing like this had ever happened before. It was even more high profile because the father was the mayor. Prominent family." Jack leaned back and gave her a penetrating look.

"I don't mind going over this, but if I'm going to share my notes with you, I'll need a good reason why. Remind me, what's your connection with this? What's going on?"

"I've been working with Claire Murray for the last week," Anne said. "She's revising her will, so I'm appraising all her belongings. Some things are stored away, and we've been going through boxes of stuff together. I'll help her sell some of it." Anne paused for a moment.

"And..." Jack prompted.

"The thing is, she's very ill and doesn't have long to live, maybe three months on the outside. And before she dies, she wants to *finally* know who murdered her son. My FBI background slipped out in a conversation, and she remembers you from the investigation. She practically begged me to talk to you about the case," she said, then paused again. "The bottom line is, she wants Danny's case reopened."

Jack thought it over. "It's about as cold as a case can get, and I'd bet my pension that no one's looked at those evidence boxes in decades. Looking for closure, is she?"

"No, Claire says she doesn't have much hope of closure. But she *does* want justice."

"Actually, I'm surprised it took the Murrays this long to try to get it reopened, especially since DNA testing is all over the news these days."

"Well, not everyone in the family is on board with this," Anne said. "But that's another story."

Jack pulled out his tattered notebook from the folder. "Dean and I were both rookie detectives back then, so we were teamed up with seasoned investigators. It was my first case. I've never really let it go, and neither has Dean. That's why I asked him to join us."

He riffled through his notes. "Let's see, on September 25th, 1990, we were called in on a Code 187 at the old adobe house—which, by the way, was the second oldest building in the county, but officials never got around to giving it landmark status. Probably because of its dilapidated state and low reputation. Anyway, it was located next to the St. Paul's K-8 school and was torn down soon after the murder.

"Since the incident was a presumed homicide, practically every cop in town was there. A thirteen-year-old kid named Scotty Hudson found the body around four o'clock, about an hour after school let out. He said he didn't touch it. He ran back to his friends, and they ran to the school office and had the secretary call the police."

"Did the other kids go near the body?"

"No, Scotty stopped them. He knew it was Tony Murray's brother who was dead, but he didn't tell him. Scotty was pretty freaked out. In interviews, he also said he heard a scream. That's what first got his attention. Then he thinks he saw a figure, maybe even two figures—he said it was all a blur—run out from the back of the adobe house. He assumed it was a kid, but he was fuzzy about whether it was a boy or girl. He didn't see the person well enough to recognize him or her, or to describe the clothing."

"Was the runner ever identified?"

"No, but we had our suspicions." Jack glanced up at the front door. "Well, look who the cat dragged in, late as usual."

Dean Diaz stood at the doorway of the diner, filling it with his large, bear-like build. He was holding a spiral notebook and scanning the room. Jack waved him over.

"Hey Mac," Dean said to Jack as he approached the table. Catching sight of Anne, he said, "Hi sweetheart, haven't seen you in a while." She stood up for a brief hug. "Not since you left the Bureau so suddenly."

Her smile faded.

"Was that about two years ago?" he asked, motioning for Jack to move over.

She searched his face for disapproval. It didn't take much to stoke her insecurities.

"That sounds about right," she said, sitting back down. She opened her mouth with every intention of saying something defensive about her exit from the FBI, but then decided she was being too touchy and clamped it shut again. Besides, Dean didn't need to know the particulars of how she'd been caught using the FBI's high-security databases to keep track of Gary during their divorce, how tempers flared when her boss confronted her and threatened suspension—and how her resignation letter was on his desk by the end of the day. It was bad enough that her uncle knew.

"But you're still keeping a hand in, I see," he said, pointing to the case file on the Formica tabletop.

"Just this one case," she said, then gave him a quick summary of her involvement with the Murrays. She studied his face: slightly pockmarked and perhaps more weathered now, but he had the same easy smile that didn't quite match up with his wary eyes. He was wearing a tan polo shirt and sharply creased khaki pants.

Kathy came over, took their orders, and headed back to the kitchen.

"The Murrays want the case reopened," Jack told Dean.

Dean shook his head slowly. "That's real nice, but families don't decide these matters, as you both well know. Are you saying there's some real reason to open it? Is there new evidence?"

"I haven't heard of any, but we don't need new evidence—we just need to get DNA tests for the evidence we already have," Jack said.

"This isn't a high priority case anymore. The department doesn't have a lot of resources to open cold cases without good reason."

"We could make it one. I could call in a favor with Joe Kessler," Jack said.

"The budget and the manpower just aren't there, from what I've heard," Dean countered.

"There's always a way."

"Time out," Anne said, interrupting the old partners. "Okay, so they didn't have DNA testing back in the day, but you had other evidence to work from—what kind? And who's Joe Kessler?"

"Kessler's the current Sonoma County assistant district attorney. He's influential in deciding which cases get reopened," Jack said. "Right before I retired, he was just starting out, and we hit it off. I gave him a lot of leads and contacts over the years."

"Take me back to the beginning, when the cops first got to the crime scene," Anne said.

"Atta girl, keep us focused." Jack grinned at Anne, then looked down and read from his notes. "The responding officers found the boy's body on the dirt ground in the back left corner of the adobe house. He was lying flat on his back with a dark blanket thrown over his legs, seemingly a hurried attempt to hide him. A red, aluminum mini-flashlight was lying on the ground nearby."

Jack stopped reading and pulled out a crime scene photo. He handed it to Anne; it was a black-and-white photo of Danny's tiny, lifeless body. His left arm was stretched out over his head; his right arm was down by his side. A dark shadow ran from his mouth halfway down to his chin.

Jack cleared his throat and continued reading. "He was fully clothed in his school uniform and had what appeared to be only minor injuries on the

28

back of his head. There were no broken bones or other apparent injuries. Scratches and round pressure marks were found on both sides of his neck. There were traces of blood-stained saliva at the corner of his mouth."

"Among all the rubble inside the adobe," Dean said, "we found fingerprint evidence on a couple of wine bottles. And there was a crumpled up, dirty paper bag with a used syringe in it. We were able to get fingerprints off those items, too. Plus, there were a lot of *Penthouse*-type magazines that were lousy with fingerprints—smudged fingerprints mainly—but the ones we recovered were from the group of boys who used the place as a clubhouse."

"The most direct evidence we found was the hair," Jack said. "A few strands were found near the boy's mouth. A few more hairs were found in his hand—these had the follicles intact, which suggests he'd pulled them out of the assailant's head in a struggle."

"Hair follicles can yield DNA, of course," said Dean. "But back then, we could only derive limited information from the hair. For example, labs could tell if the hair evidence matched the hair of any suspects in color and width by examining them side-by-side under a microscope. Also, from about eighty percent of hair samples we could learn blood types. But we couldn't determine the age, sex, or race—only DNA testing can give us that information. And even DNA can't give us the age."

"And there's a good chance there's a DNA match on some database out there somewhere," Jack said.

"Back then, did they collect hair samples from suspects to match up with the evidence?" Anne asked.

"Of course, we collected from everyone we legally could, but no matches. That information is in the original files, which I won't have access to until the case reopens," Jack said.

"And the flashlight near Danny's body?" Anne asked.

"The only fingerprints on it were Danny's, so we assumed it was his, but no one in the family remembered seeing it before," Jack said.

"Strange. Five-year-old boys don't go out and buy flashlights. If it was his, someone must know how he got it…." Anne said.

Dean and Jack shrugged. "A dead end for now," Dean said.

"What about all the fingerprints on the paper bag and syringe?" she asked.

"That was our bright, shining hope," said Dean. "We ran the fingerprints and came up with a vagrant with a long rap sheet and a history of mental illness."

"Problem was, he died of a drug overdose two days before the murder," Jack said.

"And the fingerprints on the wine bottles?"

"Again, a dead end," Dean said.

"Which is another reason to reopen the case," Jack said. "Those fingerprints should be run through the current databases, Diaz. We might get a hit."

Kathy appeared back at their table, setting down two of their plates.

"Now, that's just plain pitiful, Kathy," Jack teased the waitress. "Your mother could have balanced all three plates on one arm and our drinks on the other—while twirling the saltshaker on her nose."

"Don't be talking about my mother, Jack," Kathy said, smiling as she headed back for the third plate of food. Kathy's mother was the diner's namesake, Nell, who seemed partial to Jack for reasons known only to them—a somewhat alarming thought that Anne always willed back into the ethers. Yet the signs were there: On the menu, Jack's regular breakfast was called the *Handsome Johnny*, though Nell would never admit that it was named after Jack. She insisted it was named after her favorite singer-songwriter, John Prine. But Jack wasn't buying it. He would tell anyone who would listen, "I've never been prouder."

Between bites of his pastrami on rye, Dean picked up the threads of the narrative. "Danny was last seen in the schoolyard after his kindergarten class let out around three o'clock. He would always walk home with his siblings"—Dean glanced down at his open notebook— "his oldest brother Tony or his two sisters or his other brother Peter. I think they'd take turns. But on that day, no one in the family was with him. He was found an hour later at four o'clock. The medical examiner's report agreed that he died sometime within those sixty minutes."

"Manual strangulation was the official cause of death?" Anne asked. She poured catsup on her plate for the fries.

"Right. The head injuries were minor," Jack said. "They could be explained away as a backward fall."

"Any witnesses besides that kid Scotty who found him?"

"No one reported seeing anyone in the vicinity," Jack said. "We talked to over 200 kids, teachers and parents. A few people brought up the janitor as a possibility, a guy named Carl Pinn, mainly because he was new at the school. He acted pretty squirrelly when we questioned him."

"And the guy refused to give up a hair sample, which is a red flag—" Dean said.

"So we never found out if he was a match. There was nothing to arrest him for and no probable cause for a search warrant," Jack said.

"And didn't that janitor have some lame-ass alibi from his girlfriend?" Dean searched his notes and found it. "Right, she said she was with him in the janitor's shed, though no one remembered seeing her."

They were silent for a moment. Anne waved a French fry absent-mindedly in the air. She broke the silence by bringing up what she considered to be the elephant in the room. "The small figures who were seen running from the adobe...they were probably children, right? It's a horrible thought, but children have been known to kill."

"It's rare," Dean said, "but because of the small pressure marks on Danny's neck, it's possible that a child could be the murderer."

"So if you can identify the runners, the case might be solved," Anne said.

"Not necessarily," Jack said. "That assumes the person—or persons—seen running away were the killers, and that's not necessarily true. Maybe they were just witnesses. Maybe they just saw something and got scared. We don't know."

"But you're pretty sure they were children, right?"

"Again, it's possible. But back up, Anne. Scotty never said he was sure there was more than *one* figure. And he just assumed it was a kid. Let's not get ahead of ourselves," Jack said.

"But since that person was at the scene, he or she had the opportunity to kill," she said.

"Only according to Scotty," Jack said. "I wouldn't mind talking to him again."

Anne regarded the two former partners. "Uncle Jack, you said earlier that you two had suspicions about the identity of the person—or people—who ran from the back of the adobe."

Dean said, "We looked at the school children and friends of the Murray kids."

"And the Murray family?" Anne persisted. "Aside from the business with the flashlight, what did you learn when you talked to them?"

Jack sighed. He was letting his eggs get cold.

"Any cop will tell you that next-of-kin notifications are the worst part of the job. Nothing harder. I was partnered then with a senior detective named Bowers, and he handled the tough part of telling Claire Murray when she came to the door. She just stared at us with a blank expression, then her knees buckled, and she dropped to the floor. She let out this low, hurt-animal sound. Almost primal," Jack said, shaking his head. "I'll carry that image to my grave."

Dean said, "A few of us showed up later—Jack, you were still there too, right?"

Jack nodded.

"We took statements and asked for their whereabouts at the time of death," continued Dean, referring to his notes. "The mother was home; the father was at work. Tony, the thirteen-year-old, was with his group of friends from three o'clock until Scotty Hudson found the body. Peter, the nine-year-old, was playing tetherball at the school. Peter's twin sister Noreen walked home with a friend. The older, twelve-year-old daughter, Joanne, walked home alone."

"And not one of them was making sure Danny got home safe? He *was* the baby of the family after all," Anne said. "Who knows, maybe in a large family like the Murrays, kids get lost in the shuffle. I wouldn't know, but it's still odd, don't you think?"

"The whole thing is odd," Dean said.

"And senseless," Jack said.

"Your thoughts about motives?" Anne asked.

"Nothing. The kid was five years old. How many enemies could he have?" Jack said, pushing his empty plate to the side.

"Maybe he just made someone mad…took someone's ball away. Who knows?" Dean said.

"Back to your suspicions…."

Anne saw a look pass between Jack and Dean. Jack shrugged and finally said, "Maybe that's too strong a word. I'm not sure we should get into this now. It's just guessing and gossip at this point. If the case gets reopened, we'll pursue it. Dean, do you agree?" Dean nodded.

"Anything else you remember from talking to the family?"

"Not really. The family was devastated," Dean said. "We had to interview the mother in her bedroom. The father just sat on the living room couch with his head in his hands, weeping. He was nursing a bourbon in the middle of the day." Dean threw down his napkin. "Man, it's good to be retired."

"Damn right," Jack said as he reached into his wallet and tossed a twenty-dollar bill on the table for the tip. "But still, it would be good to finish off that case. Somewhere out there is a murderer who thinks he got away with it."

"Call Kessler," Anne said. "It's time to reopen."

"Yeah, okay, I'm sold. Call Kessler," Dean said as he grabbed for the check, then apparently thought better of it and tossed it toward Jack.

* * *

Later that day, in his musty home office—the only room in the house that his wife Dot refused to clean and hadn't remodeled—Jack held his smartphone up to one ear and leaned back in his duct-taped brown leather recliner.

He had already made his case to Joe Kessler, the assistant district attorney, and was now listening to Kessler's objections and qualifiers: the case was too old; the physical evidence might have gotten lost in the back rooms; there were no new leads; witnesses might have died.

"Not to mention," Kessler continued, "the man-hours it would take to review all the case materials, detective notes, photographs, key witness lists, lead sheets, lab documents, and results, suspect information...."

Jack was only half listening; he knew all of this already.

"And it's more than likely the evidence wasn't properly stored and has degraded to the point that it's useless for testing—"

Jack cut in. "On the other hand, time isn't always an enemy, Joe. A witness who'd been hostile might tell a different story now. Or a suspect could slip up when talking about the crime he did decades ago."

Despite the roadblocks Kessler was tossing out, Jack knew him well enough to know he was intrigued. This wasn't just any case, and anyone who'd been alive at the time—even a toddler like Kessler had been—would have heard about the crime. It was still in the air. Even all these decades later, kids would dare each other to run into the old orchard—and though the ones who took the dare all came out alive, the game never lost its thrill. Every ten years after the murder, reporters would mark the anniversary with an article in the newspaper. The case still haunted the town.

"The cold case department already has several cases lined up," Kessler said.

Jack said nothing, just waited.

"Okay, but if we reopen this, we'll need more hands on deck," Kessler said. "How serious are you about all of this? Because we can always use volunteers, retired cops like you. We might even be able to put you on the payroll as a part-timer. Maybe have you head the case."

Jack shifted in his seat and glanced at his empty calendar hanging on the wall.

"Interested?" Kessler pressed.

"Well, that's a possibility, though I'm pretty busy these days."

"That's not what your wife tells *my* wife."

"Okay, tell you what," said Jack, sitting up, "reopen the case, and I'll work on it—part-time anyway—and I'll see if I can rope Dean Diaz and my niece, Anne, into it, too."

"If Anne's willing to qualify as a temp-hire investigator with the police department, that could be doable," Kessler said.

"I'll sound them out. There might be a few blind alleys we'd like to go down."

Chapter Five

Wednesday, October 9

It was after five o'clock by the time Anne pulled up in front of her duplex and spotted a cardboard storage box sitting on her front porch. She was not expecting a delivery. She walked up the paved pathway to get a closer look: there were no address markings on the package, so she didn't pick it up—her training and cautious nature at work—but she did open the envelope taped to the top of it. The notecard inside was in Claire Murray's familiar handwriting.

> "Hi Anne,
>   I asked Peter to bring you this box from my storage unit. I'm not sure what's in it, but I thought you'd like to get a head start with your research before our meeting. No problem if you don't have time, just please bring it with you tomorrow.
>   Warmly, Claire"

Anne tucked the note inside her purse. She fumbled with her keys and opened the front door, carrying the box inside and dropping it on the coffee table.

She didn't mind that Claire was eager for her to start on the next day's work—in fact, she enjoyed rummaging through Claire's mounds of boxes. But she *did* mind that Peter was the one who had dropped it off. Now he knew where she lived. He'd never shown any interest in her or even looked up when she was in the room, but something about him set her teeth on edge. The less he knew, the better, was her feeling.

She went outside again to get her mail: bills and catalogs, one invitation, and—hallelujah—a commission check from her first job as McCormack & Co. Family Estate Sales and Services. Setting the mail on the kitchen countertop, she took another grateful look at the check. It was from Vanessa Jackson. Aside from a few odds and ends that still needed to be sold, Anne's work on the Jackson estate had been completed after a quick two weeks, and she needed to drum up more business fast. Her rapidly depleting savings, the Murray job, and the rental income she was getting from her tenant living in the second half of her duplex were all that would be keeping her afloat until she landed a few more clients.

The duplex had been a lucky find. She had scouted around for a place to buy in the Town and Country area of Santa Rosa right after her divorce two years before. A place where she could hide out and find a little peace. Her real estate agent brought her to Winslow Lane, a tree-lined cul-de-sac within walking distance of downtown shops and a mom-and-pop market. He stopped the car in front of a cute, shingle-sided duplex.

"This one may be pricier than you want," he warned.

It was, but one look, and Anne was hopelessly taken with the crisp white trim and craftsman-style front door. It felt like home. The blossoming peach tree in the front yard closed the deal, so she made an offer that day, justifying the purchase as "income property." She never regretted it, and now that rent money was a lifesaver.

She'd furnished her half of the duplex with an eclectic mix of things inherited from her parents, found at estate sales, and wrested from her divorce: a wildly colorful Moroccan rug, a miniature sailboat, cheap assemble-it-yourself bookcases, a stuffed Victorian chair no one ever wanted to sit in, sterling silver serving dishes, a white slipcovered sofa with down-filled cushions—which she could never afford now—and a light wood headboard and dresser set with matching side tables.

The late afternoon sun streamed through the paned window, warming the kitchen. She filled the teakettle, turned on the gas stove, and opened the invitation. In florid calligraphy, it cordially invited her to a baby shower for Krista Hageman.

An olive branch of sorts? Before her divorce and the Bureau inquiry had made collateral damage of their friendship, Anne would have been the one to host the shower for Krista. They had been teenage hellions together and maids of honor at each other's weddings.

Unsure of her emotions, she set the card down and took a sip of tea. Maybe it was time to let resentments go, or at least consider softening them a bit. After all, it wasn't as if she hadn't caused her share of damage and hurt. And she missed her friend. *A baby. Krista is going to be a mother.*

* * *

The battered cardboard box piqued her curiosity, but not enough to stop her from eating her Chinese take-out before opening it. Or doing the dishes. Or watching an old episode of *Schitt's Creek*. Its contents would have to wait until Anne finally unwound after an afternoon spent troubleshooting her website, renewing her driver's license, and pricing out Claire's art pieces. She scooped some chocolate chip ice cream into a bowl and brought it into the living room.

Glancing at her phone on the coffee table, she noticed a missed call and listened to the message: Aunt Dot was inviting her over on Sunday for an "informal dinner but wear make-up." Which could only mean one thing: Aunt Dot was matchmaking again. Her previous attempts—a nice accountant twenty years her senior and a still-bitter, newly divorced insurance adjuster—hadn't panned out. This was partly because the candidates weren't promising, but mostly because Anne had no intention of veering anywhere near a real relationship. Not a fan of vulnerability and heartbreak. It was altogether too soon.

Besides, she had Jim Raggle, a beefy, six-years-younger car mechanic she had met at the Whiskey Tip bar. It took them only a few dates to realize that the romance part of their relationship wasn't working—neither of them cared much about the other's hopes and dreams, nor did they care for each other's friends. But the slow, meaningless sex—the steamy nights spent making love and smoking a little weed while John Mayer's sensuous guitar solos played in the background—*that* had worked. So an arrangement was struck. He was a part of her life now, but she would not be introducing him to the family any time soon.

After shooting a quick text declining the invitation due to "prior plans," Anne contemplated the box again. Claire's possessions and the life they represented were fascinating to Anne. Every few days, she visited Claire's storage unit and brought back another box or two for them to go through together. So far, they had inventoried diamond rings, silver place settings, and numerous paintings—including the one by Fernando Amorsolo that she noticed at her first visit, which she authenticated partly by its original bamboo frame. There was also a signed Sunday comic strip worth thousands. Even some rare first edition books collected by Gerald's grandfather.

This was by far her favorite part of her new career. She remembered the first time she'd spotted her old boss, Marty Holmes—right after she left the FBI—at an estate sale his firm was holding at a posh mansion. He was running the job, but not the cash register. He answered customers' questions and policed the rooms for potential thieves. Watching him was an epiphany for her: she could do that. She could sell the items for clients and get top dollar. She could turn her avocation—her time-sapping hobby—of going to estate sales looking for undervalued silver, paintings and jewelry—into a career. She loved research, history, and art, and learning the value and provenance of big-ticket items. It was right up her alley. She could do all of that. So she asked him for a job, learned the business, and then started her own.

Anne set the bowl on the coffee table, removed the lid of the box, and peered inside. Just some old report cards, financial paperwork, leather-bound journals, manila folders, and four photo albums.

A fragile folder labeled 'Family Questionnaires, 1985-1990' caught her eye, and she lifted it carefully out of the box. Inside were dozens of pages separated and stapled together by year. The Murrays apparently had a New

Year's Eve tradition of answering a list of ten questions—the same questions every year: favorite movie, worst habit, favorite song, best vacation, happiest day, and so forth.

She could imagine them all sitting around the dining room table, each hunched over the questions, writing their responses in wildly varying handwriting styles—from Claire's elegant script to Danny's block letters written in crayon.

She looked closer at the entries for New Year's Eve in 1990, the bright beginning of the year of Danny's death later that fall. The year the tradition came to an abrupt halt.

To the question of "What was the happiest day of last year?," the patriarch Gerald answered, "the shopping center deal," while Joanne, in her loopy pre-teen cursive, wrote, "getting straight-As." Claire's lofty reply to "What's your idea of perfect happiness?" was "listening to classical music with my children at my knee."

Danny's "favorite movie" was *E.T. The Extra-Terrestrial,* and his "happiest day" was seeing it for the second time. Tony's "hero" was "my dad and then Eddie Murphy!" Nine-year-old Noreen wrote in boxy lettering that her "worst habit" was "crying too much when Joanne yells at me for no good reason." Her twin Peter's answer to "What would make your life better?" was "People should stop telling me how smart I am all the time. It's annoying."

The family's priest and two friends of the children joined in that year: Scotty, Tony's buddy; Father Patrick Dunn; and Michele, Noreen's friend. None of the guests answered all of the questions, preferring, it seemed, to pick and choose. Father Patrick's "happiest day" was "meeting the Pope in Rome." Michele wrote, in large and childish block lettering, that her "favorite vacation" was "Disneyland in France." Noreen had apparently liked Michele's answer and wrote the same. Or was it vice versa? Regardless, they seemed in lockstep. Scotty dashed off that his "hero" was "the surfer dude from *Fast Times at Ridgemont High.*"

Like the photos at the bottom of the box, the questionnaires were snapshots of a time and of a family very much like others: functional and seemingly happy with each other. A family with no idea of the devastation the coming year would bring. Or how its cruel events would expose the cracks and fissures that would tear their lives apart.

Chapter Six

Sunday, October 13

Leaning against her car, Joanne watched as her sister Noreen—on her third attempt to parallel park in front of their mother's house—finally squeezed her red minivan into a tight spot between their brother Peter's car and a blue hatchback.

In the soft mid-morning light, and from a distance, Noreen still looked something like the pretty cheerleader she'd once been, Joanne thought. But at closer range, Noreen was a bulky five-foot-three with a freckled complexion that was starting to prematurely wrinkle and jowl. Blowzy was the word that came to Joanne's mind. *As if she spends her days in a dark bar—and when she does go outside, refuses to use sunscreen.*

"I see you took the only good parking place, as usual," Noreen called out to Joanne. Their mother's narrow driveway could only fit one car, and Joanne had just parked her silver Lexus there. Joanne shrugged and reached into the back seat to retrieve a bag of groceries.

Noreen struggled out of her minivan and impatiently motioned to her fourteen-year-old daughter, Chloe, to put down her phone and get out of the vehicle.

"Gee, sorry," Joanne called to Noreen. "We should have put orange traffic cones out and saved the spot for you." Joanne instantly regretted her sarcasm and in penance, waited by her car so the three of them could walk into the house together.

Chloe sidled over to Joanne and gave her aunt a hug. "Hi, sweetie," Joanne said, kissing Chloe's forehead. Aside from her own two boys, who were still in the sweet, hugging ages but teetering on puberty, Chloe was the child closest to her heart. And it seemed nothing short of a miracle that Chloe and her sixteen-year-old brother Jake, living under Noreen and her husband's freewheeling parenting style, were both normal, happy, and seemingly on track for high school graduation and most likely beyond.

Their mother's front door was ajar. Louie came bounding out to greet them, his tail wagging so hard that his entire body wiggled along with it. Chloe laughed and scooped him up.

"Good morning, girls," Claire called out from the front door, her slender frame silhouetted against the light from the back window. She ushered them in, and they assumed their usual positions in the living room—Claire in her worn brocade armchair near the window; Chloe at her grandmother's feet, sitting cross-legged on the floor with Louie in her lap; and Noreen on the couch with the pillows pushed to the side. Joanne went to the kitchen to unload the grocery bag, then joined Noreen on the coach.

Noreen's eyes roved around the tiny living room. "Peter's still living here, right? Must be a little cramped." Noreen lived ten minutes away in a newish two-story home on the northeast side of town. "I'd let him stay at my house, but it's a zoo over there—two teenagers, a husband, a cat, two dogs—"

"Peter says it's a good thing he's living here so he can take care of me."

Although Joanne rolled her eyes at the absurdity, she realized this gave her an opening for a topic she wanted to raise. "Mom, we have to make plans for when you need real caregivers," she said. "I've gotten some good referrals from friends, and I'd like to start interviewing a few of them soon—"

"Where would they stay?" Claire interrupted her.

It had been two weeks since the prognosis, and Joanne knew her mother was determined to remain independent and upbeat for as long as possible. She made her bed every morning before coffee, fixed her own meals, still drove, paid bills, and kept her hair appointments. Her lipstick still matched her outfit. Independence to Claire was like the air she breathed, and now it was slipping away. It was inevitable, as they both well knew.

Yet Joanne couldn't get Claire to discuss any next steps—like kicking Peter out of the house or moving somewhere else. Claire would always change the subject.

"Anne, please come out here and meet my girls," Claire called out, turning toward the bedroom.

"What? Someone's been hiding out in your bedroom all this time?" Noreen asked with an incredulous look. "While we're out here talking about private family matters—"

"Oh, for Heaven's sake, Noreen, simmer down," Claire said. "Anne and I were almost through working when you drove up."

Anne emerged from the bedroom, looking somewhat sheepish, holding a cardboard box filled with first-edition books in her arms. She'd been packing them up to take home for research when Claire's family arrived early, preventing a clean getaway.

"You already know Joanne, of course, and this is my youngest daughter, Noreen," Claire said to Anne. Then gesturing toward Chloe, added, "And *this* is my favorite granddaughter in the whole wide world, Chloe."

"Your *only* granddaughter," Joanne and Noreen chorused in singsong. Chloe grinned and gave her long, caramel-colored hair a diva-like toss. She clearly never tired of the joke.

"Sit down, Anne. Stay a little longer," Claire urged. Anne settled into a chair in the far corner and appeared, in Joanne's estimation, to be unsure if she should be at this family gathering. Joanne smiled at her, thinking, *She has no idea what she's stepping into.*

"You're helping Mom with the estate, right?" Noreen said, giving Anne a perfunctory smile. "What's in that box you're taking?"

"It's just some old books," Claire said before Anne could answer.

"Mind if I get a drink?" Noreen hauled herself off the couch, and went to the kitchen to pour herself a glass of Chardonnay. "Anyone else want anything?"

No one answered because their attention was drawn to the creaking sound of a door opening. Peter stepped out of the utility room, wearing baggy red sweatpants and a school-bus-yellow T-shirt, rubbing his eyes like he had just woken up. It was close to noon.

"Morning, everyone," he said while yawning. "Quite the crowd." He spotted Noreen through the kitchen door and gave her a little salute. "Hey, twin." She came back into the living room, wine glass in hand, to give him a hug. "Hi, Petey."

"Did Mom tell you all that Anne used to be an FBI agent?" Peter asked.

"An FBI agent, really? What happened with that?" Noreen asked Anne, who just shook her head as if she wasn't about to get into it with Noreen or anyone else in this room.

"Don't grill her, Noreen," Joanne snapped.

"Just curious."

"And here's the interesting part," Peter continued, speaking as though Anne weren't in the room, "she still has some connections with the police and is trying to grease the wheels to get Danny's murder case reopened."

Peter was looking pleased with himself and in the silence that followed, headed into the kitchen with a bounce to his step. "Any coffee left?" he asked.

"Nice conversation starter, Peter," Joanne groaned. That the investigation was possibly going to be reopened was not news to her, but she dreaded hearing Noreen's reaction.

Noreen moved deeper into the room. "What do you mean, reopen the case? I thought we talked about this years ago. It was settled." Noreen's voice rose in agitation, and she turned to face Claire. "We decided there was no point to it! We've got our lives to live—"

"It isn't even decided yet, Noreen," Claire said. "Please calm down."

Noreen gestured toward Anne. "Is this her idea? Did she just go ahead, all on her own, and decide to get the case reopened?"

"No, Noreen, it was entirely my idea," Claire said. "I asked Anne to talk to her uncle about it. He was one of the detectives—"

"Seriously, Mom, what were you thinking?" Noreen gulped down the rest of her wine and set the glass down hard on the coffee table.

"Oh, I don't know," Peter chimed in, coming back into the living room with a mug in his hand, "it could be interesting. I've been watching a lot of true crime shows on TV lately, and we could help the cops to—"

"Help the cops? By doing what, exactly?" Noreen turned her fury onto Peter, who was momentarily stunned; the twins rarely quarreled.

"Well, we could help with interviewing suspects, for one thing...." His words petered out.

Joanne turned to Anne and asked, "Have you heard anything? What are the odds of getting it reopened?"

Noreen threw up her hands. "I won't have anything to do with this. I mean it! Don't you think our family has been through enough?"

"Like your mother said, it hasn't been decided yet." Anne, speaking for the first time, kept her voice steady as if hoping to calm the waters. "My uncle spoke to the assistant district attorney about it a few days ago. We should know this week if they decide it's worth opening."

"Can't we just stop it?" Noreen persisted, a vein beating in her right temple.

"Carry on, ladies," Peter said, heading for the bathroom. "I have to take a shower. I have a special guest who'll be joining us any minute now."

"Who?" Chloe called after him.

"It's a surprise!" Peter said.

Joanne ignored Peter and turned to her mother. "Mom, in a way, I agree with Noreen—but only because of your health. Maybe you have enough on your plate."

"That's right, you just don't need this right now," Noreen said, nodding her head.

"Have you told Tony about this yet?" Joanne asked her mother.

"Where is Tony, anyway? He gets to be Mom's executor, and he doesn't even bother to show up at a family meeting?" Noreen complained.

"*Gets* to be executor? Do you know how much work that is?" Joanne muttered.

"He had to be in London for a meeting. I'll see your brother tomorrow," Claire said in a low voice.

"Tony's going to have an opinion on this," Joanne said.

"Actually," Anne interjected, "the family's opinions don't really matter at

46

this point. It's a criminal matter. Once the wheels are set in motion—that is, if the district attorney decides to open this cold case—there's no stopping them. It's out of the family's hands."

Noreen's expression said she was having none of it. "But if we told them to forget it, I'm sure they would. Just tell them we won't cooperate. I mean, why can't they just go out and investigate some other cold case if they're so damn gung-ho to be opening cases? I'm sure there must be plenty of them to keep them busy."

"Why are you so against this?" Anne asked.

"Stay the fuck out of this," Noreen shot back.

* * *

The air in the room went still, and nobody moved. They all looked toward Claire, waiting for her reaction, but her eyes had shifted to the wall niche above the fireplace with the three photographs of Danny—as an infant, a toddler, a young boy.

"It all happened so long ago," Noreen tried again with a coaxing tone. "Shouldn't we be over it by now? At least a little?"

"I'm not over it," Claire said, her voice weary. "I'm just used to it. I just hide it better."

Claire turned her gaze back to them. "Do you remember Mr. Dunwoody, our neighbor when you were all kids? Well, one day, he came knocking on our door. He said to me, 'Claire, I have a problem. I think the neighborhood kids are breaking into my garage and taking things.' And I thought, oh no, that's got to be Danny. He had just turned five, but what a little rascal—your father used to call him Dennis the Menace. So I said to Mr. Dunwoody, 'What can I do for you, Jim?' And he said, 'I'd like to hire Danny to watch my garage and make sure no kids go in there. I'll pay him two dollars a week.'" Claire paused. "What a dear, wise man Mr. Dunwoody was. He understood little boys. Danny was so proud of his new job. And, of course, the mischief stopped."

Claire sat quietly for a few seconds, wondering why this story had come to mind. What was the point of it? To remind them that Danny was just a sweet, little bright-eyed boy who never meant to hurt anyone? That he wasn't perfect, he wasn't an angel? He could be a little rascal, but he was full of life and promise? Danny deserved to be remembered. And that, she decided, was the point.

Tears threatened, but she willed them away. Even after all these years, grief was relentless. Retreating for a while, and then coming back in waves, blindsiding her when her guard was down—like when she'd suddenly see a baby in a store or on TV, who tilted his head just like Danny did. Or had a crooked smile like Danny's.

Turning to her children, she continued with as much force as she could muster. "You know, I don't really care how much the investigation disrupts our lives—they're disrupted already. What's a little more chaos?" She reached for her cane. "Danny deserves justice. Finally. Justice before I die, and he stops being important to anyone. And I'll do anything I can to see that he gets it."

Claire stood up on unsteady legs. "I'm tired now, so if you'll excuse me."

She turned to Anne and said, "Please let me know as soon as you hear what the district attorney decides."

Her granddaughter leapt soundlessly to her feet, took her arm, and led her to the bedroom. Chloe left the door ajar "so Aunt Joanne can check on you later."

* * *

By the time the front doorbell rang, Noreen, Chloe, and Anne were already halfway to their respective homes; Joanne was tidying up the kitchen, and Peter was still steaming up the bathroom.

"Must be Peter's big surprise," Joanne murmured to herself as she headed to the entryway to answer the doorbell.

Opening the door wide, she saw a woman standing on the porch smiling anxiously. She was a few years younger than Joanne and petite, with brown hair in a spiky pixie haircut.

"Peter's friend, I presume?" Joanne managed a polite smile.

Then it hit her. Of course, Peter's ex.

"Joanne? It's me, Michele."

Claire's bedroom door closed quietly.

Chapter Seven

Monday, October 14

The next morning, Claire woke up to a quiet house. Peter must have spent the night somewhere else. Or maybe he had stayed at Michele's place. *Wherever that is*, she thought with a shudder. When was that relationship going to end?

Then the sound of a low moan caught her ear. Maybe it's the wind blowing through the trees outside her window, she thought for a moment. It was hard to tell. Then she brushed the idea aside. No, the sound was too close; it was coming from inside, somewhere beyond the hallway. Throwing back the covers, she eased out of the hospital-style bed with the help of her cane and slipped into her silk robe and slippers. She opened her bedroom door.

She only got a few steps down the hallway before the moaning started again. It sounded like a woman, and it was coming from behind the closed door of the utility room. Claire stood frozen, then quietly returned to her bedroom and sat on the side of her bed. The sounds stopped. She stared at the clock on her bed table and watched ten minutes tick by, then waited a few more minutes to make sure the moans wouldn't resume before she got up to open the door.

Before it was completely open, she heard muted laughter coming from the living room and then the slamming of the front door. Finally alone, Claire felt a violent anger flare up with the speed of an ignited gas fireplace. *I don't need this, and I won't have it.*

She leaned on her cane to steady herself and proceeded down the hall to the kitchen, where she sat down at the table and wrote a note:

Peter—
This is my house, and I will not hide out in my own bedroom.
You will move out tonight.
Mother

She went out onto the porch and taped it to the front door where he would see it before he walked in after work that evening.

* * *

Claire leaned against the front doorframe and waited for Tony's reaction.

"Want me to throw his stuff out on the grass, Mom?" Tony asked in a joking tone, gesturing to the note. He leaned down to kiss Claire on the cheek.

"Because I'd be glad to," he said, stepping inside. In his early forties and darkly handsome, her son had the black Irish coloring—brown eyes, almost black hair, thick dark eyebrows—that Claire always said was a throw-back gene from his father's side of the family. No one else in the immediate family looked like him.

"Do you think the note's too harsh?"

"Just remind me never to get you mad."

Tony had taken this sunny Monday morning off from work to help her with financial and legal affairs. They talked on the phone every other day, but Claire hadn't seen him in a few weeks, and from the look on his face when he first saw her—which he quickly cleared—he was surprised by her appearance. *I'm thinner, that must be it*, she thought.

"I'm sorry I couldn't make it yesterday. My flight didn't get in until late," he said as they moved into the living room. "So what's the story with Peter?"

"Same old thing, only more so. Come into the kitchen and have some cake with me, and I'll tell you all about it." In the kitchen, Claire reached inside the refrigerator and pulled out the packaged coffee cake Noreen had brought her.

"It's funny," she said, "but before my illness, I would never let myself eat a piece of cake. Too many carbs and calories. Now I try to make it a daily thing."

"Sit down, Mom. I'll get it." Tony went to the cupboard for plates, cut two slices, and brought them to the dining room table. Louie sat patiently under the table, poised for any crumbs that might fall his way.

"OK, let's hear it," he said.

"I can't have Peter living here anymore," she said, and then gave Tony the short version of last night's surprise visit from Michele and a discreet account of this morning's unwelcome interlude.

After just one bite, she put her fork down. "He has a right to his private life, but not at the expense of mine. It's been two weeks since he moved in. He was never supposed to stay here for more than a few days, but you know Peter—"

"Then we'll get him out. I'll pack up his stuff and put it on the porch before I leave."

"He has a key, so he'll just bring everything back in," she countered, slipping Louie a bite of cake off her napkin.

"I'll call a locksmith."

If nothing else, Tony was decisive. He knew how to make things happen. 'The fixer,' Joanne sometimes called him.

"But before we send him packing, let's go over some of your estate trust business and insurance." Tony cleared the dishes off the dining room table, their designated workstation, to make room for his briefcase. He pulled out a dozen forms and piled them on the table. For the next hour, the two sat with their heads together, pouring over the mountains of paper—all the complicated details that go into putting one's affairs in order. Claire asked questions and made her wishes known; Tony explained contingencies and wrote detailed, copious notes. But when it became clear that Claire's energy was fading, Tony put a halt to the work. "We'll finish this later."

"On a different subject," he said, loading the piles of papers into his briefcase. "I'm just curious, but have you heard anything from your old doctor—"

"Dr. Rose. No, he hasn't visited or even called. I'm a little hurt by that. Though I know he probably feels bad about misdiagnosing me."

"More like malpractice, if you ask me. There might be a case against him. I can look into—"

"No, dear," Claire said, shaking her head.

"You can't let people get away with things."

"It was a mistake." Claire let out a sigh. "People make mistakes." She didn't have the time to take the doctor to court, she didn't have the energy, and she certainly didn't have the heart. "There's enough trouble in this world," she said.

He held her gaze and then shrugged. Without another word, he got up and headed toward the utility room to start collecting Peter's belongings.

Claire's voice stopped him. "Are you sure we should do this? Peter's going to be so angry."

Tony came back and parked himself on the arm of the couch and waited.

"Where will he go?" Claire finally said. "Maybe I should give him a few more days."

"This is the only thing he'll understand. If you give Peter a few more days, he'll take a few more months."

Claire just looked at him.

"Don't worry, Mom, he'll forgive you."

"I don't know about that," Claire said. "Did you ever forgive Dad when he tossed your clothes out on the lawn when you were sixteen?" Tony shrugged as if that would dispel the memories.

But Claire remembered that night all too well. Tony had come home drunk from a party like teenagers do. He passed out on the living room couch and woke up—hungover—in time to see his father pitching his clothes, books, baseball card collection, even his underwear, out the front door for all the neighbors to see. Tony ran outside to gather his stuff up and shoved it into the back seat of his car. Then he spent the next two nights at a friend's house. Though Claire felt torn between them, she understood her husband's wild fury. She knew that nothing pushes a parent—especially one who's already in a downward spiral—into an open rage faster than a rebellious teenager. Yet it was still a sore spot.

"Actually, I did forgive him. I think it was last year," he said. Claire managed a smile. "Okay, point taken, Mom. Then we'll have to go with plan B," he said, raising his hands in the air as if to say, *whatever the hell that is.*

"Maybe we could take the note off the front door and move it *inside* to his bedroom door instead. That's less harsh. And I'll give him a deadline of 24 hours instead of tonight."

"Okay, and if that doesn't work, I'll give him a call. And if *that* doesn't work, we'll get the locks changed," Tony said, then shifted to a new topic. "So you saw Michele last night? That girl was a major disturber. What did she have to say for herself?"

"I didn't even get a glimpse of her," Claire said. "I just heard her voice. Which was more than enough for me after what she put our family through during her marriage to Peter—"

"—the backstabbing and petty larceny, sleeping with Joanne's boyfriend...."

"And then sending Joanne that anonymous letter to make sure she knew about it," she said.

He shrugged. "What a shitshow that was."

"I never understood that girl. She blew up her marriage and our family from the inside out. All in one fell swoop." Claire frowned.

"But at least the incident got Michele out of the family."

"For a while, anyway."

"So why's she back? I don't get it," Tony said.

"I have no idea. Maybe she came back for Peter. I hear she still uses our last name. Calls herself Michele Murray. Even though she dumped him and got married again. How Peter could ever get involved with her again is beyond me...oh, well." Her voice faded out.

She rose from the table and moved into the living room, then slowly sank into the couch. She gestured for Tony to sit down beside her, signaling the time had come to speak of weightier matters.

"Darling, I'm getting tired and will have to lie down for a nap soon. But before you leave, I need to talk to you about something." She folded her hands neatly in her lap and looked down at them.

"What's on your mind?"

"Jo says I'll need caretakers soon," she said, looking up, "and I know she's right. But let's face it, there's no room here at the house for anyone to stay. I'm not sure how to resolve this."

"Now that you bring it up, the girls and I have been talking. We decided that you can't stay at this house alone much longer."

Claire sat motionless for a moment, staring blankly at the distant wall. Her thoughts were miles away.

"Mom?"

She looked up to find Tony staring at her. She gathered herself and turned to face him. "I want to be very clear about something, Tony," she said slowly. "I will not move in with any of you kids. I will not become a burden. Absolutely not. Where I die and how I die will be on my terms." She fingered her cane and tapped it twice on the floor for emphasis.

"And I will *not* go into some damn nursing home!"

Tony seemed startled by her agitated state. He took her trembling hands in his and said quietly, "There are other alternatives out there, Mom. I've been talking to Joanne and Noreen. We have an idea."

"What kind of idea?"

"It's still in the planning stages. Before we come to you with it, I need to get more information. But we think you'll approve of it. In any case, nothing will be decided without your consent." He lifted her right hand, kissed the top of it, then stood up to leave.

"We'll do everything in our power to abide by your wishes. We'll take care of you, Mom, I promise."

He walked out the front door, ripped off the note intended for Peter, came back inside, and handed it to Claire.

"Here's your note, Mom. Now don't change *any* of it except maybe to give him more time to move. The rest is perfect. I especially liked the part about 'This is my house.' Damn right, it's your house."

She looked out the mullioned kitchen window and watched him walk to his car. *There's a swagger to his walk*, she realized with amused affection. Where had it come from—his father? Or maybe he was just born with it. She'd had aspirations for all her children, but it was Tony, much more so than the others—even the competent and gifted Joanne—who exceeded her hopes for his success. Tony was the one with the golden resume who went from a scholarship to UC Berkeley to Harvard Business School, then rose through the business ranks to become a principal of The Lans Group, an international development firm. Entirely, completely on his own. It was as if he could tap into some magical formula for success only a few knew how to access.

He had been so young after Danny's death, yet she had depended on him. But had it been fair to him? No child should be burdened to the point of sacrificing his youth to take care of the adults around him. She worried that she had done that and was maybe doing it still.

The ringing of the phone broke her reverie. It was Anne.

"Claire, hello. My uncle just called with the news: Danny's case is being reopened, effective today. He'll be contacting you soon."

Chapter Eight

Thursday, October 17

Three days later, a customer walked into Nell's Diner, breezed past the busy hostess station, and headed toward a back booth. Dirty breakfast dishes, crumpled napkins, empty cups, crumbs, and bits of egg still littered the table. Waitresses hate when people sit down at uncleared tables, the customer knew full well. *Like I care.*

A folded newspaper had been left behind by the last customer and was tucked under a plate caked with drying eggs. On the bottom of page four was a short news article accompanied by a headshot of a bright-eyed Danny Murray in his school uniform. The article might have escaped the notice of most readers, but it would pull in others like a magnet draws straight pins.

Leads Sought in Unsolved 1990 Murder

SANTA ROSA— A 29-year-old cold case involving the shocking murder of a five-year-old Santa Rosa boy has been reopened, it was announced yesterday by Sonoma County Asst. District Attorney Joseph Kessler.

"Advances in forensics technology and expanded databases warrant the retesting of evidence collected at the murder scene," said Kessler.

The public is being asked to come forth with any new information regarding the case. "We're hoping anyone who remembers

THE LAST THING CLAIRE WANTED

anything—or suspects someone—will come forward. You never know what piece of information will fit into the puzzle," said Det. John McCormack, who came out of retirement to head the investigation for the district attorney's office.

The DA's office has established a new anonymous tip line, TipLineSR, to encourage those hesitant to call the police. This third-party tip line will take the caller's information and relay it to the police without identifying the caller. A reward of up to $1,000 will be paid for useful information.

Finishing lunch, the customer folded the newspaper, tucked it inside a green backpack, and muttered, "$1,000? What a cheap-ass reward."

But a lot of people would do, or say, plenty for a lot less money.

* * *

"I forgot the newspaper," Jack said to Anne as they drove down Fourth Street on the way to their meeting at the district attorney's office.

"We'll have to go back," he said.

"Are you kidding?" she ribbed. "You're so excited by seeing your name in print that we have to drive all the way back to Nell's? And try to find a parking place to boot?"

"Never mind, I've got a newspaper at home. The photographer took pictures of me. I wonder why they didn't use one."

Anne laughed. Her uncle was in high spirits and full of himself.

"Maybe you should buy more copies," she said, "and laminate them to send out with your Christmas cards."

"Laugh it up, kiddo, but Jack is back." In his button-down blue shirt and tan khaki pants, Anne thought he was looking very sharp. Very professional. He noticed her studying his outfit and said, "Dot took me shopping at the mall last night."

Anne hadn't seen this side of him since his retirement dinner when he had been hailed as a 'cop's cop' by his colleagues ten years before. For today's meeting, Jack even brought along his old, scuffed-up briefcase, which was stuffed with files and stashed on the floor of the back seat.

Midday traffic was light, and they made good time breezing north along Highway 101. Seven minutes later, they took the Steele Lane exit and pulled into the parking lot of the county administration complex, a monolith of boxy concrete buildings with narrow slits for windows.

They were a few minutes early for their two o'clock meeting, so they decided to take the stairs to Joe Kessler's office on the third floor. Jack was breathing hard by the time they reached the reception area.

"I'm already up to 2K steps on my Fitbit today," he bragged to Anne, who raised her brows. She would wager hard cash that the count wouldn't be much higher by nightfall.

"Getting in shape to get the bad guys," he wheezed. "Which reminds me, is the police chief making you take a physical before hiring you, or is he waving it?"

"I haven't gotten that far yet."

"Well, don't drag your heels. You're the one who got me into this case—you and Claire—and you won't do me much good without police officer powers."

Kessler's secretary, busy talking on the phone, waved to Jack and motioned for them to go ahead to the office down the hallway. When they reached Kessler's open door, they saw him thumbing through a stack of papers on his desk, then look up. He smiled and leaned over the desk to shake Jack's hand.

"Joe, this is my niece, Anne McCormack, Bob's daughter," Jack said. "Anne has been working with the Murray family, as I mentioned on the phone."

Kessler extended his hand to Anne. She gauged him to be in his early fifties. He was average height, Black, with thinning hair and thick glasses. Ordinary, except for his intelligent eyes and easy authority.

"We actually met a few times when you were a kid. Your dad and I were golfing buddies."

Although having no such memories, she shook his hand and said, with a graciousness she didn't know she possessed, "Of course, good to see you again." Claire's influence, she decided.

"I understand you trained at the Bureau and were an agent for several years," Kessler said, motioning for them to sit in the two guest chairs facing his desk.

"We can use that kind of expertise on cold cases like this, or on other investigations for that matter." Kessler smiled at her while Jack settled into his chair.

"I've gone in a different direction lately. Away from investigations." Anne hesitated, not sure how much her uncle had told Kessler about her departure from the FBI. "I've started my own business. Estate services, that kind of thing...."

Anne saw a skeptical look pass over Kessler's face, and it wasn't hard to read his mind: *Then why are you here?*

A fair question, and one she'd wrestled with during the last few weeks. Her reasons started with Claire. During their hours of working together, a bond had grown between the two of them, and Anne couldn't help but be moved by the still-grieving mother and her longing for resolution. The case also gave her a chance to work with her uncle. But an even stronger, truer pull was her own fascination with crime, a bone-deep curiosity about why people did what they did, and how they did it. Besides, the job would come with a paycheck.

Still and all, she reminded herself, she was heading in a new career direction.

What Anne said aloud was as bland as the office decor surrounding her. "I hope I can bring something to the table. I'm looking forward to working with all of you—in any capacity that's helpful."

"Anne has a relationship with Claire Murray that gives her unusual access to the family," Jack said. "And as you know, casual conversations can offer up sensitive information—the kind of information people wouldn't feel comfortable coughing up in a more formal setting—"

"Like at a police station," Kessler agreed and then turned to Anne. "Your uncle tells me that you're not currently licensed, but you're working on it, right?"

Anne nodded.

"Until then, there are some limits to your involvement." Raising his hand, he used his fingers to tick off the restrictions. "One," he said, index finger raised, "you can't collect physical evidence for DNA testing. Actually, you could, but it couldn't be presented in court. Chain of custody problems. Two...."

He continued in this vein until all five fingers of his hand were raised.

"Understood," she said in a tight voice, annoyed at his condescending need to explain the fundamentals. But she caught herself and quickly ran through all the reasons not to have a chip on her shoulder about this guy: it's not personal; she is an unknown quantity to him; there's no reason for him to trust her yet; he's just covering his ass. Her therapist would be proud. Nevertheless, she wasn't liking his attitude.

"Do you have a firearm?" Kessler continued.

"Yes." She had a conceal-carry permit, but hadn't fired her Springfield Armory semi-automatic in years except for shooting practice at the range.

"You won't need it," Jack jumped in.

"The department can't take liability for your actions until you get qualified," Kessler said. "But all that said, any information or research you can pass along to Jack is greatly appreciated."

So that was it. She had her assignment: to study the dynamics of the family and tease out any information she could, whether online or in personal interviews.

"Oh, by the way, Jack, your old partner-in-crime Dean is coming on board part-time like you. He's taking the empty office next to yours," Kessler said.

"I already heard, and I'm looking forward to having him under my command," Jack said, grinning. "Do you mind if I make a quick call?" He stood up without waiting for a reply and walked to the other side of the room.

While Jack was on the phone, Kessler quietly took Anne aside.

"You know, dismissal or resignation from the FBI doesn't have to mean the end of your career," Kessler said. "I don't know the particulars of your case, but as long as the reasons have been dealt with, the FBI won't stand in your way."

"I've heard that, but it's reassuring to hear it from someone in your position," Anne said.

"And given your background, it may be easier and faster than you think to get your license from the police department on a temp assignment basis. They might want you to jump through a few hoops—like qualify to their standards at the range, but I'm pretty sure the Chief could wave that with your experience. Once that's done, we can bring you on board here at the DA's office. We hire investigators from other agencies all the time."

Kessler puzzled her. One minute he was patronizing, the next earnest and borderline deferential. She decided to settle on 'earnest' and let it go.

Jack joined them. "I just checked the tip line. Nothing yet."

* * *

"Very cozy," said Anne, looking around Jack's office. It was located directly above Kessler's office on the fourth floor, and it wasn't much to look at. It had a narrow slit of a window and furniture that looked like it had been hauled up from the storage room and barely dusted off: a basic L-shaped gray metal desk with a computer, metal file cabinets, a swivel chair, and two wobbly guest chairs. A tan, corded landline phone sat on the desk by the computer. In the corner, five white banker boxes were stacked on the floor.

"Play your cards right, and you'll get your own fancy office."

"I already have my own fancy office," Anne said. "I'll work from there."

Lifting a box onto his desk, Jack said, "Step one will be to review all the old case material—go through the chronological records, the photographs, witness lists, lead sheets, detective notes, lab docs, and so on. When I went over to the police property and evidence control unit, I was expecting to find cardboard boxes with all the case materials tossed in haphazardly. Your basic time-consuming nightmare. I knew I'd have to try to organize all of that and make copies. But know what I found?" he asked, reaching into the box.

"Can't wait to hear," Anne said with an amused smile.

"The original investigative staff had already copied the evidence and put it in labeled three-ring binders—with tabs, no less," he said, holding a binder aloft like it was lit from within. "This case was handled with kid gloves, that's how high-profile it was. Mind you, it's still going to be very time-consuming to figure out what's been done—and what needs to be done—but everything seems to be in good order. Anyway, I'm counting on it 'cause I think the culprit is hiding in that stack of old case boxes. Hiding and ready to be exposed. I can smell it."

"What about the physical evidence—the hairs, flashlight, and fingerprints?" Anne asked.

"Collected and stored in sealed paper bags, which was standard for the time. They got sent to the lab last week," he said. "Let's just hope the evidence wasn't over-handled or that it isn't just plain too old to be useful for DNA. We'll find out soon enough."

Anne sat on a metal chair with her notebook in hand.

"So what's *my* first move?"

"Aside from getting sworn in?"

"Okay, okay," she muttered.

"Talk to Claire. Ask her if there's anything she didn't tell us back then. Or if there's anyone she suspects, even a little. Even if it's someone in the family. And then go through this list of the family members and ask them the same things."

Jack handed her a list of names, all of them familiar.

"And here's a copy of the notes from their original interviews," he said, passing her a file.

"I'll study these," she said. "It'll be interesting to compare what they said *then* with what they'll say now." Anne flipped through the pages of typed interviews.

"What about their friends?" she asked. "I'd like to talk to Claire's friend, Betty Fazio. Maybe track down that childhood friend of Noreen's, Michele."

"Talk to the family first, then branch out to friends later. Report back with anything interesting. Dean and I will follow up. As for Michele Dixon, see if anyone knows where she is or how to contact her. That would give us a head start. But until you get sworn in, leave Noreen's interview to us.

We'll talk to her." Jack stood up to leave.

"What about Tony's friend Scotty? And that janitor?"

"They're on my list," he said, opening the door and locking it behind them. "Guess we're off and running."

* * *

"Slow down!" Anne snapped. "It's the next turn!" Her uncle's driving made her crazy.

"I know it's the next turn, damn it," Jack snapped back.

"And watch out for that guy on the bike—"

"I know how to drive, okay?" He grumbled.

The trip to pick up Anne's car in the parking lot—where she'd left it so they could drive together to the Kessler meeting—wasn't going smoothly. Jack turned into the lot, eased into the empty spot next to Anne's car, and then turned off the motor. She unfastened her seatbelt and reached down for her purse, poised for a quick exit.

"Wait a minute, Anne, I want to talk to you." He sounded uncharacteristically serious. She clutched her purse in her lap, her eyes trained on the floor mat.

"You seem so, what's the word..." he said haltingly. "I guess, irritable lately."

"Thanks for not saying bitchy."

"Never, Annie. And by the way, there's nothing's wrong with my driving." Jack took a breath. "It's you. Something's going on with you. Tell me."

She settled her purse back down on the floor but didn't look up. She wasn't in a hurry to meet his eyes.

"It's nothing, really. Nothing specific, more of a generalized...." She stopped herself mid-sentence. How could she explain this free-floating, low-grade depression—this sadness—that had come over her since receiving the invitation? For a baby shower, for God's sake. Such an innocuous thing, yet it triggered so much in her.

Jack waited for her to speak again.

"I don't know…" she began, looking out the car window into the distance. "It's been two years since everything—my career and marriage—imploded. I thought it would be over by now. But it never ends. The shame and the embarrassment…."

She shook her head and reached for the car handle. "I'm okay, I really am—"

"Are you? Your Aunt Dot doesn't think so. She thinks you're still upset about your divorce from Gary."

"Well, she's right, of course, but it's more than that. It's a combination of things, the divorce, and the dismissal. They're tied together."

"They didn't dismiss you. You dismissed yourself."

"Before they could."

"That's debatable. Anyway, the FBI culture is tough on people. A *lot* of agents quit or wash out. People get divorced right and left at the bureau, especially during training. Drinking problems…"

"Then I must be a textbook case. Divorce, check. Drinking, check. Although no drinking problem per se—a few incidents involving booze, but I do *not* have a drinking problem."

"OK, fine, but you've quit drinking, right?" He gave her a sidelong glance.

"For now. We'll see."

"Has Gary contacted you?"

"No, we have no contact at all. I don't even know where he lives now."

"Too bad you don't still have access to FBI databases. But you could always Google it," Jack said, then paused. "Sorry, bad joke."

"No offense taken. But I *am* a little offended that you think I'd use Google," she said ruefully. "Or even one of those cheesy people-search websites. No, I prefer the unauthorized use of high-security FBI databases for *my* stalking needs." She shook her head at the memory of how the trail of her searches to gather information about Gary had caught the attention of higher-ups and prompted her immediate resignation.

The cool fall air was seeping into the car. Jack reached over to start the engine to blast up the heater but then stopped, as if fearing the sound of it would break the mood. Fearing she would bolt.

"Is that why you're dragging your heels about the investigation? Is it about the FBI thing?" Jack asked.

Again with the "dragging heels." And yet, for all of her sound reasons for helping solve the case, her exit from the FBI did make her leery of going back into law enforcement.

Without waiting for an answer, Jack continued, "And about Gary—the lowlife was having an affair. You caught him. You went a little crazy. It happens. You were wrong to do what you did, okay. But consider this: how he retaliated was even worse, in my opinion."

"I overreacted." But then again, maybe not, she thought. Gary had tried to sabotage her credit rating and lied to their friends about her—telling them she slashed his new girlfriend's tires, broke into his home, and ripped up his clothes. All lies. Who knows what else he did or said? He had no bottom. Though she did, in truth, make some drunken, late-night calls and send angry emails with vague threats, which he promptly forwarded to their friends. Tension seeped into the muscles of her shoulders.

"Everything isn't your fault. Gary's a jerk. Always was," Jack said.

"I haven't done any searches on him since then, so I guess that's progress. I made a big enough fool of myself to last a lifetime." There was more that her uncle didn't know, and never would if she could help it.

"Everybody makes a fool of themselves sooner or later," Jack said, then started humming. "What's that song?" He snapped his fingers. "It's 'Everybody Plays the Fool Sometimes.'" He sang along to the music in his head, getting the lyrics mangled up as usual.

Anne felt her shoulders relax. Somehow he could always make her feel better. "Thank you, Uncle Jack," she said quietly.

"And think of it this way: you're still young. You've got a lot of dumb, foolish years ahead of you. You've just begun."

She opened the car door slightly but stayed seated.

"You've always been too hard on yourself," he said.

"I think *I've* got problems—most of them of my own making, I know. But then I look at Claire," Anne said. "She's handling her illness, Danny's murder case, that argumentative family of hers. Now *those* are problems. I got nothin'. And she's handling it all with grace and courage."

Jack started the engine. "Okay, kiddo. You going home now?"

"No, first I'm going to a job at a mobile park. It's called Tranquil Acres. Ever hear of it?" Anne asked, stepping out of the car.

He looked at her incredulously. "Every cop in town knows that place. Wall-to-wall pervs. You have a client there?"

"My client's mother lived there before she died. The job's wrapping up," she reassured him. "This will be my last trip there."

"If I remember correctly, that place was owned by an older couple."

"Judy Lyle and her husband. They still do. But she says they've never had a problem with her 'boys' as she calls them."

"Then they've got more luck than brains. Maybe I should come with you. It'll be dark soon."

"I'll be okay."

"Maybe you should go home first and pick up your gun."

"Nope. Got it in my car."

* * *

It was nearly nightfall when Anne turned into the Tranquil Acres mobile park, her car lights on high beam to guide the way to her client's doublewide. A sign announcing FOR RENT was posted inside Althea's front window.

This wasn't the best time of day—if there even was one—to be visiting a 'habitat for sex offenders,' as its owner Judy Lyle called it. But she would make it a quick stop, just pack up the few remaining odds and ends, and then head home to leftover pasta. Tomorrow she would turn the keys back over to her client Vanessa Jackson. *Fini.*

It was unusually windy and chilly for an October evening. Anne slipped on her down jacket before stepping out of her car. She heard the familiar creak of a metal front door. Judy poked her head out of her trailer next door, then flicked on the porch light.

"Almost done?" Judy asked, coming outside with a flashlight in hand. She directed the beam onto the front porch so Anne wouldn't trip on the steps.

"Just a few boxes left."

"Let me help."

They went inside together, removed their jackets, and spent the next ten minutes filling boxes with the dregs of Althea's worldly goods—one box for Goodwill, one for the trash bin, and the last box of framed family photos for the client. After setting the boxes on the front porch, Anne went back inside and walked through each room, opening closets and drawers. Inspecting one last time to make sure nothing was left behind.

She was in the living room when she heard angry hollering coming from outside. She stopped in front of the bay window, her eye caught by movement from across the street. Under the streetlamp, a scruffy-looking man wearing only a thin T-shirt and jeans was staring at her while he paced back and forth on the sidewalk. He turned his head after every few steps, so his eyes always stayed on her. Pacing and staring, over and over, along with some yelling, fist shaking, and fingers jabbing in the air. The effect would have been comical if he wasn't so deranged, Anne thought.

She grabbed Judy's arm and pulled her over to the window.

"Who's that lunatic? And why is he staring over here at us?"

"Pay no attention to him," Judy said, clearly annoyed at the spectacle outside. "That's just Carl. He's just agitated and drunk and wants attention. He's usually not so crazy, but today...." Judy interrupted herself to go out onto the porch and yell, "Go inside, Carl!"

He stopped pacing. Judy made shooing gestures at him. "Go!" His storm of fury spent, he slowly retreated to the inside of his trailer.

Judy stepped back inside Althea's doublewide, shut the door, and heaved a long sigh.

"Boy, it was crazy-town here this afternoon! He knocked on my door, waving a newspaper, yelling and screaming, 'The cops will be here any minute.' I told him the cops were here all the damn time, so what else was new? But he kept ranting and raving about some murder that happened years ago."

"What else did he say?" Anne said, watching her closely.

"Not much that I listened to. But I said to him, 'If you don't have anything to do with that murder, the cops won't bother you. What are you so worried about?'"

"What did he say to that?"

"Something like, 'I didn't do nothing, and if they look at my record, they'll see I don't even like little boys.' Whatever the hell *that* means," Judy said.

"What's his name?" Anne kept her voice steady.

"Carl Pinn. He's lived here about ten years. Used to be a janitor, but not anymore. I don't know what he lives on, money-wise. Maybe disability. I just know he pays his rent on time. And he's usually quiet. Keeps to himself."

Anne's heart was racing. So this was where the St. Paul's school janitor ended up. The guy who wouldn't give up his hair sample, who had a sketchy alibi, who acted 'squirrelly' when he was questioned all those years ago—he lives here now.

Which means he has a prison record, she reasoned. Which means, in turn, that his fingerprints, and probably his DNA, are registered on the nationwide sex offenders database. *Oh, lucky day.*

She squinted at Pinn's doublewide to make out the house numbers. The cold case team could find Pinn's location easily enough through records, but it didn't hurt to give them a head start.

Anne zipped up her jacket and stepped out into the chill air. She opened the car trunk and loaded up the boxes.

"I'm getting too old for this place," Judy said, heading back to her doublewide. "And now that Althea's gone, it's kind of lonely here with just my husband to talk to. Maybe it's time to sell this place."

"Thanks for all your help, Judy," Anne said, slamming down the trunk door.

"No problem, drop by anytime."

Chapter Nine

Thursday, October 17

In the pale gray light of the autumn evening, Claire was waiting for Betty Fazio in the parking lot of The Parisian hotel. Like they had done for years, the old friends would walk into the hotel's dark piano lounge together, arm in arm.

Would tonight be the last time? Claire quickly brushed off the thought in her pragmatic way. She heard Betty's car pull up beside hers, right on time. *Well, if it is, we'll make it a good one.*

She glanced over at Betty but couldn't catch her eye. Betty was preoccupied with angling her car's rear-view mirror, patting her bobbed blond hair, adding another swipe of mascara, and freshening her lipstick—all the rituals Betty usually used to fill the minutes of waiting for the perpetually late Claire.

Claire used to be punctual, almost to a fault, but that was before Danny died, and before her internal clock—along with everything else in her world—tilted off kilter. In those disorienting, grim days right after his death, a steady stream of friends and acquaintances had rallied around the family, encircling them. Condolence letters, phone calls, and flower arrangements poured in. But after a few weeks, the attention waned, and everyone got on with their own lives.

Everyone except Betty. She was the one who bore witness to the crime's miserable aftermath. She stayed by Claire's bedside for hours, holding her hand, speaking quietly or not speaking at all. She weathered Claire's fevered, angry outbursts and her inconsolable grief. She watched as Gerald gradually withdrew, locking himself in his study with bottles of scotch or whatever was handy.

Every night Betty brought the family their dinner—a baked ham, pizza, a quart of lemon chicken, homemade lasagna. And every morning at seven-thirty sharp, she would arrive at the house to drive the kids to school. Their bagged lunches would be ready for them in a cooler in the back of the van. She would pick them up after school to make sure they got home safely.

And Betty watched as the losses piled up: Gerald stopped showing up at work, so his commercial development business started to fail; he was forced to resign as mayor; the family teetered on bankruptcy. She watched as the family reeled from shock and defeat. But after a while, she also saw them struggle to recalibrate and regain their equilibrium.

After about a year, when Claire was feeling up to it, she and Betty would drive to The Parisian hotel and sit in a back booth in the piano lounge, a cozy world of dim lights, chocolate-brown leather banquettes, burnished wood, and murals of local vineyards. They would order dirty martinis and pass along song requests via the waiter.

Claire would always ask for her favorite song, the achingly lovely "What'll I Do" by Irving Berlin. Betty would urge "something more upbeat." But Claire would insist. She'd lean back, close her eyes, and let Berlin's haunting lyrics wash over her:

What'll I do with just a photograph
to tell my troubles to
When I'm alone
With only dreams of you
That won't come true
What'll I do?

"Betty saved my life," Claire would say about those days. "And I will never forget."

Betty finally looked over and noticed Claire, waved her lipstick in greeting, and got out of her car. "Good God, you're on time!" The hotel's uniformed doorman recognized them and rushed over to help Claire out of her car. "Lovely to see you two again." He gave them a slight bow. It had been months since their last visit.

The Parisian's history was part of the Murray family's history, starting in the late 1960s when Gerald and his partners developed the resort-like hotel to bring a mix of European and Las Vegas glamour to Santa Rosa. The posh Grand Opening party was attended by a lot of important people—politicians, lawyers, even a few minor Hollywood celebrities. It had even made the society page of the *San Francisco Chronicle*.

With its expanse of polished black marble flooring, gilt-edged mirrors, and blue velvet upholstered love seats arranged in conversational groupings, The Parisian was shabbily elegant, and though it still exuded some of its old glamour, the hotel was in woeful need of the multi-million-dollar makeover that was scheduled to start within a few years.

Claire and Betty passed through a brass-edged, revolving glass door into the lobby and felt as though they were stepping back in time. All the way back to their days as the town's two most stylish blondes who'd turned every man's head in the hotel's ballroom. Even in her seventies, Betty was slim and had the beautiful legs of a Broadway gypsy, which in fact, she had been for a brief time before joining the Radio City Rockettes—and before her husband Butch swooped her up and brought her out west.

Claire's beauty had faded into a fragile loveliness, having done "precisely nothing," as she would say, to preserve her looks. Betty, who was privy to Claire's regular Botox and filler treatments, said nothing; she let her arched eyebrow say it for her. Claire's smile still glowed, friends would say, like the double strand of pearls she often wore. "You don't smile, Claire, you *beam*."

It was six o'clock, the heart of the cocktail hour at the piano lounge, yet the regular Thursday night crowd hadn't arrived yet. The place was empty except for the pianist, Harry, and the bartender who was polishing the mahogany bar.

Betty led the way to the far corner booth near the piano. A waiter came over to light the candle on the table and take their orders: one martini with extra olives for Claire, one bourbon straight up for Betty.

"Is that Frank tending bar?" Claire waved to him across the room. Frank Greco nodded and winked at them. After decades of bartending, he was now the operating manager and part owner of the hotel, thanks to a substantial inheritance from the previous owner, his former boss. But on slow nights, he liked to take up his old position behind the bar. It gave him a feel for the ebb and flow of business, and a chance to visit with old friends.

A few dozen hotel guests and patrons started drifting into the room. Betty and Claire sipped their drinks and caught up with Claire's family drama (*Peter promises to move out tomorrow*), Betty's family drama (*Butch refuses to shave his beard off*), news about the investigation (*Detective McCormack called me*), doctor visits, and the seventy-fifth birthday party Claire's children were planning for her in three weeks (*It's getting bigger by the minute*).

Claire nursed her martini. Betty, now on her second shot of Maker's Mark, set her glass down and surveyed the room with a critical eye: the mood of the crowd was far too subdued for her taste. The pianist launched into "a little tune I wrote that I hope you'll enjoy," and when it was finally over, a cloud of inertia seemed to envelope the room.

"What a dirge." She nudged Claire. "Let's liven up this joint."

Claire laughed. She knew what was coming.

"Okay, but I'm begging you—anything but 'My Way,' " Claire said.

Betty gulped down the last of her drink, stood up, smoothed her black satin skirt, and with her heels clicking, sashayed across the room to the baby grand. She leaned in close to the pianist, whispered something in his ear, and reached for the mic sitting on a stand on the piano.

From behind the bar, Frank grinned. He seemed to get a kick out of Betty and her impromptu song sets and was known to say that she was actually quite good in a jazzy, late-period Rosemary Clooney kind of way.

He clinked two wine glasses to get the room's attention and announced in a booming voice: "Ladies and gentlemen, please welcome a star of Santa Rosa community musicals and a veteran of the Broadway stage, our own Betty Fazio."

The audience applauded politely and went back to their drinks.

Betty blew into the microphone, testing it, then said, "I thought I'd start with my rendition of 'My Way.' "

Claire groaned.

"No, just kidding," Betty grinned, then launched into the peppy "Put on a Happy Face" from *Bye Bye Birdie*, one of those community musicals she had appeared in.

Mild but sincere applause followed this time.

Frank wound his way around tables, pausing to chat with a few customers before he sat down next to Claire in her booth. They sat in companionable silence, listening to Betty sing a couple of torch songs about love gone wrong.

"I could stay here forever," Claire said, leaning back and closing her eyes.

A waiter came over to the table and tapped Frank on the shoulder. "Sorry, Frank, but there's a call in your office."

"Excuse me, Claire, but I've got to take this."

On his way out, Frank gestured to the bartender who'd just come on duty and—nodding toward Claire's and Betty's table—mouthed the words "On the house."

* * *

"So that's the situation," Joanne said into the receiver. She had just broken the news of her mother's illness to Frank Greco.

"Oh, geez, I knew Claire wasn't feeling well, but I didn't know it was this serious," Frank said. "This is rough, Joanne. What can I do to help?"

She outlined the family's idea: They wanted to book a double suite at The Parisian, a place where Claire could live out the rest of her life in the greatest comfort the family could provide. "We'd like her residency to be open-ended. It could be as long as three months. Or with any luck, even beyond," Joanne said.

"We've never had a request like this before. But I don't see why not, especially since it's for your mother. Let me check the room availabilities."

Joanne could hear the clicking of the keyboard.

"What about her nursing care? Will you be providing for that?" Frank asked.

"We'll arrange for around-the-clock home care. That's why we need the extra bedroom."

"Here we go. Found what I was looking for," Frank said. "You'll want the corner Presidential Suite on the top floor. She'll have views of the vineyards on one side, and the downtown skyline on the other." He described the suite as having a living room and two bedrooms with en suite bathrooms, as well as a kitchenette with a sink, refrigerator, range top, microwave, cupboards, and coffee maker.

"Month-to-month suites here are expensive," Frank said, and then quoted her a five-figure rate that amounted to almost a year's salary for some of his own hotel employees. Joanne was unfazed. She and her older brother Tony had figured it would be pricey and that, between them, they could afford it. She had a well-paying, upper management marketing job, and her husband, Mark, was an established dentist. And money wasn't an issue for Tony, a millionaire before he'd turned thirty-five. Noreen would want to contribute what she could, but Tony said that he didn't want her to stretch herself too thin, so he'd pick up the slack.

And Peter? They weren't even going to bring up the matter with him. They'd be lucky, in Tony's opinion, if Peter didn't see this move as an opportunity to take over Claire's house and sublet the bedroom, pocketing the rent. Or even grab the second bedroom of the hotel suite as his own. "I have visions of Peter lounging by the hotel swimming pool." Joanne threw in, "Margarita in hand."

She shook her head to clear the thought. She was tired of Peter's sense of entitlement and tired of judging him for it.

"That'll work, Frank," she said. "Other places might be less expensive, but this is what we want for Mom."

Joanne knew it was the right move. The Parisian held a special place in Claire's heart. Having visited the hotel for decades, the uniformed staff knew her by name. She delighted in hearing children splashing in the Olympic-size pool and looking out at the hilltop views. More important, the hotel held nothing but warm memories for her: so many family parties and Mother's Day brunches in the four-star restaurant, so many joyous wedding receptions, bar mitzvah parties, and over-the-top charity balls. Fred MacMurray, a local resident and movie star—and, as it turned out, an excellent dancer—had once spun her around the dance floor.

"This will happen fast, Frank, unless, for some reason, Mom doesn't like the idea. But I don't see that happening—"

"Hold on one second," Frank interrupted her.

She could hear him call out, "Night, ladies, drive safe." Once back on the line, Frank said, "Betty and your mother just left the lounge. They should be home before it gets too dark. Anyway, Joanne, let me know if it's a go. You know we'll take good care of her."

Chapter Ten

Friday, October 18

The following morning Jack McCormack stood outside his office door, fumbling with his keys, as the landline inside was on its sixth—and likely final—ring. "Hang on, damn it," Jack muttered out loud. He barely made it in time to pick up the call. An out-of-state area code came up on the screen.

"Lieutenant McCormack here." Jack cradled the receiver against his shoulder, struggled out of his jacket, and draped it on the back of his chair.

"Lieutenant, this is Scott Hudson. It's been a while."

It took Jack a half-second to place the caller. "Oh, hi, Scott, thanks for returning my call." Jack sat down at his desk and grabbed his notebook and pen. The last time he and Scott had spoken was nearly thirty years before, when Jack interviewed the teenager soon after Danny Murray's death. The kid had been so traumatized by finding Danny's body that he'd been largely silent. Now that decades had passed, Jack was hoping he might learn what Scott had seen and heard as a kid that he hadn't told the detectives about at the time.

"I guess it's Sheriff Hudson, now, right?"

"Yes, I'm working up here in Brookings, Oregon. A small seaside town, only around eight thousand people. Not a hotbed of crime, but then neither was Santa Rosa back in the day. My sister still lives in Santa Rosa, and she sent me a link to yesterday's newspaper article asking for anonymous tips."

"So you know why I called."

"The Danny Murray case, sure. I was wondering when it would finally get reopened. I think about that case every day. It's the main reason I became a cop. Any new developments?"

"It's coming along. DNA results will be in next week. That'll be a big tell." Jack leaned back in his chair, settling in for a long and—he hoped—enlightening interview with the kid who grew up to be a cop—and who could look back on the events with a cop's perspective. "But as you know, it's often by talking again to witness like yourself that we get some new light shed on motives or suspects."

"Sure, glad to help. Ask away," Scott said. "Not that I have much to add to my original statement. Except that over the years, I've done some speculating about it. Got a few random thoughts I'd like to share with you."

For the next ten minutes, they went over Scott's past testimony, retracing his steps from the ring of the school bell to the moment he found Danny's body. But even after decades of playing and replaying a mental film of that day—and dissecting every instant—Scott said his memories remained largely unchanged.

"So that wraps up your old testimony. Now, I'd like to hear those thoughts," Jack said. "You were close to the family and their friends, so any observations or stories are welcome. I don't care how off-the-wall they are."

"Well, if you're looking for off-the-wall, I've got it," Scott said.

Over the next few minutes, Scott told Jack a harrowing tale about what he'd seen through the crack of a door at the Murray house a few days after the murder. When Scott was through, Jack slowly set the phone receiver down.

Chapter Eleven

Saturday, October 26

C hloe stood before the framed "Grand Opening Gala" newspaper article that was hanging in The Parisian's hotel lobby. She had passed it several times since Claire moved into her suite a week before but hadn't given it a second glance.

Now she studied the youthful partiers in their late 1960s finery. She searched the black-and-white photos and spotted her grandfather, Gerald, handsome in his white tux with black cummerbund; Claire, deeply tanned in a strapless dress with a blond bouffant hairdo; Betty, barely recognizable as a glamorous brunette; and Butch, Betty's mysterious and rarely seen husband, with his arm draped casually around his wife's shoulder. Each of them held a cigarette in one hand and a drink in the other.

Strange to see them in their carefree bygone lives—so young and unhindered by the passel of children that would come later. Chloe went into the hotel restaurant, placed the breakfast order, and asked for it to be delivered to her grandmother's suite. She then peeked into the piano lounge, visited the glass-enclosed gift shop to buy a Snickers candy bar, roamed the long, marble-floored hallways, and checked to see if any other teenagers were hanging out in the pool area on this bright, clear, chilly Saturday morning. All was quiet.

Having made her usual rounds, she entered the mirrored elevator. Background music was playing softly, and since she was alone, she broke out in a tap dance—something she had seen once in a movie—until the elevator arrived at the third floor.

* * *

Chloe burst into Claire's suite and called out, "I know I've said it a zillion times, but this place is sick! I love it in every way!" She twirled exuberantly around the living room, her eyes large and bright, her joy contagious.

"Don't you love it, Grandma?"

"I *do* love it," Claire laughed, watching from her seat near the window as her granddaughter made a leaping pirouette. Claire thought her a beauty and a marvel. She ducked just in time to miss Chloe's flying arms.

Louie jumped up and barked excitedly.

"Louie, stop! You'll get us all kicked out of here," Claire said.

Louie was wearing the blue "Therapy Dog in Training" nylon vest that Chloe had bought online so she could smuggle the dog into the hotel. No such training was going on. Louie didn't need any training to be therapeutic, in Claire's opinion—although other kinds of training, like learning to heel and to refrain from jumping, wouldn't hurt.

The hotel management had obligingly approved of Louie's residence—with or without a certificate—but Claire didn't have the heart to tell Chloe. Her granddaughter was so proud of her shenanigans. Besides, Claire had a natural liking for roguish behavior. Not only did she abide a little rule-breaking, she thought it was good for the soul.

"And I love *that* view," Chloe said, stopping mid-twirl to point—like a television game show hostess offering prizes—toward the expansive westside window and its miles-long hillside view of grapevines vivid with russet and gold leaves.

"And *that* view," she said, moving over to the south window. It looked down on the city and The Parisian's own flashy sign, which was topped off with a pink neon, revolving Eiffel Tower. Around and around it went, in all its garish glory. It had infuriated city officials when it first went up. And as Claire liked to tell the story, the politicians tried to pass an ordinance to stop the rotation of the sign, but amused citizens did not agree. Claire and Betty joined them for a few pleasant hours of waving posters and chanting as they picketed City Hall. The protest made the front page of the newspaper and kept the sign lit up and turning.

"I know you liked your little cottage," Chloe said, winding down but still standing. "But you have to admit, this hotel is way cooler. It's practically a resort."

She plopped down on the couch. Louie leapt up to join her and curled up in her lap.

There was a knock at the door.

"Uh oh, busted," Claire said. It was too soon for their room service delivery, so it had to be Noreen back from the pharmacy.

"It's me, Chloe, open up," Noreen yelled through the door.

Chloe dragged herself off the couch and opened the door, saying, "Hi, Mom." Then she slouched toward the spare bedroom and closed the door.

Claire leaned forward, gripping her cane as if to stand.

"Don't get up, Mom." Noreen carried two shopping bags into the kitchen and set them on the counter. "I've got your prescriptions and picked up some groceries."

"Thanks, Hon."

Noreen emptied the grocery bags, putting items into the small refrigerator and cupboards, then retrieved Claire's plastic pill organizer from the cabinet. When she was done filling the organizer with a week's worth of pills, she stepped into the living room.

"I heard laughter coming from inside here before I knocked on the door," Noreen said. Her face was impassive. "But the minute I come in, Chloe went off to the bedroom, sulking."

"Well, fourteen is a mercurial age," Claire said.

"Mercurial? Now that's a word you don't hear every day. Is it another word for 'moody?' 'Surly?' Or maybe just plain 'bratty?'" Her tone was taking on an edge.

"You were like that at fourteen, Noreen. Spirited girls often are," Claire said, treading carefully. Her hands gripped the sides of the armchair. She wasn't in the mood for one of Noreen's eruptions.

"Really? You remember what I was like?" Noreen said, her face turning pink as she fastened her gaze on Claire.

Claire braced herself. *Sweet Jesus, here we go.* When would Noreen stop nursing old resentments? Not anytime soon, apparently. Noreen's weepy, unhinged confrontations usually came after too many drinks during holiday dinners, wedding receptions, birthday parties. Always at a public event—meaning, at least one other sibling was present—and messy.

Yet many of Claire's own memories gave weight to Noreen's grievances. She thought of the little girl who sat silently at the dinner table, who was rarely spoken to or fussed over. The girl who waited for an hour to be picked up after her soccer game.

Nevertheless, Claire resisted the bait, and silence followed.

A softened expression passed across Noreen's face. She let out a deep breath.

"I'm sorry, Mom. I'm just on edge."

"We all are, dear." Claire reached out to squeeze her hand. "Thank you for everything you're doing for me."

Another knock on the front door. Chloe came bounding out of the bedroom to answer it. "Finally, breakfast!" she said.

* * *

After breakfast, Claire was alone in her suite, sitting at her desk with a mug of black tea cupped in her hands. The day was turning out to be sunny and much warmer than a typical late-fall day in this mild climate.

She was glad for the solitude and quiet after her busy morning. She could hear nothing but the muffled growl of a vacuum cleaner in the hallway and the laughing shrieks of children drifting up from the pool area.

The late morning sun streamed onto her desktop. She gingerly moved her desk chair so she would be out of the glaring light. Of course, she could have closed the drapes, but that would have kept her from seeing the tiny blue jay hopping along the windowsill, the same one that had visited every morning for the last three days. The bird stared intently inside. *I must be a riveting sight.* Claire smiled to herself.

Unlike many of her friends, she wasn't one to believe that every blue jay or butterfly she saw was the soul of a departed loved one paying her a visit—although she found nothing odd in that belief. It just wasn't true for her. No, Claire believed dreams were the portal through which her loved ones came. In clear, lucid visitation dreams, they would appear without any foreshadowing, communicate love and peace without speaking, and then vanish before she was prepared for them to leave. Through the years, she'd had only a handful of them, yet their images lingered as if they were actual memories: Danny holding a toy truck out to her. Her parents leaning on a red convertible. A young and smiling Gerald.

So profound and real were those dreams that Claire would always awaken in tears. She longed for another one. It had been ages.

Her spiral-bound At-A-Glance calendar lay open before her on the desktop. Claire's plan for the rest of the day was fourfold. First, she would organize her activities for the coming week. Then she would fix something for lunch, maybe a plate of cheese and crackers. Then take a nap so she'd be rested when Anne McCormack arrived at two o'clock for the informal interview about Danny's case. Claire had no idea what new information she could pass along to Anne, but she would do what she could to help. Joanne would be joining them at Anne's request.

She put on her reading glasses, clicked on her pen, and jotted in the week's day-to-day activities: Sunday, grandchildren; Monday, doctor appointment; Tuesday, have her party clothes picked up at dry cleaners; Wednesday, see her attorney and sign legal documents; Thursday, talk to Father Patrick; Friday, working lunch with Tony; Saturday, hair appointment and visit with out-of-town-guests.

Another busy week, and maybe it wouldn't all get done. A lot would depend on her health and energy, and she couldn't control that. But with so little time to waste, she always felt better moving forward.

She turned to her list of long-term goals at the back of the calendar. This was an even more ambitious list and included writing her obituary, finalizing her estate, and writing individual letters to her children and grandchildren. By her doctor's most generous reckonings, she had only two more months to accomplish it all. And if she were being realistic, she really had only *one* more month in which she could expect to be active. The last month was when all bets were off.

Next, in the margins of the calendar, she added her weekly notations of activities she was still capable of doing. It was a practice of gratitude. Now, at three weeks since her diagnosis, she wrote: "Grateful I can still walk, drive, read, make my bed, take walks around the grounds, visit the piano lounge, handle pain without morphine, live alone without caregivers."

She looked over her list. Still good. She hadn't driven her car for a while but liked to think that this was by choice. She knew the last item probably wouldn't be on next week's list: Joanne was insisting that she start hospice care. And hospice services required that she have private 24-hour-a-day caregiving, either hired or family.

The week before, Joanne had arranged an interview with two middle-aged Fijian women, members of a family that was well regarded in the town's caregiving community. The sisters, Sala and Jasmine, looked remarkably alike, almost like twins, and shared the same warm smile and solid, comfortable build. But it was clear that Sala was the dominant, and probably older, sister since she took the lead on the salary and duty negotiations.

Claire had nodded her approval to Joanne. They appeared competent and relaxed and not overly chatty—which was good since, as much Claire liked company, she didn't want to feel pressured to talk all the time. She liked them; they seemed easy to be around.

And so, the arrangements were agreed upon: the sisters would take shifts—Sala on duty during the day, Jasmine at night. They would monitor Claire's pills, coordinate treatment with the hospice nurses, bathe, feed, and minister to her needs. They would share a private bedroom and bath off the living room. They could start as soon as they were needed.

Claire removed her glasses and rubbed her eyes. She walked slowly to the kitchen and peered inside the refrigerator. Nothing looked appetizing.

Well, maybe an orange, but that would mean getting out a knife and a plate and then sitting down to eat, getting up again, and then rinsing the plate. Not likely. She was more tired than hungry anyway, so she walked to her bedroom to lie down for a few hours.

She would need to conserve her energy for the afternoon ahead.

Chapter Twelve

Saturday, October 26

L ater that afternoon, Anne entered Claire's suite carrying a cardboard box and a briefcase full of notes, a laptop, and her shiny, new detective's badge. She was wearing her best baby-shower-appropriate outfit.

"Well, look at you." Claire greeted her with a smile. "I haven't seen you this dressed up since the day when you brought my husband's watch back."

"Right—hey, whatever happened to that watch?" Anne added the cardboard box to the stack on the floor by the dining table.

"It's still on Peter's wrist," Claire said with a wry smile. "But he's not getting away with anything. I'm subtracting it from his portion of the inheritance."

"Hi, Anne." Joanne entered the room from the bedroom, wearing jeans and a cashmere V-neck pullover, her blondish hair hanging loose to her shoulders.

Joanne turned to her mother and said, "Actually, Tony said he'd like to have Dad's watch, too."

"Oh, I didn't know that." Claire's voice grew low and pensive. "I want to be fair...."

"Sorry I brought it up. Maybe he wasn't serious," Joanne said hurriedly, then turned her attention back to Anne. "So where are you going after you leave us today? Because I know all of *this* isn't for us," she said, gesturing to indicate Anne's chic black dress, Murano glass necklace, heels, and dark lipstick.

Anne did a quick turn to display herself and laughed. "I'm going to high tea at the English Garden Tea Room for a baby shower."

"Well, la-di-da!" Joanne said.

"Oh, how lovely. They have the best cranberry scones," Claire said.

"Which reminds me," Joanne said as she moved toward the kitchen, "we can't talk without snacks. How about some burrata caprese salad? You don't happen to have any wine here, do you, Mom?"

"Noreen finished it off."

While Joanne was in the kitchen arranging the caprese and garlic toast on a plate and pouring glasses of iced tea, Anne and Claire took a cursory look through the box Anne had brought from Claire's storage unit. Later in the week, Claire could decide which photos and mementos to toss and which to set aside for her family.

"Help yourself," said Joanne as she carried in the tray of food and drinks and set it on the table. She dished up a plate for Claire.

Finally settled around the table, Anne began by asking, "Do you mind if I record your answers? I'll take notes too, of course, but it never hurts to have back-up." Besides, she knew Jack and Dean would want to hear this conversation.

"That's fine," Claire said, squirming against the chair's back pillow, trying to get comfortable.

Anne pulled out her phone, opened the memo app, and set it on the table.

"I'll record it, too." Joanne brought out her own phone. Anne raised her eyebrows, then shrugged; it occurred to her that Joanne might simply want a recording of her mother's voice. A voice is so soon forgotten.

"I've read the detectives' original notes." Anne brought out the files and placed them on the table. "Do you mind if we quickly review what was said back in 1990?"

"Oh my God, I was twelve then. I probably wasn't very helpful," Joanne said.

"You were interviewed only once, the day after the murder," Anne said, flipping to the interview notes. "At the time, you said you walked home alone."

"That's right."

"Although, didn't that boy—the son of Father Dunn's housekeeper—try to walk home with you?" Claire asked. "He was so smitten with you."

Joanne sighed. "Larry Brenner? He was sixteen—too old, skinny, and pimply. I brushed him off and went straight home by myself."

"Who usually walked home with Danny?" Anne asked.

Joanne and Claire exchanged a long look.

"We kids took turns," Joanne finally said. "It was the twins' turn that day—Peter and Noreen. I saw the twins together after school, but they were with Michele, one of Noreen's friends. I remember asking them where Danny was because, as I said, it was their turn. Noreen told me that he'd run off to find Tony so he could go home with him."

"Why would Danny do that?" Anne asked.

"I think because Danny didn't like being around Michele," Joanne said.

"Besides," Claire said, "he always wanted to hang around Tony. Danny idolized him. When it was Tony's turn to walk Danny home, he always did, of course. But otherwise, Tony went to the clubhouse, or hangout, or whatever they called that dilapidated old adobe shack."

"I just assumed Danny was safe with Tony," Joanne said. "I never saw him again." Her words hung in the air.

Anne looked down at the notes of Tony's original interview, and then broke the silence. "Tony said he didn't see Danny at all after school."

"I know. And like Jo said, it wasn't his turn that day. Nevertheless, Tony feels terrible about not...I don't know...." Claire's words trailed off.

"Joanne, you said Peter and Noreen were with Michele," Anne said. "But Peter told the detectives he stayed behind to play tetherball—that he didn't walk home with them."

"I *did* see them together," Joanne said emphatically. "I have no idea why Peter would say he didn't walk home with the girls. Unless, of course, he went back to the school grounds after I left them. That's possible."

"I'll clear that up with Peter when I interview him," Anne said. "Although, when I tried to call him to set up a meeting, there was no response."

"I don't keep track of Peter's whereabouts," Joanne said offhandedly, then turned to Claire. "He's not still living at your cottage, is he?"

"No, he moved out so it could be sold."

"So the house is empty?" Joanne asked.

"Pretty much," Anne said, jumping in. "Only a few items are left in the utility room. Your real estate agent wants it cleared out so she can stage it. I'm going over there later this week to pick up the remainders."

Louie was sitting patiently at Claire's feet, eying her plate. Claire nudged it away from the edge of the table, out of Louie's view. "There's nothing for you here, Lou," she said, leaning down and giving him a scratch behind the ears.

Turning her attention back to the conversation, Claire said, "Peter told me he rented a new apartment—I don't have his address yet—and is living there by himself."

"Not with Michele?" Joanne asked.

"That seems to have fizzled out, thank God."

"Fingers crossed." Joanne let out a long breath. "Michele is the last thing this family needs right now. That surprise visit to your cottage two weeks ago—and that sugary sweet smile plastered on her face—was too galling."

Anne wasn't following. Her bewilderment must have shown on her face because Claire said, "Michele is Peter's ex-wife. Michele Dixon. I'm not sure if you knew that. Although she insists on calling herself Michele Murray."

"Oh! Are you saying she's the same Michele who was Noreen's friend?"

"One and the same."

"No, I didn't know. Maybe I should have assumed that." Anne had to quickly recalibrate her thinking: the little girl—Noreen's friend—grew up to marry Peter. And divorce him. And then come back to town again. Full circle.

"Well, there are a lot of Micheles in the world," Joanne said. "It's understandable."

Claire began drumming her fingertips lightly on the table.

"Back to the main topic," Claire said to Anne, "I always wondered about what Scotty said. He claimed he saw someone running from the adobe. He thought it might have been a child. That makes sense since there were so many around the school that day. Have you learned more about that?"

"My uncle spoke with Scott earlier this week," Anne said. "Scott's a cop in Oregon, did you know?"

"That sounds vaguely familiar. Tony might have told me. They've stayed friends and go on a fishing trip together every year or so," Claire said.

"Anyway, regarding the figure—or possibly two—that he saw, Scott said he can't be any more exact in his description than he was in the first interview. It was a blur to him then, and it's a blur to him now."

"No identification, then."

"No."

"It couldn't be any of Danny's little friends," Claire said. "They would never hurt him, and they were just babies themselves. None of Tony's friends would ever—"

"Never," Joanne interjected. "They treated Danny like a mascot. He was their little buddy."

"Just because Scott saw someone running away…well, that doesn't mean they did anything other than happen to be near the scene," Anne said. "The murderer could have been someone we haven't even placed at the scene yet. Which is one reason we set up the anonymous tip line."

"Right, the one in the newspaper article. Any tips yet?" Joanne asked.

"A few, mostly from people who wanted to turn someone in—their ex-husband, a priest, a crazy uncle, a creepy neighbor. That kind of thing. Personal grudges. But a couple of the leads might turn out to be fruitful."

Anne paused, then looked intently at Claire. It was time to ask the crucial question, the reason she was here. "Is there anyone who behaved strangely before or after the murder? Anyone you suspect may have had something to do with Danny's murder?" she asked. "Even if it's just a vague feeling. Even if it's something you can't substantiate."

Claire took a moment to summon her thoughts, then said, "There was a time when I couldn't go to the grocery store without looking at the clerk suspiciously. The mailman. Teachers. People crossing the street. I suspected anyone and everyone," Claire said. "But over the years, I kept thinking back to something I never brought up with the police. In fact, I only mentioned it to a few people because, of course, it could mean nothing."

Claire then turned to Joanne. "Do you remember right after Danny died, Jo? Michele was about ten, and she and Noreen were inseparable. Michele was always at the house—"

"Lurking," Joanne said.

"Well, she came up to me once in the kitchen—I was finally getting out of bed then—and she asked me, 'Can't you stop crying?'"

"I remember."

"And another time, she asked me if I was still sad about Danny."

Claire turned back to Anne. "The strange part was that both times she'd have a tiny smile on her face when she said it. A grin."

"And you told Daddy to get her away from you."

Claire sighed. "I know she was just a little girl, but it chilled me to the bones."

"But it didn't stop her from coming around," Joanne said.

Claire gazed into the distance. "From what I remember hearing, Michele had a truly horrific childhood. Her mother a prostitute. No one knew who her father was. Something about drug use, too. Whatever happened in that household, it was bad enough to land Michele into the foster system."

"I always thought Michele wanted you and Dad to adopt her. I swear. She was constantly at the house, practically glued to Noreen. Then she just disappeared for a few years—"

"She got moved to another foster home—"

"Was that it?"

Joanne looked down at her plate. "And then she shows up again when she's twenty years old or so—sometime after she aged out of the foster system. She comes back here and starts up with Peter. Anything to get into the family, I guess." Joanne was quiet for a beat before adding, "Now *that* was a marriage from hell."

"At least it only lasted a few years," Claire said.

"Do you suspect Michele of anything?" Anne asked.

"No, not really. I guess she's on my mind because she's back in town.

91

That's all," Claire said. "And it was just so odd, the grinning and all. Like she knew something. Will you be talking to Michele?"

"No, but my uncle will, once we find her. It sounds like Peter might know how to contact her." Anne lifted her pen from her notebook and looked up at the two women.

Dozens more questions came bubbling to her mind.

"Joanne, you said Danny didn't like Michele. Why was that?"

"Something about Michele wetting the bed when she slept over. And he said she kicked the cat. Things like that," Joanne said.

"I'm sorry, ladies," Claire said abruptly, "but I'll have to call it a day." Her complexion had turned pale and ashen. Her hands were trembling.

"Oh, Mom, let me help you." Joanne stood up and brought her mother's metal walker to her side. As she led Claire to her bedroom, Joanne leaned in and said, "I've decided to contact hospice tomorrow, Mom. It's time. And I'm calling Sala tonight to ask her if she and her sister can start tomorrow."

Claire stiffened slightly, then nodded. "Okay, Jo," she said in a nearly toneless voice.

* * *

The tea room waitress lifted the pot expectantly. "More tea, ladies?" Anne's tablemates raised their cups for refills. Anne placed her hand over the rim of her cup and surveyed the room. The English Garden Tea Room was crammed with mismatched Victorian furniture and china and too many lace doilies for her taste, but the room's aroma of burning logs, freshly baked scones, and jasmine was irresistible.

Anne reached for another petit four and finger sandwich from the three-tiered cake stand in front of her and eyed a lemon tart that looked tempting. She considered wrapping it in a paper napkin and discreetly pocketing it for later.

Of the eight Peter Rabbit-themed tables, Anne's seat assignment was at the table farthest away from where the mother-to-be was holding court. Which was both perfectly fine and not at *all* fine with Anne. Hidden away in the back as she was, she could be as unobtrusive as she liked. But on the other hand, it was a little insulting. And would she even get to say hello to Krista, her very pregnant friend? It was all so uncomfortable. Why had she even been invited? She glanced at her wristwatch. Maybe she could limit her stay to an hour without seeming rude.

"So, what do you do?" asked a sharp-eyed, elderly woman from across the round table. "I hope you don't mind my asking. It's just that young women your age always seem to have a career."

"Me?" Anne pulled her attention back to her tablemates, five cheerful, middle-aged, and senior women, two of them wearing boldly colored fascinator hats. "Oh, I don't mind at all. I'm an estate liquidator."

"And that is…" the woman said encouragingly.

"I help families sell the personal items left over from estates. I work mainly with the family executors."

The flame-haired matron next to her perked up. "Fascinating. Whom have you done?"

"Done?" echoed Anne, startled by the question but even more by the correct grammar usage. Who says *whom* anymore?

"I know everyone in town. With whom have you worked?"

Anne hesitated. "Well, the Murray family is a current client." Claire had offered to give her referrals, so she assumed it would be all right to mention her name.

"Claire? How is she doing? I've been meaning to call."

At the mention of Claire's name, Anne, along with her estate business, gained instant social cachet with the group. It seemed that everyone at the table either might need her services themselves, or knew of someone who would. Her business cards were requested and passed around, and at least one woman, Lydia Smith, an old friend of Claire's, appeared to be genuinely interested in her services.

"I saw that newspaper article about Danny Murray's murder case being reopened," said a diminutive brunette named Dorothy as she passed a pot of raspberry jam to her right. "I'm debating whether to have my daughter call the tip line or not."

"You must," said the redhead, biting into her scone.

"You don't even know what the tip is, Muzzy!" exclaimed Dorothy.

"Nevertheless, since you rarely insert yourself into the action, it must be good," Muzzy said.

For a second, Dorothy looked unsure if she'd been insulted or not, but shook it off with a laugh. "Anyway, my daughter went to St. Paul's with the Murray kids. She was never questioned by the police, but says she remembers a few things they might want to know about."

"She should definitely call," said Anne. "In fact, let me take down her name and number to give to my uncle. He's the lead detective on the case." She reached for her purse and took out her notebook and pen.

"It can't hurt," said Dorothy, writing the information in Anne's notebook.

"You know, maybe this is off-the-wall," Lydia said, "but I always wondered about that teenage boy who lived at the rectory with his mother, the housekeeper. Motive and opportunity, as they say on the crime shows. What was his name?" she asked the table.

"Larry something?" Muzzy offered.

Anne looked up sharply. "What about him?" This was the second time she'd heard his name that day. "What do you mean by 'motive'?"

"Oh, nothing really, just that he always seemed to be hanging around the younger kids. And didn't he have some mental problems? Wasn't he sent away for a while?" Lydia looked around the table for confirmation and only got shrugs in return.

Anne wrote the skimpy information in her notebook, closed it, and then took a casual glance around the room. Her gaze landed on a table of young women seated near the table of honor. Two of them were part of Anne's former, pre-divorce circle of acquaintances. *Oh, perfect.* Before Anne could look away, the sharp-featured one locked eyes with Anne and nudged her friend. Anne watched as the duo look her up and down. They kept their eyes on Anne while they whispered to each other, smirked, then turned their backs and laughed.

In the space of an hour, Anne had gone from feeling like an outcast to feeling welcomed to feeling like an outcast again. But the sting of rejection faded nearly as fast as it had overtaken her, replaced by a surge of annoyance. *What ridiculous, petty women.*

Sitting to her left, Muzzy was appraising the situation, looking from Anne to the women and back to Anne again. She leaned in toward Anne and said in a low voice, "Pay them no mind, dear. Unkind people are of no interest."

"Well…"

"In fact, fuck 'em."

Anne let out a short laugh and squeezed Muzzy's arm. *Fuck 'em indeed.* She felt a little better. Nevertheless, this emotional roller coaster ride of an evening was getting exhausting. Time to leave.

She stood and waved across the room to catch Krista's eye and blew her a kiss. Krista looked a bit surprised but waved back, whispering in the ear of the woman next to her, Emily, the hostess. Anne bid goodbye to her tablemates, who were gracious enough to appear reluctant to see her leave. She slipped on her coat and headed for the door.

The early evening air was invigorating. She tucked her red wool scarf inside her coat and glanced down the street. Next door to the gentile English Garden Tea Room, the Russian River Brewing Company was catering to a wholly different type of clientele. In a line that stretched over a block long, young beer-lovers were still waiting outside the microbrewery for a taste of the latest brew release. Farther down the street, outdoor cafes were firing up their outdoor heaters, hoping to catch some run-off business from the brewery. At the Taproom & Lounge, there was a crowd lined up for the amateur comics scheduled for the open mic hour. Street lamps were glowing through the boughs of the redwood trees that lined the walkway, their trunks wrapped in strings of white lights. Fourth Street was humming.

Anne buttoned her coat. She gave a last look through the window of the tea room, its interior light softened by the lace curtains. At least the evening hadn't been a total bust: she didn't have to worry about making dinner tonight, and she was coming away with a possible new client and potential leads in the cold case. She started down the street.

"Anne, wait!" called out Emily as she rushed down the sidewalk to catch up with Anne. When she reached her, Emily took Anne's arm. "I didn't get a chance to talk to you yet...I'm so sorry you're leaving already," she said breathlessly. "Krista is thrilled you came. She would have come out here herself, but she's so big now she can barely waddle."

Now Anne felt welcomed, again. She decided to quit while she was ahead and drive home with her lemon tart.

Chapter Thirteen

Monday, October 28

Jack was the first to arrive at the third-floor conference room. His wife had sent him out the door with a bag of her homemade poppy-seed muffins and some advice: "Keep your blazer on so no one can see that gawd-awful T-shirt," Dot said with a resigned sigh, "and share the muffins."

He switched on the lights, took off his blazer, and tossed the bag of muffins on the boardroom-style table in the center of the room. Since he was a few minutes early for the nine o'clock Monday status meeting, he started brewing their first pot of coffee.

While waiting for Dean and Anne, he sat at the head of the conference table and started organizing his notes and files into piles. Original interviews. New interviews. Crime scene evidence. DNA evidence status. Documents. Photographs. Hot line tips. Random notes.

* * *

Five minutes later, Anne walked in. In her black suit, with her tawny hair pulled into a sleek low ponytail, she looked as professional as any agent or assistant DA in the building.

"Epic T-shirt, Uncle Jack," Anne said as she plopped her files down on the table. Her uncle's T-shirt collection was a source of family amusement, and today's shirt read: IT'S OK TO LET YOURSELF GO, AS LONG AS YOU

CAN GET YOURSELF BACK.

Jack grunted. "Hi yourself."

"So what do we have here?" She ignored his cranky mood and leaned across the table to pull the bag nearer. She reached in and pulled out a fresh muffin. "Still warm. I love Aunt Dot," she said, inhaling the sugary aroma.

"Give her a call. She's planning a dinner party for Sunday," Jack said. "But heads up, she's in a match-making mood again."

"I'll call, but Sunday won't work," Anne said. "That's the day of Claire's birthday party at The Parisian restaurant. Her kids started planning it before she got sick. It started out as a small family dinner, but now it's mushroomed into a huge event. Old friends and family—even me, which is nice of them. Some people are even flying in from back east."

"Is Claire up for all that?"

"Just barely, I think. She says she's good for about two hours," Anne said. "But she wants to see everyone. The good news is she doesn't have to organize anything—the kids are doing everything. All she has to do is show up."

Jack nodded, picked up a file, and slid it across the table. "I don't think you've seen these photos yet—they're of the Murray kids and their friends at the time of the murder."

"Probably not. I've just seen the ones at Claire's house," she said, opening the file and fanning the photos out on the table.

She reached for the photo of Joanne; she'd been a brunette as a child, but still had the same angular features and lean frame. Tony had curly hair and a lopsided, cocky grin. Noreen looked like a typical, plump little girl in pigtails. Peter had a goofy smile and was as thin as a blade of grass. Danny, with his straight blond hair falling into his eyes, still had his baby teeth. There were a few photos of Tony's friends, including Scott.

When she got to Michele's photo, she came to a full stop. Nothing had prepared her for this beautiful, angelic-looking child. Michele's heart-shaped face, cupid bow lips, and riveting, Mediterranean blue eyes reminded her of photos she'd seen of Elizabeth Taylor at that same age. Her expression was both shrewd and innocent, sweet and wary.

Jack's cell phone rang.

"Lt. McCormack here." Jack listened a moment, then said, "What's that again? Yeah, right." Jack was writing down the information when Dean walked in. He was wearing his usual buttoned-down blue shirt and tan khaki slacks.

Anne gave Dean a smile and a nod and set the photos aside. Dean headed over to the coffee station, poured three mugs of coffee, and carried them to the conference table. Settling into his chair, he lifted his bulky briefcase onto the empty chair beside him.

"Thanks," Jack said, ending the call. He nodded in Dean's direction. "A new lead from the tip line. Mind following up on this?" Jack said, pushing the note toward Dean.

Glancing at the note, Dean looked exasperated. "The caller suspects a priest? Father Patrick Dunn?" Dean was a practicing Roman Catholic at St. Paul's parish. "Well, why not? They seem to be everyone's favorite punching bag for every crime out there."

"If I remember correctly, Father Dunn was the Murray family priest," Jack said. "I recall meeting him the first time I was at the house. He was consoling the family."

Jack riffled his notes until he found the entry mentioning Father Dunn. "No one got his statement at the time. Too much else was going on, and apparently, no one went back for it."

"I know him from the parish," said Dean, "and there's never been any scandal or talk about him. He's well thought of. But he might have information about other priests. Santa Rosa had more than its share of bad priests—it was where other dioceses liked to relocate their molesters. That went on for decades. Worth checking."

"Speaking of leads," Anne said, "last night at the English Garden Tea Room, I met a woman who mentioned the son of the rectory housekeeper." She filled them in on what little she knew of Larry Brenner and added, "Might be worth bringing up with Father Dunn."

Dean nodded. "I remember something about that guy. Didn't his mother give him an alibi?"

"That rings a bell. I'll go through the files," Jack said.

"And I have another lead from the bridal shower—" Anne said.

"—I gotta get out more," Jack said.

"One of the women has a daughter who went to St. Paul's back then. The girl's name is Suzy Eller, and she was never interviewed. She might have some helpful information. Here's her contact info." Anne reached into her purse, pulled out the note, and held it up for grabs.

"Strange that she was never interviewed," Jack said as he reached for the note. "We carpeted the town with questionnaires for kids to fill out, and we followed up on anything interesting." He glanced down at one of the three-ringed binders from the original investigation lying on the table. "Colored tabs notwithstanding, I'm beginning to have doubts about the thoroughness of that investigation."

Jack then stood up, red marker in hand, and went to the whiteboard on the side wall. He wrote down four headings: Suspects, Leads, Motives, Assignments. He added,"Father Dunn" and "Suzy Eller" to the Leads list.

"Okay, Dean, you want to start?"

Dean took a sip of coffee. "Thanks to Anne's extraordinary...I can't call it investigative skills since it was really just dumb luck...." Anne stifled a smile. "...I was able to locate the janitor, Carl Pinn, at the Tranquil Acres mobile park without any trouble. Thanks, Anne," he said, nodding to her and doffing an imaginary cap.

"He was just as big of a mess as you reported. Hungover, and strangely both loud and sullen at the same time. He claims he had nothing to do with the murder, and to prove it—at least in his mind—he showed me a copy of his arrest reports. He said he only had *trouble*, as he called it, with little girls, so Danny wasn't in any danger from him."

"Interesting point. But it doesn't let him off the hook," Jack said, writing "Carl Pinn" under the Suspects heading. "Some child molesters abuse children of both genders. It happens."

"Although, arguably, there didn't appear to be any sexual motivation at all in this case," Dean said. "There were no clothing issues—Danny was fully clothed, and there was no semen—nothing was found that could point to sexual abuse. So it seems it was just a murder with nothing else to go along with it."

"Unless Pinn was just getting *ready* to do something and got interrupted," said Jack. "Then sexual abuse would still be a motive. He just didn't get to act on it."

"Let's say it *wasn't* about sexual abuse," Anne said, picking up her fork and sectioning her muffin into bite-size chunks. "Would Pinn have any other kind of motive? Why kill a little boy?"

"Maybe Danny saw him doing something to another kid—maybe even at some other time, some other day—and he wanted to shut Danny up. That's a possibility," suggested Jack.

Dean reached into his briefcase and produced a file.

"I talked to Dianne Simpson, the ex-girlfriend who gave Pinn his original alibi," Dean said. "Turns out she was the first anonymous tip we got last week, the one who said we should look at Pinn again. She was surprised when I showed up since she hadn't left her name. I told her we were speaking to a lot of people again, and she was just on our list. Coincidence."

Dean passed around printouts of a recent photo of Dianne Simpson.

"Whoa!" Jack fell back hard in his chair. "What the hell! I know a few decades have gone by since we last saw her, but this isn't normal aging here."

Anne studied the photo. It was like the "after" of a before-and-after of a meth addict: several missing teeth, gray stringy hair, sunken eyes, and scabs on her blotchy, wrinkled skin. Dianne looked eighty.

"She's fifty," Dean said. "Hard life. Anyway, now she denies she was with Pinn at the time of the murder. No big surprise there. And now she's doubling down and saying he confessed to her. Pillow talk, she said. No details or proof, just her word. Seems like she wants the $1,000 reward any way she can get it."

"Although, we shouldn't discount her story yet," Jack said.

"But not exactly a credible witness," Anne said.

"She also told me Pinn had a stash of Polaroid photos of little girls. They were naked, and most of them had brown paper bags over their faces," Dean said.

"Now *that's* believable," Jack said.

"Why was Carl Pinn even looked at by the detectives in the first place?" Anne asked. "Just because he was the new janitor at the school? At the time, he didn't even have a police record."

"We were looking at everyone. Besides, some parents called in about him. They didn't like his looks," Dean said. "And the way he acted under casual questioning made us focus in on him. Plus, he wouldn't give his hair sample or fingerprints," Dean said.

"There's something else about Pinn you ought to know." Jack reached for the file marked "Documents" and pulled out a stained note encased in a plastic evidence folder. He passed it to Dean, who studied it before passing it along to Anne.

"This note was found on a shelf in the school janitor's shed a week after the murder."

It was a rumpled piece of letter-sized paper with childish lettering done in red crayon. It read: "danni DEAD murder sees u. Fuk u!!"

"A rookie cop—not me, by the way—was called in by the school after the vice principal found the note when she was looking for a broom. But the rookie thought it was just a nasty prank," Jack continued.

"Not me, either, just to be clear," Dean said, "No way would I ignore something like that."

"The note stayed filed away in a sheriff's desk drawer until just before the case was closed. There was zero follow-up—no one even asked Pinn about it—and by the time anyone gave it a serious look, the fingerprints were smudged. It wasn't worth anything, at least not in terms of forensics," Jack said.

Anne studied the note. The block lettering looked vaguely familiar. The last time she'd seen such childish writing was on the Murray family questionnaire.

"The janitor's shed was usually locked, and Pinn was one of the few people who had a key," said Dean. "But if he wrote it, why would he leave it there? It's incriminating. Doesn't make sense."

"Maybe someone planted it," Jack said. "That would be easy enough if the shed door didn't stay locked all day. Dean, can you follow up with Pinn about that? And check with the school," Jack said, adding the assignment to the board.

"Sure," Dean said.

"Was any handwriting analysis ever done on the note?" Anne asked.

"Not yet. As I said, the note was ignored at the time. Nothing at all was done with it," Jack said. "Besides, there are no handwriting specimens to compare it to—as of yet, anyway. Do you have anything in mind?"

Anne described finding the Murrays' yearly questionnaires, with each answer written by hand. She said she would ask Claire for the originals for comparison.

"Good, but try to downplay the importance of them when you ask. Just tell her I'm curious. Don't mention comparisons. I don't want her worrying about her kids unnecessarily," Jack said.

"And it's a long shot," Dean said. "The note could have been written by an adult disguising his or her handwriting."

"And if it *was* a kid who wrote it," Anne said, "then it's even harder to get a match from what I've heard."

"Lots of variables. And it doesn't mean the writer was seriously involved in the case," Jack said. "Could have been just a prank like they originally thought. But it's worth a shot."

"On another subject. I have a question for you both," Anne said. "During our first conversation—back before the case was reopened—you said you had your suspicions. I'd like to finally hear them." She took a bite of her muffin and settled back for the answer.

"Sure, but remember, these were only subjective impressions, and we were young cops then," Dean said. "But when we first went to the Murray home, Jack and I both had funny feelings about the way some of the kids reacted."

Dean picked up his old detective's notebook and skimmed it for details. "Peter appeared pretty disinterested, except when he asked questions about our handguns. The youngest daughter, Noreen, seemed more excited than sad. She kept staring at the ground, then glancing up when she thought we weren't looking."

"Then, in a later interview," Jack interjected, "she was sobbing and distressed. Emotionally, Noreen was all over the place."

"And her friend, Michele, was emotionless and very intent on the questioning, just glued to our side," Dean said. "The oldest sister didn't say much; it was like she was frozen."

Jack stood up and added the names of the Murray kids and Michele to the Suspects list on the board. "Of course, they were just kids at the time, but strangulation doesn't always take much pressure or physical strength. And the younger the victim, the easier it is to do—if it's done slowly or lightly. It could leave very few marks."

Seeing the siblings' names written on the board caught Anne off guard.

"So what are you saying?" Anne looked from one man to the other. "That you're focusing on the family, here? On what grounds? We know their hair samples didn't match the crime evidence."

"Right, the hair samples gathered in 1990 from the family *did* clear them as far as being a match for hair color, width, and texture," Jack said. "But that doesn't mean they couldn't be involved. Or know more than they've told us."

"Then why not just put them under the Leads column? Of all the people in town who could have done this, are they really *suspects*?"

"Well, what do you think, Anne? You've been talking to them," Jack's voice took on a challenging edge. "Tell us what you learned from Claire and Joanne."

Anne met his gaze. Was her growing attachment to the family—or at least to Claire —keeping her from being objective? Because that wouldn't work, she needed to stay objective.

She rummaged through her purse for her phone and placed it on the table.

"Claire and Joanne don't seem to have any suspicions about other family members. But they talk a lot about Michele. She's always been a thorn in their sides."

She turned on the audio of the interview. Jack and Dean took notes and listened intently, learning about why Danny was left alone in the schoolyard.

About Michele's disturbing questions and odd grinning. About Michele's marriage to Peter (*Now we find out,* Jack said). About Danny's dislike of Michele.

"Maybe the feeling was mutual," Jack said after the audio finished.

"Michele didn't like Danny for some reason? Are you thinking of motive?" Dean asked, raising his eyebrows.

"Maybe Michele resented Danny because—in Michele's mind, at least—he was stopping her from getting adopted into the family," Anne said. "And as you just heard, Joanne always thought that's what Michele wanted all along. Joanne even thinks that's why she eventually married Peter—to have a place in the family."

"Adopted—that's so off the wall," Dean said.

"But how could Danny have stopped her from getting adopted?" Jack asked.

"We know Danny had a few gripes with her," Anne said. "Maybe he threatened to tell negative stories about her to the parents. I'm just guessing. According to the family, it was never going to happen anyway. It was all wishful thinking on Michele's part."

"Still, a possible motive," Jack said. "Noreen would know more. Anne, are you talking to her soon?"

Anne nodded, her reluctance showing.

"In the meantime, I have a little story to tell you that came from Scott Hudson, the kid who found the body," Jack said.

"You spoke to him again?" Dean asked.

"No, just once last week on the phone. But this seemed like the kind of story that I needed to tell you in person."

Jack cleared his throat and continued. "Anyway, Scott hung out at the Murray house a lot in the days following the murder. About a week after Danny died, Scott walked by the den where the father, Gerald Murray, was holed up. He did a lot of drinking back then. The room was dark, but the door was cracked open, and Scott looked in and saw Murray sprawled out, asleep on the couch. Scott said Michele was there, just looking down at him. Then she got on her hands and knees and crept up to Murray and unzipped his pants and started—"

"Holy Jesus," Dean muttered.

"Scott said Murray jerked awake and pulled himself away from her really fast. He started yelling stuff like 'Get the hell off me!' Michele just froze up and got really upset. Started crying. Murray tried to calm her down, saying, 'Don't worry, it's all right. Just don't do that again.'"

The oxygen seemed to have seeped out of the room.

"That's one for the psychiatrist's couch," Dean said.

Stunned, Anne picked up Michele's photo and studied it again. "But it makes sense in the context of her wanting to get adopted. In Michele's mind, by seducing the father, she was trying to cement her place in the family. Maybe manipulate him into a situation that she could use to her advantage later," she said. "Blackmail or something."

"Very disturbing and interesting thought, but pretty far-fetched," Jack said. "But there's another way to look at it: we know Michele had been in the foster system, bouncing around to at least three foster families over the years. She was taken away from a mother who was a prostitute. Michele obviously saw too much as a kid. She seems to have all the earmarks of a sexually abused child. She had very few boundaries—she thought sex was what men expected of her. Maybe she thought she was doing her job."

"Or maybe she was just testing him. Seeing if he was like the other men," offered Dean. "Any way you look at it, that's one disturbed child."

The three were silent for a moment, each lost in their own thoughts.

Jack broke the silence. "I've saved some bad news for last. The DNA results just got postponed, sorry to say. We got bumped. Now we're expecting them next week."

"They're taking their sweet time," Dean said.

"Well, cold cases aren't high on their list," said Jack. "I'm optimistic, but if we get no matches, then—"

"That means the murderer probably hasn't gotten into major trouble with the law, at least in the last thirty years since they've been collecting DNA," Anne said.

"But that doesn't mean we're entirely out of luck," said Dean. "We'll keep interviewing people and following up on tips. Keep building a case, in other words. Then if we can narrow in on the suspect with solid evidence, we'll be in a position to get a search warrant for their DNA."

"And if *that* doesn't work—if we can't pull a legal warrant—we'll just pick a suspect we like, toss them into a room, strap them to a chair and make them spit into a cup. Cause if there's no DNA on file, we'll *get* it on file," said Jack.

"Cop humor," Dean muttered to Anne.

"But we probably already have Pinn's DNA on file," Anne said.

"Right, so things could wrap up soon," Jack said. "But it's also possible that when the results come in, he could be cleared."

"And then Dianne will be *really* pissed off. That woman wants her $1,000 reward," Dean said.

"I'm rooting for Dianne," Anne said.

"How's everyone's schedule?" Jack asked as they started packing up their briefcases. For the next few minutes, they divvied up assignments: Anne off-loaded Noreen's interview (*She's got major issues with me—you two would do better with her,* she said), said she'd talk to Peter, and volunteered to join Dean's meeting with Father Dunn (*Not necessary, but sure,* Dean said); Jack would track down Michele Murray (*Bet she's got a record,* Jack said) and follow up on Anne's tea party lead.

They cleared the dishes from the table and tossed the dirty napkins into the trash. Jack switched off the lights.

Chapter Fourteen

Tuesday, October 29

St. Paul's rectory, home to parish priests, stood bastion-like near the busy corner of Wilson Lane and Randolph Drive. The parking lot across the street was filling up with parents waiting to pick up their children from the parish school.

While Dean knocked on the heavy, carved wood front doors, Anne surveyed the rectory's neatly manicured front lawn and row of potted geraniums on the porch. Looking to the north of the parish property, she could make out school buildings and part of the fenced-in field beyond.

They heard a shaky female voice call out from the other side of the door, "Your guests are here, Father." After a minute, a plain, elderly woman wearing a floral-print bib apron opened the door and stepped back so they could enter the modest foyer.

"Hello, Father will be down soon," she said. "Would you like coffee or tea?"

Before they could answer, Father Patrick Dunn came into the foyer. "Thank you, Catherine," he said to the housekeeper. "Coffee all around, please." He was a roundish man, his thinning hair the color of ash, his manner avuncular.

Dean offered his hand to the priest. "I don't know if you remember me, Father. I'm Dean Diaz. My family and I attend St. Paul's."

"Ah, yes, of course. And didn't your children go to school here?" Father Dunn shook his hand.

"They did indeed. And this is my colleague, Anne McCormack."

Father Dunn smiled broadly at Anne. "I feel like I know you. Claire Murray has told me some wonderful things about you." He shook her hand and gestured that they should all enter the room off the entry, a formal sitting room overcrowded with two facing leather sofas separated by a coffee table. The room smelled of Pledge furniture polish. Its glass windows sparkled.

Dean sat down in the center of one sofa, his legs spread apart, leaning forward with his notebook in hand. Anne took a seat on the opposite sofa.

"I actually expected a call sooner," Father Dunn said, lowering himself onto the sofa next to Anne. "Claire told me the murder case was reopened and said some detectives might contact me. Not surprising since I'd never really been interviewed about the case, and I was close to the Murrays."

Catherine came bustling in from the kitchen, set a silver carafe and tray down on the coffee table, and poured three cups. A loud crash, sounding like plates hitting the floor, came from the direction of the kitchen. Catherine's head jerked up.

"It's nothing," a man's voice called out.

"Oh dear," Catherine muttered and hurriedly left the room.

Anne glanced up in time to see a balding middle-aged man, overweight by at least fifty soft pounds, come lumbering out of the kitchen. He turned the corner and disappeared up the stairs.

"Excuse me, Father," Anne said, tugging on the priest's sleeve, "but who was that?"

"Oh, that's Catherine's son, Larry Brenner. He's visiting her for a few weeks from Idaho." He paused a beat, then called out, "Larry? Why don't you come on down? Meet our visitors." No response.

Anne exchanged a look with Dean.

"Well, anyway," Father Dunn shrugged. He stood and retrieved a silver flask from the side desk drawer. "Care to join me?" he asked as he poured a half shot of bourbon into his coffee. Anne, busy writing "Call Larry Brenner" in her notebook, shook her head. Dean declined, too, but pointed to a dish of Halloween candy on the coffee table.

"Help yourself, detective. Now, what can I do for you?"

"We're here to follow up on a tip," Dean said, unwrapping a fun-size Butterfinger, "so if you don't mind, we'll go through our list of questions."

"What was the nature of the tip?" Father Dunn asked in a tight voice.

"Well, I wouldn't ordinarily tell an interviewee much about the tip, but since I know you...." Dean let the sentence fade while he bit into the candy. "All they said was that a lot of priests lived here at that time. Also, that you were close to the Murray family. In the current environment, even that is suspicious to some folks."

"The Murrays are friends. That's no secret." Father Dunn's face relaxed.

Dean flipped open his notebook. "Just answer as best as you can remember." He began by asking Father Dunn where he'd been at the time of the crime? (*In the rectory. My witnesses were the housekeeper Catherine and another priest, now deceased*) Had he gone to the adobe house that day? (*No*) How had he heard about the murder? (*The school secretary*). What did he do next? (*Went immediately up to the Murray home to comfort them*).

Father Dunn sipped his concoction, returned the cup to the table, and then abruptly stood up. "It's a beautiful day outside. Why don't we take a stroll over to the school and finish up the interview there? It's almost three. School's about to be let out."

The trio stepped outside into the late afternoon sun, the sky still clear and blue, and headed north past the church toward the school grounds. With the children still in the classrooms, the campus was utterly quiet except for the distant hum of traffic.

"The school hasn't changed much since Danny Murray attended all those years ago. Even the uniforms are basically the same," Father Dunn said as they stood facing the rows of flat-roofed, concrete classrooms that were built in the 1960s.

Dean nodded sagely. "I know all about those uniforms: I paid for new ones nearly every year for eight years for our three growing kids."

Father Dunn chuckled.

The sharp ring of the school bell interrupted them. Within seconds, children of all sizes and shapes were hollering and laughing, streaming out from the classrooms with whoops of joy like cries of freedom.

Father Dunn smiled at the kids racing past, a few of them yelling out, "Hi, Father!"

"Look at them, running around without a care. Believe it or not, this is where the Los Angeles archdiocese sent its problem priests. Can you imagine doing that?" the priest asked.

"They called our diocese the 'dumping ground,'" Dean said. "They left us to clean up the mess and pay the court settlements." Like most locals, Anne knew the history: since the diocese was founded in the early 1950s, more than twenty-five priests had been accused of the sexual abuse of over one hundred parish children. "The diocese paid out more than $29 million in legal settlements to abuse victims," Dean continued.

"Less than half of those settlement costs were covered by insurance," Father Dunn said.

"Right, the rest came from the pockets of us parishioners," Dean said. "And we were fit to be tied. Not only were our kids put at risk, but we were supposed to pay for it."

"Many families dropped away from the Church." The priest stood motionless for a moment, then threw his hands up in exasperation as if railing against the unimaginable. "You have to understand, we didn't know for sure the abuse was going on." He sighed. "And it was so unthinkable. In hindsight, of course...."

"Tell us about some of those priests," Anne said.

"Sorry I even brought it up. Danny's death wasn't related to any of that," Father Dunn said, as if that would ward off further speculation. "A sad story from a miserable time, but the murder was an anomaly."

"It might be related. We don't know yet."

Father Dunn stopped and faced them. "If it helps, I'll give you a DNA sample."

Anne was startled by the priest's out-of-the-blue offer. "You're not a suspect, Father. But a DNA sample would end any speculation."

"I'll take a polygraph test, too. What I *won't* do is tell you anything I've learned in confidence," Father Dunn said. They turned to walk back to the rectory.

"We're not asking you to reveal anything you heard in confession. But otherwise, you should tell us what you saw or heard," Dean said.

"You know, of course, that Claire Murray is the driving force behind opening this case, right?" Anne said. "I'm sure she'd want you to shed any light that you can."

Glancing back to the schoolyard, Father Dunn seemed to come to a decision.

"There was one, Austin Timmons, a newly ordained priest. I watched him closely. He was paying a little too much attention to Danny, for my taste. Trying to pull him aside and talk. Maybe it was harmless, but I'd heard some rumblings about him. Timmons used to invite boys to overnight camping trips—I didn't like the sound of it, so I'd quietly take parents aside and advise them to steer clear of certain invitations from certain overly ingratiating priests. And, of course, I reported it to the bishop, who said it would be handled. But it never was.

"So anyway, I told Timmons to leave Danny alone, but Timmons said it was all in my imagination. I also told Tony to watch over his little brother. The attention seemed to stop."

"What happened to the priest?" Anne asked.

"He ended up facing charges a few years later. He was defrocked and moved to Belgium for a while, I think. That's the last I've heard of him."

"Father Timmons hasn't been—"

"Don't call him Father. He lost that honorific," Father Dunn said sharply.

"Timmons hasn't been on our radar at all," Dean continued, adding the name to his notebook.

"But there's something else." Father Dunn stopped walking and turned to face Dean and Anne. "I was at the Murrays' home the day of the murder. Right after they got the news. The kids were in the backyard, and I heard them yelling, so I went back there and saw them fighting and shoving each other. They usually didn't do that. Then I saw a friend of theirs—I think her name was Michele—throw the youngest Murray daughter to the ground and spit in her face. Tony ran over and pulled her off Noreen and broke it

112

up."

Father Dunn resumed walking and said, "But it could mean nothing. It was an emotional day."

Chapter Fifteen

Tuesday, October 29

An hour later, while driving to Claire's vacant cottage to retrieve the few remaining boxes, Anne's phone pinged with an incoming text.

Oh well, I need gas anyway. She took the next freeway off-ramp, pulled into a Chevron station, and dug her phone out of her purse to check the text.

It was from Chloe: "Got your number from Aunt Joanne. Secret assignment! Meet me at Grandma's old house?"

Too many logistics for texting back and forth, Anne decided. She sent back, "Okay, I'll call you." Chloe picked up on the first ring.

"You're so old-school, Anne."

"What's up?"

"Grandma says there are still some boxes of old photo albums at her cottage and that you're going to pick them up today."

"Right, I'm on my way there now," Anne said.

"I need to get into Grandma's house and look through the photo albums."

"Why not just wait and see them at your grandmother's? What's all the rush and secrecy about?"

"It's because we're making a video for Grandma's birthday party," Chloe said in a hurried voice, "and I need old family pictures to scan for it. It's going to be about her whole life, from when she was just a baby, then college, then her wedding, and up to being a grandmother…and it's going to have all the music she likes best. And she can't know we're doing this!" Anne grinned. If a voice could do somersaults and twirl at the same time, it would be Chloe's.

"It's a total surprise! My brother's even helping me make it on the computer. And our cousins are helping. I need to pick out the photos I want before you bring the boxes to Grandma," she continued breathlessly. "Mom's going to drop me off there at four-thirty. Is that okay? And maybe you can give me a ride home when I'm done?"

Whew, good thing we didn't try texting all of this, Anne thought, but said to Chloe, "Yep, see you in fifteen."

* * *

A real estate sign announcing FOR SALE BY BRENDA MORAN was posted on the front lawn of Claire's vacant cottage. The house was freshly painted that year's hottest trend color—a slate gray/blue—the lawn was neatly mown, the bushes pruned, and brightly colored flowers were planted along the walkway. Lights inside the house were set on timers to keep burglars away. Brenda, the real estate agent, had plopped down a new welcome mat on the front porch. Next week she would stage the interior with furniture to make it easier for buyers to imagine living there.

Anne parked on the street right in front of the house and waited for Chloe, savoring the first peaceful moments of the day and checking her emails. After a few minutes, she talked herself into leaving the warmth of the car and going into the house to turn on the heat so it would be warm when Chloe arrived.

Anne got out of the car and stretched her arms lazily, then stepped beyond the hedges that obscured the house. She lifted her gaze toward the cottage, catching a flash of movement coming from inside the kitchen. It couldn't be the realtor because there was no car in the driveway. Who else had a house key? Peter? Wouldn't he be at work now?

Anne quickly ducked back behind the hedge to stay out of sight, then pulled open the car door and reached into the back seat to grab her semi-automatic and waistband holster. After tapping a full magazine into the handgun, she fastened the holster around her waist and slipped the gun into it. She edged along the perimeter of the exterior walls until she reached the front porch.

She tried the front doorknob. Unlocked. She opened it quietly, alert to any sound coming from inside. Nothing. Then she heard the creaking of floorboards, seeming to come from the far corner of the living room. The faint smell of cigarette smoke carried through the air. She stopped, felt for her holstered gun, and peered around the open door. From the dim foyer, she was able to see straight through to the living room and the back window.

That's when she saw the figure, darkly silhouetted by the late afternoon sun that streamed through the window, veiled by the smoky haze of a lit cigarette. Without thinking, she pulled her handgun waist-high, pointing it downward.

"Don't move," Anne called out, taking two long steps into the room. Her eyes quickly adjusted to the low light, and she could dimly make out a woman, a smallish one, leaning back casually against the windowpane. As if she hadn't a care in the world.

"Who are you?" Anne demanded, nudging on the light switch with her left elbow.

"I'm a friend of Peter's." The woman's face was expressionless, her tone flat. If she noticed the gun, she showed no sign of it.

"You're Michele Murray, aren't you?" Anne didn't wait for an answer. Of course it was Michele, older and no longer the cherub-faced beauty of her childhood, but definitely Michele. The delicate features had coarsened. The mouth no longer resembled a rosebud—it was now a hard thin line. The ocean blue eyes were unmistakable, though; they were the giveaway.

"What are you doing here?" Anne asked, lowering the gun to her side.

"I'm just picking up something for...." Michele left the sentence hanging. She stepped away from the window, dropped the lit cigarette on the floor, and stubbed it out with her foot.

"How did you get the key to the house?" Anne asked.

No answer. Michele bent down to retrieve the cigarette butt and dropped it in her coat pocket.

"Or did you break in?"

They heard a car pull into the driveway, and the short beep of a horn.

Michele suddenly straightened up and leveled her gaze at Anne. "And who are *you* anyway? And what do you have to do with anything?" she challenged, and then gestured with disdain toward Anne's lowered gun. "Overreacting, much?"

Michele bent down and picked her purse up from the floor, slinging it onto her shoulder as if ready to leave this conversation behind.

As Anne holstered the gun, the front door creaked open, and Noreen breezed in saying, "I'm dropping Chloe off now, and I'll be back—" Noreen stopped cold. She looked quickly from Anne to Michele, seeming not to believe what she was seeing.

Behind her, Chloe stepped in. "What's going on?" she asked, her eyes widening. No one answered her.

Michele looked neither right nor left, brushed past all of them, and headed quickly out the front door. Without a word, a grim-looking Noreen followed Michele out and slammed the door behind them.

Their muffled arguing grew increasingly louder, but not loud enough to make sense of it from behind the closed door.

"Chloe, I'll be right back," Anne said. "Go ahead and pick out the photos you want." She pointed to a stack of boxes and left Chloe alone in the living room.

Now was her best chance to find out about the relationship between the two—if there was one anymore—and to see Michele in action. Anne put an ear to the front door, and when that wasn't sufficient, opened it a crack. Just enough to see and hear without being seen.

"Didn't I tell you to get out of town?" Noreen asked.

"Leave? And why should I? I'm not going anywhere. And if I do leave, it won't be before I get what I came for."

"And I told you, I gave you everything I could. There *is* no more."

"Get the rest from Tony. Or Joanne. I don't care where you get it," Michele said, her voice rising sharply.

"Not so loud," Noreen said, "and leave my family out of this. How many times do I have to tell you? If I get you more, then will you leave?"

"Maybe I will. Who knows? But not until after the party." Michele's tone was petulant.

"After the *party*? Are you fucking *kidding* me?" Noreen was now in a fearless fury. She took several lurching steps closer to Michele, who didn't budge.

"Now *you* keep your voice down, Noreen, unless you want that gun-toting bitch inside the house to hear. Peter said we should go to the party together. The family has to get used to the idea—"

"Used to *what* idea? You're not showing up anywhere near that party. If you think for one minute you're going to—"

"Here's the thing: Peter expects me to go, and I don't see any harm—"

"Peter? Just leave Peter alone," Noreen spat out in a lowered voice. "I'm telling you, once and for all, you're not wanted around *any* of us."

"Peter seems to want me around. What are you so damn worried about?" Michele said sharply.

"The same thing you *should* be worried about."

"See, Noreen, that's the difference between you and me."

"Leave town *now*. I'm warning you!"

Michele laughed in Noreen's face. She turned her back and headed down the paved walkway, yelling out her parting shot: "You've always been such a whiney wimp, Noreen."

Anne gently closed the front door, leaning her back against it. She closed her eyes, then stepped away from it and went into the living room. And waited, knowing Noreen would walk in at any second. Only after looking into Noreen's eyes, gauging her body language, sensing her mood, would Anne know whether now was the time to press her for details about the day of the murder, or save questions for another day.

Noreen opened the door slowly and stepped halfway into the living room, her face a mask of exhaustion and defeat, her voice low. "Chloe, are you done yet?"

"Not yet, Mom," Chloe said without looking up. She was sitting on the floor, engrossed in foraging through the boxes and sorting photos into piles.

"Can Anne give me a ride home?"

"Fine."

Noreen turned and walked out the door without another word.

* * *

"Maybe you should ask your mom," Anne finally said to Chloe. She had spent the entire ten-minute drive to Chloe's house dodging questions about the "strange woman who had the *nerve* to break into Grandma's house."

"Wait 'til I tell Grandma. She'll freak." Chloe jumped out of the car the second it came to a stop in front of her house. Her air of indifference back at the house had apparently just been a teenage ruse to be invisible to the adults, the better to observe and ferret out their secrets.

"Thanks for the ride, Anne. See you at the party on Sunday!" Chloe dashed into her house without looking back.

Anne sat quietly for a moment before backing out of the driveway. She turned her car toward home and drove on automatic pilot, barely registering familiar landmarks along the way. Her mind was wandering, playing and replaying the scene at the house. Noreen and Michele were clearly bound inextricably together—to the terror of Noreen. But bound by what, exactly? Secrets, certainly—and they were so menacing that Noreen was bowing to blackmail. What had Noreen done, and why was it so dangerous to her now? Why was it so urgent that Michele should clear out of town *right now*? But apparently, Michele was not in the same danger, or didn't think she was, anyway. And what was Peter's connection to all of this besides being a besotted suitor?

Pulling into the driveway of her duplex, Anne took out her notebook and jotted down the women's conversation while it was fresh in her mind.

Her phone pinged with an insistent text. It was from Jim Raggle, her sometimes-boyfriend, hoping to come by tonight after dinner. Well, of course, *after* dinner—he wouldn't want to pick up a dinner check, or even split one—now, would he? He rarely gave her this much lead time. Usually, he just showed up and knocked at her door. And she usually wouldn't let him in. She had her standards. At the moment, she was not feeling warmly toward him, and it occurred to her that, given her snarky new attitude, they weren't going to last through the holidays.

Not tonight, buster. Tonight, she had plans to meet Krista for dinner.

Chapter Sixteen

Tuesday, October 29

Krista was already seated by the window at Le Jardin restaurant, her back to the front door, when Anne came in and spotted her from across the room. It was hard to miss Krista's glossy black hair hanging in a single braid down her back.

"I see her, thanks," Anne told the hostess. She threaded her way around waiters, customers, and crowded tables in the teeming restaurant, which food critics raved about as offering "deceptively simple" French fare. Anne might have chosen a quieter, less trendy restaurant, maybe even the Chinese eatery where the two of them had spent hours, often late into the night, analyzing family role dynamics and rehashing their latest men. But this was Krista's choice, the new favorite of her new friends.

Anne approached the table, blew out a short breath, and tapped Krista on the shoulder before sitting in the chair facing her. The friends smiled at each other.

"It's so good to see you!" Anne said.

"I'd get up to hug you, but I can't," Krista gestured toward her hugely pregnant stomach. "I may never get up again!" she laughed.

"Pregnancy looks great on you, Krissy. How much longer?"

"Two weeks to go, and I cannot wait. No one ever tells you how tiring it is lugging around…well, actually they do!" Krista said. "In fact, I'm getting nothing but sympathy and advice from other women."

Dressed in well-cut, expensive maternity jeans, and a black cashmere turtleneck sweater, Krista looked as casually chic as ever. Menus arrived, Krista made recommendations, orders were taken: poached salmon for Krista, coq au vin for Anne. Their waitress sailed off toward the kitchen.

For a while, they talked of the current state of their lives: the bridal shower, Anne's business and work with the Murrays, Krista's pregnancy and her husband's business, and Anne's dating prospects.

"Actually, I'm seeing someone," Anne said, then reconsidered. "No, that's putting it way too strongly." She told Krista about Jim and their arrangement. Krista groaned.

"I'm not judging, believe me," Krista said, waving her left hand so the light glinted off her three-carat diamond engagement ring. "I've been there, as you well know."

She leaned in toward Anne to offer her advice, a habit that wasn't just allowed, it was a tenet of their friendship: they freely gave each other unsolicited advice that neither of them ever felt obliged to take.

"It's been two years since your divorce," Krista said, "there's got to be something better out there than friends with benefits—at our age? And you and this Jim guy weren't even friends, to begin with."

Anne shrugged. "Okay, first of all, I'm just starting to be ready for something serious. Not even sure I'm there yet. And second, the group of eligibles out there is *not* good. You found Mike in the nick of time, Krista," Anne said, warming to the subject. "You know what's out there now? Guys who are either married or gay. Or—and this actually happened on my last blind date—they'll look at you, all sad-eyed, and complain how hard dating is because 'all the good ones are taken.'"

"Yikes, that's a date-ender!" Krista leaned back and laughed. "Guess you'll just have to wait for the first round of divorces to happen. And from what I'm hearing, that won't be long."

While she filled Anne in on the marriages expected to bite the dust soon, the waitress brought their drinks to the table.

"Iced tea and sparkling water. This is *so* not like us," Krista sighed theatrically. "After the baby's born, they'll find me passed out drunk on the floor of our wine cellar. I have a lot of catching up to do."

Anne laughed and thought back to the days when the two of them actually *did* hide out in Krista's custom-made wine cellar, eager to escape another dull party for business associates of Krista's high-powered husband, Mike.

"And I'll be happy to join you there," Anne said off-handedly.

Krista tilted her head and paused, then said quietly, "Oh, I thought maybe you'd quit drinking. That you'd left that behind you."

"Oh, well, I've definitely cut back." Anne managed a weak smile, but a tinge of anger was building. Why should *she* be the one on the defensive here? Did Krista expect her to apologize for something? And why was her drinking any of Krista's business?

Their food arrived, and they ate in near silence. On the drive over, Anne had rehashed the scenes that had changed everything in their friendship. Her ex-husband's phone calls—actually more like preemptive strikes—to their mutual friends, telling them lies about her. Lies that Krista apparently believed if her actions indicated anything. Her texts and calls to Krista that were never returned.

Should she bring up the rift in their friendship? Anne wanted to hear Krista's side of it. Maybe she'd learn something. But then, does talking really resolve anything or just stir things up? Maybe it's better to leave the past in the past. Talking about something isn't the same as fixing it. On the other hand, how they talked about their feelings, how honest and forgiving they were, would decide whether they would remain friends or part ways. That was the theory, anyway—her therapist's theory. Anne wasn't convinced, but nevertheless.

Back and forth she went.

She decided to plunge in. She put her fork down and dabbed the corners of her mouth with her cloth napkin. "Krista, I'd like to clear the air about what happened back then—"

"Do you really want to get into this? We're having such a nice time," Krista said.

"It's not that I want to lay blame."

"Because there's plenty of blame to go around."

That expression always set Anne off. "That's a false equivalency, don't you think?" Anne asked. Krista's sharp look warned her off. Softening her tone, Anne continued, "I just felt that after all our years of friendship, it was...hurtful that you and Mike took Gary's side over mine. I never would have done that to you."

"I didn't take Gary's side."

"I know he called you and all our friends—even my aunt and uncle—telling outrageous lies about me. Lies about how I was a raging, crazy drunk, and no wonder he had an affair." She paused. "And you apparently believed him."

"I didn't believe him."

"Then why did you stop taking my calls and texts? You simply turned your back on me. Stopped our friendship cold." Anne felt tears welling and composed herself. "I just want to know why."

Krista dropped her napkin onto the table and looked Anne directly in the eye. "Gary said a lot of things, some of them true, I suspect, but most of them lies. It wasn't about Gary or what he said. I never for one moment believed that you put a gun to his temple."

"What?"

"And I never thought you slashed his girlfriend's tires. Or threw bleach on his brand-new suits. None of that. I knew he was lying through his teeth. No, it wasn't about Gary," Krista said.

Stunned, Anne covered her face with her hands momentarily. She hadn't heard the stories about the gun or bleach. *That son-of-a-bitch. Well, no wonder.*

"What was it about then?" Anne wasn't sure she wanted to hear the answer.

"Well, those late-night phone calls you made, venting on and on about Gary, didn't help. Starting at two o'clock in the morning and continuing all through the night, for three nights in a row. Those drove Mike crazy."

"I'm sorry—"

"He thought *you* were crazy. And he started to believe all the stuff Gary was saying. I told Mike, 'No way, Annie wouldn't do those things. I've known her all my life. A person doesn't change that much.' I defended you to him and to all our friends."

"I didn't know," Anne said. "But if you didn't believe Gary, what changed between us, other than the late-night calls? You and I had only one argument."

"One argument?" Krista sounded weary. "Are you serious? Don't you remember my birthday party at my parent's house? How sloppy drunk you got—I'd never seen you like that. Remember the toast you gave? Telling stories that I'd told you in confidence. And you called me a...." Krista's eyes were swimming. "I'm not even going to repeat it. But I could handle all that. I could even understand, because you were so upset about your own life. But you said those things in front of my parents. My *parents*, who had always loved you, Anne. And when I saw the look on my father's face, it broke my heart."

"Oh, Krissy, I'm so sorry. I don't remember any of that. I swear." Anne sank down in her seat. She struggled for any memory of that day but came up with only darkness. Then suddenly, a brief image of a wine glass breaking.

"Did I throw a wine glass?"

"Anne, it's in the past. I want it to stay in the past. I really do."

Now it all made sense. The times Krista's parents ignored her when they ran into each other in public. Just days ago, they crossed the street to avoid her.

"I'll apologize to your parents. I need to do that."

"That would be good."

Krista reached for Anne's hand across the table. "In spite of everything...."

"And there's been a lot," Anne agreed, shaking her head.

"I've missed you. And that's why I asked Emily to invite you to the shower."

"I'm glad you did." She squeezed Krista's hand. The waitress cleared their dinner plates and dropped the check off on the corner of the table.

"But there's something else," Krista said, taking her hands back, folding them in her lap.

Anne braced herself, waiting for fresh grievances to come flying out of left field.

"We need to work on your love life." Krista gave Anne a sly grin. "How about that Tony guy, the oldest Murray son? I hear he's loaded and very good-looking."

"Ha! I haven't even met him yet." Anne laughed with relief. "And you know me, money's never the big draw. Besides, he's married and much older."

"He's Mike's age! They went to high school together. And wife number three is on her way out from what I've heard," Krista said as they laid their credit cards inside the folder. The waitress swooped in and carried it off.

How Krista could know this was beyond Anne, but she didn't doubt it for a minute. It was as though Krista had eyes everywhere, informants everywhere. And it had always been this way. It was something of a gift.

"He sounds difficult. Three divorces at what—forty-two years old?" Anne said.

"Of course, he's difficult. All men are difficult," Krista said. "I haven't seen him myself, but Mike says he looks like Colin Farrell, the actor, only taller."

"I can barely handle a twenty-six-year-old car mechanic who still lives with his mother. I'm sure Tony Murray, with all his money and movie star good looks, is way out of my league."

Krista dismissed the notion with a wave of her hand. "He's absolutely *not* out of your league! If anything, he's probably not good enough. Too much baggage."

"Like I don't have any...." Anne said while they finished settling their bill.

"But maybe you're right. He could be too old for you. Don't you have a seven-year age difference rule? Which always seemed so arbitrary to me...."

"And right now, that tops out at thirty-nine years old."

"Ridiculous. Well, if anything develops between the two of you, I can walk you through it. I haven't lost my touch."

"I'll keep that in mind." Anne smiled, wrapping her wool scarf around her neck. "You'll be the first to know if there are any sparks between us."

"Come visit me after the baby's born—"

"Of course I will. I'd love to."

"And we'll leave the baby with Mike and go out for brunch." Krista laughed as she shrugged on her jacket. "We were always good at brunch."

Chapter Seventeen

Wednesday, October 30

"Don't go," Claire heard herself say out loud. She was waking up and resisting it, longing to drift back into the dream. Gerald was there, wearing his black tuxedo, a dog at his side. Her collie, the one she had taught to help her herd the dairy cows on her father's ranch. Gerald smiled at her tenderly, asking without words, in the way of dreams, "Are you ready for the party? Everyone will be there, even the dogs."

She was confused. Did he mean the birthday party on Sunday? Dogs won't be there. Not even Louie. No, that didn't seem right. He just smiled.

Then it was over. The morning's insistent light seeped through the drawn curtains and onto her pillow. Tears were streaming down her cheeks. She resigned herself to being awake. Alone in her room.

* * *

"Still going out for a walk, Miss Claire?" Sala tapped lightly on Claire's bedroom door and waited for an answer. If Claire didn't respond soon, Sala would ask again, and wait again. Only then would she peek inside.

Sala had sized up Claire on their hiring interview: *This one needs her privacy.* Twenty-five years of taking care of the sick and dying had taught her to read people. She knew which ones would be demanding, needy, gracious, kind, cruel, or vulnerable. Which ones would turn on her, be in denial of dying, or accuse her of stealing.

Claire would be one of the stoic ones, Sala would bet her pay on it. She tried again. "Might want to go soon, before it gets too cool outside."

Sala also knew about families. Some gathered around, comforting and loving, not wanting to have any regrets they would have to live with later. Some never came around. And some families hovered, afraid to leave the dying alone for one minute, afraid they might call a lawyer and change their will, or say something private and spill family secrets.

She had seen adult children back up in driveways with rented U-Hauls to load up the bedroom sets, sofas, and precious keepsakes. Second wives who screened visitors jealously and ruthlessly kept the children from a final visit with their dying father. And in every family, at least in her experience, there was the greedy one. The one who would sneak valuables out of the house when their siblings weren't looking. The one who tried to extract promises from the dying. And on and on.

She had seen people at their best and at their worst. And having seen everything, she knew there was no drama like family drama—and no family drama like death.

* * *

"I'll be out in a minute, Sala," Claire called from the bedroom, still shaking off her dream of Gerald and moving slowly.

"Let me know if I can do anything," Sala said.

"Put the leash on Louie, please?"

Behind her closed bedroom door, Claire sat on the edge of the bed, gathering her strength. She slowly rose and began to get dressed. Sala and Jasmine's arrival three days before, along with the visits three times a week by hospice personnel, meant she could have no more illusions that she could carry on as usual. But she still had the strength to visit the piano lounge every night with Betty and to take strolls along the nature trail behind the hotel. Those were still on her list of things she was grateful she could do. And do them, she would.

"It's a glorious day outside," Claire said cheerfully to Sala as she entered the living room. She leaned down to remove Louie's THERAPY DOG IN TRAINING vest as his tail thumped the floor. "You're off duty now, Lou," she said, handing the leash to Sala.

Louie followed the women out the front door, stepping into the cool, bracing air. Claire stopped after a few feet to secure her wool plaid scarf around her neck. Taking Claire's left arm, Sala placed it in the crook of her own. They started down the flat dirt trail, cushioned underfoot with fallen oak leaves and pine needles. The trail, part of a county park devoted to native plants, trees, and wildlife, wound around the hotel and backed up to acres of open space. Only a few locals—and hotel guests clued in by the concierge—knew it existed.

Claire looked up at the late morning sun breaking through the mist and breathed in the pungent smell of pine and damp earth. With her right hand firmly gripping her cane, she turned her gaze to the ground and walked with the careful precision of someone always on guard against falls and pain, wary of tripping on loose rocks or tree roots. Louie ambled along at her heel, occasionally straining at the leash to sniff at boulders and tree stumps.

They fell quiet until Sala, a woman of few words, ventured, "Are you happy to see your guests soon?"

"I'm more excited than I thought I'd be, actually," Claire said.

Claire's family would be arriving for her birthday party in three days, coming from as far away as New York, Kansas, and Chicago. Among them were her brother, two cousins, nieces and nephews, and an old college chum—all staying at The Parisian in a block of specially discounted rooms.

The week before, Claire had almost called the party off. She probably would have, except that over cocktails at the lounge, Betty ticked off the reasons why canceling would be "horribly, horribly selfish." Guests would get stuck with airline cancellation fees. Restaurant deposits would be lost. Claire would be depriving herself and everyone she loved of the chance to be together one last time—and that was exactly what they all needed right now.

But it was Betty's final argument—accompanied by a theatrical flinging of her arms skyward—saying, "the show must go on!" that had Claire rolling her eyes to the ceiling, but ultimately caving in. She could never win an argument with Betty. And heaven forbid she ignore a plucky old show business axiom, not while Betty was around.

So the party plans accelerated. Noreen was designing the flower arrangements, a skill she'd picked up at the florist shop where she worked part-time. Joanne was finalizing the menu and arranging the seating chart. Tony was adding items to the menu and paying most of the bills. Peter would chauffeur the out-of-town guests. Claire's four grandchildren were up to something—a project that had them whispering, giggling, and airing creative differences.

So while all that was going on, Claire forced herself to relax—her only responsibilities were to keep her hair appointment, dress up in her new silk outfit, apply her makeup, and be as rested and well as possible.

They had arrived at the stand of redwoods, the halfway mark of their walk, and were turning around to head back when they saw Peter jogging up the trail to meet them. Claire was startled by his sudden appearance: she knew Peter wouldn't show up in the middle of the afternoon and track them down on a trail if it was good news. He was out of breath by the time he reached them, his tan windbreaker flapping open and his face ruddy with exertion.

"What's wrong?" Claire asked. She came to a full stop, leaning on her cane. Sala stepped away to give them privacy, feigning interest in the furrowed bark of a redwood tree.

"Nothing, nothing! It's all good," he answered, catching his breath.

"Then what's going on?" Claire waited.

"I called Joanne to ask her to add another guest to the party. She said she wouldn't do it. Can you freaking believe that?" Peter shook his head as if in shock and disbelief. "Big deal, one more guest!"

"Who's the guest?" Claire knew Joanne was a whiz at squeezing in guests she liked.

"It's Michele. I want her to come," Peter said, using the same wheedling tone he'd used to cajole Claire into letting him move into the utility room.

"She's practically a member of the family. After all, she's my ex-wife, and maybe even more soon if I play my cards right."

"Absolutely not," Claire said, starting to walk again toward the hotel. Sala and Louie were right at her side. Peter turned to follow them.

"I have to agree with Joanne. There's no extra room. None," she said.

"I told Michele she could come." Peter stepped in front of Claire, blocking her progress. "What am I going to tell her now?" he asked as he threw up his hands in helplessness. "That no one in our family has one ounce of forgiveness in their hearts after all these years?"

"Oh, Peter…" Claire stepped around him. She had nothing more to say. The matter was settled.

"She's waiting in the car in the hotel parking lot. She wants to talk to you," Peter said to his mother's back.

Then it's going to be a long cold wait, Claire thought and kept walking.

Chapter Eighteen

Thursday, October 31

The next morning, Anne was sitting alone inside the Parkside Diner, looking out the window and drumming her fingers on the Formica tabletop. Peter had finally agreed to meet with her—on the condition they meet near his job and that it would not interfere with his lunch hour. She offered to pay for breakfast before his shift started, so they made the date.

For the last twenty minutes, over fried eggs and hash browns, she had questioned Peter about his whereabouts on the day Danny died and the whereabouts of anyone else he could remember. She asked him for contact information for Michele and managed to get a cell phone number, though he said he couldn't guarantee that it was her latest. He also said he didn't know where she was living—but wherever it was, it wasn't with him.

Then he excused himself to go to the restroom. That was ten minutes ago.

Her phone rang: it was her uncle.

"How's it going?" Jack asked.

"He's sticking to his story that he wasn't anywhere near Noreen and Michele after school that day. Still says he was playing tetherball—which isn't how Joanne remembers it."

"So who are you gonna believe?" Jack asked.

"All in all, Peter's given me nothing—he's a fount of non-information. Doesn't know where anyone was. Doesn't know where Michele is living.

132

Has no opinions. Heard nothing." Anne sighed, keeping her eyes on the restroom door. "He's not exactly forthcoming. Oh! But he *did* offer his services in helping solve the crime. He says we can brainstorm with him anytime."

Jack barked out a laugh.

"Tell him if he really wants to help, he can start by coughing up Michele's address. It turns out Michele isn't in the system since she's never been arrested," Jack said.

"That's kind of surprising. Anyway, I don't believe for a minute that he doesn't know where Michele is staying."

"Me neither. So tell him to spill her address and her *real* cell number, or we'll be forced to pull search warrants or maybe start surveillance on him," Jack said.

"He won't fall for that," Anne said.

"Give it a shot."

"Gotta go, he's coming back."

Peter sauntered back to the table and slid into the booth, his plaid shirttail hanging out. "Sorry about that. Sometimes things take longer than you expect," he confided with a wink. Anne wondered, not for the first time, how Claire could be his mother.

"Let's see, where were we?" Anne looked down at her notes, pretending to read them. "Oh, right, we were talking about Michele. I ran into her the other day at your mother's house. She was inside the house, alone. Did she get the key from you?"

Peter sat back, crossing his arms and narrowing his eyes. "I don't see what this has to do with anything. If I gave Michele a key or not, that's between me and my mother. That's Murray family business."

"You seem to be in touch with Michele—"

"Not really. Not anymore."

Anne leaned forward. "Here's the deal—straight from the lead detective—you either give us her address and current cell number, or we get warrants. Or maybe even put a tail on you."

"You can't do that," he said, jutting out his chin. "Where's the probable cause for a warrant? And a warrant for what—my phone, my apartment? And you don't have the manpower for a tail. It's all ridiculous." He sat back, raising his chin even higher, so high he was literally looking down his nose at her.

"Okay, then how about this—I'll tell your mother you aren't cooperating in the investigation that she herself instigated."

"Oh, so now you're going to tell my mommy on me?" His voice dripped with sarcasm.

"That's right."

Peter hesitated. Then, as if sensing the inevitable, finally said, "Let me see what I can do."

"Well, do it fast."

* * *

To the casual eye, Santa Rosa might seem like a bedrock of normality, a fine place to run a business, and a safe place to raise a family. Jack McCormack and Dean Diaz liked to think it was safer than most—they'd spent their careers working toward that end—but there was nothing casual or starry-eyed about the way they saw their hometown. They knew the crime rate was down. Nevertheless, they would zero in on what appeared shady—like the rail-thin guy loitering on the bus bench with darting eyes and a facial tic. And though they saw the delight in their grandkids' faces when they rode the carousel and miniature train at the city park, they also saw the used condoms and needles littering the ground under the benches.

They were sitting in Dean's pride and joy, a 1962 red Corvair, in the late morning, drinking coffee in the shopping center parking lot facing College Avenue. Snazzy old cars, circa their youth, were among the many topics they liked to shoot the breeze about. They'd be content to sit here all day in front of the Coffee Hut—talking gas mileage, comparing golf scores, rehashing old cases—if it weren't for their upcoming noon appointment with Noreen Murray Grindel.

Through the sun's sharp glare bouncing off the windshield, they spotted a long-haired driver with neck tattoos in a beat-up Toyota on the fast-moving street in front of them. Motoring along a little too cautiously, below the speed limit, signaling before changing lanes.

Their wives would joke that if Jack and Dean didn't spot an ex-con they'd helped to put into prison within thirty minutes of sitting down to enjoy a restaurant meal, well, it just wasn't a successful night out, in their estimation.

They were trained observers, Jack and Dean would tell them, and they couldn't turn it off. They couldn't help it any more than a teacher, when observing a group of children, couldn't help but know which ones were being bullied, which ones were being hurt, and which ones were oblivious to the bullying. Or any more than a graphic designer could keep from guessing the fonts being used on random store signs or magazine covers.

"If I was twenty years younger, I'd tear out of this parking lot and do a three-point turn and go after that guy. What do you wanna bet he's holding?" Jack said, relaxing back into the plush leather seat, leaning his head on the headrest.

"Oh, yeah," Dean said.

"But these days, we'd need a probable cause to stop him."

"Maybe, but we could still do the illegal three-point turn," Dean said helpfully.

The two detectives had spent their morning following up on the tip by Suzy Eller, Danny's classmate at St. Paul's. Her information had turned out to be mostly hearsay and rumors about which kids at school were troublemakers.

But one memory was hers alone. About two weeks after the murder, she saw Tony and his friends, "the cool kids" as Suzy called them, corner the new school janitor in the hallway. She saw the boys kick him a few times and call him a murderer, then run away. "The younger sister was also there," she had added. "I remember she went into the janitor's shed while the argument was going on, and the janitor yelled at her to get out. I'm not sure what that was about."

The detectives thanked Suzy Eller for her help, encouraged her to contact them if she remembered anything else, and then drove off to the Coffee Hut.

They were on their second cups, just waiting for Anne to show up. After her interview with Peter, she had decided to join them for Noreen's interview at the last minute.

Jack added more sugar to his coffee. "Peter Murray. Now, that guy bothers me."

"Yeah, one of those high-IQ types who can't hold a job but thinks he can do ours better than us." Dean nodded genially. "Yeah, I'm bothered by Peter too, but he seems pretty harmless—other than he's hiding something."

They heard Anne's car pull into the parking space next to them. She gave a short honk. Jack stepped out of the car and folded the front seat forward so Anne could wedge herself into the tight rear seat of the Corvair. "Thanks for letting me tag along," she said as she angled her knees sideways and felt around for a seatbelt that didn't exist.

"So, what changed your mind?" Jack asked.

"Curiosity. I want to see if Noreen cooperates with you—which she *never* will with me because she hates me, as we all know," Anne said. "Every time I've seen her, she's been aggressive. Even belligerent."

Dean looked skeptical. "Noreen seemed like a quiet, scared little kid. At least, that's how I remember her. Always hiding behind her older brother Tony." He drained his coffee cup, then cocked his head to a philosophical tilt. "But people change."

"I'll just stay in the background and not interfere. I won't say a word."

Jack snorted. "Ha!"

"I'll be a fly on the wall. Quiet as a mouse."

Jack looked down at his phone: a text was coming in from Noreen. "Noreen's running late. She wants to change the appointment to two o'clock. Hell, that's running a lot late—that's almost three hours from now." Jack turned to Dean and Anne. "Okay with you guys?" They nodded, and Jack wrote back to say they would see her at two instead.

"Maybe we could go for a walk in the meantime," Anne suggested. The two men simultaneously shook their heads.

"Or maybe go back to the office," Dean said.

"Or maybe go get some lunch," Jack countered.

"It's kind of early for that," Anne said. "While we mull it over, I'm going into the coffee shop to get a latte. Anyone want more coffee?"

They both nodded. Within a few minutes, she was back inside the car with three paper coffee cups and a hefty, greasy bag of donuts.

Jack pried open the lid of his cup and emptied a few packets of sugar into it. "By the way, Anne, did you get Michele's address out of Peter this morning?"

"Only after threatening to bring Claire into it."

"Playing the Claire card, huh?" Jack said. "He's probably worried about staying in her will."

Dean laughed. "Are we cynical, or what?"

"But Peter wasn't sure Michele was still at the address he gave me," Anne said. "According to him, she bounces around a lot. Anyway, Peter made it very clear that Michele isn't with him anymore. They aren't a couple. Apparently, Claire nixed the idea of Michele coming to the birthday party, and she went ballistic. Blamed Peter. He almost got teary-eyed when he talked about it." Anne texted the two detectives the address for their records.

"But here's what's interesting: the address he gave me was that of her old foster home—the one she got removed from when she was eleven. Only a few months after the murder," Anne said. "Peter said Michele always stayed in touch with that couple. The father is dead now, but Michele sometimes stays with the mother when she's in town."

"I remember that couple from the original investigation. Nice people," Jack said.

"Right. He was a doctor here in town," Dean said. "When we questioned Michele back then, he was her legal guardian and had to be present. He was very protective."

"The woman's name is Faye Lockwood. Peter gave me her phone number, so I plan to call her today and see if she'll meet with me—or us, if you want to come," Anne said.

"We have a few hours to kill. What's the number? I'll give her a call and see if we can go up there now," Jack said. Anne passed him the note with the phone information on it. While Jack placed the call, Anne took a bite of her donut and watched as its powdered sugar drifted off and landed on her dark slacks. "Damn," she muttered to herself. Her attempts at brushing it off only resulted in a white powdery smear.

"That's why I only eat cake-style donuts," Dean said smugly.

Jack ended his call. "We got lucky. Mrs. Lockwood is between doctor appointments and can see us now."

Dean shook his head and begged off, saying he should finish some paperwork back at the office. That left Jack and Anne to handle the Lockwood interview, but the trio agreed to meet up at one-forty-five at the office and drive to Noreen's house together.

Anne collected the used coffee cups and dirty napkins and stepped out of Dean's car to toss them in the trash while Jack headed toward Anne's car. Watching Dean drive off, she hesitated a beat before getting inside her car. A fleeting thought came to mind, a thread tying together sundry clues and motives. Just as quickly, it disappeared. She stood still and stared off into the distance, trying to call back the thought. The random connections. But poof, gone.

"Any problem?" Jack called out to her.

"No, just thinking." She stepped inside the car.

* * *

"Oh my, I thought we were in for another dreary rainy day, but look at that sweet sunshine peeking through the clouds," Faye Lockwood said, smiling mildly at Anne and Jack as they stepped onto her front porch.

She ushered them inside her large, once fashionable house set on a valuable piece of hilltop property in the Bennett Valley area of Santa Rosa. There was the aroma of chicken noodle soup coming from the kitchen and the drone of a political talk show from the television in the living room.

Anne judged Faye Lockwood to be around eighty-five, about a decade older than Claire. She had the weathered skin of a sun lover, was slender but not frail, and moved about with the physical confidence of one who had been an athlete all her life. She wore tan, calf-length cargo pants and an oversized nubby red sweater. She turned off the television.

"Can I offer you some lunch? It's just soup and wheat crackers, but—"

"Thanks, but we've eaten," Jack lied. "But you go ahead."

"That's all right, I'll wait."

"Thanks for seeing us on such short notice," he said.

While the two talked, Anne ventured toward the mullioned north-facing window and looked out toward the houses located higher up on the hill. She knew the Murray family had lived two doors up from the Lockwoods on this street at the top of the hill, but the garish house she saw planted there did not in any way resemble the modern, glass-walled house that Claire had described.

"Is that the old Murray house?" Anne asked. Mrs. Lockwood went over to Anne's side to view the house in question.

"Oh, heavens, no," she replied. "The new buyers tore down the Murray house ten years ago—it was too tasteful, I guess—and built that monstrosity. They just wanted the lot and the views that went with it."

Jack sat down on the couch, took out his notebook, and cleared his throat. Anne and Mrs. Lockwood took the hint and settled into the armchairs facing him.

"Just a few questions," Jack said. "You and your husband were Michele's foster parents during the years surrounding Danny Murray's death. Can you tell us about that?"

Mrs. Lockwood settled back into her tufted red velvet chair, her hands folded in her lap.

"Let's see, we started taking in foster children when I was in my late forties. Our children had left for college, and my husband and I were at loose ends, missing them. We felt we had something to offer those kids. It wasn't for the reimbursement money. We didn't need the money. My husband made a good living as a doctor, so we put nearly all of it aside for Michele when she turned eighteen. That way, she'd at least have something to start her life with. Most of these foster kids have nothing. No safety net, no money, and certainly no family that was worth a hill of beans."

She pointed to the framed photos of children on the fireplace mantel. "We put money aside for all our fosters, and we made a good home for them while they were here," she said, "We had three altogether. Michele was our last one."

"Why was that?" Anne asked.

Mrs. Lockwood sighed. "My husband didn't have the heart for it anymore. We had Michele for just two years."

"Why was it terminated?" Jack asked.

"You have to understand—when we got her, she was very emotionally damaged. Lord, the things that girl had lived through. Her mother apparently brought her clients—strange men—into the home for God knows what. Even worse, she had Michele, when she was as young as four years old, perform sex acts for her clientele. Can you imagine exposing a child to all that?" She shook her head and continued without waiting for an answer. "The child services people told us that they first learned about her when they received a report that she was going to neighbors' houses and begging for food. When they looked into it closer, they learned about the mother's prostitution and all that and placed her into the foster system. Michele was nine years old when we got her, and already she was quite sexualized."

Anne suspected Mrs. Lockwood would keep rambling like this all day if she didn't repeat the question. "Why did you end the placement?"

Mrs. Lockwood continued as if she had not heard. "Michele was a handful, and she lied all the time and was aggressive with other children. We were always getting complaints from the teachers. Sometimes kids who are abused become the abuser, you know? That's not unusual. And she was very skittish here at the house, couldn't tolerate being hugged or touched. She always kept a chair wedged under the doorknob of her bedroom—like she was expecting us to barge in on her and do God knows what."

Mrs. Lockwood leaned forward. "Anyway, back to your question. All that kind of behavior was to be expected, considering her start in life, but when she started spreading rumors about my husband—well, that was the final straw. We couldn't have his reputation ruined. He was crushed."

"What rumors?" Jack asked.

"Well, there was simply no truth to them, you know, but Michele told a teacher that he asked her to take a shower with him. And that he snuck into her bedroom at night, and she had to threaten him with scissors to make him leave. All lies."

"You know that for sure?" Jack asked.

"Oh yes. I was always here. I made a point of it. Nothing happened, and Michele has apologized for saying those things. She's apologized many, *many* times. Too little, too late as far as my husband was concerned, but nevertheless. Besides, if those things had really happened, why would she beg us to take her back? She never stopped calling us after she left."

"Did she seem overly attached to the Murray family?" Anne asked.

"Funny you should ask. After she became friends with the youngest daughter—"

"Noreen."

"Yes, like Elmer's glue, those two. Michele started telling us about how Noreen's parents were so young—compared to us, anyway—and how great their house was. Michele even suggested that I dye my hair blond to look more like Claire Murray." Mrs. Lockwood managed a laugh.

"But one time, we really got into it because I was a little hurt. I told her that she should just move in with them if they were so great. Michele told me that she planned to. Imagine that?" She was quiet for several seconds, then said, "Now that I think of it, maybe that's why she said those awful things about my husband. To force a move. Well, it forced a move all right, but not how she wanted it."

"Peter Murray said she lives here with you now. Is that right?" Anne asked.

"No, not entirely. She stays overnight sometimes and keeps some of her things here. I have a spare room where any of my children and fosters can stay if they need to. But just for a visit."

"Is she visiting now?" Anne asked the same question, different words.

"Yes. She's very quiet, no trouble at all."

"When will she be home?"

"She has a key. She comes and goes as she pleases," Mrs. Lockwood said, crossing her arms.

"Can we see her room?" Jack asked.

"I'm not comfortable with that."

"How long has she been here?" Anne asked.

"Just a few weeks, on and off. But she's moving out this weekend. I told her my family was all coming here for Thanksgiving and I needed the room. Besides, it was time for her to find a permanent place to live."

"Do you have her new address?"

"Maybe you should ask her for it," she said, tilting her head, her guard dialing up. "I thought you were just going to ask me questions about the murder investigation, not about Michele's private life now as an adult. And as far as the murder investigation goes, I don't really have anything to add. She was just a damaged, abused child. And she's adjusted as well as can be expected. She got married a second time, went to beauty school...."

"Of course, Mrs. Lockwood," Jack said in a soothing voice.

"Where does she work?" Anne asked.

"I don't know the name of it, but it's a beauty salon at the Fulton Market Center next to Party City. She's probably there now. She does pick-up work, mostly walk-ins, since she hasn't established a clientele."

"If you could provide her new cell phone number, we'll be on our way," Jack said.

"I didn't mean to be rude or short with you, detectives. It's just that Michele's been through a lot." She paused a beat, then stood up. "I'll get it for you." Mrs. Lockwood went over to the roll-top writing desk in the corner of the room, thumbed through her address book, and wrote down some numbers.

"Here you go," she said as she handed a slip of paper to Anne. Then turning to Jack with a smile, she asked, "Before you go, detective, could I ask you for a big favor? Would you mind giving me a hand with a box in the garage? It's heavy, and it has all my fall and Thanksgiving decorations in it, you know...a cornucopia, wreath...."

"It'd be my pleasure. Lead the way."

Anne watched them go out the sliding glass door and head toward the garage, situated just steps off the back deck. Once they were out of sight,

Anne hurried down the hallway, which was lined with bedroom doors on both sides. She wasn't sure what she was hoping to find—and knew she shouldn't be there—but her curiosity was in overdrive. Trouble was, there were four closed doors, and she hadn't a clue which one was Michele's. And she only had Mrs. Lockwood's word for it that Michele wasn't home.

But it was now or never. Anne knocked lightly on the first door on the right. No answer, so she peeked inside: a double bed with a floral, ruffled bedspread and framed family photos covering every surface. Obviously, Mrs. Lockwood's room.

The faint sound of laughter and voices came from the direction of the garage. She knocked on the next bedroom door. Again, no answer. So she opened the door slowly and scanned a small, impersonal room with a definite "guest room" vibe. Moving boxes were stacked in a corner, and a green backpack had been tossed on the queen-sized bed. Michele's room, no doubt. Was there time to search the backpack?

Anne jumped at the sound of the sliding glass door being pulled open. She was backing out of the room when she spotted a sheet of paper—a lease or contract of some kind—on the otherwise bare dresser next to the door. The logo at the top read "Vineyard Apartments."

She heard her uncle asking, "Where do you want me to put the box?"

"On the table, thanks."

Anne quickly shut the guest room door and turned the corner into the living room in time to see both of them staring at her. Her uncle's eyebrows were raised.

"Were you looking for something?" Mrs. Lockwood asked.

"Just using the restroom. Hope that's okay."

Mrs. Lockwood nodded curtly, then showed them to the front door with barely a goodbye. Once out on the porch landing, Jack turned to Anne and said with a sarcastic edge to his voice, "Well, that went well."

She glanced down at the cell phone number Mrs. Lockwood had provided—it was different from the disconnected number Peter had given her. So that was progress. And now she knew where Michele was moving to: Vineyard Apartments.

"Actually, maybe it did," She said.

Chapter Nineteen

Thursday, October 31

Noreen took a desultory swipe at the coffee table with a dust rag, sending cookie crumbs flying onto the carpet. She fluffed a sofa pillow and kicked the dogs' chew toys under the skirted floral armchair. She picked up the dirty drinking glasses, still half filled with milk, from the floor where the kids had played board games, and set them in the kitchen sink.

Her attempt at straightening the living room was interrupted by loud barking, crashing noises, and the trampling of children's feet bounding up and down the stairs.

The detectives would arrive in fifteen minutes, and she wasn't ready. Not physically—the house was overrun with messes, children, and dogs, and she hadn't even showered or combed her hair yet.

And not ready mentally, either. Her mother wanted her to talk to these cops, and that was the only reason she was doing this. To her way of thinking, nothing good would come from this. They were wasting their time. Noreen's stomach churned as if she had stuffed one too many towels in a washing machine. But at least, she reassured herself, she wouldn't have to talk to that pushy Anne, the one who had insinuated herself into all their lives and started this whole fiasco of a crime investigation off and running—and at a time when the family least needed it.

Noreen longed for a cold Chardonnay and for this to be all over.

"The police detectives will be here any minute. Keep the noise level down!" she yelled up to her children, Chloe and Jake. They weren't alone up there in the playroom. Their two younger cousins—Joanne's two boys, Kai and Artie—had spent the night so they could work together all day on the video they were creating for their grandmother's birthday party. On a Thursday, no less. Noreen shook her head. Here she was, stuck with four kids on what should have been a school day, all because their school declared, willy-nilly in Noreen's opinion, to make a four-day weekend so teachers could go on a retreat. Why weren't the parents consulted?

"And if you don't behave, I'll send the cops up to the playroom," she yelled. Her teenagers laughed derisively. Even to the ears of her eight-year-old nephew, Kai, the threat rang hollow. "Yeah, right," he snickered, barely loud enough for her to hear. But hear it, she did. Noreen sighed. The days of threatening the kids with police action had sadly passed.

"We will, Mom. Don't worry about us. We're busy up here," Chloe called out.

"It's crunch time," Jake shouted.

"Do you have any more munchies?" Kai yelled.

They had already finished off the Cheetos and store-bought cookies. Those kids and their voracious appetites were the reason her food budget was already shot for the month, she fumed. But did Joanne even *think* about chipping in? Maybe consider tucking a few lousy dollars inside her kids' backpacks? *Hell, no.*

"Come down and look for yourself. I'm not your servant."

She caught sight of herself in the hall mirror. She ran her fingers through her flyaway copper-colored hair and noticed some new gray at the roots. A few more crow's feet, too. She was still the beauty in the family, she thought, but maybe she'd add some sunscreen to the shopping list. She grinned at herself in the mirror, then shrugged and headed to the bathroom for a quick shower.

By the time the doorbell rang, she was made-up and dressed in black leggings and a peasant top long enough to hide her ample backside. Music was blasting from the playroom, along with insistent voices squabbling about which tunes for the video best represented "Grandma's childhood—not *your* childhood, you moron!" The dogs were barking again.

"Keep it down, I'm warning you!" Noreen shouted up one last threat. *What a mad house.* She squared her shoulders and opened the door, her palms perspiring.

Jack and Dean stood patiently on the porch, silhouetted by the afternoon sun. Someone was behind them, partially hidden. They wore practiced smiles and carried black leather folders.

"Come in." Noreen smiled back. *A smile is disarming,* her father had always said. But her smile turned sour at the sight of Anne. She stepped aside and motioned for them to enter the living room.

She had a vague memory of dashing young cops coming to the Murray home on that awful day. That had been nearly three decades before, but these two senior citizens, though nice enough looking for their ages, couldn't possibly be them.

"Nice meeting you again," Jack said. "I don't know if you remember us, but I'm Detective McCormack, and this is my partner, Detective Diaz. We haven't seen you since you were about nine years old. And you know Anne, of course."

Noreen nodded. "Okay, have a seat," she said. They took the beige sectional couch, and Noreen sat opposite them in a straight-back chair. She noticed a crumpled bag of chips peeking out from under the coffee table in front of her and nudged it out of sight.

"How's the case coming? Any hot new leads?" Noreen said, letting a bit of snarkiness into her voice. *Tone it down,* she told herself.

"It's coming along," Jack said mildly. "Thanks for seeing us today."

"I hope this doesn't take too long," She smiled tightly at the two men. "We're having a big party in a few days, and I haven't even gone clothes shopping yet."

Sounds of whooping laughter reached them from the upstairs playroom.

"Okay, we'll get right to it." Jack reached into his pocket for his phone and turned on the recording app. "You don't mind if I record this, do you?"

Noreen nodded her assent.

"After school let out on the day of Danny's murder, what did you do?" Jack asked.

"Walked home, that's all. Except a friend and I stopped at the drug store for snacks to eat on the way home. We did that almost every day."

"It was your turn to walk Danny home—yours and Peter's—and yet you didn't take him with you—"

"No, he didn't like Michele, so he ran off looking for Tony."

"Michele was your best friend, right?" Dean said.

"I guess so, then."

"When did you stop being friends? Or did you?" Jack asked.

"She had to move to a new foster home, so she changed schools. That was when we were eleven. We just drifted apart like kids do."

"Did she ever tell you she wanted your family to adopt her?" Jack leaned forward.

"No, that's crazy," Noreen said, surprised.

"Your sister seems to think she did," Anne threw in, looking ready to duck.

"Joanne thinks *a lot* of things," Noreen spat out.

Jack traded a quick look with Dean.

"From what Joanne's told us, and what you just said yourself, Danny didn't like being around Michele. But how did Michele feel about Danny? Did she like him?" Dean asked.

"What? Sure, everyone liked Danny. Why are you asking all these questions about Michele?" Noreen fidgeted in her seat.

"Are you still in touch with her?" Dean asked.

Noreen breathed out a sigh. "No, but I used to text her—like every few years—when she lived in Texas, but not since she moved back to town. I saw her by accident a few days ago. Anne was there." She shot Anne a quick look.

"We heard. Why did she move back to Santa Rosa?" Jack asked.

"Who knows?" Noreen let out an exasperated sigh. "She left her husband about six months ago. I guess she wanted a new start. She said that she and Peter had unfinished business. Whatever."

Noreen suddenly stood up. "Can I get you anything to drink?"

They all declined. She went into the kitchen, coming back with a glass of wine in her hand. She sat down and took a sip, then sipped again. Her face relaxed.

"Where was I? Oh yeah, I told Michele it was a lousy idea and discouraged her," Noreen said. "I told her my mother would have a fit. I stopped talking to Michele after she moved back."

"Why?" Jack asked.

"I told you. I didn't think she should start things up with Peter again. I didn't want to encourage her or anything, or let her think she had friends in town. I didn't want her to settle in."

"I overheard you and Michele arguing outside the house," Anne said. "She wanted something from you. Money? What was she threatening you about?"

"Whatever you *think* you heard, you heard wrong. I don't remember anything like that," Noreen abruptly stood up, glass in hand, and walked toward the window. "And why were you eavesdropping on a private conversation anyway?"

"Michele said she wants to go to the birthday party on Sunday—" Anne said.

"Fat chance. Listen, she and Peter have broken up."

"Why?" Anne persisted.

"Why?" Noreen echoed with a how-should-I-know shrug of her shoulders. She sat down again and looked with tunnel vision at Jack and Dean, as if she could make Anne disappear if she only willed it hard enough.

Jack returned her gaze and picked up the questioning. "Where was Peter after school on the day of the murder?"

"I don't remember. You'll have to ask him."

"Do you recognize this note?" Jack pulled out the copy of the letter with the childish scrawl, the one found in the janitor's shed that said "danni DEAD murder sees u. Fuk u!!"

"No. Never saw it before." Noreen's cheeks turned a dull pink.

"Do you recognize the handwriting?" Dean asked.

"No. It's just a kid's messy writing, isn't it? Doesn't their scribbling all look the same?"

"A classmate of yours said she saw you go into the janitor's shed. Were you putting the note in there?" Jack asked.

"What? No way. Whoever said that was wrong. Like I said, I never saw it before."

Noreen stood up again as if to signal the end of the interview. The detectives and Anne stayed seated.

A prolonged silence followed until Jack said at last, "Back to the day of the murder...do you remember seeing anyone suspicious that day?"

"No." She sat down again, rubbing her hands on her thighs, then reconsidered her answer. "Maybe. What about that janitor? I saw him heading toward that adobe house where Danny was found."

"What time, any idea?" Jack asked.

"I just remember it was right before I left to walk home."

"Did you see him near the chain link fence that blocked off the house?" Dean asked.

"I really don't remember."

"Maybe you remember that flashlight that was found near Danny's body—" Anne began.

Noreen cut her off. "Oh, *please*. I was just a kid, and it was a long time ago. I don't remember." She stood again. "I'm sorry, but I have to call an end to this. I have plans for this afternoon."

They looked up at the rattle of a truck engine shutting off in the driveway, followed by the creak of the front door opening. A tall, burly man, wearing jeans and a plaid flannel shirt and carrying a red tool case, stepped into the room. "Hey, doll," he called out.

Noreen joined him at the door, turning her cheek to him for a kiss. She gestured to investigators in the living room and introduced them. "Babe, these are the detectives I told you about. Detectives, this is my husband, Ron." She watched while everyone shook hands, then turned to walk up the stairs.

"I've got to check on the kids. I'll be right back," she said over her shoulder, leaving them alone.

They sat and looked at each other. No one instigated small talk. Then Rod blurted, "Does it look like the case will wrap up anytime soon?"

"It's coming along," said Jack, nodding agreeably.

"How soon will you know who killed the boy? Will you know before Claire dies?" Ron asked, then paused, looking embarrassed. "Sorry, that came out wrong."

"It's understandable," Dean said.

"It's just that with these two things—my mother-in-law dying and the investigation—coming at the same time…." He rubbed his face with rough hands, then looked directly at them. "It's been hard on Noreen. She doesn't sleep at night. She's on the computer until all hours of the morning. It's been hard on everyone in the family."

"It won't be long now," Jack said. Anne gave her uncle a questioning look.

Noreen came downstairs, ducked into the kitchen, and returned to the living room with a bottle of cold IPA beer. "The kids are almost done with that video, thank God," she said, handing the beer to her husband. "They're going to show it to us tonight, but Chloe says we can't make any changes or even make suggestions."

"I think they've finished what's referred to as the 'director's cut,'" Jack said genially.

Ron gave him a blank look, then muttered, "Whatever."

"I don't mean to rush you, but as you can see, there's a lot going on here," Noreen said with a hand gesture that loosely encompassed the entire house.

"Just one last question, if you don't mind," said Jack. "Have you heard anything through the years—or seen anything—that could point to a suspect?"

"No," she said, leading them to the door. "Sorry I couldn't be of more help."

"We appreciate your time."

The door closed behind them. They walked slowly to where Dean's car was parked on the street in front of Noreen's house. Dean slid into the driver's seat, and Jack squeezed into the tight back seat. But Anne stayed outside. She stood there by the car door for a moment, studying her own shadow on the pavement, lost in thought.

"Thinking again?" Jack called out.

Anne opened the car door, got in the passenger seat, and slammed the door shut. She laid the palms of her hands on the glove compartment, silent for a moment, then turned to face Jack and his old partner.

"I think I know what's going on here."

It took only a few minutes for Anne to explain her theory of the case. They sat without speaking for a long time, watching the occasional traffic go by. The silence was broken only occasionally as one of them asked a question or played devil's advocate. More silence, then some back-and-forth about hidden motives and contradictory statements, followed by more silence. The theory was holding.

Dean started the engine.

"Well, if you're right," Dean said, pulling the car out into the flow of traffic, "and if the DNA results back it up, the next question is: what are we going to do about it?"

Chapter Twenty

Friday, November 1

A bracing wind added to the chill factor in the morning air. Bundled in a too-thin navy jacket and wool scarf, Anne stood in front of her bank's ATM machine, waiting for her debit card to produce cash. Why hadn't she worn a few extra layers? It was going to be a cold winter, a real record-breaker according to the news. She tightened the knot on her scarf and blew on her fingers.

A large figure stepped in front of the machine next to hers. In her peripheral vision, she could tell it was a middle-aged man. Vaguely familiar. She glanced over to get a better look. It was Larry Brenner.

Just a week ago, she'd never even heard of him—now he seemed to be everywhere.

He casually reached into his back pocket for his bank card, looked over, and did a double-take. "I know you," he said. "You're one those cops who came to the rectory."

"And you haven't been answering my calls," she said with all the casualness she could muster. She punched in her password.

"Was that you?" He slyly looked her up and down. "If I'd known that, I'd have picked up my phone."

"I left messages."

"Didn't get them."

"Can we talk now?" She nodded toward a bench a few yards away. She didn't really have the time—she was already running late for her lunch at Claire's—but this was too good of an opportunity. "Let's sit down. I have a few questions."

He just stared at her, and she stared back. "I understand you had some run-ins with the Murray kids," she said, baiting him.

"Listen, if you want to talk so bad, why don't you follow me back to my room at the rectory where we can have some privacy?" His wet lips glistened.

She turned her head away at the sight. He seemed to take that as a sign of shyness.

"Well, why not? Worried about your reputation?" He chuckled. "As my mother always says, 'What happens in the rectory, stays in the rectory.'"

She let out a short, derisive laugh. "Not likely."

"That was a joke, by the way. Nothing happens at the rectory these days, believe me. Most boring place on earth."

Anne tried again. "Let's move this conversation over to the bench. It'll only take a minute. I just want to know what you remember about the day of the murder. And why you wouldn't join us in the interview when Father Dunn invited you in?"

"Now it's my turn to laugh." He stepped closer. She could feel his hot breath and smell the mixed odors of sweat, cheap aftershave, and weed.

"You know the only reason you guys were even there asking questions—*fi-nally*—was because of me. That anonymous tip? That was from me—and I didn't send it because I wanted to help that Murray family get justice. Don't get me wrong, I don't hate them, but they're all goddamn snobs. No, I plan on getting that cash reward, though it's not much. Pretty cheap of them."

"You were the one who called it in? You think a priest was involved? What do you know?" She reached for the cash spitting out of the machine. "The more you tell me, the likelier you are to get a reward."

"Listen, you want to know more, you know where to find me. I'll be at the rectory all week." He winked and turned away.

Heading back to her car, Anne took a backward glance at him and found that he was doing the same. She waited a beat, then reached for the door handle.

"The invitation's still open," he called out.

* * *

With practiced hands, the hotel waiter flung a starched white tablecloth onto the round dining table by the front window of Claire's suite. Louie's ears perked up. He leapt into the air to bite the corner of the cloth but missed and landed hard. He slunk away, crawled under the table, and rested his head on his paws.

"Next time, Louie," Claire said.

The servers put out place settings for three guests and then stood back, waiting for Claire to decide on the menu for lunch. Without much thought, she ordered Italian cuisine—Caesar salad and a light pasta—because you can never go wrong with Italian. But the wine? It had to be a local Sonoma County wine.

A fire was blazing in the fireplace, the drapes were pulled back to let in light and views, her medications were taken, and she was dressed and ready for the day. She checked her watch. Almost half past eleven. Her son Tony would be here at noon. But Anne would be here sooner. In fact, she'd be here any minute.

The plan was for Anne to help her finish—at long last, Claire hoped—sorting and boxing the photos and mementos she wanted to pass along to her family. Then the three of them would sit down for a nice lunch. Followed by estate work with Tony. Then a long nap.

"I'll be going out now," Sala called out. "Back at two, but call if you need me."

"Thanks, Sala. Please leave the door unlocked."

Claire sat in the armchair by the fire and gazed at the pile of boxes in the corner. Her relatives and guests were flying in the next morning for the party, and she wanted to concentrate on *them*, not on these boxes crammed full with the flotsam and jetsam of her seventy-five years of living. Enough with these photos of long-dead relatives, old recipes, newspaper clippings, and graphs of family trees, she thought.

She had hoarded them for too long—time to let other people hoard them.

A knock on the door meant Anne had arrived, so Claire called out, "It's open, come in." Anne entered the room, her face still ruddy from the cold wind outside. "It's so nice and toasty in here," she said, stripping off her jacket and scarf. She went over to where Claire sat. They reached for each other's hands and squeezed lightly.

"Lovely to see you," Claire said. "Now get comfortable because there's work to do, young lady!" Claire pointed to several black Sharpie pens on the table. "Let's plow through these boxes fast. Lunch is in thirty minutes."

Anne grabbed a marker pen, moved the boxes close to Claire's feet, and took her place on the floor with her legs crossed in a yoga pose. Box by box, they emptied the contents out on the floor, sorted the items, and placed them into new shoe-size boxes—one box for Cousin Sue, one for Cousin Jean, one for her brother, Willie, and so on.

"They probably won't even want these things," Claire said with a sly grin, "but they'll be too polite to refuse. But if *they* don't take them, who will? My kids don't know who half of these people in these photographs are. I wish more of the portraits had the names and dates written on the backs. Anyway," she said, shaking her head, "all the mystery photos go to my cousin Jean. If anyone knows who's who, it'll be her."

A sepia-toned photo, white-veined and browning at the edges, caught Claire's eye. "Oh, but look at this one: my grandmother with her favorite jersey cow," she said, handing it to Anne. "She was one tough old bird. I was raised on a dairy farm just outside of town. Did I ever tell you that? My brother might like this one." Anne nodded and dropped it in Willie's box.

"Where are all the old 8mm home movies?" Claire asked suddenly. "I know I had them in one of these boxes. Dozens of them! Not that they were viewable. No one has one of those old projectors anymore." Claire dug through the boxes, growing increasingly frantic. "They are *really* important. Those home movies go back to college days and when my husband and I were first courting."

Anne raised her hands in a time-out gesture. "Claire, no worries. They're safe, I assure you—and that's all I'm at liberty to tell you." Chole had sworn

Anne to secrecy about the home movies, which were being digitized for the grandchildren's surprise birthday video.

Claire tilted her head and considered Anne closely. Then she shrugged and continued sorting, picking up a folder of family recipes. "My cousin will like these," she said, pointing to Sue's box.

Anne reached for the folder labeled 'Family Questionnaires, 1985-1990' and handed it to Claire. "These are priceless. I told my uncle about these. Do you mind if I borrow them for him? I'll make copies and return them."

"For Danny's case? Whatever for?" Claire glanced up, studying her from over the rim of her reading glasses.

"He's just curious."

Claire hesitated, then said, "Of course, that's fine. But I'd like them back soon." She flipped through the stapled pages, stopping to read a section, then stopping again. "I want to spend some time reading these again."

She ran her hand slowly over a page, lingering. Recalling the New Year's Eves that the family had spent in front of the fireplace, laughing and kibitzing over their answers. After a moment, Claire handed the fragile folder back to Anne. "We'll never get done if I keep this up," she said, "And Tony will be here any minute."

"I think we *are* done," Anne said as she stood up to carry the full boxes to the corner of the room. Anne finished scrawling the names of the new recipients in thick, black marker ink across the sides of each and taped them shut. "Done!" Anne said triumphantly and dusted off the job with her hands.

"Hmmm. I don't know. There's still all that stuff in the storage unit," Claire reminded Anne. Lamps, vases, tables, books, dish sets, old clocks, ad nauseam.

They both groaned. Then Anne said, laughing, "But the good news is, that's Tony's problem!" The items in storage were to be divided among the four siblings—and that headache belonged to the executor.

"*What's* Tony's problem?" Tony entered the room, a suspicious smile spreading over his face. He headed to where Claire sat to give her a kiss on the cheek.

Behind him, in the open doorway, two waiters stood beside a rolling room service cart. "Just in time," Claire said, motioning for them to enter. The waiters set out the silver domed entrees, poured water and wine, and left the room.

"Let's sit down for lunch, and you two can get acquainted," she said to Tony and Anne. Over plates of steamy pasta puttanesca, they made small talk, steering clear of any mention of Claire's health or the murder investigation. The trio agreed that Sala was wonderful (*I'm getting first-class care*, said Claire), that over forty people were expected at the party (*What do you mean, your wife won't be there?* Claire asked Tony), that the weather was challenging (*But reports say it will be sunny for the party*, said Anne), and that Claire certainly had a lot of stuff.

"Actually, you weren't kidding about the storage items being a problem," Tony said, setting his napkin down. "I'm not worried about dividing up the big items, like the house. We'll sell it, and each of us kids will get an equal share in the proceeds. Simple. And as for the grandchildren, I'll set up trusts so they can't blow through their inheritance before they're twenty-one years old—"

"Prudent. Maybe even stick it away for college." Claire then turned to Anne and said, "The grandchildren get the proceeds from the paintings, books, and everything you just sold for us."

Anne reached down into her shoulder bag and fished out an envelope. "I don't know if this is the right time to bring it up," she said, "but I have a check for you. After all the commissions were subtracted, here are the proceeds from the sales."

She handed the check along with the backup receipts to Claire. "The auction house sold the paintings, the ivory Buddha, and the Sunday cartoon drawing for about twice what we estimated. The auction rep said our timing was perfect. The market on artwork of this caliber has exploded recently," Anne said. "And the rare books dealer was practically drooling over your first editions. He said he could place them immediately."

"This is much more than I expected—actually, I'm a little shocked," Claire said, passing the check and receipts across the table to show Tony.

Tony whistled low. "I remember all those wild spending sprees Dad would go on after making a big business deal, buying you jewelry and fur coats—"

"Those furs, I can't even *give* away now," Claire said, then a sudden wave of nausea hit her. She stared down at her plate of uneaten pasta as if it were pickled seaweed. The nausea passed, but her appetite was gone.

"And when the family would visit Carmel," Tony said, "he'd stop at every art gallery on every side street along the way. He almost always came home with an original oil painting."

"He could be extravagant, yes," Claire said, pushing her plate away, "but at the time, we thought we were rolling in money—and for a while, we were. And at least he showed good taste in what he bought."

"They turned out to be great investments," Tony said, passing the check back to Claire.

Claire held the check in her hands again, mentally calculating the amount each grandchild would receive. For years she had despaired of leaving an inheritance behind for her family. After Danny's death, the family's financial circumstances started deteriorating, and they only grew worse after Gerald's death four years later. That's when she discovered that not only did they owe back taxes to the Internal Revenue Service, but that Gerald had let his life insurance policy lapse. To top it off, because Gerald was such a profligate buyer of unneeded things, there was less than a thousand dollars left in their bank accounts and precious little equity in their over-mortgaged hillside home. Betty and Butch offered a gift of money to tide her over, but Claire insisted it be a standard loan. They countered with, "Fine, but interest-free."

Only Betty knew how furious Claire had been with her late husband. How could he have left her with four children to raise and a mountain of debt and unpaid bills? She was angry at herself, too, for having turned a blind eye to their finances for all those years. It took her over a decade to do it, but she paid off every dime she owed to all the creditors, including Betty and Butch—by working long hours as a paralegal in law offices and selling the house and practically everything in it. Gradually her fury dissolved and gave way to pride. She had accomplished solvency by sheer grit. She was able to buy her beloved cottage and nearly pay that off as well.

But through it all, no matter how cash-strapped her circumstances, she held on to several of her favorite art pieces and the rare books. She refused to give up the beauty they represented, the reminder of more gracious, better days. A reminder of who she was.

And thank God she had, she thought, handing the check back to Tony. He tucked it in his folder marked ESTATE BANK ACCOUNT and set it aside.

Turning to Anne, he said, "If the grandchildren never get around to thanking you—and they probably won't—the family thanks you." Claire put a hand on his arm, saying, "Of course they will."

"But back to me and my problems," Tony glanced Anne's way again and grinned. "As I said before, it's the storage unit items—the furniture and all of that—that keep me up at night. How are we going to divide those things without a full-out war, resentments, crying fits, and…."

"Just as long as it's fair," Claire said. "I know my children. If it's fair, they'll be fine."

Tony looked skeptical and muttered, "Easier said than done."

"That's one of the reasons I wanted you and Anne to meet today. She's had lots of experience with estates and how best to distribute the assets to siblings. She told me about a method that reduces much of that tension."

"It's basically a Top Ten list system," Anne said, "It works like this: each sibling makes a list of the ten items they most want to inherit. The items should be listed in the order of importance to them. Then you all meet at the storage unit, and everyone draws a number from a bowl to determine who chooses first. When someone picks their item, they attach a colored sticker to it. And once everyone gets a turn, it starts over again until the top ten lists are fulfilled."

"What if an item, say a gold watch that belonged to their father, is on more than one of the lists?" Tony asked, looking over at Claire.

"The person whose turn it is gets it," Anne said. "However, it often happens that people do trades. They work it out."

"And what happens if one sibling—Peter, for instance," he said pointedly to his mother, "wants all the expensive stuff, and another one just wants keepsakes that aren't worth very much, money-wise, like, say a jewelry box? How do we make that fair?"

"You would keep track of the monetary values of what everyone's getting." Anne passed Tony the appraisal folder. "Almost everything's been appraised, and if it isn't, you can just ballpark the value. For instance, if Joanne wants a fur coat—"

"You'd mark it as worth twenty-five dollars," Claire said dryly.

"After everyone's done with their lists, you tally it up. Any differences would come out of the proceeds when the house is sold. It would get evened out then. Also, any leftover items can be chosen by the same method. Then I'll hold an estate sale for the very last items—things no one in the family wants—and you can divide the proceeds."

"It sounds like a workable plan," Tony said, standing to stretch. "Could I get your business card?" Anne reached into her folder, withdrew one from the card slot, and handed it over.

"Oh! And one other thing," Anne said. "No in-laws at the meeting. Absolutely none. Just the four of you with no outside interference. Saves a lot of fights."

Checking her watch, Anne reached for her purse. "Claire, I'm sorry, but I've got to run off to a meeting. Thank you for the wonderful lunch."

Before Anne could stand, Claire leaned forward, taking Anne's hands in her own. "Thank you for everything you've done, Anne," she said in such a tender, motherly voice that Anne briefly averted her gaze. "You've been a blessing."

A few seconds passed before Anne, close to tears, spoke. "Anything I can do, I will. I'm always around. All you have to do is ask."

"Thank you, dear. Now off with you."

"I guess I'll see you at the party on Sunday," Tony said to Anne as she rose and went toward the door.

"I'm looking forward to it." She turned and gave a wave to Claire. "Nice to meet you, Tony."

"I'll walk you out," Tony said, a few strides behind Anne.

Claire raised her eyebrows. "Coming back?"

"Right back, Mom."

* * *

There wasn't far to walk. Only twenty steps down the hall to the elevator. Anne glanced over at Tony, thinking he was indeed movie star handsome. Krista's husband Mike had called it.

"Tell me about your firm," Tony said while they waited for the elevator.

"It's just a small business. Not much to say," Anne said.

"Don't do that," Tony said.

"What?"

"Downplay your business like that," he said. They heard the elevator car ascending to their floor.

"And I know I'm overstepping my bounds here a little," he said, "but you might want to shorten your company name. It sounds like you're trying too hard." The elevator doors opened.

"Any other advice?" Anne asked with a tight smile. She stepped inside and pushed the down button. The doors closed on his amused face.

Now that was a little galling. Yet she was unsure if that was all she thought. Maybe in his blunt, presumptuous way, he was trying to be helpful. Maybe even a little flirtatious. But one thing she *did* know—and that was good business advice when she heard it.

Reaching the first floor, she stepped into the lobby just as her phone went off. She headed to a nearby armchair to take the call. It was her uncle.

"Sitting down?"

"Yep."

"The DNA results just came in. So you and I will be making a little trip out to the Tranquil Acres mobile park on Monday."

"No kidding. Carl Pinn, the janitor? His ex-girlfriend Dianne will be thrilled."

"It's not what you think."

II

PART TWO

Chapter Twenty-One

Sunday, November 3

They had arrived at the restaurant thirty minutes early. The noonday sun was out, as promised by weather reports. The long banquet table, laden with candles and vases, was already set and smelled fragrantly of the flowers that Noreen had spent the early morning hours arranging. The hotel manager had closed off the main dining area for the party and placed a PRIVATE EVENT placard on an easel at the entrance.

"It's all about timing and pacing," Betty Fazio, hands on her hips, instructed her co-hostesses Joanne, Noreen, and Chloe. Betty was wearing a simple, black velvet sheath so as not to outshine the blue silk suit Claire would be wearing.

"Think of it as a Broadway show," Betty continued. "We've got two hours to do all three acts: first act, mingling and cocktails; second, toasts and food; and then third, the private screening of the fabulous—how could it be otherwise?—video while we eat birthday cake."

Chloe's face lit up at the show of confidence.

"Precisely. We *cannot* go overtime. Mom's just not up to it," Joanne said. Although Claire was still able to walk on her own, she had reluctantly agreed to arrive and leave in a wheelchair to conserve her strength. But she refused to sit in the wheelchair during the reception or at the banquet table.

They scanned the room for signs of unreadiness. Was the champagne being chilled? The guestbook set out? And by now—it was fifteen minutes to noon—shouldn't the candles be lit? Why wasn't the background music piping through the sound system yet? Joanne went into the kitchen to give last-minute instructions to the wait staff.

They were as ready as they could be.

"Let's have a glass of champagne and kick back," Noreen suggested as she headed to the bar and lifted a bottle out of the bucket on the counter. A waiter hurried to her side and claimed the bottle, saying, "May I?" He popped the cork and poured her a glass.

"I'm in," Betty said, picking up a glass from the bar.

"Why not?" Joanne said, holding up a glass. The waiter gave each glass a healthy pour. "Cheers, ladies," Betty said, clinking her champagne glass with theirs. After a few sips, she snuck her glass to Chloe for a taste.

Sounds of laughter and greetings floated in from the lobby. The guests had arrived, and they seemed to have all materialized at once—a steady stream of family members, old friends, neighbors, past co-workers, and members of Claire's painting class and book club. Through the French doors, the hostesses could see them crowding around the guestbook to write birthday wishes—laughing and chatting as if they all knew each other, which, for the most part, they did. Children raced past the adults, jostling them in their rush to reach the outside courtyard garden, where they hoped to avoid adult supervision until lunchtime.

A few minutes later, a cheer went up in the lobby. "She must be here," Betty said. "Show time, ladies."

They crossed to the lobby and watched as Sala slowly wheeled Claire through the room, pausing every few feet for warm wishes, hugs, and cheek kissing. The guests trailed behind Claire's wheelchair as it wound its way toward the dining hall. Stationed at the French doors leading to the hall, two tuxedoed waiters greeted guests with glasses filled with champagne, wine, and local beers.

* * *

Anne, arriving a little late on the scene, followed a group of fellow stragglers

166

into the brimming dining hall. When they made a beeline for Claire, she veered off into the crowd and spotted Chloe and Joanne standing near the back of the room. Chloe gave her a two-handed wave, and Joanne gestured for Anne to join them.

"I've seated you next to my most eligible male cousin," Joanne said after Anne reached her side. "You probably won't like him, but who knows? His name is Sean. Anyway, Muzzy will be on your other side, and she's always entertaining, so all will not be lost."

"Sean is *not* her type, Aunt Jo," Chloe said definitively.

"Well, maybe she likes bad boys," Joanne replied with an airy shrug, then turned back to Anne. "I have to check on the food, Anne. Now, go have fun. Mingle!" she said as she turned away to greet other guests.

With a glass of sparkling water in hand, Anne resumed her wandering. She caught sight of some familiar faces: Muzzy, her friendly tablemate from the bridal shower, attired in a siren red dress that went with her hair color and effervescent spirit, was air-kissing her friend Dorothy. Anne spotted yet another tablemate from the bridal shower, Lydia Smith—a possible new client—and gave her a wave from across the room. Peter, Anne noticed, was leaning against a wall, frowning down at his phone and texting.

While the buffet was being set out against the back wall, guests began searching the banquet table for their name tags. The seat assignments, Joanne had informed Anne, were both carefully planned and haphazardly intuitive, with the talkative seated next to the listeners, the easily shocked next to the irreverent. As promised, Anne would be sitting between Muzzy and the mysterious cousin named Sean. Anne idly wondered what her seat assignment meant, then shrugged. Claire would be seated in the middle of the table, where she could see and hear everything.

"Lunch is served," announced the head waiter. Anne saw Noreen go outside to herd the children in from the courtyard.

As Anne moved toward the end of the buffet line, she noticed Claire's oldest son Tony standing in the far corner of the room, deep in conversation with a muscular man with deep-set brown eyes and neck tattoos peeking out from his collared shirt. It was a curious sight. Two men of the same approximate age, but with no other similarities that she could fathom: Tony, so urbane and professional, while the other more closely resembled a convict than a family friend. What could they possibly have in common? Tony looked up and noticed her watching him. He smiled and motioned her over.

"Anne, glad you could make it."

"Wouldn't miss it."

"This is Sean Brutrain. We practically grew up together," he said to Anne, then turned to Sean. "And this is Anne McCormack. She's helping with Mom's estate and also with the police investigation into Danny's death."

"I think we'll be sitting next to each other," she said, offering up small talk. "Joanne mentioned that you were a cousin."

"Not really," Sean said with a dead-eyed stare, as guardedly as if she had demanded his social security number.

"Actually, he's the son of my dad's former business partner," Tony said with a smile, clearly amused by the interaction. "Not a cousin exactly, but like family."

Sean crossed his arms and looked her up and down slowly. "Are you a cop?" he asked Anne. "You look like a cop."

Although she wasn't offended, she knew she was meant to be. She was used to this kind of impertinent comment; it usually came from young men with the need to deflate, challenge, or even seduce—men who expected rejection from an uppity woman, so they struck first. It annoyed her.

"And you look like a felon," she said, scanning him right back, from the top of his slicked-back red hair down to his alligator boots.

Tony busted out laughing. "Don't mess with her, Sean. She can bite."

Anne shrugged at Tony, turned away from them, and joined the buffet line.

After everyone was seated for lunch, but before they could start eating, Father Patrick Dunn stood and offered grace. Eating commenced until halfway through the meal when Tony rose from his chair and clinked his glass of bourbon. The group quieted down and gave him their full attention.

"Family, friends, Mom," Tony said, looking down at his prepared notes. He then set them aside and began his toast by thanking them all for coming. He went on to praise Claire's virtues as a mother, wife, and active community member, and ended by saying, "As is evidenced by her many old friends who've traveled far and wide to be in this room, it's clear that our mother has what's known as the gift of friendship. Mom, there's a quote from the Irish author, William Butler Yeats, that I think could have been written about you: "And say my glory was I had such friends.""

He lifted his glass to her. "La´ breithe shona duit! Which means—if I have my Irish right—happy birthday, Mom."

As applause filled the room, Tony gestured to Claire's brother Willie to stand up.

"You're up next, Uncle Willie."

While Willie wrestled with his chair and stood, Noreen drained her glass of champagne and reached for the bottle of wine in the center of the table. She poured liberally into her glass, then lifted the bottle to her tablemates, offering, "Anyone?"

Sean, who had been silent throughout the meal, shook his head, then pushed his chair back away from the table and stood. He sucked in air through his teeth, murmured a good-bye, and faded off into the lobby and out of the restaurant.

"Won't take up much of your time," Willie said in a deep, gravelly voice. Wearing his pressed jeans, new plaid shirt, and turquoise bolo tie, Willie looked as rough-hewn and dandified as a ranch hand dressed up for a fancy wingding. Nailed it, Anne thought.

"Got a little story about my kid sister I'd like to tell you."

He cleared his throat, puffed out his barrel chest, and began. "You may not know this, especially by the fancy designer clothes she wears now, but Claire was raised on a cow ranch. Me, I stayed in the ranching business and worked on a dude ranch in Nebraska. One time Claire and Gerry brought the kids to Nebraska to visit the ranch—what year was that, Claire, 1980?" Claire nodded and smiled at him.

"Remember Cloud, that old mare on the dude ranch, Claire? Beautiful horse. All levels of riders rode Cloud, but mostly bad ones. That poor horse was always patient but grew pretty forlorn. But on that day, the minute

Claire climbed in the saddle, grabbed the reins, and whacked the stirrups against Cloud's belly, that horse's head shot up so high and proud. She started prancing around, showing off for Claire. Cloud knew she finally had a real rider on her," Willie laughed. "But then when Claire climbed off, the poor horse gave her the saddest, most love-struck look I ever saw. I swear, Claire, that horse never did get over you." Willie laughed again and raised his glass.

"Here's to my little sister, a real cowgirl. Happy birthday, Clarabelle."

Claire touched her fingertips to her heart, then blew him a kiss.

An astonished Kai cried out, "Is that Grandma's real name, Clarabelle?"

"No dummy," his older brother said, slugging him in the arm. "It's a nickname, just like yours is 'dummy.'" Over the floral arrangements, Joanne gave her boys a withering look that could have straightened out Charles Manson. They looked down at their plates, momentarily penitent, while their cousin Jake snickered.

Betty stood up next and, once all attention was on her, raised her glass.

"Here's to my dearest, most loyal friend. We've been pals ever since I first got talked into moving to this backward frontier town, away from the bright lights of New York City," said Betty with a side-eye and wink to her husband. "Ever since then, Claire has been Thelma to my Louise and vice versa. Who's had more fun than us, Claire? I don't think anyone has, not ever! Happy birthday, sweetie. Love you."

Claire flashed her a radiant smile.

Noreen sat up straighter and placed her palms on the table, preparing to push off and stand. Well into her second bottle of Chardonnay, she was ready to give her toast.

But Peter beat her to it. He leapt to his feet and spread his arms out wide to encompass the entire room. "I know you all are expecting a grandiose, enlightening toast from me, quoting a Shakespeare sonnet or something like my big brother Tony did, but all I really want to say is: 'Yay, Mom!'" Polite applause and a bit of snickering followed.

Noreen's turn. She clinked her wine glass with a spoon, and as she struggled to her feet, her chair tipped back dangerously. Willie leaned over and righted the chair before it hit the ground.

"Is there time for my toast? Or is this show already running too late?" Noreen said with a slow slur in her voice.

"Sweet Jesus, take the wheel," someone muttered.

"Because I have a little story to tell," Noreen said, rocking from one foot to the other. Her struggle to stay balanced had Anne worrying she would tip over like a sleeping cow.

"Lord have *all* the mercy," another quietly enjoined.

"Whenever I stayed home from school, sick with the flu or something, as a kid," Noreen said, "no mother could be more loving. She'd put a cold, wet hand towel on my forehead and give me 7-Up. She'd coo at me. She even called me sweetheart. Of course, the rest of the time—when I was well, she didn't really know I was around. So like I always tell my husband, it's amazing that I'm not a hypochondriac."

She paused, waiting for laughter that didn't come, then said, "Get it? Because if I only got attention when I was sick, I'd want to be sick all the time, am I right?" Her laugh took on a slightly maniacal edge.

An uneasy silence enveloped the room. "I have another story you might like—about the time she forgot me at Walgreens drug store…." But before Noreen could continue, Uncle Willy stood up and was by her side.

"Hey, darlin', come sit by me," he said softly as he put his arm around her shoulders and gently lead her back to the empty seat next to his.

"It was a joke, for chrissakes," Noreen said to him as she sat down.

Claire sat with a frozen half-smile on her face, stung. Joanne quickly signaled to the waiter and mouthed the word "cake" and pointed to the sideboard.

"Everyone else gets applause for their toasts," Noreen whined to Chloe, who was sitting to her left. "But what do I get? Look at them all staring at me…."

Anne saw Chloe shoot her aunt an imploring look from across the table, a pleading for some kind of rescue. Joanne abruptly stood up. Smiling a little too widely, her face showed a steely determination to salvage the situation, to make sure that Noreen's foolish toast would not be all that would be remembered of the day.

"Before Mom's birthday cake comes out," Joanne said with forced cheer, her voice carrying farther and louder than usual, "I want to thank everyone for being here on this very special occasion—some of you came from as far away as New York—and to let you all know that all her grandchildren have worked very hard to create...." She was saved from prattling on when the kitchen doors were flung open wide, revealing two waiters holding a large, two-tiered cake ablaze with a dozen lit candles.

"Here we go!" said Joanne, looking relieved as the room lights dimmed and all eyes turned to see the cake carried triumphantly into the room. The crowd spontaneously broke into singing "Happy Birthday to You" while the waiters set the cake down in front of Claire.

"Make a wish!" came a shout from the back of the room.

"Speech!"

"Blow out the candles!"

"No speech, I'm afraid." Claire motioned for her grandchildren to join her. "And I'm not blowing these candles out by myself."

The four grandchildren leapt up and gathered tightly behind her chair. On the count of three, they blew heartily, extinguishing the candles to cheers and applause. The cake was whisked away to be cut into pieces. Within minutes, coffee and cake-filled plates were placed in front of the guests.

"It's time for the video!" cried one of the grandkids.

Standing behind their grandmother again, Jake and Chloe introduced the video.

"I picked out the music, Grandma!" Kai called out.

"You did not! We all did," Artie said.

Chloe ignored her cousins and continued, "We learned a lot about you, Grandma, while we were making this film. And we're so proud to be your grandchildren. This is our birthday toast to you."

"So here goes," Jake said, activating the video system from his laptop computer. The lights were dimmed, and the room quieted. Claire sat up straighter for a better view.

For the next twelve minutes, the look on her face was pure joy. There on the screen was a photo slideshow with her parents, her as a baby, the ranch, her cousins, her brother, and her old childhood friends—together capturing the narrative arc that was her young life. There she was at her high school prom. At her lavish wedding held at Gerald's parent's winery, there was Gerald with his arm draped around his best man's shoulder, a beer in his other hand. Bridesmaids in flowery, empire-waisted gowns. Claire, glowing in her white satin dress, throwing her bouquet.

Halfway through the video, while they were lulled by a Frank Sinatra ballad accompanying sweet photos from their honeymoon, the video abruptly stopped—interrupted by five seconds of mayhem, dancing, singing, and fooling around by the grandchildren. Then just as suddenly, the video resumed with more romantic photos and songs. The audience burst out laughing at the shenanigans.

"That was my idea!" Kai yelled out. His brother just lowered his shaking head.

Music from the 1980s played in the background as the video transitioned into silent home movies that Claire hadn't seen in decades: Danny's baptism presided over by Father Dunn (*You look so young, Father*, called out Muzzy). Ski weekends at Lake Tahoe. Peter making devil horns above his kissing parents. A teenage Tony flirting with a cheerleader (*Nothing's changed*, said a cousin). Claire and her daughters wearing identical Easter dresses. The kids clowning around in Halloween costumes, with Noreen holding a lighted flashlight below Danny's chin, casting scary shadows on his face.

Anne drew in a quick breath, not sure of what she was seeing. Was that Danny's flashlight—the one found at the murder scene? Was it red? The image had flashed by so fast she couldn't be sure. No one else seemed to notice, but then why should they? It was just a small piece of evidence that was "not remembered" by the family. She looked over at Noreen, who was blandly smiling, and then over at Claire, who seemed fully immersed in the video. Anne brought her own gaze back to the screen.

Out of time sequence, a college-aged Claire appeared on the screen wearing a modest two-piece bathing suit and giving a girlish little wave to the camera. Hoots and whistles rang out in the room. "Hubba hubba!"

Butch hollered, to which Betty leaned in and said, "You're dating yourself, honey." Claire's college pal, Georgia, said, "Claire always had the boys lined up."

Joanne's oldest son leaned over the table to ask Claire, "Was that really you, Grandma?" Claire laughed. Turning back to the screen, she looked incredulously at her twenty-year-old self.

Ending with a flourish, the "Birthday" song by The Beatles in the background, each grandchild held up a one-word sign. When standing side by side, it read "Happy Birthday To Grandma."

The lights went up. Claire joined in the applause, then gripped the arms of her chair as if to stand, but quickly gave up the effort and remained sitting. "That was the best birthday present ever. Ever!" she said to her beaming grandchildren. "I can't believe how creative and talented you all are."

Two hours had passed since Claire's arrival at the party, and she was visibly flagging. Sala appeared next to her with the wheelchair as if on cue, and they worked their way out of the room. In their wake, guests called out birthday wishes, then gradually found their way to the lobby and out into the parking lot beyond.

In the after-party buzz of departing guests, Anne wandered over to a quiet corner in the lobby and settled deep into a feathery couch, her mind still on the flashlight. Maybe it was the same one; maybe not. She looked up from her reverie to find Joanne plopping down beside her, looking totally exhausted. They sat together quietly, unable to muster the energy to talk. A few minutes later, the rest of the adults in the family straggled over, leaving the kids to fend for themselves out in the courtyard.

"I need a drink," Joanne suddenly announced from the depths of the couch.

"To the lounge!" her husband Matt said.

"What'll we do with the kids?" Joanne asked with a groan.

"Let them stay out in the courtyard. They'll never know we're gone," Matt answered.

"Ron, are you coming?" Tony asked Noreen's husband. "Where's Noreen?"

"She's in the diner drinking some coffee," Ron said. "Sala came and told her that Claire wanted to see her back in the suite."

CHAPTER TWENTY-ONE

"Uh oh," Joanne said.

"So she's sobering up before she goes up—" Ron said.

"Good call," Tony said.

Peter begged off, saying he had to visit a friend.

"Anne, you coming?" Tony asked.

"Right behind you," she said.

The five of them made their way to the piano lounge next door. The older contingent—Betty, Muzzy, Butch, Willie, and Claire's old college mate—had beaten them there and were already whooping it up at a table in the darkest corner. Betty and Willy, who hadn't seen each other since the last Murray family wedding, were re-bonding over a shared fondness for Maker's Mark and Hank Williams. But it was Willie Nelson's "Crazy" that drew them to the piano for a duet. No piano player was in sight, so Betty took over the keyboard while Willie grabbed the microphone. Butch was too busy feigning interest in Muzzy's photos of her Labradoodle to show any jealousy over the twosome who were trading verses and eye contact.

The mood at the younger table was more subdued. Sitting quietly in their large corner booth, Anne, Claire's children. and their spouses smiled over at the impromptu lounge act and nursed their drinks. The family was recovering from weeks of party planning. Relieved it was over.

"Mom loved it," Tony finally said.

"She did," Ron said.

"We pulled it off," Joanne said.

They talked about having weeks of worrying about Claire to come, and years of grief to follow. But this day, a day of gathering loved ones around Claire for a final time, had been important. This much was done.

* * *

The party at The Parisian was still winding down when real estate agent Brenda Moran arrived at the Murrays' house in the hills above the hotel. She had work to do.

The Murray house was Brenda's favorite kind of real estate sales listing:

the neighborhood was good, the views spectacular, and the owners were already packed up and gone. With or without all the curb appeal improvements she had made—and she'd made plenty, in her opinion—this house, though on the small side, would practically sell itself.

Brenda left her husband sitting in the passenger seat of her Audi Q7, settled in for his afternoon nap with a baseball cap propped over his face, while she headed inside the house with her retractable measuring tape in hand. Today's job: take measurements for the furniture she'd need for staging and decorating the rooms before potential buyers got a look. She wanted the house ready to be on the market next week, sold by the following week, and in escrow before the start of the traditionally sluggish holiday season.

She jiggled her keys, located the right one, and opened the front door. Time to get a lock box, she thought. She stepped in but didn't get very far before she was hit with a rank odor emanating from within. Sometimes her overactive sense of smell was a curse; this was one of those times. Covering her nose with her hand, she ventured slowly beyond the foyer.

There, in the center of the living room, on the newly refinished hardwood floor, sat a heaping pile of wet and decaying vegetables, rotting fruit, coffee grinds, raw chicken innards, egg shells, and other festering compost next to an empty black yard bag. Two rats scurried away at the sound of her footsteps. Inching closer, she saw tiny white maggots crawling on potato peels.

Topping the slimy pile was a gnawed-at cupcake with a half-smoked cigarette butt stuck in the frosting where a birthday candle should go.

With a shutter, Brenda quickly backed out onto the porch. She looked up and down the street for someone to blame. No one in sight, she went to her default suspicion: "Damn teenagers."

She glanced over at the black mailbox perched atop a wooden post in the front yard. A white envelope was jutting out from the lid.

* * *

Tony was leaning back in the leather booth, unwinding with a bourbon when he took Brenda's call. "Jesus," he said every few seconds, varying it now and then with, "Disgusting."

On the other end, Brenda's agitated voice grew so loud that he held the phone away from his ear. Loud enough that Anne, sitting next to him, could hear the conversation. When she caught the gist of it, she tugged at his sleeve and hurriedly interrupted him.

"Ask her what she did with it."

"Huh?" he gave her a funny look.

"Ask her!" Anne insisted.

Tony took a deep breath and exhaled into the phone. "What did you do with it?"

"What do you *think* I did with it?" Brenda said in a horrified tone. "I had my husband gather it up and toss it out in the trash."

He repeated this to Anne. She reached out and grabbed the phone from Tony's hand. "You didn't toss the cigarette butt, too, did you?"

"Who are you?" Brenda demanded of Anne. "And are you *kidding* me? Of course, we threw it away! And we cleaned the floor, and I lit some sage. My next call is going to be to my energy clearer so she can come over here and start chanting."

"Damn, damn, damn," Anne muttered. Perfectly good DNA tossed away.

"Put Tony back on the phone," Brenda said. "There's more."

Tony took the phone back and frowned as he listened to Brenda. Hanging up, he addressed the four others sitting in the booth. "Whoever did this also apparently left a birthday card in the mailbox."

"Oh, for God's sake. How sick. Was it signed?" asked Joanne.

"Nope, no signature. Just some corny pop-up balloons and the word 'Surprise.'"

Chapter Twenty-Two

Sunday, November 3

"Y ou really should be resting now, Miss Claire," Sala said as she walked to the stovetop and put the teakettle on to boil.

"She'll be here soon," Claire said.

It was three o'clock in the afternoon. The birthday party had ended an hour before.

Claire sat in the armchair by the window, the sun warming her neck. She shrugged off the shawl Sala had draped over her shoulders. A small black velvet box lay on the side table, along with an envelope with Noreen's name written on it.

"Why don't I try texting her?" Sala suggested. "Maybe she forgot you wanted to see her. She might have enjoyed too much wine…."

"She didn't forget. She'll be here."

Sala sighed. "Maybe you can go ahead and lie down. I'll wake you if she comes."

"I'll wait for just a few more minutes."

Claire sat back in the chair, picked up the box from the table, and opened the lid. Her engagement ring was inside, the heirloom three-diamond ring Gerald had slipped on her finger when he proposed to her over fifty years before. During all this time, she had never removed it from her finger—not until recently, when her weight loss made the ring too loose to wear.

Gerald's grandmother, the wife of a wealthy California vintner, gave it to him for his engagement to Claire. The elderly woman's only request was that it be passed down to female descendants so the ring would stay in the family. Only one of Claire's children had a daughter to whom the ring could be passed, and that was Noreen. But Claire reasoned that she couldn't give it to Noreen, the logical choice, because that would seem unfair to Joanne. Her plan was to give the ring directly to her granddaughter Chloe. No one could object to that.

But today had changed her thinking. As she watched and listened to Noreen giving her disastrous toast, she saw clearly—perhaps the first time she let herself—that her daughter was someone who lived in a nearly constant state of pain, jealousy, and self-loathing. Someone who deeply felt a sense of her own lovelessness.

Gazing out the window, the words of author Toni Morrison came to mind: "When a child walks into a room, does your face light up? Because that's what they're looking for."

Of course, she loved Noreen, but now she had to admit the truth to herself: it was a smaller love, less intense than what she felt for her other children. And her face rarely lit up when Noreen walked into a room. This was the emotional truth that fueled her daughter's outbursts of self-pity, her embarrassing scenes. Despite being a parent herself now, Noreen was still, in many ways, that anxious child who felt unloved. The child who worried she could not hold her parent's attention. All those feelings were still close to the surface.

Claire felt a gathering sense of urgency. If she had time, she'd be able to make things right in a gradual way, slowly, so the love could sink in. But she didn't have time. Noreen needed to receive the ring. Claire needed to be forgiven. And it all needed to happen now.

Sala came in and laid a mug of tea on the side table. As she reached for it, Claire was suddenly gripped by a sharp stomach pain, followed by an exhaustion that began at the party and now overcame her with snowballing force.

"On second thought, I think I will lie down," Claire said, setting the mug down. Before standing, she picked up a pen and scrawled a few words on the front of the sealed envelope containing her letter to Noreen. A few days before, she had written letters to each of her children. This one for Noreen was sincere, and as loving and kind as truth would allow. It might help.

She handed the envelope and velvet box to Sala.

"When Noreen shows up, please give her these."

* * *

Noreen sat alone in the hotel parking lot, staring out the windshield of her minivan at the late afternoon comings and goings of hotel guests. The tiny jewelry box felt heavy in her lap. Her head was throbbing, and the exhaustion of the day had seeped into the muscles of her neck.

She finally opened the lid, expecting to see vintage earrings or an old charm bracelet inside. Noreen drew in her breath at the sight before her. *This* she had not expected—her mother's most valued possession, her diamond engagement ring. Why on Earth would she give it to *her*? By mistake?

She lifted the ring out of the box, turning it over and over, mesmerized by how brightly the diamonds reflected the sun's glancing rays. Then she placed it back in its velvet slot and closed the lid.

She looked down at the envelope. Her name was written in black ink. But above it, her mother had written "My darling" in blue ink. And below her name, in that same blue ink, Claire had scrawled, "Much love."

Must be some kind of afterthought, she thought with a sigh. She hesitated a few beats before opening the envelope. Taking out the letter, she braced herself for anything.

Dear Noreen,

I don't know if I ever told you how proud I am of you and what you've made of your life. I admire your wonderful, long-lasting marriage to a good man. The happy home you've created. Your beautiful children, whom you've raised to be loving and kind—with maternal instincts that sometimes escaped me. Your quick wit, intelligence, loyalty, and resilience.

I wish we had spent more time together, just the two of us. But I will always treasure special moments like your wedding, the soccer championship game, the birth of your children, and the time we laughed until we cried talking about how men act when they're sick (Life is better when you stop trying to make them happy, you said!).

You were the most beautiful baby and child, and now woman. Did you know that your father always called you his wild Irish Rose because of your ginger hair and sparkling eyes? You have brought such joy to my life. These last few weeks, especially. Your kindness has overwhelmed me. You have been such a help during these difficult days, without ever being asked. I know you'll be designing the flower arrangements for the party, and I know they'll be stunning, with not a gladiola in sight.

I love you dearly,
Mom

Noreen felt ambushed, broken open, stunned by the tenderness. Tears ran down her cheeks as she leaned forward and hugged her arms to cradle her stomach, rocking back and forth rhythmically. She hadn't been prepared for kindness.

Oh my God, what have I done? What can I do? She straightened up after a few minutes, lifted a tissue from her purse, and blew her nose. Taking out her phone, she wrote a text message to her brother: "Can we meet and talk soon?" Then hit send.

She took in a long, deep breath and slipped the ring onto her finger.

Chapter Twenty-Three

Monday, November 4

"It's close, but no cigar," Jack said to Dean and Anne. They were gathered around the conference room table for their Monday morning status meeting, and Jack was debriefing them on the official DNA results: no exact DNA match for the hair sample was found in the nationwide system.

Jack had already given them a verbal, pared-down version of those results after he received them last Friday, but since he'd hinted that they'd be visiting Tranquil Acres today, Anne and Dean knew there was more to it.

"Did I ever tell you where that saying came from?" asked Jack, an enthusiastic spreader of arcane knowledge. Anne and Dean groaned, having heard, one too many times, about how county fair carnies in the 1930s gave out cigars as prizes for games of chance. Losers were told they were "close, but no cigar."

"So what we've got here is…." Anne prompted, flipping through her copy of the full report that Jack had handed Anne and Dean as they'd walked into the room.

"—disappointing, but not a major setback," Jack said. He led them through the contents of the report. It disclosed that the hair follicle evidence found at the crime scene, so carefully preserved for twenty-nine years, had been tested for DNA by the local lab and was found to be viable. The DNA profile data had then been uploaded to the FBI's Combined DNA Index System, known as CODIS.

"We now know that the DNA profile is that of a female Caucasian," Jack said.

"And I see here," Dean said, running his finger down a page, "that CODIS has given us some investigative leads...."

"Right," said Jack, taking a sip of coffee. "CODIS output two close familial matches—both males with lengthy police records. And *one* of these guys shared enough genetic markers to make him the likely father of the female suspect."

"Randall J. Crane, who goes by "Rambo," Anne read from the report. She stood and wrote his name on the whiteboard under the Leads header.

"So the likely father of the suspect is a convicted sex offender, fifty-eight years old," Jack said. "Rambo's been out of prison for a little over a decade. He lived in Santa Rosa before and during his offenses. After he was released, he moved back to Santa Rosa and now lives at—where else?—Tranquil Acres."

"Your old stomping grounds, Anne, home to Santa Rosa's finest," Dean teased. "One way to find out more about this guy is to go there and talk to him—"

"—and find out about his daughter. See if he can give us a name," Jack said.

"If he even knows he *has* a daughter," Anne said.

"Yeah, what are the odds he'd even know? Guys like that hardly ever do," Dean said.

Jack did some quick calculations in his head. "Let's see, he's fifty-eight years old now, and if he had a child when he was around twenty, that means his daughter probably would be about thirty-eight years old now or a little younger—but the daughter can't be *too* much younger or she would barely have been alive at the time of the murder twenty-nine years ago. But let's say he got an early start—say he became a dad at eighteen—then she would be forty now. So that means that the female suspect's likely current age range is thirty-eight to forty."

"Which means that at the time of the murder, the daughter would probably have been no older than eleven. And most likely, a little younger," Anne said.

A deep silence spread over the three like a heavy blanket. Now they knew it was almost certainly a child—a girl—who had left strands of her hair behind at the scene of the crime. Someone around Michele's age. The DNA could belong to any number of Santa Rosa girls, they knew, but they were closing the circle of evidence, and Anne's theory of the crime was still holding. All they needed was more DNA to tie a bow on it.

Jack said, "While we're at Tranquil Acres, we should drop in on Carl Pinn and give him the good news that he's off the hook—at least as far as physical evidence goes."

"Good news for him. Bad news for Dianne. Who's going to tell her she's not getting any reward money?" Dean asked as he gathered and disposed of the usual meeting debris of coffee cups and dirty paper plates and napkins.

"You're big buddies with her, Dean. I think she'd want to hear it from you," said Anne. Dean groaned.

"Yeah, well, what about that Larry Brenner guy?" Dean shot back, grinning. "Guess he's out of luck too, now. You should drop by the rectory and let him know, Anne."

"Not a damn chance."

Anne pulled out her phone from her purse and sent a text message to Judy Lyle, the owner of Tranquil Acres, giving her a heads-up that they were on their way over there, but got no reply.

* * *

One look at Judy Lyle and Anne knew something was up. She leapt out of Dean's car and hurried down the gravel driveway to reach the trailer porch where Judy was standing as still as a hunted rabbit except for the visible trembling of her arms. Her eyes were huge and wild.

"Judy, what happened—"

Judy just shook her head, motioning for the trio to move quickly up the narrow wood stairs. "Come inside," she said in a near whisper.

"Who did this?" Dean asked, indicating the dent in the front metal door. "Looks like someone tried to kick it in." Judy didn't answer.

Jack took a sweeping look down the street before entering. Not a sound, and no movement except for the drawing back of curtains at a few windows. "What's going on here?" he said as they followed her in, crowding into the compact kitchen.

The curtains were drawn against the bright morning sun and the prying eyes of neighbors. Anne noticed the beginning of an angry red swelling above Judy's left eyebrow.

Dean automatically felt for the handgun he carried concealed under his jacket, clipped to his belt on the left side. Jack teased him mercilessly about always carrying a gun when he was working the cold case. Anne's gun was locked inside her car. So here he was, the only one of them armed and ready.

Except for Judy. Dean nodded toward the semiautomatic on the kitchen table.

Judy shook her head and said, "It never occurs to me to bring my gun outside while I'm gardening in the broad daylight, especially when my husband's here. But he's out of town today. But I'm glad I didn't bring it outside. I might have killed that son-of-a-bitch."

The son-of-a-bitch was Carl Pinn, she told them. She'd been out in her front yard digging up weeds when he crossed the street and started yelling at her, falling-ass drunk. He accused her of telling lies to the police and trying to set him up for a crime he never committed. He didn't have a gun with him, at least not one that she saw. But Pinn was shaking his fists, calling out threats, and advancing menacingly. It wasn't like her to be frightened, she told them, but then she had never seen Pinn act like that before. She dropped her gardening trowel, fell on the porch steps and hit her head while she was running to get inside, and then bolted the door with two locks. He tried to kick in her door—that's when she ran to her bedside table, grabbed her gun, and reached for her phone.

"I was just calling the police when I got your text, thank God," Judy said, gingerly touching her forehead. "Carl hasn't been himself for weeks now. Something's been building up inside of him, like he's going to explode like a shaken beer can—God knows there are enough of those lying around on his porch."

185

Anne put her arm on Judy's trembling shoulder.

"I've got to get rid of that son-of-a-bitch," Judy said.

Anne said, "There are some things we can do today: we can get officers out here who can request an emergency protective order so Pinn can't come near you while you are in the process of applying for a temporary restraining order—"

"Can't you just arrest his ass?" Judy was starting to get the color back in her face.

"That's for you to do," Jack said. "You can make a citizen's arrest just by asking for it. Which you just did."

While Jack called the police dispatcher to send a backup patrol car to the address, Dean explained the law to her: because Pinn's actions constituted a misdemeanor and not a felony—and because the police weren't present when it happened—a citizen's arrest would be required.

Judy reached for her gun. "Okay, so you want me to go over there—"

Jack suppressed a smile and assured her, "No, we'll go talk to him. Then, with your delegation of authority, the responding officers will inform him of his arrest and take him into physical custody. You *are* delegating your authority to the police, right?"

"Just get him out of here," Judy said.

"I'll stay here while we wait for the officers to come and take your statement," Anne said. "After that, we have to take care of other business here at the park."

"What other business?" Judy asked.

"Anne can fill you in on it," Jack said, then turned to Anne. "Could you stay here and get any information about Rambo?" She nodded.

"Okay, let's go see what Pinn has to say for himself," Jack said to Dean. He looked out the front window toward Pinn's trailer. No signs of life. Then the curtains moved slightly.

* * *

While Jack knocked on Carl Pinn's front door, Dean leaned against the wooden porch railing and discreetly felt for his weapon under his jacket.

"Mr. Pinn," Jack said, knocking again. "We're detectives McCormack and Diaz. Would you open the door, sir?"

The detectives remained motionless, staring down at the wooden porch slats; they were used to being kept waiting at front doors. Almost imperceptible sounds came from inside. They knew Pinn was standing on the other side of the front door, peeking through the keyhole. Then they heard the sound of a lamp crashing to the floor and a slurring voice mutter, "Shit!"

Dean stepped up to the door, pulled out his ID case, and flipped it open. He pressed his badge against the keyhole and knocked more insistently. "Open the door, Pinn. We need to talk to you," he said, clearly tired of niceties.

"What do you want now, Diaz?" Pinn asked. Dean's visit to Tranquil Acres two weeks before had ended with a hungover Pinn trying to convince Dean of his innocence in the Murray case by saying he only had "trouble" with little girls.

"We came all the way out here to Tranquil Acres to give you some good news, Pinn," Jack said, stepping to the front.

The door cracked open. All they could see was Pinn's bloodshot eyes and a sliver of his dingy white T-shirt. He hadn't said a word, but the stink of cheap wine was coming off him. After years of transporting drunks to the county jail, they were familiar with the smell of bodies so saturated with alcohol that it oozed through the pores of their skin.

"Can we come in?" Dean asked.

"Think I'm some kind of fucking idiot? No way."

"Well, okay then," Jack said, his soothing tone in sharp contrast to Dean's aggression. The good cop/bad cop strategy wasn't an act in their case; it was more a function of their differing temperaments, views about human nature, and whatever mood they happened to be in. The older Dean got, the crankier he got, going from zero to sixty when he felt like he was being played or lied to. Jack was usually more even-keeled; he assumed most people had some larceny in them and were hiding something, so he just didn't take it personally when he was proven right. He wasn't one to let it ruin his generally good mood.

Jack sauntered over to the two molded plastic chairs on the porch, sat himself down, and stretched his legs, crossing them at the ankle. Getting comfortable. Dean took Jack's cue and moved away from the front door and nonchalantly leaned against the railing again.

"What's the good news?" Pinn asked, not budging from the doorframe.

"Can't hear you," Jack said. Coaxing Pinn out of the trailer would give the responding officers a clear path to make the arrest when they arrived. Otherwise, the officers would need a warrant to enter Pinn's trailer, and that would take up more time than any of them wanted to spend. But Jack couldn't accomplish that by asking Pinn straight-out to step outside as a trade for the "good news." No, a smart defense lawyer could argue that he'd used subterfuge to lure Pinn. And then, the citizen's arrest could be jeopardized, and any evidence found after that could get tossed.

The law is a complicated and holy thing, Jack thought, not for the first time.

"Bullshit, man. Just tell me," Pinn said, still not moving.

Jack leaned back in his chair and made a big show of yawning. Finally, Pinn stepped out onto the porch.

"Join me, have a seat," Jack said, patting the seat of the chair next to him as if he were the genial host and Pinn a welcome guest. Pinn lurched unsteadily to the chair and dropped into it. "Okay, so what's the good news?"

"Thought you'd like to know your DNA didn't match the evidence at the murder scene."

"Well, duh, I could have told you that," Pinn said, "so now you're gonna get off my ass, right?"

"This *could* have been your lucky day, Pinn—the last you saw of us," Jack said, "if only you hadn't started in on your landlady this morning. She's real eager to slap a citizen's arrest on you, Pinn."

"For what? I didn't touch her."

"Drunk and disorderly, property damage, threatening violence...." Dean rattled off.

"Mrs. Lyle is itching to give a statement to the officers who, by the way, should be here any minute now," Jack said to Pinn. "Some neighbor must have heard the commotion—we'll get their statements—and there's property damage to her front door. I tell you, her case is building."

Pinn narrowed his eyes at the detectives, taking their measure. A thin stream of spittle leaked from his mouth and dribbled down his chin. He smeared it away with the back of his hand as he said, "Maybe we can settle this some other way."

"What other way?" Dean asked.

"Maybe I have something to trade."

"Like what?" Jack asked.

"Like about the murder of that kid, Danny. I might know something."

"Let's hear it," Jack said. He spotted a patrol car cruise to a stop in front of Judy's home.

Pinn hemmed and hawed for a few minutes, then got around to telling them about his hobby of paying young schoolgirls to pose for nude Polaroids. It was slim pickings at St. Paul's grade school, he told them, and he had to be careful about which girls to approach. "But I had a real instinct for it and singled out Michele right away. Besides, she was pretty," Pinn said.

"Get to the point," Dean said.

Pinn shot him an annoyed look but continued at a faster clip. He said he would approach Michele and other girls—only when they were alone—and take them to the janitor's shed and have them take off their uniforms. Then he would take a few snaps and hand over five dollars for each session. Never took more than five minutes. A simple transaction. And he never touched them, he insisted.

The day Danny died was a bit different, he told them. He had Michele already positioned on the chair with her clothes off, but he forgot to lock the door. Hell, he was so excited he forgot to even close the door all the way.

"That little brat Danny was looking in at us through the crack in the door, all bug-eyed. He said really loud, 'Is the devil tempting you?' What a stupid thing to say! When I yelled at him, he ran off, and Michele put her clothes back on real fast and tore off after him. And that's all I know."

"Anyone else around?" Jack asked, watching the patrolmen disappear inside Judy's trailer.

"No one that I saw."

"Did you see where they went?" Dean asked.

"No, I slammed the door shut after they left."

"So why didn't you tell us all of this back then?" Jack asked, knowing the answer but wanting to gauge how drunk and dimwitted Pinn was.

"Ha, good one. Because you would have had me arrested for taking those photos. But guess what, fellas, the statute of limitations has expired now." Ex-cons knew that kind of thing.

"Can you show them to us? Let us see if there's any deal we can help you with," Jack said. He had little doubt that Pinn still had the photos. He could have destroyed them, but that was unlikely—pedophiles hate parting with their stash.

Pinn looked confused. He leaned back and scratched his bare, freckled and wrinkled arms. Jack could tell that somewhere in the back of Pinn's disoriented, inebriated mind, he sensed a trap. What it was, Pinn probably hadn't figured out. So he was stalling for time until it came to him.

"Statute of limitations!" Pinn repeated.

"We need to make sure it's Michele in those photos," Jack cajoled. "We need to make sure you're telling us the truth."

His eyes shifting side to side, Pinn started muttering to himself, "Show the photos, and they'll arrest me for possession. Think I'm a fool."

"No can do," Pinn spoke with a bit of smugness.

"Then no deal. But thanks for the information," Jack said, watching the two patrol officers cross the street toward them. The uniform officers stepped onto the porch, read Pinn his rights, handcuffed him, and lead him across the street to one of the patrol cars.

As Pinn angled his shoulder into the back seat of the car, he glared at Dean and Jack and yelled out, "I didn't kill that kid, but I sure as hell wasn't sorry it happened."

At that, Dean spun around quickly and started down the porch steps. He stopped midway to toss Jack his car keys.

"Take my car. I'll meet you guys back at the office later."

Jack caught the keys, saying, "And I'll get a warrant going so we can toss Pinn's place and find the photos. That'll keep him locked up for a while."

"Wait up," Dean shouted to the patrolman in the driver's seat. "I'm coming along."

* * *

It was nearing noon by the time Anne and Jack climbed the stairs to the mobile home belonging to Randall "Rambo" Crane. He opened his front door before they had a chance to knock.

Crane's long graying hair was pulled high into a man-bun, a style usually worn by young men. His shoulders were narrow and his stomach protruding, but Anne had no doubt: they were looking at Michele's father. Same ocean blue eyes, same thick dark lashes, same thin-lipped mouth. No DNA comparison was necessary.

"Is this about all that ruckus up the street this morning? I didn't see it, but I sure as hell heard that Pinn guy making an asshole of himself," Crane said, motioning them inside. "Is Judy okay?"

"You're Rambo Crane, right?" asked Jack, holding up his badge, though it was likely Crane had made them as cops on sight.

"No one calls me that anymore," Crane said quietly after a pause. "I go by Randall now." The muscles in his jaw tightened. Rambo was his prison name.

"We're not here about the disturbance, Mr. Crane," Jack said. "We're here about your daughter." They glanced around the neat and almost empty living room.

"Terri? What's happened to her? What's wrong?" Crane asked, panic edging into his voice.

"Terri? No, we're here to ask about your other daughter—" Anne said.

"Possible other daughter," Jack interrupted.

"I don't have any other kids, only Terri. She lives in Reno. What's going on here?" he asked.

"Do you remember a girl named Sandy Dixon? From high school?" Jack said, pausing to give Crane a chance to let the name sink in.

"Who?" Crane scratched his head, then shrugged. "Oh yeah, okay. I kinda remember her. She was in a class or two below mine. Kind of a loose one."

"Are you aware that she gave birth to a daughter thirty-nine years ago?" Anne asked.

"Hold on. We may have gotten together a few times, but there weren't no baby. Is that what she's saying after all these years? Me? Believe me, it coulda been a dozen guys."

Anne briefly related the details of the DNA testing and the odds of his possible paternity. She handed him a photo of Michele as a child.

Crane studied the photo and shrugged. "I don't know. I mean, I see the resemblance. She looks like my sister did as a kid, but..." he left it hanging, then handed the photo back. "Why are you looking at this woman? What did she do?"

"Nothing that we're sure of." Jack shook his head as if he hadn't a clue.

"Well, whatever it's about, leave me out of it."

The interview was over. Jack and Anne thanked him for his time, left their business cards behind in case he wanted to contact them, and drove out of Tranquil Acres in Dean's Corvair.

They had gotten what they came there for. They had the familial DNA connection that led them to Crane, and now they had—by virtue of the strong physical resemblance and a past sexual relationship between Crane and Michele's mother—a probable father/daughter connection between Crane and Michele. Together with the growing mountain of anecdotal evidence, they might have enough to ask for a probable cause warrant to get Michele's DNA for testing.

But getting a warrant from the DA's office wasn't a sure thing.

"After we drop Dean's car off, let's grab some lunch at Nell's and figure out how to get a sample of Michele's DNA," Jack said.

"You mean, skip the warrant—" Anne said.

"You got it. Skip the warrant. For now, anyway. The DA's office might have a problem justifying a warrant. But if we bring them a sample that tests right—"

"And if Michele's DNA matches, then a warrant would be easy to get, and testing could be repeated in a more controlled situation," Anne said, nodding. "Proper chain of evidence and all that for court."

"If it ever gets there. Kessler and the district attorney are going to have problems with this whole thing anyway—DNA match or no DNA match. But at least we can get our ducks in a row and argue it out later."

Thirty minutes later, over lunch, Anne and Jack hashed out how much information to pass along to Claire when Anne met with her on Wednesday. They agreed Claire should know about the results of the DNA and fingerprint testing.

But some things, they decided, Anne would keep from Claire: she would not be told about Danny being a witness to Carl Pinn's nude photos session with Michele in the janitor's shed. Nor would Anne tell her that Michele was blackmailing her daughter Noreen, threatening some kind of exposure.

"Not at this point in the investigation—and maybe never. There are some things a mother doesn't need to know," Jack said.

Chapter Twenty-Four

Monday, November 4

Michele Dixon Murray had been sitting on the metal street bench, waiting for hours. Or so it seemed to her. Downtown Fourth Street was mostly empty. The temperature was dropping, and the wind was picking up, so she unwrapped the sweater she'd tied around her waist and slipped it on.

An old woman, her curly black wig sagging to the right, rolled her small shopping cart to the bench and sat down next to Michele, carefully securing her bulging cart between her veiny legs. *As if I'd want your crap, you old bag,* Michele thought, edging herself away from the woman. She resisted the urge to give the woman a quick swat, one she could deny, and kept her attention on the front door of Nell's Diner.

She checked her phone: only twenty minutes had actually gone by since she went into the diner and headed to her regular table. Luckily, before she advanced too far, she saw the girl—the one who had pointed a semiautomatic at her face—with an older guy who looked like a cop, sitting there in her booth. They were laughing with the waitress.

She'd beat a quick retreat through the front door and made it out onto the sidewalk before they could see her. She would wait here on this bench for them to come out. No matter how long it took. Those two were tied in with the Murray family, and the investigation. Of that Michele was certain.

She wanted to keep them in her sights—though why, she wasn't sure. She wasn't sure of anything anymore, but she knew she was being hunted. Her foster mother had called and warned her. Peter had warned her. She was getting daily phone calls from a cop, which she'd be crazy to return. Every hardened instinct in her told her to leave town ASAP and head back to Texas. Get as far away from the Murrays as she could.

But she couldn't stay away.

She lit a cigarette, took a deep drag, and watched the smoke drift away in front of her. Her bench mate leaned in close and asked, in what she doubtless hoped was a well-bred voice, "Got another one of those?"

"Why don't you get lost?" Michele's tone carried a hint of menace. She pulled her green backpack closer, so it touched her hip and looked down at her phone to check for text messages.

Finally, a message. Her therapist from Texas, who usually refused to communicate with her by text, had answered her. Twice in the last two months, they'd used Skype for phone sessions, but that took money that Michele didn't have. *But it won't be long now,* she thought, *Noreen is practically shitting in her pants.*

"Why do you say you're going backward?" Her therapist wrote. "In what way? What happened?"

Michele dropped her head and closed her eyes, suddenly overcome with shame at the memory of her visit to the vacant Murray home. Just yesterday. If only they hadn't been so cruel, refusing to let her go to the party. Shunning her that way. She began to sob.

The old woman looked over at her as if she were deranged and quickly got off the bench and shuffled off down the street.

"I'm so mad, and all I do is cry. My feelings are all in a jumble. I do things, crazy things, but I can't help myself. And I can't sleep, and when I do, my dreams are nightmares," Michele texted back.

The terror of last night's dream had stayed with her all morning, and she couldn't shake the images: she was standing on the edge of a cliff with the wild ocean churning below. A crowd gathered behind her. She had done something to make the people yell and scream at her. Something wrong. She began climbing down the cliff's mass of rocks, trying to get away from them, but her foot lost traction, and she began to slide. A faceless person appeared out of nowhere and threw her a rope. A lifeline. She grabbed it. Then he smiled at her as he opened his hands, letting the rope trail off in the wind, and left with the others.

"What happened?" her therapist repeated in her text.

"I did something. It was childish, but I tried to be nice to them, and nothing works. NOTHING. The mother won't talk to me, and I don't know what else I can do. I feel so alone."

A tear ran down her face, and she quickly wiped at it with her sweater sleeve. She glanced at the diner door but saw no one come out.

"Why don't you come home?" the therapist texted.

"If I could just talk to the mother and explain everything. I'm so tired, and they won't listen except for Peter. They should be sorry for the way they treat me. Why can't this ever be over? What do I have to do for it to be over?"

"Don't do anything until we talk."

Michele looked up and saw the door to Nell's Diner open. The man and woman walked out and headed in the other direction down the street. She felt a tugging compulsion to follow them, to find out where they were going and what they knew. But she stopped herself. *What's the point?* She took a final drag on her cigarette, crushed it beneath her shoe, and kicked the butt under the bench. She remained seated.

"I don't know what's happening to me," she texted her therapist.

Chapter Twenty-Five

Wednesday, November 6

"I 'm not in any pain yet," Claire said to Anne, "or at least not too much. I still only need oxycodone. Maybe I can stay this way for a while."

Sala was standing beside Claire's cushioned patio chair, her expression noncommittal. Claire noticed Anne and Sala exchanging glances.

"Of course, I'm a realist," Claire said, "and I'll probably be drowning in liquid morphine by next week." Looking from Anne to Sala, she added with a gleam in her eye, "From the looks on your faces, I can see I'll have to work on my gallows humor. It's my delivery, isn't it?" Anne managed a short laugh.

The changeable fall weather was on the warm side this midweek afternoon, hovering near a sunny seventy-five degrees. They were taking their lunch outside on the wrap-around terrace, one of the advantages of having a corner suite.

Now in her sixth week since the diagnosis, Claire was devoting much of her time to grandchildren, lists, naps, and pain management. And dodging phone calls from friends and acquaintances who wanted closure. Yet as casual as she was about theirs, she sought closures of her own. Not in terms of grief—she had long lost faith in that kind of closure. But closure in terms of making amends for things she regretted having done.

So she set about making amends. She wrote a letter apologizing to a man for standing him up at an important dinner held in his honor, simply because she got a better offer. She wrote to her favorite cousin, apologizing for not having asked her to be a bridesmaid—even though they had fantasized about being in each other's weddings since childhood. But when the time came, Claire simply forgot. Why? Because she was young and self-absorbed. Besides, they hadn't seen each other in a year. *As if that were any time at all*, she thought now. From that day forward, her cousin avoided her. Another letter went to a well-intentioned woman who had offered syrupy condolences after Danny's death. Claire lashed out at her. There was such hurt on the woman's face that it stayed with Claire all these years, along with deep regret.

Regrets, for Claire, were almost always about unkindness.

She resolved to return all those phone calls. No more dodging. She didn't need to add more regrets to her pile. And along with them, more amends to make.

"But you're not here to listen to a blow-by-blow of my health problems," Claire said to Anne. Sala set their ice teas on the glass bistro table and went into the kitchenette to get their lunches. Their estate work together was done, but Claire had invited Anne over for business of another kind.

"Tell me, what's happening with the case?"

"The big news is the DNA and what it tells us," Anne said, then gave Claire a rundown of how the hair evidence led to Randall "Rambo" Crane and will, in all likelihood, lead to Michele. But that they still needed her DNA.

Sala returned with an avocado spinach salad for Anne and a bowl of pumpkin soup for Claire. Sala waved off an invitation to join them, saying she would be in her room watching game shows and to ring the bell if they needed anything.

As Anne started telling Claire about their plan to gather Michele's DNA "on the sly without a warrant," her phone pinged with an incoming text. She reached down into her purse and pulled it out.

"Sorry, thought I'd turned that off." Anne glanced down. "Hmmm…it's from your son," she said to Claire.

"Oh, Tony?" Claire said, striving to sound uninterested.

"It's about business. He wonders if I'd be interested in a referral in San

Francisco," Anne added, turning the phone off. She took a bite of her salad.

"Oh, how nice," Claire said, losing interest. Claire took a sip of iced tea, then brought the subject back to the investigation.

"The family questionnaires that I gave you to show your uncle...did he find them helpful? What was that really all about?"

"The questionnaires contained handwriting samples. I'm not sure if you knew about the anonymous note that was left in the janitor's shed." Anne opened her manila folder and withdrew the copy of the "danni DEAD murder sees u. Fuk u!!" note written in childish block letters. She handed it to Claire.

Claire slipped on her glasses. As she read the note, her growing shock deepened the lines between her eyebrows.

"This is horrifying," Claire said. "Why haven't I seen this before?"

"Well, it wasn't taken seriously back then," Anne said, then went on to explain how the note had been filed away in a sheriff's desk because he thought it was just a nasty joke. It was only toward the tail end of the investigation that the note was even looked at, and by then, any fingerprints it may have contained were too smudged for testing.

Claire searched Anne's face. "So you wanted to see if one of my children wrote it? Is that it?"

"We wanted to compare the handwriting—"

"The handwriting of *my* children with that piece of garbage?" Claire felt her face reddening, the note trembling in her hand.

"Michele's handwriting, Claire," Anne said in a low, insistent voice. "*Michele's*. It looked similar. Look at the Fs and Ds." Anne pointed to the letters on Michele's answers and the corresponding ones on the note. "But the forensic handwriting expert said he couldn't conclusively match up any of the samples in these documents. That's mainly because children's writing is notoriously difficult to work with. As a rule, penmanship doesn't get unique until the late teens or so."

"You mentioned other fingerprints at the crime scene," Claire said in a calmer voice, eager to move on.

"Right, fingerprints were on the wine bottles found in the adobe. Unfortunately, they weren't able to get a match on the database."

They sat in silence for a moment. Pushing her half-empty soup bowl to the side, Claire placed her bread plate in front of her and tore the sourdough roll into bits. Louie sat up and whimpered.

"So where does that leave us?" Claire asked as she tossed a bread piece lightly in the air. Louie made a Nureyev-caliber leap and snatched it in his teeth. She patted the excited dog's head and turned back to Anne.

"We have no hard proof yet—" Anne said.

"But you and your uncle think Michele killed Danny, don't you? I know there's more you aren't telling me, but that's what you think."

Anne said nothing.

Claire exhaled a long sigh. "In all these years, it truly never crossed my mind that Michele killed Danny. I think maybe she *knew* something—maybe witnessed something, heard something—because she was acting so strangely, but I've never thought she could actually be involved," Claire said. "And apparently, no one else did because, during the entire original investigation, there was never any mention of Michele as a suspect. Never. Besides, she was so tiny. It was unthinkable."

Then Claire looked past Anne to the redwood trees outside her window. "I remember that her hands were big, though, at least in proportion to the rest of her," she said eventually. "And I remember them encircling Noreen's neck once, choking her. She stopped when I yelled out the kitchen window. But oh my God, how could someone so close to us murder Danny? Why? And then to keep coming back to our home, eating at our table, watching us suffer. Even marrying Peter, for God's sake. What kind of monster would she have to be?"

Claire fastened her gaze on Anne. "Could it have been an accident? Is that possible? I'm not ready to accept this, Anne. It's just too...unfathomable."

"We don't know enough yet. We still need to tie the DNA evidence to Michele, as I mentioned. Or get a confession, which seems unlikely."

"That anonymous tip line didn't produce anything, I take it."

"Nothing concrete about Michele. Mainly stories about what she was like as a child. Even with all the children who were around that day, no one has come forward to say they were an eyewitness."

"A witness..." repeated Claire, a dark thought crossing her mind. "You're not thinking that one of my children saw her doing anything, are you? Because I'll tell you right now, no child of mine was involved. If any of them saw anything, they would have told me. They loved their brother."

"Right now, we're concentrating on getting Michele's DNA sample," Anne said.

"I know she's a smoker," Claire said. "Peter sees her now and then, maybe he can grab a cigarette butt." They looked at each other and almost laughed at the irony: Peter would be their least reliable, least helpful accomplice.

"You know, I can get her here for you," Claire said suddenly. "She wants to talk to me. All I have to do is give Peter the word."

"Thanks, but I think we can do it another way—old-fashioned surveillance of her home and workplace. In fact, we plan to start tomorrow. But if that doesn't work out, your idea would be a good plan B—that is, if you don't mind talking to her," said Anne as she stood up to leave.

"Any idea what Michele wants to talk to you about?"

"Whatever it is, I'm ready to hear it."

* * *

On the drive back to her office, Anne debated between two ways to spend the rest of her afternoon: She could devote hours researching antique values at the Invaluable.com website for her new client, Claire's friend Lydia, or she could catch up on her bookkeeping. Neither option sounded good. Besides, the weather was too lovely to be indoors sitting at a desk.

So on a whim, she drove down Hwy. 12, took the Fulton Road exit, and headed north for the strip mall where Michele worked at the BeFabulous Salon. When Anne called the salon earlier that morning, the receptionist told her that Michele made her own schedule, but to try again later. "She comes and goes as she pleases," she said, "so we never know when she'll be here. But it's *never* before noon, that's for sure."

Anne harbored no great hopes of seeing Michele on this trip, but if nothing else came of it, she would get a feel for Michele's stomping grounds, and maybe pick up some groceries at the Raley's market located next door to the salon. She turned into the strip mall, parked near the front of the beauty salon, and sat watching its comings and goings for a mind-numbingly sluggish thirty minutes.

If Michele was working inside the lighted salon, Anne couldn't see her. But in the off-chance she was, Anne came prepared. She popped the trunk of her car and retrieved a bag containing a blonde wig, clear-glassed, horn-rimmed glasses, and a Giants baseball cap. She slipped them on and hoped they would be disguise enough. A few more minutes dragged by.

She was about to start the engine when she saw Michele leave the salon and walk toward an ancient, tan Camry—a car so thoroughly commonplace it would be the ideal getaway car for a bank heist. A hard car to follow in traffic. Michele reached into the back seat, pulled out cloth shopping bags, and headed into the grocery store.

Anne drove to the far end of the parking lot, near the only exit from the shopping center, and waited. From this vantage point, she couldn't miss seeing Michele's Camry getting onto Fulton Road. She only hoped Michele wouldn't go directly home and decide to hole up for the night.

Twenty more minutes went by before Michele came out carrying grocery bags. She loaded them in the trunk and headed out of the parking lot. Anne waited a beat, then turned into the far right lane onto Fulton Road and stayed a few cars behind her.

Michele was a slow yet distracted driver, unpredictably swerving now and again as if she were reading text messages or trying to keep a tray of cookies from spilling off the passenger seat. One by one, the cars behind Michele changed into the faster lane on the left, leaving Anne directly behind her, with no choice but to pull over to the side of the road and let a few cars go by before getting back into traffic. No sooner had Anne gotten back into the flow of traffic, with four cars between them, than Michele swerved left into the next lane, followed by a sharp veer into the farthest left-turning lane—all without signaling. Michele was apparently turning left onto Sally Lane, the start of a subdivision of middle-class ranch homes that was miles from where Michele lived. The light turned red.

There was no way to maneuver through traffic fast enough to get behind her, so Anne turned right and did an illegal U-turn, then headed straight onto Sally Lane. She got there in time to see Michele's Camry stop in front of the Live Oak Park, a city park bordered on two sides by residential streets—Sally Lane and Stevens Avenue—and on the other two sides by stands of oak trees and bushes. The park had a grassy knoll, park benches, and playground equipment, and on this day, no other visitors in sight.

Anne turned onto Stevens Avenue and stopped beneath a large, leafy oak tree on the opposite side of the street from the park and out of Michele's line of sight. She watched as Michele got out of her car, leaned down to look into the side-view mirror, and touched up her lipstick. Michele tossed her purse into the back seat, locked up, and then set off up the hilly knoll. When she reached the park bench at the top, she shaded her eyes, and looked around like she was expecting someone.

Within minutes a black, late-model SUV carrying two passengers parked behind Michele's Camry. A tall, lean man stepped out. He was wearing mirrored glasses, wrinkled Bermuda shorts, a baseball cap, and a turquoise windbreaker with a white shirttail hanging below it. The other passenger stayed in the SUV.

Given the distance and the casual clothes, it took Anne a moment to recognize him. *What the hell is Tony doing here?* That wasn't his usual vehicle—Claire told her that he owned a BMW—and that outfit wasn't like anything she had seen him wear. She watched as he slowly advanced up the hill toward Michele, who didn't raise a hand in greeting when she saw him. In fact, she seemed startled and unnerved and took a step backward, nearly stumbling.

Anne watched them closely as they came together, facing each other. Tony took a few steps closer to Michele and leaned in. He held a white envelope in his hand and was doing all the talking. Michele stepped backward. He pressed even closer. She looked ready to bolt. This was a graceless dance of power and intimidation, and fear. Michele raised her hands up in surrender, but then quickly lowered them and made a grab for the envelope. He held onto it tightly and kept up his stream of talking. She reached out for the envelope again and said something loud enough for the sound to carry down the knoll, but Anne couldn't make out the words.

Tony released the envelope without another word, turned away from her, and walked down the hill. Michele stood motionless, the envelope clutched in both hands. She remained there as if frozen until his car drove off. Anne kept her eyes on Michele and waited for her to walk down the hill and get into her car.

Michele had carried nothing up the hill, and she left with nothing but the envelope. There were no cigarette butts to collect, no coffee cups to save.

* * *

Juggling her keys, a grocery bag, and the mail, Anne paused on her front porch and looked toward the horizon, a sight she rarely slowed down long enough to take in. The sun was setting, streaking the fiery sky with wild purples and oranges. No sounds carried from the street or the adjoining duplex, but that was normal. Her renter was a quiet widow with a teenage son who never seemed to be home.

Finally opening the door, she was met with a stale, closed-up-all-day house smell. She set the groceries and mail onto the kitchen countertop and went through all the rooms, opening the windows to let in the soft evening breezes.

Back in the kitchen, she reached into the grocery bag. Rescued a pint-sized tub of ice cream and stuck a spoon in it: tonight's dinner. After putting away the rest of the groceries, she plopped an oversized pillow onto the floor between the coffee table and couch. She set the ice cream on the coffee table and eased herself onto the pillow, her legs in a lotus position, her back leaning against the couch. She dug into the ice cream and ruminated on what she had seen that afternoon.

After Tony had left the park, Anne followed Michele to Vineland Apartments, a shabby, wooden three-story apartment building in the Roseland area of town, and parked along the street facing the lobby entrance door.

After two hours of monitoring zero activity at the building, she decided Michele was probably in for the night, so she headed home.

Anne had little to show for her day of surveillance—nothing really, except more questions, and most of those were about Tony. What could have been so important about this meeting with Michele that he would make the drive all the way from his home in San Francisco? That's a two-hour round trip at the very least. And why did they choose this secluded, yet still public, place to meet? Why his disguise, half-hearted and lame as it was?

The envelope contained the blackmail money Michele demanded from Noreen—that much seemed sure. But what was the blackmailing all about? What did Michele have hanging over Noreen's head? From the start, Anne had a nagging hunch that Noreen had somehow been involved in Danny's murder, or at the very least, knew more than anyone else in the family. She must have been desperate to enlist her older brother's help. How much—and what—did Noreen tell Tony to get him to step into the middle of this mess? Whatever it was, Anne could only conclude that he was now fully on board, that he was taking charge of the blackmail threats for Noreen—not just by providing the funds, but also by sending the message to Michele to stay away. A very clear message, from what Anne saw in the park.

Anne ate the last spoonful of ice cream, then picked up her phone. She owed Tony a text message. She might as well do a little fishing for information at the same time. See how far she gets.

"Thanks for offering a referral," she sent.

A few minutes later, he responded. "Sure. Interested?"

"Are you in Santa Rosa? Maybe we could meet."

"What makes you think I'm in SR?"

"Your mother said she'd be seeing you soon," she lied.

"No, I'm not. Do you want the lead?"

"Of course. Thanks for thinking of me."

"I'll give them a call, and they'll contact you. Good luck."

Well, that was a whole lot of nothing, Anne thought as she headed back to the kitchen to open a bag of cookies.

* * *

Anne's phone rang just as she was sprawled out on her pillowy white couch, working the remote to surf TV channels. Anne checked the ID screen and picked up.

"Hey there, Krista."

They'd traded a few friendly texts since their dinner over a week before but hadn't actually talked before this.

"I've got some news...." Krista's tone sounded serious.

"Aww...the baby was born? That's so—"

"Oh God, I wish! Six more grueling days to go. Or even longer. No, I'm calling to give you a heads-up." Krista paused dramatically, then said, "I've heard through the grapevine that your ex-husband's new girlfriend wants to talk to you. I think she's going to call. And by the way, it wasn't me who gave her your number."

"What on God's earth for? I don't even know her." Anne was sitting up now.

"Actually, I feel bad for her. She and your ex have been going out on and off for about three months now—which is just enough time for Gary to start showing his true colors."

"And let me guess: she doesn't know if he's the crazy one or she is," Anne said as she went into the kitchen and poured herself a glass of organic kale juice to counter-effect the ice cream.

"She needs to talk to someone who knows Gary," Krista said. "I guess he told her some bad things about you, but the longer she's with Gary, the less she believes them."

"I don't know if I want to get involved."

"Well, who would? But on the other hand, Annie, don't you wish you'd talked to his ex-girlfriend, the one before you? Just to get some perspective on him?"

"You mean the one who tried to kill herself after he dumped and ghosted her?" Anne took a sip of the bitter green juice and shuddered. She poured it down the drain.

"I remember," Krista said. "And that's even more reason to talk to this girl, don't you think? She should know what she's up against with him. She's very nice. Her name's Grace. She was at my baby shower, so maybe you talked to her."

Anne thought back to the gathering at the English Garden Tea Room, and though she didn't remember seeing Grace, she clearly remembered those two snide women and wondered if they were friends of Grace.

"I'll have to think about it."

"Anne McCormack, Relationship Counselor." Krista laughed. "It has a nice ring to it."

Chapter Twenty-Six

Sunday, November 10

Sunday brunch was The Parisian's busiest, showiest event of the week. Brunch there was a family tradition passed down through generations of Santa Rosans, and the pool-side restaurant was always packed. Families started arriving after the nine o'clock mass at St. Paul's Church and kept coming in a steady stream until around three in the afternoon.

At seven a.m., hours before brunch started, Jack stood outside the main front entrance with Frank Greco, listening in as the hotel manager barked orders into his cell phone.

"Did you find those old standing ashtrays yet?" Frank asked his maintenance supervisor. "Yeah, the ones with the sand on top. They need to be rolled out right now." The Parisian was a no-smoking hotel, and even the outdoor ashtrays had been banished to the storage room years ago so smokers wouldn't get any ideas.

Jack had made his request to Frank the night before. Without giving specifics about *why* he wanted what he wanted, Jack asked for two ashtrays—one to be placed at the front entrance and the other at the side entrance leading to the hotel rooms.

"No, we *gotta* have the sand," the manager demanded into the phone. "Try a hardware store or a garden shop or something."

Jack nudged Frank. "And ask them to hang up some EXTINGUISH YOUR

CIGARETTES HERE signs while they're at it."

* * *

Three hours later, Anne approached the hotel's side entrance, took note of the round cylinder ashtray outside the door, and mumbled under her breath, "Is that kitty litter?"

She entered the hallway and rode the elevator up to Claire's suite.

"Come in, Anne," Sala greeted her at the door. Anne returned Sala's smile and handed her a bag of blueberry and pumpkin-spice muffins from Flour Power, Claire's favorite bakery.

"Miss Claire is extra tired today. She didn't sleep well last night. Maybe she's nervous about that woman coming to visit," Sala said as she carried the bag into the kitchenette.

"I hope she isn't too worried. I'll be here all the time," Anne said.

But nervous or not, Claire was proving to be an adept partner-in-crime, Anne thought. The night before, on the phone, Claire had passed the word along to Peter: she was willing to see Michele the following morning, Sunday at eleven, but only if Michele came alone. Peter could drop her off at the hotel, Claire told him, but he could not come up to the suite. He whined, as was his habit, but Claire gave no explanations and held fast: that was the condition.

Michele's visit would give the cold case team its best shot at collecting discarded items for DNA testing, so Anne and Jack were double-teaming it. They agreed that Jack would wait in his car in the hotel parking lot, where he would have a view of both entrances. If he saw Michele extinguish a cigarette in an ashtray, he would pull on his gloves, extract the butt, and slip it into an evidence envelope.

For Anne's part, she would hide in the bathroom adjoining Claire's bedroom. Not just to collect any discards for testing, but also to act as a witness to the meeting—she would be able to hear everything through the crack in the bathroom door—and to protect Claire if the need arose; Michele was a wild card.

With only a few moments remaining before Michele arrived, Claire and Anne went over their strategy. Anne took out her phone and opened the recording app.

"What will you do with the recording?" Claire asked, straightening up in her bed.

"In case something important gets said, I want my uncle and Detective Diaz to listen to it. But technically, it isn't legal to record Michele without her consent."

"Even if I give *my* consent? And it's being recorded in my residence?"

"Not in California. This is a two-party state—meaning, both parties have to agree. And technically, I shouldn't be hiding out of sight and listening in, either."

All the legalities of what you can and cannot do—what's allowable evidence and what isn't—which seemed to change with each new legislature, weren't among the things Anne missed about full-time law enforcement. One positive thing about her new business was that no one tells you—or cares, for that matter—how much you can charge for a client's silver tea service or Tiffany lamp. It's all about what the market allows. It's still the Wild West.

"I don't care about legalities. I want you here," Claire said. "Go ahead and hide behind the door and record all you want." She pulled her robe tighter across her thin chest as if the silken fabric could act as armor.

"But let's say you get a call when the phone's recorder is on," Claire said. "The noise will alert her." Anne assured her that the phone was on mute.

"And if Michele asks to use my bathroom while you're in there, then what?"

"Good point." Anne considered it for a few seconds, then told Claire she would instruct Sala to offer Michele the use of the other bathroom when she first arrived. Anne headed to the living room to tell Sala of the plan.

Then they settled in to wait—Claire on the hospital bed, Anne behind the bathroom door. After a few minutes, there was a knock at the suite's front door, and Anne could hear Sala talk to Michele in the living room through the cracked door.

***

"She's having a bad day," Sala said to Michele. "Real bad earlier this morning, but she's more comfortable now. I don't know if she can visit for long today. Maybe stay only a few minutes?"

"Okay." Michele nodded. Her gaze darted around the suite, alighting on family photos in silver frames.

In the far corner, Louie glanced up at the new visitor, but stayed sprawled out in his fleece doggie bed, his chin resting on the rim. The constant comings and goings of visitors in the suite—nurses, waiters, lawyers, and so forth—seemed hardly worth a tail wag anymore.

Sala briefly sized Michele up, taking in her quick movements, her nervous energy. *She looks like a bird. A bird of prey.* The blue of Michele's eyes reminded Sala of the wings of a Collared Kingfisher, a bird native to her island homeland of Fiji.

"Would you like to use the restroom? It's over there," Sala said, pointing to her own private suite. Michele looked at Sala as if appalled by such an indelicate suggestion, then cleared her expression and declined with a shake of her head.

Claire's bedroom door was cracked slightly open, but Sala tapped on it anyway, and when no response came, opened it wider. "Miss Claire, your visitor is here."

Michele stood in the bedroom doorway, waiting there until Sala told her, "Go ahead in." Sala left the room but kept the door open a crack.

***

Claire lay perfectly motionless except for her left hand, which made a small gesture for Michele to sit in the wooden chair next to the bed. Michele ventured near, tentatively, and then settled into the chair.

Michele's gaze traveled around the bedroom suite, taking in the opulence of the high-beamed ceilings, double French doors that opened onto a private patio, expensive furnishings, gas fireplace, and autumnal views of the vineyards below. Then her gaze fell on Claire. Michele's eyes widened, as if not believing that the pale, thin, almost shrunken woman in the hospital bed was really her ex-mother-in-law.

"Hi, Claire. I wanted to see you because Peter told me you were sick."

Claire did not react, her face impassive, but her eyes locked onto Michele's face.

Michele said nothing for a moment, taking a deep breath. Then the words rushed out: "I wanted to say some things, like I'm sorry about everything that happened all those years ago. I know how much I hurt your family while I was married to Peter, but I'm older now, and I've changed."

She paused to catch her breath, then continued, "We shouldn't have gotten married so young. My fault. But that thing with Joanne's boyfriend? *He* came on to *me*. It was all his idea. I was just young and flattered, I guess. Peter forgave me a long time ago, and now we're working on a future together again. You want that, don't you? For him to be happy?"

She paused for an answer that did not come. "A-anyway, I know you and Joanne couldn't let go of that affair, like that one mistake was the end of the world or something. Joanne always thought her shit didn't—" Michele cut herself off.

She leaned in for a closer look at Claire.

"Can you talk?" she asked.

Claire looked past Michele to the fan on the ceiling, then closed her eyes.

A prolonged silence followed, then Michele said, "I guess not. I didn't know you were so sick. I'm sorry for that. I don't know how much you can understand. Do you understand what I'm saying?"

Michele inched her chair closer to the bed and took Claire's hand in hers. Claire tensed slightly at the touch but did not pull her hand away. She opened her eyes and kept them on Michele.

"Anyway, one of the saddest things of my life is that I never could have children, not after the abortion," Michele said. "Did Peter ever tell you about that? We just decided we were too young. And Peter could never hold a job anyway, so it all would have fallen to me. Then later, after me and Peter got divorced, when I tried with my new husband, I couldn't get pregnant.

212

But I wanted a baby so bad. I just longed for a baby. You know that feeling? That's when I started thinking about Danny all the time—about what that must have been like for you and Mr. Murray to lose Danny like that."

Michele began to cry softly. She released Claire's hand and reached for a tissue from the box on the bedside table. She dabbed her eyes and curled the tissue in her palm.

"I feel bad for you, Claire, I really do, and I can't stop thinking about it. The thoughts are like worms in my brain. I guess Danny's death will never be over for you. It will never change. And nothing I can do will make any difference. But you have to understand, I was just a baby myself then. I was ten—just *ten!*—when it happened. Danny was going to tell on me...those silly nudie photos. He was going to ruin everything. So I had to chase him into that house to stop him, and he tripped and fell...."

She paused to blow her nose.

"Then he started hitting me and pulling my hair and calling me a nasty girl...all kinds of names, so I slapped him. He wouldn't stop! He said he was going to tell you everything, so I hit him some more. Then he screamed, and I *had* to stop him. I only pressed his throat a little bit. Maybe more than a little bit...." She paused, as if entrapped in the past, then shook her head defiantly. "If Danny had just minded his own business that day, if he hadn't threatened me and been so mean, it never would have happened. I know it sounds like I blame him, but I don't really...no one's to blame. No reasons make sense, not to us as adults anyway. I didn't mean any harm. I'm just sorry...oh God, I'm sorry. Only words, that's all I have."

Her elbow hit a glass on the bedside table, and a little water sloshed over the rim. "Clumsy—no wonder you didn't want to adopt me," she said with a nervous laugh, wiping up the droplets with the sleeve of her sweater. "I don't know whether to laugh or to cry...." Claire's eyes flew open at that, and her lips tightened in rage, but Michele seemed not to notice.

"But what about Noreen?" Michele continued. "I never told anyone she was there, not even Peter. So she gets to go on with her life and have a family and a husband, and a house, and nothing happens to her. Everyone thinks she's so perfect. Well, it's time for her husband and kids to know who she really is! If she thinks she can just—"

Michele stopped talking, as if realizing she would be better off not continuing down this perilous road. But she started up again anyway.

"Don't you think?" Michele asked.

Still no response from Claire, who had closed her eyes. Both women seemed drained, exhausted by emotion. "I wish this could be over," Michele said, more to herself than to Claire. She gave out a long breath, then dabbed her eyes again.

"I guess I better go now." She stood up, her eyes lingering on Claire's face. "Goodbye for now."

Hearing "goodbye" from behind the bathroom door, Anne picked up her phone and hit the Stop button on the recorder. But Michele kept talking. "If you want to talk later…." So without looking at the phone, Anne went to press the Start button to keep recording. But instead, her finger slipped, and she pressed Play.

Into the silence, Michele's recorded voice could be heard, sounding far away and muffled, saying something like, "Hi Claire."

"What's that?" Michele's head jerked up.

Anne quickly scrambled to stop the recorder. She held her breath.

"Is someone in the bathroom?" Michele stood abruptly, clearly about to move in search of the sound, when the living room door burst open, and Sala barged into the room, noisily declaring that the hospice nurses were coming earlier than usual.

"Time to go, sorry!" Sala said firmly to Michele, taking quick strides into the room. She planted herself in front of the bathroom door, standing there as solidly as a redwood tree to block Michele's entrance.

Michele wavered for a second, looked past Sala to the bathroom, then shrugged. She said goodbye to Claire again, to no response, then moved slowly out of the bedroom. Sala followed closely on her heels and closed the door behind them.

* * *

Once they were alone in the living room, Michele placed a hand on Sala's arm, leaned in, and said in a near-whisper, "I thought I heard something coming from the bathroom. A voice."

"This is an old hotel, lots of ghosts."

Michele hesitated for several seconds, then shrugged as if Sala's explanation was as good as any. "Maybe I imagined it. Anyway, why didn't you tell me that Claire can't talk? She didn't say a word to me," Michele said in a low confiding tone. She searched Sala's eyes and held them briefly before adding, "She's much worse than Peter told me. That's so sad."

"It is sad. Miss Claire is a good woman," Sala said.

Leading Michele to the front door, Sala's eye was caught by the used tissue peeking out of Michele's sweater pocket.

"Take a muffin with you," Sala said, steering Michele over to the plate of muffins on the side table by the front door. While Michele was busy wrapping a muffin in a paper napkin, then wrapping another one, Sala moved to her side and deftly lifted the soiled tissue out of her sweater pocket. Sala held the tissue behind her back, opened the door for Michele, and closed it behind her.

She went to Claire's bedroom and knocked on the door.

"Come in, Sala," Claire called out.

Sala entered and looked from Claire, who was straightening herself up in the bed, to Anne, who was stepping out from the bathroom, and delicately held up the clean edge of the soiled tissue between her thumb and index finger.

"She dropped something," Sala said.

Chapter Twenty-Seven

Sunday, November 10

Two slight nip in the air didn't keep the kids from taking running leaps and cannonballing into the hotel's Olympic-size pool. The Sunday brunch was at its noontime peak, and dozens of groups sat around the umbrella-covered tables located along the south end of the pool, positioned just outside of splashing range.

Anne and Jack were among them. Lounging poolside with cold drinks and chips, they were recounting their morning adventures in DNA scavenging. Both brought something to the table.

Anne told Jack of the accidental playback of the audio—a near-disaster but for Sala's eavesdropping and quick thinking.

"My kind of woman." Jack gave a thumbs-up, chuckling. "But tell me, what would you have done if Sala hadn't stopped Michele from finding you in the bathroom?"

Momentarily embarrassed, she finally said, "All I can say is that I had one hand on the toilet handle, and I was ready to flush."

"Sounds weak, Annie." Jack raised one eyebrow.

"Anyway, if she had found me there, what was she going to do? Overpower me? Grab my phone?"

"If she realized you were recording her illegally, she could have claimed she was the 'injured party' and sued you in civil court—that's what she could have done."

"That's a stretch, Uncle Jack," Anne said, raising her own eyebrow. "Well, luckily, none of that happened. Sala came through for us—and with something else, too." Anne bent down and retrieved the evidence envelope from her purse. She handed it to Jack and gave him a blow-by-blow of Sala's cunning in gathering the soiled tissue.

"Sala is sticking to her story that the tissue just happened to drift—"

"Accidentally, I'm sure—" Jack cut in.

"—out of Michele's sweater and onto the ground."

"Not sure if we need to use it, seeing as it might be problematic, legally speaking," Jack said. "But God love her, as my Irish grandmother would say." He tucked the evidence envelope into his jacket pocket.

"Maybe not problematic. Who's to say how Sala got it?"

"Yeah, right. But whether she took it, or it dropped accidentally, it doesn't really matter. It's just semantics since we're not taking it to court. We're just getting it tested. But we have something else to show for today."

Jack reached into his other jacket pocket and produced an envelope containing the cigarette butt Michele had extinguished in the ashtray before entering the hotel. Peering inside the envelope, Anne wrinkled her nose at the smell. "I was right—that *is* kitty litter they used instead of sand."

"It didn't get on the wet saliva end of the butt. That's all I care about," Jack said.

Anne handed the envelope back and sat quietly for a moment, her good mood quickly dissipating. It was time to share the audio recording of Michele's conversation with Claire. She pulled out her phone, turned the recording app on, and slid the phone across the table to Jack. Though the sound was low and garbled, they could make out most of the conversation.

Listening to this rambling confession again—this raw unburdening of despair, shame, self-pity, and obsession onto a dying woman—was nearly unbearable. Anne could almost hear the ripping open of Claire's unhealed wounds.

When the recording stopped, Jack turned off the phone and pushed it back toward Anne. "We're almost there," he said quietly. "The case is winding down."

She gazed at the pool and the kids swimming, barely hearing the loud shrieks of laughter or even what Jack was saying.

"So how's Claire taking it?" he asked.

Anne shook her head at the memory of Claire sinking back in her pillows, looking small and hugging her arms to her chest.

"After Sala gave me the tissue and left, Claire and I sat and talked for quite a while. I asked her why she hadn't said a single word—seriously, not one word—to Michele. She said it was because she didn't want to give Michele the satisfaction. That's the word she used, *satisfaction*. Claire said, 'If Michele thinks she's getting any kind of reconciliation or forgiveness from me, she's sadly mistaken.'"

"So she was expecting Michele to ask for forgiveness—"

"—for all the havoc she caused while she was married to Peter. That's what she was expecting," said Anne, running her fingers idly along the wet rim of her glass. "I think it took Claire by surprise when Michele brought up the murder. Confessed to it. Part of her couldn't believe Michele really did it. It was just too shocking of a thought—that Danny's murderer was so close. Had once been a part of the family. She had to hear it for herself to believe it.

"Anyway, Claire was very torn, very upset about what she learned from Michele. You know what she said to me? 'It was all about some stupid photos. My baby was murdered over some stupid, goddamn photos.'"

Jack looked off into the distance and waited for her to continue.

"I was at her bedroom door, about to leave," Anne said, "and then I looked back at her. Claire was sitting there on the side of her bed wringing her hands—*literally* wringing her hands. I went back in and sat next to her on the bed. She looked so defeated. Claire told me that part of her has sympathy for Michele. That she knows Michele was just a child then. But that doesn't really change anything. It doesn't make what she did to her family any less horrible. And Michele's not done yet. She suspects Michele was the one who trashed her home with garbage—and that happened just last week.

"Then Claire told me, and I'll never forget her words: 'Michele is still after my family. In her jealousy and sickness and cruelty, she's still after us.'"

* * *

CHAPTER TWENTY-SEVEN

"Noreen, what the fuck?" Peter shouted into the phone.

"What are you yelling about?" Noreen asked as she stepped out of her minivan and slammed the car door shut. "Unless this is really important, I'll call you back when I get the groceries inside the house."

"Damn right, it's important—"

Overcome by a fiery surge of impatience, she disconnected the call. She had no time for his shenanigans. No doubt this had something to do with Michele, and she was sick to death of hearing about Michele or having her in their lives. Everyone in the family was of the opinion that Michele was the one who had left that stinking pile of garbage in the house. Everyone except Peter.

Noreen popped open the trunk, picked up a grocery bag and a jug of milk, and headed into her house. Opening the front door, she called out to her two teenagers to "Turn off those damn video games and come get the rest of the groceries. Please!"

"Video games? As if!" Chloe called out, leading Noreen to suspect that Chloe was upstairs watching the 1995 movie *Clueless* again.

Noreen ignored her. "I'm not kidding, you two!"

Noreen was emptying the box of popsicles into the freezer when Peter called again.

"That was rude. I don't hang up on you," Peter said.

Noreen waited a beat until his petulance wore off, then asked, "Okay, what's going on?" She grabbed a diet drink from the refrigerator, pulled the tab, and took a sip from the can. Chloe and Jake trudged past her on their way to the car, slamming the front door on the way out.

"What's going *on* is that I brought Michele to visit Mom this morning—"

"You did what?" Noreen said, straightening up.

"Mom wanted to see her."

"Are you kidding?" Noreen frowned and pressed the cold can to her forehead. "I can't believe Mom agreed to that. What did they talk about?"

"I wasn't allowed in, so how should I know? Girl talk? But Michele said she had to do all the talking—that Mom was too sick to say anything. Which sounds like bullshit to me. I just talked to Mom last night, and she sounded as tough as nails."

"Did you tell Michele that? What did she say to that?"

"I didn't tell her, of course. It would just hurt her feelings—and she was already upset about the visit. She wouldn't even let me into her apartment. Can you believe Mom would play these games? Pretending not to talk? What bullshit! So here's what I want to know: what the hell is going on with Mom?"

"Why are you asking *me*? Why didn't you just call her and find out?" Noreen spat out. Then a sudden thought occurred to her, causing her to change directions with the speed of a cutting horse. "Never mind, I'll call her myself," she said.

She disconnected from Peter's call and leaned against the kitchen counter, staring down at her phone. What lies and delusions had Michele fed to her mother behind her back? A slow, desperate fear began to wash over her, as if a noose was tightening around her neck. She could lose everything that meant anything to her—her husband, her children, her mother's love. She could be ruined. Disgraced. All because of Michele.

She punched in her mother's phone number.

"Hi Sala, can I talk to my mother?"

"She's sleeping, Noreen. Can I ask her to call you back?"

"I heard she was very sick today."

"Yes, rough day. Tired."

"Too sick to even speak. Is that right?"

"What?" Sala recovered quickly. "Oh yes, could not talk. That's right! But she's better now. Don't worry."

Chapter Twenty-Eight

Monday, November 11

The Monday morning meeting of the cold case team was minus one member.

"Diaz called. He can't be here today," Jack announced to Anne as they plopped their files onto the conference table and dropped their respective leather bags onto the floor. He placed a battered shoebox on the table with deliberate care.

"He's still on his wife-imposed R & R," Jack said.

"Dean's wife? What's going on?" Anne asked as she headed to the coffee station. She hadn't heard a word from Dean for the past week, and frankly, she realized, she had been too busy to notice. Aside from her cold case work, her estate business was finally gaining some ground, and her work schedule was verging on hectic. A big estate sale was planned for the coming weekend, and she still needed to hire more sales help.

"Fallout from last week's high jinks with Carl Pinn, that's what's going on," Jack said. "Remember how Dean chased down the patrol car, drove to the police station with Pinn, stayed for all of the catch-and-release festivities, and then joined me in tossing Pinn's place looking for evidence? Remember all that?"

"Hard to forget, but no one could have stopped him." Her uncle had filled her in on the action-packed aftermath. During the few hours Pinn was in custody that previous Monday, Jack requested, and was issued, a warrant to search his trailer for the photos of Michele that Pinn claimed he'd taken twenty-nine years prior. Less than fifteen minutes after Pinn arrived home from the police station, Jack and Dean were at his front door. One look at Pinn's frantic expression told them he wasn't ready for their visit and that finding his child porn stash would *not* test their police skills—or take much time at all. Pinn stayed mute, nervously scratching his arms as he followed Jack and Dean from room to room while they searched under the couch and bed, rummaged around in his drawers, opened cupboards, and looked behind posters.

On the floor in the rear of his bedroom closet was where they'd found the two shoeboxes labeled "StPaul pics" and "Misc nudes." Each box contained dozens of Polaroids of nude, underage girls. "Can't believe you labeled them," Jack had said to Pinn, who'd just stared back, wide-eyed.

Anne filled the coffee maker with grounds, poured water in, and pressed the brew button. "Something about Pinn seems to hit a big, raw nerve in Dean."

"He has two daughters and a granddaughter. He takes any case involving kids personally—always has," Jack said. "But according to his wife, the stress of dealing with Pinn and running around last week made his blood pressure shoot through the roof. Janie's worried about his health. She's putting her foot down and keeps reminding him he isn't thirty years old and hasn't been for over thirty years now."

"Well, that's the damn truth."

"He says he'll be back. She says he won't," said Jack, slipping on latex gloves and passing a pair over to Anne. He opened the shoebox lid and fanned out a few photos onto the tabletop. "I only brought one of the boxes with me because the other one is practically identical—full of young girls, metal folding chairs, covered faces, bad lighting, nasty intentions."

Anne, gloves on, gave them a cursory look, picking up a few and noting that the backs were dated and initialed in Pinn's thick handwriting. The initials were for the name of the child in the photo, she assumed. Some Polaroids dated back years before Danny's murder. The most current ones were ten years old, probably taken right before his arrest for sexually abusing a minor girl.

"Why weren't these found when Pinn went down for that charge? It says here," Anne said, looking down and reading the case files, "that Pinn's place was searched back then, and nothing was found. Strange. Where did he hide them? Or did he give them to someone for safekeeping? Maybe his ex-girlfriend hid them for him?"

But she dismissed the notion as soon as the words flew from her mouth, "No way. He must have given them to some pedo friend of his to hide, or maybe put them in a storage unit."

Needing relief from the toxic images, Anne peeled off the gloves and headed to the coffee station to check whether the coffee was ready. She came back carrying two steaming mugs.

Jack took a sip of coffee. "Anyway, doesn't really matter what he did with them then—they were back in his possession yesterday. This one is of Michele," he said as he picked up an envelope that was tucked along the side of the pile and lifted out the photo. Smudged with old fingerprints—most likely, Pinn's—the Polaroid showed her without a brown paper bag over her face.

Anne gave it a quick glance and looked away. *Jesus.*

"What a pitiful life that girl's had," she said.

"No doubt," Jack said, setting the photo back in the box. "But that photo goes straight to motive. This is proof that the photo was taken just like Pinn said it was. And the date on the back is the date Danny died. Of course, it doesn't prove the rest of Pinn's story about Danny—that Michele chased after Danny that day—but it makes it more likely. Together with the DNA evidence we collected yesterday—"

"Did you get the items to the lab?"

"This morning. They estimate we'll get the results in a day or two. They're getting faster. Hired new staff at the lab from what I've heard," Jack said. "But don't count on any of the evidence seeing the insides of a courtroom."

"That refrain is getting old," Anne said, drumming her fingers on the table. "All this work we've been doing—the interviews, DNA, recorded confession, motive—will anything ever get in front of a jury?"

"We're getting to the bottom of the case," Jack said. "And isn't that the point—to solve the murder? Find out who did it and if we get lucky, find out why? Other than that—whether it goes to trial or not—it's all out of our hands." Jack stood up and stretched lazily, as if to suggest that they might as well relax. "That's all we can do right now."

Jack leaned over the table and gathered the photos into a pile, and put them back into the shoebox. He fit the lid back on and glanced over at Anne, his eyes meeting hers. "Getting justice for Claire and her family may never happen, Annie, and that's just a fact."

Anne lowered her gaze and pursed her lips. In silence, they cleared their mugs off the table, gathered up their files and bags, and headed toward the door.

She finally said, "Maybe we can get Dean to sneak out of the house for our meeting at the DA's office next week. We need all the help we can get with Kessler."

"I'll give Dean a call," Jack said, turning out the lights, "and hang up if his wife answers."

Chapter Twenty-Nine

Wednesday, November 13

Anne's unanswered emails and texts were piling up. At nearly two o'clock, she poured her final cup of coffee for the day and settled in front of her computer to catch up on business. For the next hour, she set up interviews for sales help for the coming weekend's estate sale, then she phoned in some beefy classified ads that listed hot-ticket items like KitchenAid appliances, baseball card collections, and lightly used Chanel bags.

At last Saturday's estate sale, cars had been lined up at seven-thirty, an hour before the doors opened. The night before, her unflappable new assistant Britney, who'd previously worked at a department store makeup counter, spent hours lovingly arranging items so that they were just-so. She did everything but put key lights on the jewelry to pick up the sparkle. When Anne arrived at the client's house just after Britney finished up, she took one look and muttered *no, no, no* under her breath. She thanked Britney profusely for her efforts and obvious talent, then directed her to tone it all down—estate sales clientele weren't looking for elegant presentations; they were hunting for bargains and finds and didn't trust fancy trappings that suggested that the sellers knew the value of what they were offering.

And instead of putting the "smalls"—the inexpensive, leftover items—together in groupings, Anne told Britney to mix them in with more valuable items to make it all seem haphazard. Customers liked to sort past the smalls in search of the treasures. It was all about the thrill of the hunt for them.

After answering text messages from clients, Anne tackled the emails. She didn't hurry to check phone messages—hardly anyone made business calls anymore. Except, she reminded herself, her older clients who refused to text and hated emails. She checked, but there were none. Then she did a quick online search for new office space. Perhaps two rooms in a downtown suite, with the use of a conference room included. *Dream on.* Business was picking up, but not enough to justify a move. Especially since part-timer Britney worked mostly from home.

Anne turned off the screen and stood to stretch her legs. Gazing outside her window, she noticed the wind was beating through the trees, threatening to topple the squirrel that was struggling to keep its balance on a wobbly dry branch. *You and me both, buddy,* she thought in sympathy.

Her phone pinged with two new texts while she was reaching into the mini-fridge to grab the sack lunch she'd brought from home. She tossed it on the desk, settled into her swivel chair, and punched in her password.

The first text was from Mike Hageman, Krista's husband, and now, from the looks of the message, an excited, brand-new father: "Krista says to get your ass down to Mercy Hospital and see the world's most beautiful baby boy born this morning!"

Feeling a rush of joy for the new parents, she texted back, "Congrats! Much love, and see you in a few hours." If she finished work soon, she could grab some flowers at the corner florist shop and make it to the hospital before visiting hours were over.

The second was from a woman who wanted to "talk about Gary." Anne groaned. *Oh, right, the new girlfriend.* She'd get to it later, if ever.

Her phone pinged again, this time a text from Tony, Claire's oldest son.

"Did my friends call you about their family estate job yet?"

"Not yet. Should I call them?" she keyed in.

"No. I can have a brunch at my place in SF to introduce you. Interested?"

"Sounds great."

"Sunday the 24th good for you?"

"That works. After eleven? LMK details. Thanks."

Here was a chance to meet a potential a new client—along with a chance to feel Tony out about the case and the blackmail payoff to Michele. Besides, one of Anne's new clients owned an intriguing jade carving they wanted to sell. Anne had been intending to visit her San Francisco dealer for an appraisal of it and perhaps even make a direct sell.

So yes, a trip to the city would indeed work.

* * *

A party was going on inside Krista's room at The Birth Center at Mercy Hospital, and the mood was as buoyant as the mylar "Hello Baby" balloons that floated around the room and bounced among visitors. The proud father stood sentry over the baby's bassinet, telling harrowing birthing stories (*Krista was a champ*, Mike said) and introducing people as though he were hosting a cocktail party. Anne crowded in, nearly toppling the stuffed bears and bouquets of flowers that lined the window ledge.

A young male nurse peeked his head inside and rapped twice on the wooden doorframe to get the crowd's attention. He cleared his throat. "Sorry, folks, but I'll have to ask you to leave." His words were greeted with groans from the dozen or so family members and friends who were gathered around Krista's bed and the bassinet.

"Mrs. Hageman and baby Leo need some privacy with the doctor," he continued politely.

"We just got here," complained a man with a stringy gray comb-over.

"You can come back in fifteen minutes," the nurse said firmly but with a smile.

Looking relieved and more than a little tired, Krista smiled and waved gamely to the group as they filed by the bassinet for a last look at the sleeping baby before emptying out into the hallway.

Anne had just found a seat along the wall of the long hospital corridor near the entry when she was approached by a dewy young woman in her early twenties. She was dark-haired and petite with thick, arched eyebrows and the wide-eyed anxious look of a cornered fawn. She was wearing a short boho print dress and a beaded leather bracelet that partially covered a *0.00* tattoo, a reference to the amount of alcohol in her bloodstream, on the inside of her left wrist. She made Anne feel ancient.

The young woman smiled nervously and introduced herself. "My name is Grace Hanson. I hope I'm not bothering you, but I'm a friend of Krista's."

Anne smiled noncommittally. Of course, she knew who Grace was: her ex-husband's new girlfriend. "Hi," she said seconds later. "I'm Anne McCormack."

"I know. You used to be married to Gary. I've been dating him for a few months now. I left you a few text messages—"

"Oh, right. Sorry I haven't gotten back to you," Anne found herself saying. "I've been really busy." *Too busy to get involved in this mess.*

"I met him at an AA meeting."

Anne resisted rolling her eyes. *So now he's trolling meetings for dates.* Not for one single second did she think he was genuinely into recovery.

"Anyway," said Grace, sitting down in the chair next to Anne and planting her Italian leather backpack on the floor. "I'm kind of confused, kind of out of my depth, and wanted to get your advice. You know Gary better than almost anyone, and I've never met a guy like him. He told me he loved me on our first date—who does that? But I'm beginning to wonder about him—like if something's wrong with him." She paused a beat before adding, "Or maybe it's me."

Anne cast a wary eye at Grace. Krista had vouched for her, so maybe all the young woman wanted was clarity and a shoulder to cry on. And yet Anne's more skeptical side was weighing in. What if Grace was just a shit disturber sent by Gary—or those snarky friends from the baby shower—to trap her into saying God knows what?

But whether Grace was treacherous or not, trouble was bound to be the outcome if she got involved. At the very least, Anne feared that her own anger and shame, now just starting to lose their power, would get stirred up again. And then there was the possibility—no, probability—of backlash when Gary found out she was talking to Grace. And he *would* find out: Grace wouldn't be able to resist tossing her name around the next time she got into an argument with Gary. And then what would he do? Then what would he say? And when would all of this ever stop?

"I can almost guarantee that it's not you," said Anne, surprising herself by plunging into the current against her better judgment. "What's he doing?"

"For one thing, he tells people we've broken up. Even when we aren't. Or at least he never tells *me* we're broken up."

"Other women." Anne nodded. "It's about other women."

"Then when I confront him, he says they're lying, or they misunderstood. And once, at a meeting, he got up to talk to a roomful of people and said, 'I wish I could find someone to trust, someone who hadn't slept with half the men in AA.' And I'm *sitting* right there, and everyone's looking at me! It wasn't true, and he knew it." She waved her arms in exasperation, her emotions building.

It sounded all too familiar: the love bombing, the drama, the gaslighting.

"Also, he'll say horrible things out of the blue," Grace said. "Like once, he said that if my nose weren't so big, I'd be pretty."

Anne eyed the perfectly normal nose. "Your nose is fine. You *are* pretty. It's just his way of tearing down your self-esteem. Getting control. And he's just warming up."

Grace looked away, tears welling up.

"How many times have you actually broken up—and I don't mean when he's just telling other people that you've broken up?" asked Anne.

"I'd say five times in the last three months. We're off right now. It's been a week, but he's starting to call again and drive by my house. Sometimes I think he's following me." She glanced toward the glass hospital doors.

"Why not just make a clean break?" It was really just a rhetorical question since Anne already knew every possible answer Grace could come up with.

"Maybe this was a mistake," said Grace, sounding wary of disapproval. She started to stand, then sighed and then sat down again. "When things are good, it's like something out of a fairy tale. And when we break up, I miss him so much it's almost like an addiction, and I mean, the sex is amazing—"

Anne cut her off. "Here's my advice, Grace: if you don't have an AA sponsor, get one. If you don't have a therapist, get one. You're going to need all the emotional support you can get when you're dealing with this narcissistic bastard."

Anne leveled her gaze at her and continued, "But what you really need to know, more than anything, is that you'll never change him. It will never work out, and you should cut off all contact with him."

"I'm not ready for that."

Anne could tell by Grace's glazed expression that she wasn't hearing what she wanted to hear; Grace wanted to hear about strategies that would make Gary change, make him kinder, sweeter, more like he was in the beginning of the romance.

Anne was fresh out of strategies. All she had were survival tactics.

A light-colored car pulled into the hospital lobby's circular driveway, the glare of its headlights bouncing off the automatic glass double doors. "Maybe that's Gary." Grace stood up, practically bouncing on her toes.

"Seriously?" Anne groaned, reaching for her jacket.

Grace's face fell as the car drove away. "It wasn't him."

"Good." Anne let out a breath she didn't know she was holding. Glancing down at her silenced phone, she noticed a new text message. From her uncle. *When did he learn how to text?*

"Results back. Michele's DNA. Talk later."

Anne leaned back in the chair. While the news wasn't surprising, it signaled a solid tightening of the case. They already knew Michele had been at the murder site because of her confession to Claire, but this proved it. What it didn't prove was if she'd deliberately murdered Danny. Or if she had been alone when he died. And the broader legal issues about Michele's culpability left Anne with more questions than answers. Monday's meeting with Kessler, the assistant DA, might answer a few.

"Can I call you sometime?" Grace asked.

Anne looked up, distracted. "Huh?" She tried to focus on the anxious young woman in front of her. Shaking her head, she finally said, "There isn't anything more to talk about. Other than swapping stories—"

CHAPTER TWENTY-NINE

"Yes, I'd love to hear—" Grace cut in, her face lighting up.

"No, I was kidding," Anne said quickly. She didn't intend to be harsh, but neither did she intend to have anything more to do with this drama. Gary was *her* problem now. "I've told you everything I know about what you can expect from Gary. And I know you won't follow my advice, anyway—I wouldn't have listened to anyone when I first started dating him. But I do wish someone had told me *then* what I just told you tonight. What I really hope for you is that when it gets rough, you'll remember what I said: that it's not you—you're not the one at fault here—it's him. And then maybe you'll cut yourself some slack."

When had this clarity of hers taken root? Maybe her years of weekly therapy sessions had finally cemented new insights and self-acceptance. Now they felt bone-deep and sure. She might even follow her own advice someday, she thought ruefully.

They were interrupted by the sound of Krista's husband bellowing down the corridor. "You can all come back in now!" A passing nurse threw him a sharp look, but Mike just shrugged and beamed back at her.

Anne and Grace gathered their purses and stood facing each other.

"One more thing, Grace," Anne said, slipping on her jacket. "Do me a favor: don't mention my name to Gary."

"No, of course not," she said. "Thanks for talking to me. I know you don't approve, but he wants me back, and I'll probably...well, I have to go where love takes me."

Anne held back a laugh. The girl was a walking romance novel. They said goodnight and parted ways: Grace, heading back to Krista's hospital room, and Anne, to the parking lot.

Anne turned and looked toward Krista's room and promised herself she would visit the new family in the morning. She slipped out through the automated double doors into the cool evening air and felt unexpectedly liberated.

Chapter Thirty

Monday, November 18

Anne looked up from her seat in the reception area of the district attorney's office to see Dean Diaz casually strolling in. Instead of his usual button-down oxford shirt and tie, he was wearing a bright Hawaiian shirt, freshly pressed by his wife, who was probably under the impression that he was attending a Rotary Club meeting this morning. He radiated a new spirit of aloha and greeted Jack and Anne with his pinky and thumb extended in the hang-loose hand gesture.

"You look refreshed," Jack said, wiggling a hang-loose sign back at him.

"Mahalo. What you're looking at," Dean said, "is what a week of enforced rest and watching reruns of *Hawaii Five-0* and *Seinfeld* will do for you. Janie even sent me to a massage therapist."

"That's one understanding wife you've got there," Jack said with a mischievous glint.

"It wasn't like one of those parlors we used to raid," Dean replied with a snort.

While they continued in this vein, Anne hunched over her notebook, jotting down notes about the news they'd received last week: The hair follicles found at the scene of the crime came from Michele Murray's head. Definitively.

Joe Kessler's secretary came breezing into the reception area.

"Okay, you intrepid investigators, you're on," she said. "Follow me." She led them down the hallway, stopping midway and pointing to the second office on the right.

"You know, we've been to Joe's office many times. We could have found it by ourselves," Jack said.

"I need the exercise. Besides, I don't want you wandering the halls unescorted."

By the time they stepped inside Kessler's office, their bantering mood had dried up. No one, Anne could tell, was looking forward to this meeting, probably least of all Kessler, the assistant district attorney who was on the phone with his back to his three visitors. Hearing them enter, he swiveled in his chair to face them, holding up one finger.

"Right," he said into the phone. "Right. Got it. Okay, Nicole."

Dean pulled a chair out from along the wall and moved it next to the two chairs facing Kessler's desk. The three sat in silence, closely watching Kessler's face as he talked to his boss, Nicole Collins, Sonoma County's no-nonsense district attorney. His brow was furrowed, but his expression remained impassive.

"Nope, that should do it," Kessler said into the phone, sounding resigned. "Later. Thanks."

He put the receiver down and sighed, signaling that he had just heard the inevitable. He put his elbows on the desk, his fingers forming a tent below his chin. The detectives waited in silence.

"Okay, the word has come down from on high, and it's exactly what we expected," Kessler said. "Nicole won't prosecute—regardless of the fact that the new DNA evidence from the cigarette butt and Kleenex are matches with the crime evidence. Regardless of all the anecdotal evidence, Michele Murray's background, the Pinn photos that show motive. Hell, even with all the evidence in the world—" Kessler stopped mid-sentence, removed his glasses, and rubbed his eyes.

"But you can bring Michele Murray in for questioning if you want," Kessler finally said as if throwing them a bone.

"But that would just be spinning our wheels, right?" Jack asked.

"If your goal is to bring Michele Murray to trial, then yes, it's a waste of time. Because that won't happen. No DA in the state will file this and take it to trial—and we all know it. Or at least no DA that I know, would. But if your goal is to wrap up the case with a bow, then carry on."

Anne leaned forward and asked, "But let's say we brought her in and got a formal confession from her, wouldn't that change things?"

"It's a moot point as far as prosecution goes," Kessler said. "Don't get me wrong, in my opinion, this case is already solved. In all likelihood, Michele Dixon Murray murdered Danny Murray. And there's no evidence to show that anyone else was involved—despite her vague pot-shots at the Murray daughter, Noreen. But like I said, even with all that evidence—and even with a signed confession—this is not a crime that any reasonable district attorney would want to take in front of a jury."

"Why?"

"Two main reasons," Kessler said, picking up a pencil and tapping it on the table. "First of all, if Michele had been older at the time of the murder, it might be a very different story. But at ten years old, she was just too young—in a legal sense. At that age, she didn't have a 'guilty mind' because she couldn't grasp the moral enormity of the crime. She had a child's undeveloped sense of the world and didn't have the ability to form criminal intent. So we can't prove intent to murder. And since we can't prove intent, we can't prosecute.

"However, having said all that," Kessler continued, "there is a gray area here: let's say she gave you a signed confession admitting that she *did* intend to kill—"

"Not likely, but go ahead," Jack said, nodding.

"In that case, it's possible that an aggressive district attorney might want to pursue it and try to get some kind of manslaughter charge on her. But even with an aggressive DA, that's a very unlikely scenario because of the *second* reason: every prosecutor is taught the ethical standard of prosecution—and that is, to only prosecute a case they believe has a reasonable chance of getting twelve jurors to vote guilty on," Kessler said. "As prosecutors, our job isn't to win, it's to ensure justice—not just for the victim but also for the suspect. There's a saying in DA circles: A prosecutor can strike hard blows, but not foul blows."

These words might have sounded hollow coming from a prosecutor with a lesser reputation, but Kessler was known for his professionalism and earnest integrity. His three visitors just nodded in agreement.

"Bottom line," Dean said, "a jury isn't going to like this case—she was just a kid."

"And there's not enough societal pressure to go forward," Kessler said.

"Not nearly thirty years after the fact. And not to convict a practically middle-aged woman with no subsequent criminal offenses," Jack said, leaning back in his seat.

"So if Michele is never going anywhere near a courthouse, then why did you even suggest that we bring her in for questioning?" Anne asked with an edge of irritation in her voice. "What would be the point of doing that? In fact, what was the point of all this investigation we've been doing if the DA knew all along that nothing would come of it?"

"The point is, this case needed to be solved," Dean said.

"The police and DA wanted to know if she committed the murder. We want the evidence and the information to be in the file," Kessler said.

"Because if she murdered once, she could murder again," Jack said.

"Exactly, and *that's* the point," Kessler said. "No murder case is closed unless there's a conviction, but this case is about as closed as it will ever be."

Kessler stood up, indicating that the meeting was over. "You can let the case go—unless like I said, you want to tie it up even tighter. Get a confession." He shrugged. "Your choice."

He walked to the door and held it open for them. "Michele Murray is considered 'a person of interest' and that's all she'll ever be. No matter what happens, or what we do, she'll be able to go home to her ten cats or whatever, no worse for wear."

"Home free, is that it?" Anne asked, though she had a feeling Michele would never be home free.

Jack stopped in the middle of the doorway, blocking everyone while he stood there, thinking. When he finally stepped on through the doorway, he said, "Maybe it's the old cop in me, but I don't like the idea of Michele knowing that the case is stalled and she's off the hook. I don't want her getting comfortable. I want her to keep looking over her shoulder, to keep waiting for the knock on the door, wondering when we're coming for her."

Dean nodded. "Yeah. I don't like anyone thinking they got away with murder."

"Same here," said Kessler. He shook hands with his visitors and waved them off as they walked down the hallway.

The trio rode the elevator to the first floor in silence. Anne's thoughts went to Claire, wondering how much to tell her about this sudden resolution. Shouldn't Claire, at the very least, be informed about the DNA evidence and know without any doubts—at long last—who killed her son? And shouldn't she also know why the case was coming to a full stop—about the legal restrictions that protect Michele from prosecution? Claire surely deserved that.

Anne turned to Jack and Dean as they exited the elevator. "About Claire—"

"I know," Jack said. "I was just thinking of her. Maybe it would be best if the news came from you. Go ahead and tell her the DNA results. And that Michele won't ever be charged, but ask her to keep that part confidential. I don't want that particular news getting to anyone who would tell Michele."

"Like Peter," Dean said.

Anne said after a moment, "I wonder if Claire will consider this any kind of justice."

"You never know," Jack said, "maybe she'll think of it as closure."

"She hates that word," Anne said.

* * *

Claire sat propped up in bed by down pillows, her gaze never wavering from Anne's face. After listening silently while Anne told her about the meeting with Kessler, Claire stared off into the middle distance.

"So that's it. No one can touch her," Claire said finally, looking back at Anne.

"Yes, that *is* pretty much it. But the DA's office doesn't want Michele to know that she's off the hook—"

"Why?"

"It's a matter of—" Anne stopped mid-sentence, hesitating. The unvarnished truth usually worked best with Claire, so she finally blurted out, "They don't want Michele to think she got away with murder."

Claire nodded. "As good a reason as any," she said.

"And another thing, Claire: they've requested that you don't tell your children, especially Peter. He might pass it along to Michele."

"Okay, I won't tell Peter. That makes sense—he would just run to Michele with the news that she's getting off. But I think my other children deserve to know why she won't be prosecuted. And I'll ask them to keep it from Peter."

"And you think they will?"

"It's their favorite thing to do: keep things from Peter." Claire gave a rueful smile.

Anne managed to smile back. The Claire in front of her scarcely resembled the woman she had met just seven brief weeks before, and the last two weeks, in particular, had brought a sharp decline in her health. Her eyes were still luminous but were at half-mast, sunken in her pale face. Her breathing was audible.

Before she'd entered the bedroom, Sala informed her that Claire was now on morphine. Luckily, it was working for the pain but made it hard for Claire to concentrate and caused her to sleep on and off all day. Claire had not left her suite, even to meet Betty in the piano lounge, since the day before the visit from Michele. That visit had taken its toll.

"I'm sorry your family won't have justice," Anne said, holding onto Claire's hands with both of hers. She felt the slight warmth of her delicate skin.

"Whatever *that* is," Claire said. "Sometimes, I think justice is just another word for revenge. And I don't want revenge. I'm beyond that now. I just want her to leave my family in peace."

Chapter Thirty-One

Sunday, November 24

Tony Murray lived alone in a top-floor condo in the city's posh hilltop Russian Hill neighborhood. His mid-century condominium was not large, just a two-bedroom, but in San Francisco, that hardly mattered. Square footage was always trumped by a swanky location and bay views, and his condo had both.

Anne stood in front of the eight-foot-tall, north-facing window, took a sip of latte, and watched as Tony pressed the remote that controlled the solar window panels. The black shades rose slowly, revealing a glittering sheet of water that spanned from Alcatraz Island to Angel Island to the Golden Gate Bridge, and then beyond to the Pacific Ocean. The standing telescope was trained on the lone sailboat out in the bay, bobbing along on gentle waves, slowly going nowhere on this windless, cloudless Sunday morning.

"Must be wonderful waking up to this every morning," she said, realizing there was no point in bringing up the blackmail payoff since the case was already solved—and he'd just deny it anyway. Small talk was all she had left.

Tony shrugged. "Sometimes, I take it for granted. Make yourself comfortable while I check on the food," he said, heading to the kitchen. "The Cunninghams will be here soon." The Cunninghams were Louise and Julian, a married couple in their mid-fifties, cofounders of the international real estate development company The Lans Group, and his bosses. They were the reason Anne was wearing her 'interview blacks' as she called them—black jacket, slacks, a tucked-in cashmere sweater, and a printed silk scarf for color. An outfit as safe as they come. Her laptop was tucked inside her leather bag in case the Cunninghams wanted to talk business.

Left alone, Anne turned her back to the window and studied his living room, taking in every tasteful, expensive, subtle design detail: the chevron-patterned gray rug, sleek rosewood entry table, linen-covered modular sofa, and the distressed Russian oak coffee table that held a row of remotes—one for the solar panels, one for the gas fireplace, and a universal remote for the television. Furnished like an expensive hotel room in neutral tones of creams, grays, and charcoal, the effect was clean and modern. Understated. Nothing extraneous cluttered the surfaces.

Enticing aromas drifted in from the kitchen where the brunch food, delivered by a Zagat-rated restaurant, was keeping warm in chafing dishes set on the honed granite kitchen countertop. The white wines and champagne and juice for mimosas were being chilled; coffee was just a button-push away from brewing. And in the dining room, a round glass table was set with silverware and china plates for four. Tony had it all under control.

Her gaze went to a stray paperback lying on top of the other books on the bookshelf. Stepping back into the living room, Tony spotted the object of Anne's attention and shook his head. He picked up the paperback, brought it to the hall closet, and tossed it onto the pile on the floor. "It's my wife Deborah's. She just moved out."

"Oh," Anne said, pretending not to know that Tony's third wife had left a few weeks ago after a two-year marriage. This had been confided to her by Claire during one of their long afternoons spent sorting items, talking about men and life. Tony's latest wife had left without much drama, according to Claire, leaving behind little imprint on the decor or the way the household ran (*Typical*, she said). Since Tony's marriages and relationships only lasted one to two years on average, his sisters called him a textbook romance junkie—in it only for that heady, first chemical signaling in the brain that is nature's way of ensuring the species. Even Claire had urged him to break through the two-year romantic barrier (*At least once, just for the experience*), but he never could. It's not that he was intentionally unkind when his romances were over, Claire told Anne, just bored and dismissive. So many women had come and gone through the years that the family never even bothered to learn their last names. Which was embarrassing for him when he brought a girlfriend to a family gathering, but he understood.

"He knows this about himself," Claire had said, "which is why he's leery about letting women, even his wives, settle in with their artwork or mementos, much less their furniture. It's his home, his friends, his money." Claire sighed. "And no amount of counsel from me is likely to change that."

The doorbell rang, and Tony headed to the door.

"Come in, glad you could make it," Tony said, greeting his guests.

"It's about time we saw your condo." Louise Cunningham gave him a kiss on the cheek. Wearing a ruffled white silk blouse, black slacks, and a multi-color embroidered coat, she swept in with her husband Julian trailing behind her.

"This is a beautiful place you have here, Tony," she said, then added with a laugh, "Someone must be paying you very well." Tony laughed and took Louise's coat and draped it over the couch. He motioned for Anne to come closer. "I'd like you to meet Anne McCormack."

"So you're the young lady Tony's so eager for us to meet." Louise beamed.

"And you must be the Cunninghams," Anne said, shaking their hands.

"What can I get everyone to drink?" Tony took their orders and then headed into the kitchen to fix the drinks. Julian melted into the sofa and smiled pleasantly, obviously content to let his wife do the heavy social lifting. He had a handsome, squarish face with shrewd brown eyes and wore a custom-made gray suit that telegraphed a healthy balance sheet.

Louise moved to the window and beckoned Anne to join her. "Have you ever seen anything like this?" she said, indicating the staggering bay views. They stood in front of the window together for several minutes, pointing out watery landmarks and trading observations about how the city had changed (*Where's the culture, the fashion, the street cleaners?*" Louise vented), while Tony passed out drinks and Julian sank deeper into the sofa with a bourbon on the rocks in hand.

Minutes later, Tony announced that brunch was served. "By which I mean, help yourselves." They stepped into the kitchen, where the buffet was laid out and filled their plates with bagels, fruits, and omelets, and then settled around the table.

The conversation was easy and companionable, but mostly about people Anne didn't know. Between bites of melon, she looked around the apartment again. Her gaze sought out, as it usually did, personal photos. Tony's were lined up in identical silver frames on a bookcase shelf. Tony was in every one of them. Only two photos showed him with another person—one was of Tony and his mother Claire; the other was of him as a small boy with his father. In the rest, Tony was alone—sailing, playing tennis, giving a speech, wearing a tuxedo, graduating from college; there was a slick corporate headshot probably taken for an annual business report. She found it odd.

Anne's attention was drawn back to the table when Tony leaned in toward her.

"Anne, tell Louise and Julian a little about your company. Anne has done a great job for our family, as I've mentioned," he said, leaning back.

Anne set down her fork, turned toward the Cunninghams, and gave them her practiced two-minute spiel about her business—just long enough to trigger questions if they were interested, but not so long that it would bore them if they weren't.

Louise was interested. Something about Anne's brief pitch, combined with Tony's recommendation, had clearly put Anne in the reliable category and gave Louise confidence in Anne's ability to handle the family's estate. Louise began describing the personal property as "belonging to my recently deceased mother—"

"Mrs. James, the war bride," contributed Julian.

Louise looked at her husband fondly but rolled her eyes. "He loves the sound of that: Mrs. James, the war bride. But it's true, of course. She was a beautiful young English Rose when she met my father on the streets of London near the end of World War II. She came to California with him and proceeded to buy up the finest silver tea services in the city, among other things, of course—all between raising three of us kids."

"Mrs. James, the war bride, never saw a tea service she didn't like," Julian said, nodding.

"Anyway, if you're interested in the estate assignment," Louise said, "we can meet at the house and talk about it some more."

Anne was interested. And so they spent the next few minutes exchanging information and discussing possible meeting times. A phone rang in the bedroom, and Tony excused himself to take the call.

While he was out of hearing distance, Louise leaned in toward Anne and said conspiratorially, "Julian and I think the world of Tony. He's the whole package—brains, looks, savvy. We just wish he'd settle down."

"Oh, well, not all of us are cut out—" Anne left the sentence unfinished.

"He's spoken so highly of you that I wouldn't be surprised if he was interested in you personally, Anne."

If he was, Anne had seen zero signs of it. "Really?" she said vaguely as Tony reentered the room. He looked past them and headed into the kitchen. Came back with a bottle of Veuve Clicquot champagne and opened the cork's wire cage with six quick twists of the wrist. "Anyone care to join me in celebrating?" he asked.

"Celebrating?" Julian asked.

"Old friends, new friends, a beautiful Sunday afternoon, family, whatever," Tony said, filling the fluted champagne glasses. He raised his glass. "To whatever."

* * *

Sixty miles north in Santa Rosa, Michele Murray was taking an early afternoon walk along a dusty side trail at Spring Lake Park. It was called the "Jack London Trail" because of its semblance to the back-country trails winding around the Jack London State Historic Park in Glen Ellen.

But this trail was back-country in spirit only. It was close to civilization, looping through the upper woods behind the lake for a quarter-mile before emptying out onto the asphalt walkways that led to the busy concession stands. Michele sometimes came here on her days off. It was solitary and peaceful, lined with black oaks and bigleaf maples, and it had a rickety wooden bench located mid-point along the trail where she could sit and think. She reached the bench and sat down, plopping her backpack next to her.

Digging out her phone, she wrote a text: "I need to talk to you."

A few minutes passed before her therapist in Texas responded.

"You mean a Skype phone session? You're still in Santa Rosa?"

"Yes. Can we do it today?"

"It's Sunday. Is this an emergency?"

Michele paused, thinking, *To me, it is.*

"I can't take this pain anymore," Michele texted.

"Not today. How about tomorrow morning at ten o'clock?"

Michele chewed her bottom lip and frowned. She looked up from her phone, catching movement coming from a few yards up the trail to her right. She noticed a tall, scruffy young man as he came out from the underbrush that lined the trail. He stepped out onto the pathway and was walking toward her. She looked back down at her phone, unconcerned about the intrusion; she figured he was a homeless man who camped out in the woods and wanted his privacy as much as she wanted hers.

"Okay, I'll Skype you then," Michele keyed in.

He sat down on the bench, so close that his hip touched her backpack, and draped his arm casually along the top. She glanced over, annoyed. She dropped her backpack onto the ground and edged herself as far away from him as she could get. She hit the send button.

Someone else stepped out from the bushes behind her. "Done?"

"What?" Michele looked up, startled.

"Done texting?"

She started to jump up, bent on flight, when a pair of heavy hands on her shoulders pushed her down hard.

"Have a seat, Michele."

No one was around to hear her scream. And even if they were, they might not have paid attention because her mouth was quickly taped shut after that one brief scream. In mere minutes, she was efficiently hustled through the back trees and out of the park.

An elderly couple walked along the trail five minutes later and saw nothing amiss. No signs of a struggle. They sat down on the bench, opened their brown paper bags, and ate a late lunch.

III

PART THREE

Chapter Thirty-Two

Monday, November 25

The staircase was narrow and dark, its grimy beige walls streaked with random black smudge marks. The squeak of its loose wooden steps would alert anyone in the apartment building that someone was either coming or going.

The two police officers ascended the stairs single-file behind the slow-moving landlady who was grabbing the sticky hand railing for support each step of the way and chattering non-stop. She appeared to be in her late-fifties, and by the looks of the three-inch gray roots in her otherwise coal-black hair, she had stopped caring about her appearance about six months before.

"Gotta fix these stairs one of these days. But just try and find a handyman worth a good God damn. Good luck with that. Mostly they just wave around a hammer while they're casing the place. Why is it you want to get into her room again?"

"We got a request to make a welfare check," said the first officer.

"I'm pretty sure she's not home. I haven't heard a peep out of her today. Last saw her yesterday morning, I think. Sunday. Are you looking for drugs? She always seemed depressed, so I wouldn't be surprised if she was on some meds, though I wouldn't take her for a street—" she let the sentence hang while she caught her breath from the exertion of climbing the stairs.

Stepping onto the landing of the second floor, the officers noticed the hallway smelled of cigarettes, sweat, and boiled cauliflower. Not as bad as some they had smelled. They followed the landlady to the end of the corridor.

Taking out the master keys from her pocket, she knocked on the door of apartment 24.

"Michele?" she inquired. No response.

The landlady sighed impatiently. "I have nine tenants here. Not a damn one of them is friendly. I usually have to knock on their doors about ten times before they'll even answer," she complained as she knocked again, then chuckled to herself. "Ever see that TV show, *The Big Bang Theory*, where that guy Sheldon knocks on his neighbor's door over and over...."

"Ma'am? Unlock the door, please," insisted the second officer.

She gave the door one last courtesy knock, inserted the key, and pushed it open. "Do your business," she said to the officers, stepping aside.

* * *

"Got a call from a sergeant—remember Jim Sloan? He just got back to the station from a visit to Michele Murray's apartment. She wasn't there." Jack leaned back in his cracked leather recliner with the footrest up, his phone to his ear.

It was late Monday afternoon, Jack's first day off the Murray cold case, and he was shooting the breeze with Dean Diaz. Filling him in on the latest news.

"What was Sloan doing at her apartment? And why do we care?" Dean asked.

"Welfare check. They got a call around eleven this morning from Michele's therapist, a woman named Jane Wilcox. It seems Michele missed their therapy session this morning. It was a phone session because the therapist is located in Texas," Jack said.

"And why is missing a therapy appointment such a big deal?"

"Ms. Wilcox wasn't very forthcoming about details. You know thera-pists—they're always worried about client confidentiality. But she did say she was worried because Michele was really insistent about talking to her as soon as possible. And Michele'd never missed an appointment before."

"Maybe she forgot—"

"Ms. Wilcox also said she had reason to believe that Michele was suicidal. Yesterday she got a text from her that sounded pretty desperate. She can't believe Michele would miss this appointment because it seemed so important to her. Something drastic must have kept her from it. That's the therapist's opinion, anyway."

"Huh." Dean seemed to consider the suicide angle for a second. "But why tell us? Not that I don't appreciate being kept in the loop, but the Murray case is on ice again. And for all we know, Michele could be off on a weeklong Caribbean cruise with Peter Murray."

"And then they got a second call. From Peter."

"Don't tell me: he called the cops because his girlfriend didn't pick up the phone?"

"Close. Peter reported that she's been acting depressed for the past week. She hasn't returned his texts or calls since yesterday around noon. So this afternoon, he stopped by her job at the beauty salon. No one had seen her since the previous Friday. The cops wouldn't have paid any attention to him, except that the therapist had already sounded the alarm," Jack said.

"Okay, so what do they want us to do? Look for her?"

Jack sighed. Something about this whole thing felt wrong. He rubbed his day-old beard. "No," he said after a moment. "Let's just sit tight. She'll show up."

* * *

Brenda Moran, the Murrays' real estate agent, was stumped. This was something new to her, this rare confusion, these seeds of doubt about her real estate instincts.

By every real estate maxim she held dear, the Murray cottage should have sold during the Open House she'd held two Sundays before. Hundreds of people had trooped through the house. Of course, many were just curious neighbors—but still, with such a large showing, Brenda expected to entertain multiple purchase offers by the end of the week. She would have bet her real estate license on it. In fact, she had been so confident she canceled the second Open House.

She was still waiting for those offers. A young newlywed couple, who were probably shopping beyond their price range, were the only ones who called for a private follow-up tour. Brenda told herself it was still early in the game. The house had only been on the market for ten days. Besides, it had everything going for it: a great location, hillside views, and a charming layout. So what was the hold-up? The sluggish November market? Did she price it too high? Was there a lingering odor from the slimy garbage she found in the living room three weeks before? *No, that's ridiculous.*

Brenda pulled her Audi into the driveway of the cottage, shut off the motor, and checked her watch. She was almost an hour early for her appointment with the newlyweds. She always liked to arrive ahead of time to air out the house and replace any faded flowers with a fresh arrangement.

Stepping onto the front porch, she punched the security code into the lock box and removed the house key. She swung open the front door, and before she got two steps inside, was met with a blast of a powerful odor—so vile she couldn't back away from it fast enough. She slammed the front door shut. Outside in the fresh air again, she leaned over with her hands on her knees, willing herself not to vomit on the grass but not succeeding. After wiping her mouth with a tissue, she took a deep breath and straightened up.

Just like last time, she thought. That rank and pungent smell. Only this time, many times worse. This was unholy. Like a stew of rotting eggs, spoiled meat left to ferment in the hot sun, and raw sewage. All douched with cheap perfume.

She knew she had to go back inside and find out what was in there. She considered calling her husband—*where was he when she needed him?*—but decided to forge ahead alone. Get it over with. She grabbed another tissue from her purse and held it over her nose.

She opened the front door and followed the smell. It led her through the hallway and into the living room, where the gas fireplace was burning. The room was empty and uncomfortably hot, and the only sound was the low buzzing of flies.

The heavy air was unbreathable, causing her to move quickly as she turned the corner from the living room into the dining room, batting away stray flies as she went. The dining table was pushed back against the wall. A lone dining room chair was lying haphazardly on its side on the floor. A backpack and rolled-up sweater were on the table.

But those were just peripheral sights, and it was only later that she remembered having seen them at all.

What she saw was a woman hanging by her neck from a thick rope attached to the ceiling fan.

Brenda's knees buckled, dropping her heavily to the floor. She was not sure how long she lay there before she came to and found the strength to struggle to her feet and make it out of the house. She slammed the door shut behind her, staggered to her vehicle, and pulled out her phone. Her hands trembled as she punched in 911.

Staring blankly out the windshield of her car, her thoughts out of focus, she sat motionless for what felt like forever until a patrol car finally arrived. The officers entered the house, came out, and radioed for assistance. Within a few more minutes, patrol cars pulled up, and soon after that, the house was cordoned off with yellow police tape. The grounds were swarming with cops.

An officer tapped on her window.

"We'd like you to remain here until we can ask you a few more questions," he said. And so she sat and waited, her hands shaking and her mind racing with disjointed thoughts. Trying to make sense of this horrific scene.

Whoever this dead woman was, Brenda reasoned, she probably had access to a house key. Maybe a former housekeeper? Perhaps a dog sitter or a friend of the Murrays? Could the dead woman be the same trespasser who had defiled the house weeks before? Two break-ins in three weeks seemed like too much of a coincidence.

She wished to God that she had changed the locks right after that fiasco. But sitting there, turning it over in her mind a bit more, she began to reject the idea that any of this was her fault. Maybe the woman had *not* used a key to get in. She could have broken a window or picked the locks—although Brenda saw no signs of broken windows or forced entry. She sighed and decided to leave it to the cops to figure out.

She looked out the side window and saw an ambulance pull up and park in front of the house. The coroner had arrived. Three paramedics rolled a collapsible gurney inside.

An officer came to her window and asked a few more questions about what she had seen (*No, I didn't see anyone else around*) and if she knew the victim (*No, absolutely not*). Brenda asked the officer if she should contact the Murrays (*After all, it happened in their house*), and he told her not to bother since the police department would be in touch with them. Then he said she was free to leave.

This is not going to help sell this house, Brenda found herself thinking. The thought startled her, even dismayed her a bit, especially considering the enormity of the events playing out in front of her. A woman was dead, and she was thinking about real estate values. And keys. Sometimes she wondered about herself.

As she started her engine, she suddenly remembered her appointment—the young couple was on their way over. Another hard call to make. She cut off the engine, punched in their number, and told them they would have to reschedule the appointment.

"Sorry, but now is not a good time," she said.

She glanced back at the house just as three men rolled the body out on a black gurney.

Chapter Thirty-Three

I t was the day before Thanksgiving, and had this been any other year, the early morning hours would have found Anne in the hills of Trione-Annadel State Park taking a bracing three-hour hike in the autumn air. It was her annual tradition, a preemptive strike against the gluttony that was sure to follow the next day at her aunt and uncle's house.

But not this year; she was too busy brandishing a knife. She'd made a rash promise, motivated by pride and a dare, to her Aunt Dot: she would bring a pumpkin pie, made entirely from scratch, to the family's Thanksgiving dinner.

Chef's knife in hand, she took a stab at the pumpkin, cutting out a circle at the top as if carving it for Halloween. She gutted the cavity, reached in and grabbed handfuls of stringy wet seeds, and plopped them onto the newspaper that covered the countertop.

Stray hairs fell over her eyes, obstructing her view of the recipe video playing on her propped-up iPad. She blew the hairs away just in time to see the plump farm wife, star of the video, throwing together some spices, molasses, liquids, and baked pumpkin into a food processor—*what food processor?*—and then pouring the lumpy filling into a pre-baked, from-scratch pie shell. *This will take all damn day.*

She decided she needed a break, so she set the knife down and wrote a text to Krista: "Making pumpkin pie from scratch. Have you ever? This is

253

some crazy shit."

No immediate response, so she went back to the pie. She arranged the cut-up pumpkin pieces on a cookie sheet and slid it into the oven. Then she crumbled up the soaked newspaper, tossed it in the trash can, and wiped down the countertop.

Time for another break. Seeing yesterday's soggy *Press Democrat* reminded her to check out this morning's edition. It had been two days since Michele Murray's body was found, and since the newspaper hadn't covered the story in yesterday's edition, it would likely be in today's. She brought the folded newspaper in from the porch step and carried it, along with a mug of coffee, to the dining room table. Flipping through the pages, she found the story at the bottom of page five.

Apparent Suicide Related to Murder Case

SANTA ROSA— Santa Rosa police said a woman found dead from hanging in a vacant house on Monday has been identified as Michele Dixon Murray.

Ms. Murray, 39, was considered a person of interest in the unsolved 1990 murder of five-year-old Daniel Murray, according to the district attorney's office.

Preliminary autopsy results show she died from asphyxia due to hanging. The time of death is estimated to be between Sunday at ten a.m., when she was last seen alive by her landlady, and four p.m.

Responding officers found no signs of struggle or foul play. "There is no evidence this was anything other than a suicide, but a final determination won't be made until the toxicological analysis is released," said a police representative. No suicide note was found, but anonymous sources said Ms. Murray had recently sent texts that indicated she suffered from depression and anxiety.

Claire Murray, mother of Daniel Murray and owner of the house in which Ms. Murray was found, declined to comment.

The investigation into the death of Daniel Murray is ongoing.

That Claire would decline to comment was no surprise to Anne. Claire was in no shape or mood to talk to any reporter—if, in fact, Claire even knew that a reporter had called for a comment. Her daughters and Sala were acting as gatekeepers. They kept away anyone who would upset Claire any more than she already was: the news of Michele's death had disturbed her deeply.

Anne was the one who had delivered the news. She'd driven to The Parisian hotel on the morning after Michele's body was found, anxious to give Claire a heads-up before the police could arrive with questions. Anne had worried that the sight of police officers arriving unexpectedly at Claire's doorstep would be a traumatic reminder of the day Danny died.

When Claire heard the news about Michele, she closed her eyes briefly and made the sign of the cross. "May God forgive her," she said quietly.

The ping of an incoming text drew Anne's attention back to the present.

"Look at you, a real mountain momma," Krista texted. "Sure, I've made it from scratch. Just roll out the Pillsbury pie dough, open a can of pumpkin filling, dump it in, and ta-da."

Anne smiled, then turned back to the newspaper article and read it over again.

So this is the official version they were sending out into the world. Suicide. A clean ending to the case, however sad.

There was no discussion, at least in the public realm, about the possibility of Michele's death being a homicide. In four to six weeks, the toxicological test results would be in, and those might tell the tale. If no drugs were found in Michele's system, then it could be safely assumed she acted alone in hanging herself. The same would be true if a moderate amount of drugs were detected—after all, she might have taken tranquilizers to give herself the courage to do the deed.

But if Michele had significant drugs in her system, enough to incapacitate her, it would point to homicide. But a sloppy homicide, not the work of a true professional. A professional would have walked the line: given Michele just enough drugs to make her compliant, but wouldn't have drugged her to the point that she couldn't have strung up the rope herself. Real pros made homicide-by-hanging a tough crime to prove.

Anne shook her head, telling herself that these were absurd thoughts and there was no reason to go off on wild and dramatic tangents.

It was simply a sad ending to a very sad life, and that was that.

* * *

Helped along by huge dollops of whipped cream, the pumpkin pie was surprisingly good. A little lumpy, but good. So Aunt Dot designated Anne as the family's official pie maker. The table of ten friends and relatives, knowing how much Anne hated baking, gave a loud cheer.

Carrying the last piece of pie in one hand and a snifter of brandy in the other, Jack motioned with his chin for Anne to follow him into his home office. Dot refused to come into his office to clean, which is why dust and cobwebs had taken over. Anne made a beeline for the lumpy plaid sofa, like she always did, and would have curled up for a nap if Jack hadn't been so intent on talking shop.

"How's it feel to have the case wrapped up?" he asked, swirling his brandy.

"You think it's wrapped up?" she asked back.

"Why, what are you thinking?"

"Danny's murder case is solved, yes. But Michele's death by suicide? I'm not so sure," she said, sitting up. Something about the circumstances of the death, the timing, and the place where it happened bothered her.

"Looked like a suicide to me. There was no sign of a struggle. She let herself in with the key that Peter gave her. By all accounts, she was depressed. Seems like a slam dunk," Jack said.

"Did the neighbors see anyone entering the house?"

"Not that I know of," he said. "But officers did search her apartment for drugs and found some anxiety medication in her dresser drawer. So it looks like she was in possession of drugs. That means if those kinds of drugs were in her system, they were probably hers. Let's see what the toxicology test results tell us."

"Right, okay." She set her drink down on the dusty side table.

"Why are you going down this road? Who would have a motive to kill her?"

"She was blackmailing Noreen. We never found out what that was about. Maybe Noreen—"

Jack cut her off with a laugh. "That's a joke. What is she, five-foot-three? Or maybe you're thinking she hired someone to do the job? Professionals? Noreen isn't in that world. She works for a florist, for God's sake." He paused. "Who else have you got your sights on?"

"Maybe someone arranged it for her. To protect her."

"Like who?"

"Her husband? Tony? Peter?" Anne ventured. With her index finger, she idly wrote "who" in the fine layer of dust on the end table beside her.

"You're grasping at straws, honey. This is all just speculation, and could be dangerous speculation at that. Until the toxicology test results come in, we might as well relax." He polished off his brandy. "By the way, the police chief had nothing but good things to say about you and wants you to stay on."

She gave him a half-smile. "Good to know I still have police powers as I go after Michele's murderer."

Jack just shook his head.

"Michele's funeral is tomorrow. I might go," Anne said.

Jack lifted an eyebrow. "Why would you do that? You only actually talked to her once, and that was when you pulled a gun on her."

Anne was quiet for a half minute before saying, "I'm not sure, really. Guess I just hate the idea that the only people there will be the priest. And Peter, of course."

* * *

The morning sky was thick with gray clouds, threatening rain and hiding the sun. Closing her jacket against the chill, Anne made her way up to the top of the slight knoll where the graveside service had just begun. She took her place under the white canopy, sitting a few empty rows behind the other four mourners.

Peter was there. Anne also recognized Mrs. Lockwood, Michele's former foster mother. The other two mourners were young Asian women, probably Michele's co-workers from the beauty salon.

The priest gave a brief reading from the scriptures and blessed the casket, sprinkling it with holy water. He then asked if anyone would like to say a few words.

Peter stood up, facing the others. He was wearing a dark suit and tie and was clean-shaven. He looked mournfully at the tiny group. "Michele was the love of my life. The wife of my heart. That's why I'm paying for this service and the coffin and everything. I had to borrow money to do it, but I wanted to take care of her. I wanted to be that person, that man for her."

He broke down in sobs. One of the young women helped him back to his seat.

Mrs. Lockwood stood up next. "On every Mother's Day, I would get a card from Michele. She was the only one of my foster kids who ever remembered. She had a sweet side to her that I don't want anyone to forget. I'm not saying Michele was perfect. She was a lost and tormented soul, but she didn't deserve what she got in life. I don't know why they took that cheap shot at her in the newspaper, practically calling her a mur…" She shot an accusing look at Anne. "Well, I'm not going to repeat it here. Why couldn't they just let the poor girl rest in peace?"

As the casket was being lowered into the ground, the priest recited from Psalm 34:

The Lord is close to the brokenhearted;
and those who are crushed in spirit He saves

Chapter Thirty-Four

Thursday, December 5

J oanne sat alone in the living room of her mother's suite, the room the family referred to as the "waiting room." This was where they passed the time reading magazines, squabbling, and kibitzing while Claire was being tended to by Sala, hospice workers, doctors, and soon, Joanne hoped, a team from the right-to-die nonprofit, Compassion and Choices.

The spiral notebook on Joanne's lap was filled with one list after another of things she needed to do. She ignored it for now. She just wanted to sit quietly in the window seat for a few minutes, to slow down and feel the warmth of the afternoon sun on her face.

She heard Betty Fazio's bawdy laughter coming from the other side of her mother's bedroom wall and smiled. They were in there watching a movie together, *American Graffiti*, her mother's favorite from the 1970s. She called it "The best movie in the best movie decade," which Betty would sometimes dispute, countering with *The Godfather*, but you can't argue with love.

The two of them had been behind closed doors for hours. Joanne suspected that her mother slept through most of the visit, but whether she was asleep or awake, Betty was welcome company. Joanne had always admired Betty, her mother's loyal friend and partner-in-crime. Betty earned her honorary aunt status when she'd stepped in quietly after Danny died and became the family's emotional life support system. But Joanne never loved Betty more than now, on the days when she would breeze into Claire's suite for a visit and—just by being there—light up the room and charge it with energy and laughter, glamour, and drama. The moment Betty left, it was as though the very molecular energy of the air would deflate, leaving those left behind to wonder where the party had gone.

Joanne looked down at her notebook and pulled out some folded forms tucked inside. These were the final authorization forms needed for Compassion and Choices, a nonprofit that helps terminally ill, mentally competent patients to obtain end-of-life medication to peacefully end their suffering if it becomes unbearable. Claire had requested this, saying that she would probably never take the aid-in-dying medication, but wanted the comfort of knowing it was there.

She had asked Joanne not to tell Father Dunn, her friend and confessor. "I don't want to argue with him," Claire said. "I know what he'll say—that the Catholic Church cannot condone suicide. But how is this suicide? I'm not choosing to have this cancer; this is God's doing. I'm dying in God's time, just with a little assist."

Joanne sighed. These forms should have been completed weeks ago and may never be relevant. Her mother, now down to ninety-two pounds, was losing the battle faster than any of them had anticipated. Claire had been expected to join the family at Thanksgiving dinner at The Parisian restaurant but was too weak to venture from her bed. And without their matriarch, it was a grim affair, particularly when the realization hit them all: this would be the last Thanksgiving Day Claire would be alive to plead for better table manners and to smooth over their differences.

The movie's soundtrack reached her through the walls. "All Summer Long" by The Beach Boys was playing over the movie's closing credits, and that meant Betty would be coming out soon.

* * *

"Well, that was fun," Betty said to Claire as she turned off the television with the remote and then drew open the curtains. "But good as it is, I've always had a bone to pick with *American Graffiti*...."

Claire smiled. She had heard this rant before.

"...the epilogue tells the audience what every single *male* character ended up doing in life, but not a *single* word about even *one* of the girls! They could have at least shown something about the Laurie character or Debbie, for God's sake...."

Betty stopped short, seeming overcome by a sudden realization. Knowing Betty as she did, Claire could sense what was bothering her: Here they were chatting away as though this were just another lazy afternoon in the lives of two old friends. But it most assuredly was not. This would be one of their last days together. And no amount of pretending or acting normal could change the trajectory of the illness Claire was living through. Dying from.

Betty shook her head.

"No, go on...." Claire said. "I like to hear it."

"Okay, well, it's just that it was just such a boys' club back then," Betty said haltingly. "Women these days wouldn't put up with...." Then in a voice turned suddenly wistful, "Oh, Claire, don't you wish we'd been teenagers together?"

She sat down on the edge of Claire's bed. "We would have torn up this town, cruising up and down the strip in my daddy's red convertible," she added with a laugh.

"Or *my* daddy's rusty pickup." Claire managed a faint smile.

Betty smiled back and then looked at her watch. "Geez, it's four o'clock already, and I still have to stop and pick up some groceries. Butch likes his dinner at five o'clock these days, can you believe it?"

"You have the envelope, don't you?" Claire asked.

Betty patted her purse. "Got it."

"I licked the envelope, didn't I? Sometimes I forget things," Claire said.

"Well, of course, you did. But if you're worried that I'll open it, please don't be."

"No, it's not that...." Claire let her words trail off, then said, "And you'll remember what to do, won't you? If it's necessary."

"Of course, sweetie. I'll do everything exactly the way you asked me to."

Betty looked at her with a concerned expression that deepened the lines between her brows. Claire knew she looked more tired than usual, ragged even. Her last few nights had been especially rough. Ever since her birthday party—*Was that only a month ago?*—she had slowed down alarmingly.

Claire had one more request to make. She beckoned Betty to lean in closer, then nodded toward the armchair in the corner of the room. In a near whisper, she said, "Gerald won't stop talking about the party he's planning for me. He says everyone's coming. Danny, too."

Betty looked over at the chair, plush with green velvet upholstery. She waited for Claire to continue.

"Could you ask him to leave?" she asked Betty in a hushed tone. "He's been here for hours. I could barely hear the movie."

Betty got up and walked over to the chair, looked back at Claire, and then back at the chair. She stood in front of it and said firmly, "Gerry, honey, Claire needs some alone time."

Betty looked back at Claire to see if this had worked.

It had. The chair was empty. "Thank you," Claire whispered. With that, she closed her eyes, spent.

Betty kissed her lightly on the forehead. "Have a nice evening, Clarabelle," she said as she left the room. "I'll be back to visit tomorrow."

Chapter Thirty-Five

Saturday, December 7

It had been raining all that day and Chloe was sick of it. The day was overcast and depressing and she had a bad feeling about it, the whole entirety of it—from the breakfast that she ate alone in an empty house to the way that no one here in her grandmother's suite, not even her Aunt Joanne, was looking her in the eye. The knot in her stomach didn't help.

It occurred to her that everyone in the room thought they had a special relationship with Claire. They were, in Chloe's opinion, kidding themselves: hers was the special relationship. Of course, if she and her grandmother had been peers, they might have been more critical of each other; they might even have nitpicked about each other's clothes, jokes, or friends. But their sixty-one-year age difference was a buffer to any such pettiness, and they had been devoted allies since Chloe first smiled up at Claire from the bassinet. They adored each other.

No one knew this better than Noreen. When she would occasionally vent to Claire about her daughter's messy room or smart mouth, she would be met with silence.

"I know, Mom," Noreen would invariably say with a dramatic sigh, "you don't think Chloe has any faults."

"None that I can see," Claire would agree.

Chloe sat leaning forward, her arms folded over her knees, growing more frantic by the moment. She hadn't had a chance to say her goodbyes yet.

She glanced toward her grandmother's closed bedroom door and tried to telepathically hurry along the nurses so she could get in there.

Claire had stopped eating and drinking the day before, and although Chloe knew this was entirely her grandmother's decision, she had brought along two chocolate-covered macaroons to tempt her. Now, sitting there, she rethought her strategy. *What a stupid idea*, she scolded herself, *just stupid*. Hadn't the hospice nurse, who had seen countless people die and could pinpoint the timing better than most doctors, advised the family that it was time to gather? Claire's death was imminent, she told them. Today or tomorrow.

Chloe stuffed the bag of macaroons back into her backpack and looked up as the door opened. They were finally leaving.

* * *

Claire finally had a moment, one blessed moment, alone.

She had never felt so weak and tired in her life. It wasn't just her failing body, she knew, it was everything. She was weary of strangers bathing her, touching her private parts, turning her over, parceling out meds, adjusting the tubes that wound around the bed. She was tired of their constant chatter as they went about their business. Tired of being talked about as though she couldn't hear them.

Yet as much as the pain and discomfort, it was the indignity and tedium she could not bear any longer. She knew she should be grateful, and she was: no one could ask for better care than her children had arranged for her. She wanted to cherish these last moments with her family, but all she felt was exhaustion. She wanted desperately for it to be all over. "Sick and tired of being sick and tired," she recalled Gerald saying. Was that something he'd heard during one of his many attempts to stop drinking? She tried to bring back the memory, but her mind kept wandering, drifting off randomly, and besides, what difference did it make when she was so tired, and her eyelids were so heavy? She fell asleep.

The creaking sound of the bedroom door as it opened jarred her awake.

"Grandma?"

Claire tried to open her eyes, tried to listen to Chloe as she stood by the bedside, telling her that she was her favorite person in the world and how much she would miss her. But it was impossible. Her eyelids felt leaden, as if tiny fingers were pressing lightly down on them, and all the effort in the world couldn't pry them open again. And though she struggled to focus on what Chloe was saying, her own thoughts and visions and waves of euphoria were pulling her gently, seductively away.

* * *

Claire slipped into unconsciousness. For three hours, they gathered around her bed—her children, grandchildren, Father Dunn, and Betty—and watched the quilt rise and fall with her every breath. On the half-hour, Joanne would feel her wrist for a pulse, and they would fixate on the delicate lace edging at the wrists of her silk nightgown.

Chloe stood toward the back of the room, motionless, her arms wrapped tightly around Betty's waist, her head on the older woman's shoulder. A sudden thought gripped Chloe, reminding her that there was something she had to do. And it was a matter of great urgency. She untangled herself from Betty and walked purposefully to Claire's bathroom. A minute later, she came back carrying her grandmother's brown eyebrow pencil and a perfume bottle. She set them on the side table and leaned in close to Claire.

"Grandma," she said as she removed the glass stopper from the bottle, "you have to get ready for your party." She dabbed a bit of perfume on Claire's neck and then lightly drew in her eyebrows. Chloe stood back to look at her. "There, you're ready now, Grandma. You look beautiful."

Chloe took a place by the bed and spoke softly, rushing through all the important things she still needed to say: she would take good care of Louie. She would always love her. She would take her advice and always hold her head up high and act like a lady. And always tip generously. She would be kind to her mother.

After a few minutes passed, Joanne went to Chloe's side, touching her arm. "Honey, she can't hear you anymore."

∗ ∗ ∗

Three days later, Claire's obituary—which she never got around to writing, so her children did, together—appeared in the *Press Democrat*. It mentioned her memorable holiday parties, many club and charity board memberships, graduate studies in art history, her love of travel, Irish ballads, dancing, coconut macaroons (*Flour Power lost a loyal customer,* it read), and above all, family and friends. It thanked Sala and Jasmine, along with the hospice nurses, for their "loving care."

Chapter Thirty-Six

Friday, December 13

The following Friday, Father Dunn presided over the funeral mass at St. Paul's Church, just as Claire had wanted. The hymns, scriptures, altar flowers (*Spare me the tacky gladiolas*, she instructed), pallbearers, and the order of speakers had all been specified in her detailed instructions.

A crowd of nearly three hundred ventured out in the December cold to honor Claire, and the family was astonished and touched by the turnout. Given Claire's age and the private nature of her last years, they expected far fewer people to attend. The greeters ran out of programs.

Those attending included two former Santa Rosa mayors, judges, old friends, doctors, neighbors, her hairdresser and landscaper, her children's former classmates and teachers, her husband's ex-business partners, the curious, and a large contingent from The Parisian hotel staff, including Frank Greco, who donated the catering for the reception following the service. Anne sat in a back pew with her uncle and Dean.

Father Dunn officiated over the centuries-old Catholic funeral rites of prayers, two readings, the liturgy of the Eucharist, blessings, and sprinkling of the casket. His words about Claire were warm and personal, recalling the days, decades before, when Claire was a young wife and mother. He was followed by eulogies from Betty Fazio, who spoke of Claire's sorrows and joys, and by Claire's brother Willie, who broke down after only a few words.

Claire's four children then stood together at the podium, each sharing a single, favorite memory of their mother.

Claire's casket was accompanied out of the church by pallbearers while the strains of her beloved "What'll I Do?" filled the church.

* * *

Two funerals in less than three weeks had Anne in search of a drink. Like all good Irish-Catholic funeral receptions, this one provided an open bar. It was set up on a long, fold-out metal table near the back, where a professional bartender was taking orders from the crowd.

But it was Peter, standing alongside him behind the bar table, who was doing most of the pouring. Noreen was leaning against the table, sipping white wine, and advising her twin brother on the ingredients for the Manhattan he was making for one of the former mayors.

Noreen spotted Anne in the crowd and waved her over.

"All alone?" Noreen asked.

"My uncle and Dean had to leave."

"What'll you have?" Peter asked Anne.

She looked at the wine in Noreen's glass and sighed. "Sparkling water, thanks. How are you two holding up?" The twins simultaneously shrugged. "Not great," Peter said, handing Anne her drink.

Noreen took Anne by the elbow and led her to an empty round table facing a large, flat-screen television. It was playing the video made by Claire's grandchildren for her birthday on a continuous loop. The two sat in metal folding chairs, sipping their drinks, neither of them speaking. The silence grew more awkward by the minute, and Anne couldn't fathom why Noreen, who usually did everything in her power to avoid her, had sought her out.

Noreen's blue eyes were swollen from crying. She kept them fixed on the birthday video as she began talking. "I never did thank you for helping Mom. Also, I need to apologize for the way I treated you. I was a little stressed out by everything—Danny's case, then Mom's illness...it was all too much. But it's over now." She shifted uneasily in her chair.

"The family has been through hell," Anne said.

"Yeah, that's putting it mildly. But some good has come from it—not from Mom's death, I don't mean that. Believe me, her death's been really hard on everyone in the family." She pointed to the table where the four grandchildren were sitting with her sister Joanne. Chloe was crying on Joanne's shoulder, and the three boys were preternaturally quiet and well behaved. No goofy faces, no bickering, no food tossed across the table.

Noreen took another sip of wine. "No, what I meant was that something good came from the murder investigation, believe it or not. I finally looked at what I did as a child and have come to grips with it—and after all these years of hiding it, I now realize I'm not the monster I always thought I was. I was just a scared nine-year-old kid."

"What happened back then, exactly?"

"I finally told my husband. He was amazing about it. I thought he'd leave me, but all he said was, 'Is that all? I thought it would be worse.' I was so relieved. But I never want my kids to know. Promise me you won't tell them."

"Promise."

"They would never look at me the same way."

Noreen took a deep breath and released it slowly. "Anyway, on that day, Danny was with me and Peter and Michele after school. Then Danny took off in one direction, looking for Tony. Peter went in another direction, and that left just me and Michele. Before we started walking home, Michele said she wanted to get some money from the janitor first. I didn't know what the hell she was talking about, but I waited while she ran off. After a few minutes, I got mad, so I started walking home by myself. Next thing I knew, I heard a yell and turned around and saw Danny running out into the field toward that old adobe house, and she's tearing off after him. I just stood there. For five minutes or more. Finally, I went and crawled under the fence to see what was going on."

Noreen paused and closed her eyes. "It was quiet in the adobe when I looked in. Dark. But I could see Danny on the ground, not making a sound.

And Michele was standing over him. I knew he was dead, I just knew it. Don't ask me how. I screamed, and she ran over and hit me. Pushed me out of the door. We ran. That's all…that's all…."

"But you never told your parents or the police what you saw," Anne prompted.

"I was terrified. I didn't tell anyone ever, not even Peter."

"Because you were trying to protect Michele?"

"Oh, God no, that's not why. No, Michele scared me to death. I thought if she could do that to Danny, kill him like that, what could she do to me? She warned me to keep quiet. Said I was as guilty as her and that I would go to jail. I know better now, of course, but not then."

"You're saying that's all you did?" Anne asked. "That's all she had on you?" Noreen nodded.

"But you were just a witness. She's the one who committed the crime, and she was blackmailing *you*? It's so counterintuitive."

"So counter-what?"

"I mean, you were a witness to *her* crime. If she talked, it would have landed her in trouble. Why would she risk that?"

"She needed money, obviously. She told me unless I paid, she would say I was the murderer. Her word against mine. I know it doesn't make sense—not unless you knew her. Michele was reckless. She told me that even if no one believed her, they couldn't do anything about it. She felt safe. I didn't—and she knew that. She knew me."

"Michele was a wild card, so you paid up."

"She would have opened it all up," Noreen said. "Or at least I thought she would. I had too much to lose. She had *nothing* to lose."

They fell silent. Then after a moment, Noreen said, "On our way home, we stopped at the drugstore to buy popcorn like we always did. Michele was hungry."

"Hungry?"

"It sounds ghoulish now, but back then, it was kind of reassuring. As if nothing bad was really happening. Just another normal day."

"The flashlight near Danny's body—"

270

"Yeah, I vaguely remember owning one like that. Danny might have taken it from my room or something. Who knows?"

"Did you deliver that note to the janitor's shed a few days later? Your classmate said she saw you in there."

"The note they thought was a prank? I'm not sure, honestly. I never saw the note before the detectives showed it to me. If I delivered it, it must have been in a bag or something because I would have remembered it. Back then, when Michele told me to do something, I just did it. So maybe."

"Michele's death must have been a shock...."

"More like a relief. Maybe that sounds cold, but it's true." Noreen stared for a beat at the wine in her glass. "In one way or another, she's run my entire life. Now it's over. And now you know everything—everything I've felt guilty and ashamed about. I'm just glad Mom never knew any of this. At least I hope Michele didn't tell her. I couldn't bear that. And of course, my kids—they can *never* know."

Noreen held up her hand, flashing an heirloom diamond ring on her right index finger. In a quiet voice, she said, "Mom gave me her engagement ring."

Looking up at the video screen, a smile broke out on her face.

"Funny, I never noticed that before. See that?" Noreen asked Anne. She picked up the remote from the table, pointed it toward the screen, and paused on a still photo. There was Claire standing behind a small girl, obviously Noreen, her arms draped across her daughter's chest, hugging Noreen close. They were both laughing.

"Pretty soon, I'm gonna start saying 'Mom always liked me best.'" Noreen laughed outright. "That'll be a switch. Maybe I'll go over and say that to Joanne just to shake her up." Noreen stood up and smoothed out her skirt.

"See you later, Anne. Don't be a stranger." Noreen drifted off to greet a group of former classmates who were waving her over.

Anne sat alone for a moment, gazing at the milling crowd, lost in thought. Coming into this room an hour ago, she couldn't have imagined having a polite conversation with Noreen, much less this conversation—one that revealed Noreen's longest-held, most guarded secrets. Many questions were answered, including the one she had asked her uncle a few weeks before:

could Noreen have possibly killed Michele? No, she could not have. Anne felt sure of that.

Anne saw Tony standing near the bar across the room. He was deep in conversation with Sean Brutrain, her sullen tablemate at Claire's birthday party. While her attention was trained on them, she felt a light touch on her arm and turned to see Betty ease into the chair beside her.

"Hi Anne, glad you came," Betty said, her eyes glistening, but her mascara intact. She was wearing a simple navy blue dress and what seemed to be all of her diamonds: rings, earrings, pendant, and tennis bracelet.

"Of course. Your eulogy was lovely," Anne said.

"I'm just glad it's over. Not just the funeral, I mean the months of suffering for Claire. I'm sure she told you, but she was very happy with the work you did on her estate. Not to mention, solving the case. Of course, it's sad that Michele had to die. I guess she couldn't live with herself."

This was the opening Anne was waiting for. "You knew Michele since she was a child, so do you really think it was suicide?" Ann asked, then instantly regretted having put it so bluntly. This should have been played with subtlety. Too bad that wasn't her strong suit.

"Of course, it was suicide. What else?" Betty asked.

"Well, there's been some speculation—"

"Oh, really? How very interesting. Well, Anne," Betty said abruptly, "it's been good to see you." And with that, she excused herself and wandered off.

Anne turned back to the video screen for a few minutes, then glanced around and spotted Betty with a group of chatting women. Betty was just standing there, staring at her. They exchanged quick smiles, and then Betty broke eye contact.

Strange. What was that about? Whatever it was, it nudged Anne into deciding it was time to leave. She slipped on her jacket, grabbed her purse off the floor, and headed toward the bar area to drop off her empty glass. As she reached the busing station next to the open patio door, she heard two male voices coming from just outside on the patio: Tony and Sean Brutrain.

"Any of that stuff left over?" Tony asked Sean.

"Benzos? Shit, no. Why let any of that go to waste?"

Anne set down her dirty glass down in the plastic busing bin, turned around, and left by the other door.

Chapter Thirty-Seven

Thursday, January 24

T he toxicology report finally came back a month after Michele Murray's death, and Anne was arguing with Jack about it while they ate lunch at their usual booth at Nell's Dinner.

"Doesn't mean a damn thing," Jack said, spearing a pickle off Anne's plate. "A few drugs in her system won't change the case. In fact, there *is* no case: the report says the drugs did *not* contribute to the cause of death, and the medical examiner declared Michele's death a suicide. Period."

"Nevertheless," Anne said, waving a fork in one hand and the report in the other, "the toxicology report found that Michele had taken a 'substantial amount of the sedative Butalbital, sleeping pills, and four doses of Lorazepam,' which is known as the anxiety medication Ativan, or Benzos on the street."

"All borderline amounts," Jack said. "The drugs in her bloodstream weren't enough to incapacitate her. She was still able to walk around and could have fought off an attacker. But there was no evidence of a struggle. Therefore, no attacker. Besides, those same drugs were found in her apartment. They were hers. It makes sense that Michele would take them to relax. Who wants to kill themselves with a clear mind?"

"Maybe. Or maybe they were planted there by someone who wanted her dead. Make it *look* like they were hers."

He leaned back in the booth. "Why are you going down this rabbit hole,

Anne?" Don't you have enough going on in your life with that new business of yours? Just let this go."

Anne put the report down and sighed heavily. "Maybe you're right."

"Hey, did I tell you? Dot and I are thinking about taking up the RV lifestyle. Traveling around the country, maybe even selling our house if we like RV'ing enough."

"Sounds fun," she said distractedly, fiddling with the saltshaker. "I wonder if Claire's friend Betty has any thoughts about this?"

"She doesn't seem like an RV kind of gal."

"Not that. What I mean is, Betty knew Michele since she was a kid. She knows the Murray family better than anyone. Claire confided in her. Claire's kids think of her as an aunt. I think Betty could be the key," she said, leaning in toward Jack. "Of course, I'd have to be careful how I asked her the questions, how I phrased things. Or..."

Jack looked at her like she was batshit crazy. "Oh, for God's sake!"

"...maybe Sala knows something...."

* * *

Four days later, outside in the bright noonday sun, the air was clean and crisp. But inside The Parisian piano lounge, the air smelled of bourbon and the Chinese takeout the off-duty waiters were eating for lunch on the mahogany-topped bar.

It took a moment for Anne's vision to adjust to the dimly lit room. She spotted Betty sitting by herself in a back booth and waved. They hugged briefly, and Anne settled into the booth beside her.

"Thanks for coming, Betty."

A waiter came over to their table and took their drink orders.

Betty surveyed the room. "I haven't been here since the last time I came with Claire. Looks a little seedy by day, doesn't it? Especially stone-cold sober."

"You're probably wondering why I asked you here," Anne said.

"You mean aside from the pleasure of my company?"

"That too, of course." Anne smiled. "But I've been thinking about Michele. The way she died. I'm wondering how the family is doing with it. If they know anything—"

"Know anything?"

"For instance, did Michele leave a suicide note behind for Peter?"

"Not that I've heard." Betty shifted in her seat.

"Well, since you're so close to the family, have you heard anything of a suspicious nature?"

Betty just shrugged, so Anne continued, "Do you have doubts that it was suicide? I have some doubts myself. That's why I wanted to talk to you."

"Hmmm...I guessed as much." Betty reached into her Chanel purse and pulled out a white business envelope. She set it on the table, placing her left hand protectively over it.

Their drinks arrived, and after the waiter left, Betty raised her shot of bourbon and offered a toast.

"To Claire."

"To Claire," Anne said. They clinked glasses. "It's hard to believe it's been only two weeks since she died."

"Feels like two years. Very difficult," Betty said with a you-don't-want to-know wave of her hand. She took a sip of bourbon.

Anne glanced at the envelope and saw her name written on the front. She waited for Betty to bring it up.

"Okay, back to why we're here. I was given a mission by Claire," Betty said, as if she'd been the one to convene the meeting instead of Anne. She patted the envelope. "Claire wrote this letter a few days before she died. She wanted me to give it to you."

"But why now? Why not right after she died?"

"Now is the right time," Betty said in a voice that brooked no argument.

Anne picked up the envelope and studied the spidery script. She knew Claire's handwriting well; she'd seen it often enough during the months they worked together on her estate. But this version, while unmistakably hers, was shaky and thin, siphoned of any strength.

"Claire said if you had questions, this would answer them," Betty said.

Anne started to open the envelope, but Betty put a gentle, restraining hand over Anne's. "Please don't read it yet, honey. Not until I leave."

"You're not curious? I don't think Claire would have minded," Anne said.

Betty just looked at her and took a beat. "I have an idea what's in there, but it's better if I don't know for sure."

Betty drained her bourbon, gathered her purse and coat, and bid Anne goodbye.

Anne watched Betty pass through the door, then tore open the envelope and removed the letter. It wasn't much, just a few lines.

To whom it may concern,

I hired people to kill Michele Murray. I acted alone in this. No one in my family was involved or knew about it. I am writing this of my own free will.

Claire Frances Murray

Date: December 4, 2019

Anne groaned and set her glass down hard. Droplets splattered the table. "Damn it, Claire," she said aloud.

* * *

An hour later, Anne sat on the worn plaid couch in her uncle's home office and watched his face closely as he read the letter.

When Jack finished, he looked at her in amazement. "Not a chance in hell," he said. "Is this authentic?" He turned the letter over, examined the envelope, and then set it down on his desk.

"It's Claire's handwriting, all right."

"The envelope was sealed, so there's probably saliva there that could be tested if we needed to prove it," Jack mumbled to himself.

"What galls me is that Claire thought we'd buy this," Anne said. "Like we'd fall for the idea that she could arrange a murder? In her condition? Not possible."

Jack pushed himself out of the recliner, stood up, and started pacing around the small room. "Just *writing* this letter must have taken a herculean effort—"

"—And aside from the ridiculousness of her masterminding a murder, there's the bottom line: Claire just wasn't capable of killing anyone," Anne said. "Not even the person who murdered her son. And as angry as she was, her feelings about Michele were complex. She felt some real sympathy for Michele. No, Claire would never do this. Never. It goes against her character."

"I agree. But she wrote it for a reason. Why?"

"To protect her family. What other possible reason? Because that *is* in her character. That's perfectly in her character. She would do anything for her family. And she was obviously so worried that one of them murdered Michele that she decided to do this end-run. On her death bed, no less. She thought this would stop us from looking at any of them as murderers—which makes me even more suspicious."

"So, who do you think she wanted to protect?" He stopped pacing and faced Anne.

"Maybe Noreen. Claire worried about her," she said.

"But Noreen wasn't a likely killer. We've discussed this."

"But Claire couldn't have been sure. She probably thought Noreen had reason to want Michele dead. Or maybe Claire was trying to protect someone she thought was protecting Noreen. Anyway, I think this letter was her blanket protection—for any and all of them."

"If anyone killed Michele—and I'm not saying anyone did—who would it be?" Jack asked, sitting back down in his recliner.

"Not the daughters. Not Peter—he was in love with Michele."

"Sometimes that's a motive right there," Jack said.

"Tony is the most logical one," Anne said, thinking back to the funeral reception. "I heard him talking to a sketchy family friend—his name's Sean—the type of guy who could pull off a murder. Or at least know someone who could. I overheard Tony asking the guy if there were any Benzos left."

Jack raised his eyebrows, as if leery of going down this pot-holed road but curious anyway.

"And another thing," Anne said, "the day Michele died—at probably the exact time—Tony was hosting me and some other guests over at his condo in San Francisco for brunch. He could have arranged that for an alibi."

"Although that kind of alibi would only prove he didn't do the actual killing himself."

"Right, it doesn't prove he didn't hire professionals," Anne conceded.

"If this is a homicide—and I'm not saying it is—it was a professional hit. No clues were left behind," Jack said. "But why would Tony want to get involved and risk his career and life over this?"

"Joanne once called Tony 'the fixer.' He was used to making things happen. He thought of himself as the man of the family, the protector. We already know he wanted to protect Noreen against Michele when he paid that blackmail money."

"But why set up a murder-for-hire? Why not just pay Michele more money—buy her a car to get out of town and out of their lives forever?" Jack offered.

Anne mulled this over while idly pulling a loose thread on the sofa's fraying upholstery. "He tried money. Michele wouldn't leave. And even if she left, that wouldn't guarantee her silence. She could just come back for more. But maybe it was about *more* than just protecting Noreen. Maybe he wanted revenge for Danny's death. He knew the courts wouldn't do it. Maybe he just didn't like the idea of her getting away with murder."

"Could be, but we'll never know. The lady outfoxed us." Jack picked up the letter and waved it in the air. "This letter, this signed confession, accomplishes everything Claire wanted it to accomplish."

"How's that?"

"It stops us cold."

Anne paused a moment, collecting her thoughts. "But does it? I know that's what Claire wanted, what she intended. But like I said, it just makes me more suspicious. Something's been overlooked."

Chapter Thirty-Eight

Monday, January 28

I t was still early afternoon when Anne placed a call to Sgt. Jim Sloan and asked him to pull the files on the Michele Murray case. "And please find out if the neighbors were interviewed. I'll hold."

Two minutes later, Sloan came back with, "No, it wasn't necessary since it was clearly a suicide."

Just as she suspected. Homicides by hanging are so rare that it's common for the initial responding officers and ambulance crew to assume suicide. And once investigators hear the word *suicide*, it's like a switch goes off, and they start taking shortcuts. Follow-throughs with testing or interviews don't always happen.

"I'm in that neighborhood, so I'll ask around."

"Knock yourself out," Sloan said.

Which is how Anne ended up on the porch of the house directly across the street from Claire's former cottage. The neighbors had one of those shiny new doorbells that turned away visitors with a friendly automated voice: "We can't answer the door right now, but leave a message."

Sounds of activity were coming from inside the house, so Anne spoke into the intercom. She stepped back, held up her badge, and waited. A gray-haired woman, somewhere in her eighties, poked her head out through a crack in the door and, after giving Anne a quick once-over, swung the door open wide. "Can I help you?" she asked.

Anne introduced herself, asked the woman her name (*Mrs. Alice Arata,* she replied), and inquired if she'd seen anything unusual two months before, around the time the police had converged on the Murray cottage. That was all she had to ask to get Mrs. Arata talking.

"Claire and I always looked after each other's houses when the other one was away. I was looking over there—this was the day before the girl's body was found—and I saw two men entering Claire's house. Anyway, I recognized one of them, a big redheaded fella, from seeing him at Claire's birthday party, so I wasn't too concerned. But I kept watching anyway. A minute later, I saw the garage door roll up. The redhead walks out through the garage, gets into his black SUV, and then he backs it into the garage. Pretty soon, the garage door closed, and I couldn't see anything."

Mrs. Arata paused to catch her breath. "A few minutes later, the garage door opened again, and the SUV came out, and they drove off. They left the tan car, the one the skinny guy drove, in the street." *Michele's Camry, found at the scene.*

"I have photos," she said, pulling her phone out of her apron pocket.

"Photos?" Anne was caught so off guard she could barely breathe. "And you never told the police about this?"

"Well, until you showed up, the police never asked. Besides, it didn't seem to have anything to do with that suicide, which is what the newspapers called it…" Mrs. Arata pulled up the photos and handed the phone to Anne. "I almost deleted them."

The first photo showed Sean Brutrain, clear as day, with an unknown companion entering the house. Swiping left, the next photo showed the garage door up.

"And there's a video too. My son says to always take video."

Anne hit the play arrow. The video verified Mrs. Arta's story: It showed Brutrain leaving the garage, then stepping into the SUV and backing it into the garage. Then the garage door closed—for privacy, no doubt, while they unloaded Michele's body and carried it through the backyard and into the house.

She scrolled again to the still photos. The SUV's license plate was barely visible on one, but it was visible enough to be digitally enhanced. Anne asked Mrs. Arata to send copies to her phone. After she emailed the attachments, a kitchen timer went off. "Excuse me, but I have something in the oven." Anne thanked her and said they'd be in touch.

* * *

Alone on the porch, Anne looked across the street to Claire's vacant cottage. The FOR SALE BY BRENDA MORAN sign on the front lawn was now topped with a rider that announced: IN ESCROW. She crossed the street, went around to the side fence, and entered the back yard. She tried the door leading to the garage. Not surprisingly, it was locked. Peering through the glass in the door, she saw nothing inside but darkness.

It wasn't as if she was expecting any evidence to have been left behind—Brenda would have most certainly cleared everything out. Still, it was too bad the search warrant issued after Michele's death had already expired.

She called Sgt. Sloan and told him about the photos and video. "They'll provide all probable cause we need for obtaining warrants to search Brutrain's house and SUV, and also for a reissue of the search warrant for the Murray house." They agreed to meet back at the station.

* * *

Once Sgt. Sloan and the police chief saw the photos and video, things happened fast. An additional detective was assigned to join forces with Sloan and Anne, and search warrants were issued and executed.

The black SUV alone was a treasure trove: In addition to the flakes of dry leaves found stuck in its rear cargo net that matched the specks of vegetation in Michele's hair, detectives found a crumpled-up suicide note under the front seat. It was a sorry attempt at forgery: Not only was Michele's name misspelled with two "Ls," but the handwriting didn't match up with Michele's. In Anne's opinion, "They probably knew how lame it was, so they tossed it." But what *did* match up were the fingerprints on the note with those of Sean Brutrain.

Then there was Brutrain's background. He was a convicted drug dealer, and a house search turned up the same drugs found in Michele's body. His army background could account for the "military roll" of Michele's sweater found near her body. More damning, the rope used for hanging Michele was a match for the rope coil found in the junk drawer in the kitchen.

But the clincher was the confession of his accomplice, Les Thomas, a known felon who was brought in after being identified from Mrs. Arata's photos. Under questioning, Thomas claimed, "Someone hired Brutrain to kill her. All I did was help carry her and stuff."

Brutrain was arrested and booked for drug possession and homicide and read his rights. During questioning, the officers laid out the evidence, showed him the photos, and played the three-minute video.

With first-degree murder charges on the table, Sgt. Sloan informed him, he could face the death penalty—or, best case scenario, life without the possibility of parole.

"Either that, or you can plead guilty, save us all the hassle of trial, and give up your accomplice," Sloan said. "Now, I can't promise you anything in return if you decide to cooperate—that's totally up to the DA's office—but DA Collins might remove the death penalty and reduce your sentence to life with the possibility of parole."

Brutrain decided to cooperate. "No way am I going down for this alone."

What he planned to give to the DA was a name (*A big one*, he said), along with secret phone recordings he'd made of his accomplice "for insurance," which, though not admissible in a California court, would back up his statements and lead to some strong corroborating evidence. They'd both used burner phone apps, Brutrain said (*We're not dumb*), so their cell phone bills wouldn't disclose the numbers they called. But those phone records *would* disclose the time of the calls and the length of the conversations—and he assured the detectives that his calls would definitely match up with those of his accomplice.

"But before I hand all this over, I want to talk to my lawyer," he said.

* * *

Three weeks later, while Sean Brutrain and his lawyer were finalizing a plea deal with the DA's office, Tony Murray was sitting in first-class on a flight en route to Sarajevo—the capital of a nation with no extradition treaty with the United States—sipping champagne, flying safely out of U.S. law enforcement's reach.

Epilogue

A
nne, though not particularly religious, said a brief prayer at
Michele Murray's grave and then bent down and laid a red rose
on the modest gravestone.

Now nearly three months after the two funerals, Anne and her uncle were paying their respects at Calvary Cemetery in the hills above Santa Rosa.

A light breeze kicked up as she turned and headed down the knoll to where her uncle was waiting for her in front of Claire's headstone. During those hundred yards or so, her thoughts kept returning to the events of the last few days, to the amazing speed at which the case had morphed from an apparent suicide to a solved murder.

The news media was having a field day. "Murder Suspect Flees Country" was the headline of the *San Francisco Chronicle* that morning. The story, covered by all local television and radio stations, online news sites, and newspapers, was sensational: The DA's office had filed multiple charges against Tony Murray, including conspiracy to commit murder and first-degree murder.

"It's just a matter of time before he wants to come back home," Joe Kessler, assistant DA, was quoted as saying, "and we'll be waiting for him."

Anne was just thankful Claire wasn't around to see this. It was the last thing she would have wanted for her family, this disgrace and pain. The Murphys were understandably stunned by the charges against Tony and had closed ranks. Maybe they knew Anne was involved in uncovering the crime, maybe not. But if any of them had heard from Tony, they weren't sharing the news with her. Or anyone else outside the family, as far as she could tell. Certainly not with reporters.

As Anne approached Claire's grave, holding a bouquet of flowers, she noticed Jack watching her closely. When she reached his side, he said, "You're still wrestling with this, aren't you?"

Anne looked down at Claire's headstone and nodded. "I can't stop thinking that Claire's letter was her way of telling us to stop, that she didn't want anyone going after her family. Not any of them, for any reason. She wanted all the pain to stop. It was her last request, her dying wish. So how could we deny her that? And yet we did. *I* did."

"Anne, stop it. This isn't your burden to take on," he said. "All you did was go after the truth. You didn't start trouble for the Murray family. There already *was* trouble—and Tony's the one responsible for that. Not you. You did what a good cop does, you looked for the truth. Even when everyone else was calling it a suicide. Even when I was trying to discourage you. You went after the truth. We don't get to pick and choose where that truth leads us, or who gets justice. The chips fall where they may."

"Thanks for that."

"Well, you know what I'm saying is true," he said quietly. "And if it means anything to you, Annie, I'm very proud of what you did."

She felt tears well up, so she blinked them away. "Sometimes I wonder if Claire regretted asking for Danny's case to be reopened," she said.

"Instead of just letting sleeping dogs lie?"

"Something like that. But at least she found out what happened to her son, so that's some kind of resolution. As for Michele's death...."

"There's justice for Michele," Jack said firmly. "And wherever Claire is," he added, while making a vague gesture toward the heavens, "I'm sure she'll forgive you for your part in getting it."

It was such an un-Jack-like thing to say that Anne just shook her head. But she liked hearing it anyway. She hoped it was true.

They fell silent. After a while, Anne bent down and laid the mixed-flower bouquet on Claire's grave. She could almost hear Claire's voice in her head, in the wind.

A whisper of a thought came to her, and she smiled.

"I think I'll take these gladiolas back home with me," she said, "and just leave Claire the roses."

"Whatever," Jack said, shrugging.

He watched as she plucked out the offending flowers and laid the rest on the grave. Then he took her by the arm and said, "Come on, kiddo, I'll buy you some lunch."

A Note from the Author

Those familiar with Santa Rosa will notice I've taken liberties with geography and have inserted streets, apartments, and parks where none exist. Neither, to my knowledge, does a mobile park like Tranquil Acres exist in Sonoma County. Restaurants, motels, schools, and other institutions have been altered or invented to suit the story and should therefore be regarded as entirely fictitious.

Acknowledgements

Since writing *The Last Thing Claire Wanted*, I've learned just how much of a team effort publishing is and how many wonderful people there are to thank. Here goes:

Thank you to the remarkable team at Level Best Books, the Dames of Detection—Harriette Sackler, Shawn Reilly Simmons and Verena Rose—for making this book a reality from edits to cover art. Thank you to the brilliant, no-holds-barred independent editor, David Samuel Levinson. Thanks also to Kristen Weber for her encouragement and sharp editing eye.

Every mystery writer needs a cop in the family, and I lucked out with John Leach, a retired homicide detective and co-grandparent. Huge thanks to John for sharing his expertise, generating creative ideas, and answering every off-the-wall question that I emailed his way. Thanks to Gretchen Paul of Gretchen Paul Family Estate Sales & Services for giving me the inside scoop on the estate sales business. Thanks also to Mike Hudson for generously sharing his insights into the workings of a DA's office. Any errors or inaccuracies are most definitely my own.

Thanks to Sisters in Crime, Guppies chapter, and their network of talented writers and educators who welcomed me, shared writing tips, and gave advice on navigating the publishing world. Special thanks to Dr. D.P. Lyle, Susan C. Shea, Judy White, Simon Wood, Laurie Schnebly, Arlene Miller, and Annie Bomke. Special thanks the gifted Amanda Jayatissa, who swapped manuscripts with me and passed along insightful comments that made a world of difference.

Thanks to Jim Dunwoody, my trusted first reader, cheerleader, and neighbor, who gave me invaluable feedback and kindly let me use his name.

And thank you, in no particular order, to family and friends who never failed to cheer me on, even when there was zero proof this book would ever see the light of day (I still have some of your notes taped to my computer!): Jon Ianziti, Virginia Adams, Margaret McCaskill Visek, Connie Jackson, Dr. Whimsey Anderson, Gene Helfman, Candice Oman, Tina Fruiht, Kai Tierheimer, Sharon Fitzgerald Kane, Pauline Bartholomew, Harley Tierheimer, Nicole Tierheimer, Jack Sanford, and Maura Mattoon Sanford. And to my lively, funny and supportive book club sisters: Barbara, Cathy, Darlene, Eileen, Kathleen, Pauline, Kathy, Justina, Katie, and Mary Beth.

Most of all, thanks to Allen, my husband and best friend, for believing.

About the Author

Karin Fitz Sanford was born in New York, but grew up in Northern California's Wine Country, the setting for her debut novel, *The Last Thing Claire Wanted*. A former advertising copywriter and ad agency principal, she is a member of Sisters in Crime and lives in Northern California with her husband.

SOCIAL MEDIA HANDLES:
  Facebook: Karin Fitzgerald Sanford
  Instagram: karinfitz8

AUTHOR WEBSITE:
  FitzSanford.com